Sharon Kendrick once won a national writing competition by describing her ideal date: being flown to an exotic island by a gorgeous and powerful man. Little did she realise that she'd just wandered into her dream job! Today she writes for Mills & Boon, featuring often stubborn but always *to die for* heroes and the women who bring them to their knees. She believes that the best books are those you never want to end. Just like life…

Growing up near the beach, **Annie West** spent lots of time observing tall, burnished lifeguards—early research! Now she spends her days fantasising about gorgeous men and their love lives. Annie has been a reader all her life. She also loves travel, long walks, good company and great food. You can contact her at annie@annie-west.com or via PO Box 1041, Warners Bay, NSW 2282, Australia.

D0865890

BOUND TO THE SICILIAN'S BED

SHARON KENDRICK

CONTRACTED FOR THE PETRAKIS HEIR

ANNIE WEST

MILLS & BOON

First Published in Great Britain 2018
by Mills & Boon, an imprint of HarperCollins*Publishers*
1 London Bridge Street, London, SE1 9GF

Bound to the Sicilian's Bed © 2018 by Sharon Kendrick

Contracted for the Petrakis Heir © 2018 by Annie West

ISBN: 978-0-263-93522-6

MIX
Paper from
responsible sources
FSC C007454

This book is produced from independently certified FSC™ paper
to ensure responsible forest management.
For more information visit www.harpercollins.co.uk/green.

Printed and bound in Spain
by CPI, Barcelona

BOUND TO THE SICILIAN'S BED

SHARON KENDRICK

For darling Pete Crone, who is a constant inspiration to this sometimes (!) frazzled writer, and has many of the attributes of the romantic hero.

And for Charlie Bell, director at Vardags—the amazing law firm with the amazing view over London—who provided invaluable help for this story.

CHAPTER ONE

Rocco Barberi felt anger pumping through his veins and it was enough to stop him in his tracks. Because he didn't *do* anger. He was known as a man of cool calculation. His implacable Sicilian features were notorious for never betraying a flicker of emotion and his business rivals often said he would have made a world-class poker player. So why was rage flooding through him like hot lava as he stood outside a tiny art shop in some God-forsaken Cornish town?

He knew why. Because of her. His wife. His mouth twisted. His *estranged* wife. The woman who was standing inside the shop studying some sort of vase, her thick dark curls cascading down her back, leading the eye naturally to her narrow waist and the luscious curve of her bottom. The woman who had walked away from him without a qualm, uncaring of his reputation and everything he had done for her.

He pushed open the door and the doorbell jangled loudly as he walked in. He saw her look up, her face freezing with shock—and Rocco enjoyed a brief moment of pleasure as he read disbelief in those green eyes, which had once so bewitched him. He heard her suck in an unsteady breath and as she put the vase down he noticed her fingers were trembling. Good, he thought grimly. *Good.*

'Rocco,' she said breathlessly and he could see her throat constricting as she swallowed. That long, pale neck he had once covered in urgent kisses before moving on to the infinitely softer territory of her breasts. 'What...what are you doing here?'

The deliberate pause he allowed was just long enough to increase the sudden tension, which had gathered like a storm cloud in the small shop. 'You've just served me with divorce papers, Nicole,' he drawled. 'What did you think would happen? That I would just sign over half my fortune and let you walk off into the sunset with a toss of your pretty curls? Is that what you were hoping?'

She was brushing a dark spiral of hair away from a face flushed pink—acting with the self-consciousness of a woman who was uncertain about her appearance and Rocco was unprepared for the sudden wave of lust which washed over him. Would she have taken a little more care with her clothes if she'd known he was coming—worn something a little more flattering than those faded jeans and a filmy white shirt, which concealed far too much of those luscious breasts?

'Of course I wasn't,' she answered, still in that faintly breathless voice. 'I just thought...'

'Yes?' His voice rang out flatly and he saw her flinch.

'That you might have given me some kind of warning.'

'You mean, like you did when you walked away from our marriage?'

'Rocco—'

'Or when your lawyer sent me those papers last week?' he continued relentlessly. 'You didn't even do me the courtesy of a phone call to let me know you were about to file for divorce, did you, Nicole? Which naturally led me to the conclusion that you were the kind of woman who favoured surprises. So here I am,' he finished softly. 'Your big surprise.'

Nicole felt dizzy. Faint. And not just because of the steely accusations which were slicing through the air towards her. She met the blaze of his eyes and wondered how, after just a few seconds in his company, she was already feeling mixed up and at a disadvantage. She hadn't seen Rocco Barberi for two whole years yet his impact was as devastating as it had ever been. Maybe even more so. She'd forgotten the way he could dominate the space around him and make any room seem to shrink whenever he walked in. She'd forgotten because she'd forced herself to forget the man she had loved even though duty had been the only thing on *his* mind when he'd slipped that wedding band on her finger. She licked her lips. Maybe she'd been foolish to expect anything deeper when their relationship had been doomed from the start—because those kinds of relationships always were. Rich man/poor girl was all very well in theory, but in practice...

She thought about the fuss which had surrounded their unlikely marriage and all the lurid newspaper headlines which had been splashed around. It had been a big story at the time. *'Sicilian Billionaire Weds Cleaner'*—and the inevitable: *'Fairy Tale Marriage*

Turns Sour'. And then it had ended as abruptly as it had begun. She'd walked away from him and their marriage because she'd needed to. The gulf between them had widened to such a distance that she'd known there was no going back, and when she'd lost the baby there had been no reason for them to be together any more. She'd needed to break free in order to survive.

She had told herself that over and over again in those early days after she'd left Sicily. At first every painful minute had seemed like an eternity but gradually the days had drifted into weeks and eventually months. She hadn't taken Rocco's phone calls or answered his letters because she'd known that a clean break was the only way she would have the courage to end it, although it had felt like torture at the time. When the months had turned into years she'd assumed Rocco had accepted they were better off apart, just as she had done. Yet here he was, just turning up out of the blue. In her shop and in her life. It felt as if someone were crushing her heart between their fingers. It brought the pain of the past rushing back so fast that she had to remember to breathe.

And that was what she needed to focus on—her brief tenure as Rocco's wife. The reality—not the fairy tale, which had never really existed anyway. When even her choice of clothes had been dictated by the influential Sicilian billionaire who had treated her like an old-fashioned chattel he'd been forced to purchase against his better judgement.

But that didn't stop her looking at him. From letting her gaze drift over his muscular physique, clad today in one of those expensive charcoal suits he favoured, which emphasised every honed sinew of his remarkable body. Her throat dried as she registered the pale shirt which contrasted so vividly with his olive skin. Had she hoped she might have acquired some kind of immunity to him in the intervening years? Of course she had—because hope was the one emotion which defied logic, the one which could make you get up in the morning and put one foot in front of the other no matter how dark the world seemed outside. Yet Rocco seemed even more dazzling than she remembered— as if absence had only added an extra dimension to his powerful sexuality.

His glowing skin was dark and his startling blue eyes spoke of a distant Greek ancestry. Eyes which could fell you with a single look. Which could undress you in seconds before his hands accomplished the task far more efficiently. The last time she'd seen him Nicole had felt numb with pain and an emptiness which had left little room for anything else.

But now?

She could feel the erratic thumping of her heart. There was no such numbness now. Her senses felt as if he'd kick-started them into life without even trying. She could feel it in the prickle of her breasts and the molten rush of heat to her belly. A familiar restlessness entered her body as it shivered into life and memories of being in his arms were enough to bring a renewed flush of colour to her cheeks. But those thoughts and feelings were nothing but a distraction—as well as a waste of time. There was no point in desiring Rocco. She was nothing to him and she never had been. Just the woman he'd married who had failed to give him the child she'd been carrying. It was over. It had never really begun. So don't prolong it or drag it out and make it any worse than it needs to be. Keep it cool and businesslike.

'So what can I do for you, Rocco?' She looked at him enquiringly, trying to keep her expression neutral. 'Is there something in particular you wanted to discuss with me—and if so, don't you think it might be better done through our lawyers?'

'I'm here,' he said slowly, 'because I think we might be able to do each other a favour.'

She studied him warily. 'I don't understand. We're separated—and separating people don't really do each other favours.'

Rocco ran the edge of his thumb over his bottom lip. He was fully aware that some people might describe what he was about to do as emotional blackmail—but so what? Didn't his shallow, green-eyed wife deserve everything she was going to get? He felt the beat of a pulse at his temple. Wasn't it time she discovered that you didn't cross Rocco Barberi unless you were prepared to pay the price? That was why he had come here today, intending to tell her exactly what he wanted, knowing she would be forced to grant him his wish if she wanted her damned divorce.

He'd thought it would be easy. Straightforward. A simple equation of $A + B = C$. But he had failed to factor in desire, hadn't he? A desire which had taken him completely by surprise. He had imagined he would look at her as he might any other ex-lover—with a cool impartiality, which had always served him well in the past, because once you had repeatedly tasted a woman's body your appetite for her inevitably diminished. But that wasn't happening. He wondered what it was about her which was making him grow as hard as rock, so he was having difficulty concentrating on anything other than what it would feel like to be deep inside her again— riding her until she shuddered out his name. Was it because she had once worn his wedding band and the significance of that went deeper than he'd imagined?

His voice became hard. 'I need you to do something for me.'

'Sorry, Rocco. You're talking to the wrong person.' She shook her head so that all those thick dark curls shimmered around her shoulders. 'I don't have to do anything for you. We're getting divorced. Remember?'

'Maybe we are,' he answered softly. 'Or maybe not.'

She blinked at him in consternation. 'But the law says we can divorce after two years of living apart.'

'I know what the law says. But that can happen only with the agreement of both parties.' There was a pause. 'Think about it, Nicole. You need my consent to terminate our marriage. I could drag it out for years if I wanted.'

As she heard the unmistakable threat behind his words, Nicole's instinct was to turn and run. To run so far that he'd never be able to find her. Until she reminded herself that instinct had never served her well where Rocco was concerned. It had led her into his arms and into his bed, even though she'd known deep inside that he'd only wanted her for sex. And she had been right, hadn't she?

But she was no longer that woman. The star-struck virgin who had allowed her powerful boss to seduce her. Who had fallen victim to the practised heaven of his touch. The innocent young cleaner who had believed the smooth lies which had flowed from his sensual lips and allowed herself to be guided by them. Who had obediently worn the crotchless panties he'd bought for her from shops in London's Soho and bucked with pleasure when he'd slid his fingers inside them. She'd even pretended to enjoy the light lash of a whip caressing her bare buttocks because she had wanted to bring him as much pleasure as he brought her. Because she had wanted to *please* him. To be his perfect lover in the hope that one day he might care for her as much as she'd begun to care for him. Yet soon after she'd given him her virginity, Rocco had begun to distance himself. Had started avoiding her at work. Suddenly there had been pressing business trips which had desperately needed his attention—something which apparently was a ploy of his when he was trying to get some needy lover off his back.

In fact, he probably would have gone out of his way never to have seen her again if nature hadn't intervened and cast them both in the unexpected roles of parents-to-be. She swallowed as the painful memories crowded into her mind and tried to remind herself that was all in the past. Things were different now. She was getting used to life as a single woman. And yes, it was a struggle to exist on the pittance she earned from this little art shop she'd opened with the help of a grant from the local council—but at least she was following her dreams instead of living a nightmare. She didn't need Rocco Barberi or his billions—or his cold, emotionless heart.

Drawing her shoulders back, she tilted her chin to meet his sapphire gaze. 'Why on earth wouldn't you give me your consent when we both know our marriage is over?'

'Is that why you didn't answer any of my letters? Because you'd come to that decision all on your own?'

'It was what we both knew in our hearts!' she defended. 'I just couldn't see the point in dragging it out any longer.'

His body tensed and he opened his mouth to respond when the sound of the shop bell punctured the atmosphere as a middle-aged woman opened the door. Did she pick up on the fraught atmosphere? Was that why she glanced uncertainly from Rocco to Nicole as if she were gate-crashing a private party?

'I'm sorry,' she said, automatically prefacing her sentence with the ever-present apology of the English. 'Are you—?'

'We're closed,' said Rocco shortly, watching as Nicole opened her mouth to protest—but by then it was too late because the woman had scuttled out again, murmuring yet more words of apology.

And then his estranged wife turned on him, all her studied politeness a distant memory, her emerald eyes spitting fire at him.

'You can't do that!' she declared indignantly. 'You

can't just march into *my* shop and order prospective customers to leave!'

'I just did,' he said, without any hint of apology. 'So let me put this to you carefully, just so that there can be no misunderstanding. You have a choice, Nicole. Either I turn the shop sign around to say you're closed, or you agree to meet me when you've finished work. Because I don't want any more interruptions like that when I put my proposition to you.'

'Proposition?'

'That's what I said.'

'And if I refuse?'

'Why would you refuse? You want your freedom, don't you? The precious freedom which is so important to you. It might be in your best interests to…what is it that you English say?' He rubbed a reflective finger over the hint of stubble at his chin. 'Ah, yes. *To keep me sweet.*'

Nicole felt herself stiffen because his voice had taken on that velvety caress which used to have her hurling herself into his arms and raining kiss after kiss all over his rugged features. Well, not any more. That ship had sailed. No matter how much her body might be longing to feel him close to her again, she was going to fight that attraction with every fibre of her being. And he was right. Another customer might walk in and it didn't look very professional to have a divorcing couple slugging out their differences. Surely it wouldn't hurt her to listen to what he had to say. To humour him a little in order to facilitate her freedom.

'Okay,' she said, with a sigh. 'How about I meet you

for a coffee when I've finished work? There's a café at the far end of the harbour which will still be open. It's got a red and white awning at the front—you can't miss it. I'll see you in there.'

'No.' He shook his head and his mouth hardened. 'I'm not meeting you in public in some damned *café*. I want to visit your apartment, Nicole. To see for myself the place you have chosen above your Sicilian home.'

It was on the tip of Nicole's tongue to tell him that the lavish Barberi complex had felt more like a prison than a home, but what was the point of upping the ante? Mightn't it drive home how serious she was about this divorce if she showed Rocco where she lived? Mightn't he get it into his stubborn head that wealth and privilege meant nothing, not when you measured those things against peace of mind?

'Very well, I live in the flat above the tea shop on Greystone Road. Number thirty-seven,' she said grudgingly. 'But don't come before seven.'

'Capisce.' He nodded his dark head.

He was just on his way to the door when he paused in front of a small display of pottery, picking up one of the pieces to study it. It was a glowing terracotta jug with a handle fashioned to look like the twisted leaves on a lemon branch. Raised yellow fruits dotted the surface and in the background was the flash of blue—an artistic representation of the distant sea. Slowly he turned it around in his olive fingers to study it, before glancing up to meet her eyes.

'This is good,' he said slowly. 'It reminds me of Sicily.'

She nodded, the sudden clench of her heart making

her wish he hadn't made the connection. 'That's what inspired me.'

'Perhaps I should buy it,' he reflected. 'You certainly look as if you could do with a few more customers.'

'Particularly when you drive away the ones I do have,' she observed acidly. 'Anyway, it's not for sale.'

She pointed to a bright red sticker, though in reality nobody had bought it, because it had never actually been for sale. It was the last remaining piece of the collection she'd made when she'd returned from Sicily, feeling heartbroken and empty. Her bestselling collection, as it happened, but she wouldn't tell him that. Just as she wouldn't tell him about the tiny, hand-embroidered romper suit she'd bought soon after she'd had her first pregnancy scan, which was lying shrouded in tissue paper in one of her bedroom drawers. She was planning to sell the jug just as soon as the ink was dry on her divorce papers. The romper suit she suspected she would never be able to part with.

He replaced the piece and all Nicole was aware of were those amazing sapphire eyes searing into her. He was always the most beautiful man she had ever seen and nothing about that had changed. He could still make her heart beat fast. Still make her shiver and her breasts swell into vibrant life against her lacy bra. Just as he reminded her of the darkest time in her life and her fear that she would never be able to recover. But she *had* recovered. And she'd done it without him—because they were no good for each other. She had accepted that. It was time that Rocco did, too.

And suddenly she wanted him out of the shop, before

she gave into the pain which was welling up inside her and threatening to spill over. Before it dissolved into bitter tears, which would remind her of everything she had lost.

CHAPTER TWO

TWO CUPS OF herbal tea and a stern reminder that getting emotional would accomplish nothing meant Nicole's nerves were less jangled by the time she arrived home to find Rocco waiting outside her apartment. She'd told herself that getting sucked in by dark memories wasn't going to help anyone. She'd told herself she needed to be calm and impartial when it came to dealing with Rocco, but maybe that was just too big an ask with a man like him.

She thought how out of place he looked in the narrow Cornish street, his powerful body drawing attention away from the cute little houses which surrounded him. Every property had window boxes full of colourful flowers dancing in the breeze, but her estranged husband was a study in unmoving darkness—the whiteness of his silk shirt the only thing lightening his shadowed body and rugged features. Her heart began to pound as she walked towards him.

The usual batch of holidaymakers was spilling out from the tea room below her tiny apartment and others were strolling along the pavement on their way to eat fish and chips, or drink dark pints of bitter in one of the iconic little pubs close by. Yet every person turned to glance at Rocco—men and women alike—as if recognising the powerful stranger in their midst. And even though he was head of one of the world's biggest pharmaceutical companies and one of the world's wealthiest men, Nicole suspected he would have attracted attention even if he possessed nothing. And she mustn't forget that. She mustn't forget that underneath all her swarm of painful feelings, she was as susceptible to him as the next woman.

And he could hurt her all over again.

His sapphire eyes were fixed on her and Nicole felt stupidly self-conscious as she reached him.

'You're early,' she said, reaching into her bag for her keys.

'You know what it's like. I couldn't keep away,' he said mockingly.

She gave a tight smile. 'Then you'd better come in.'

Rocco stood back to let her pass, unable to stop himself from reacting to her unique scent as she pushed open the front door, a scent which had nothing to do with perfume. It was the essence of *her*, which he had once found so intoxicating. Still did, if he was being honest—and he really hadn't expected that. But then, Nicole had a talent for making him do the unexpected, didn't she? Her green-eyed look of provocation had lured him into breaking every rule in the book, just as her abundance of curves had made her seem more feminine than any woman he'd ever met.

When he'd seduced her he'd thought she was experienced. Why wouldn't he—when she'd flirted like crazy with him after their initial meeting? Yet he hadn't touched her until their fourth date, something which was unheard of for him. Despite the fact that she'd clearly wanted him—what woman didn't?—he'd forced himself to wait. He still wasn't sure why. Maybe he'd just wanted to delay gratification for as long as possible, in an attempt to preserve that delicious state of desire she had aroused in him.

And then he'd discovered she had been a virgin and that had been a whole new ballgame. It had blown him away. Intimacy with Nicole Watson had eclipsed every other sexual encounter he'd ever had and Rocco was tempted to pull her into his arms to see whether she felt as good as he remembered. To lose himself in her soft and feminine body and thrust into the wet heat which had always awaited him.

But she had deserted him.

She had thrown everything back in his face.

The memory of that was enough to dissolve his desire as he followed her up a rickety old staircase—unable to prevent the moue of scorn which escaped his lips as he entered the cramped living room. His mouth twisted. She had chosen to live *here*? A Barberi occupying a place such as this? Why, a medieval servant would have boasted of something finer!

He looked around. It was small. Unbelievably small. A tiny sofa had been covered with a brightly coloured throw—but nothing could disguise the battered surface beneath. There was a sagging armchair, an old-fashioned electric fire and an archway leading into a cubbyhole of a kitchen. And that was it.

The only photograph on show was an old one he recognised of her mother but there were none of him. Rocco's mouth hardened. Did he really think there might have been? Perhaps a shot of them standing outside the Sicilian cathedral, a white tulle veil billowing around her dark curls and Nicole's flat stomach concealing the fact that she was several weeks pregnant?

His jaw tightened as he wondered what had made him start thinking about such a taboo subject but, with the ruthlessness born of practice, he pushed the powerful image to the back of his mind as he stared at the woman in front of him, thinking how different she looked. Gone were the elegant clothes which had crammed her wardrobe during their short marriage and in their place was the distinctly Bohemian look she had always favoured. Clothes he had found attractive enough in a mistress, but which had been unsuitable for a Barberi wife. Silver hoops gleamed amid the wild tumble of dark curls and the lush sensuality of her mouth was fixed and unsmiling as she returned his stare.

'So,' she said. 'What exactly is this all about, Rocco?'

He thought of chastising her for her lack of courtesy. He had lifted her out of the gutter and given her the chance of a better life. He had taught her everything. *Everything*. What to wear and how to behave. When to speak and when to remain silent. And now she was treating him with the barely disguised impatience she might show a persistent salesman who had shoved his foot in the door.

'You don't even offer me coffee?' he drawled.

'There won't be time. I wasn't planning a long visit. Were you?' She looked at him enquiringly. 'You told me you had something you wanted to say, so why don't you just say it?'

He sat down on the arm of the sofa, stretching his long legs out in front of him. 'I need you to play a part for me,' he said.

'A part?' she echoed non-comprehendingly. 'What are you talking about?'

'As my wife.' He gave a mirthless smile. 'Or rather, my reconciling wife.'

'Your reconciling *wife*? Are you crazy?'

Rocco thought back to the number of times he had asked himself the same question, wondering how he could have fallen for someone like her. Why, despite the eager attentions of women of his own class, he had allowed himself to become transfixed by this one—a humble cleaner at his London headquarters. Because of her he had behaved in a way which still had the power to make him shudder as he remembered locking the door to his office and taking her over his desk. He remembered her curving hips facing upwards in a silent plea for him to remove her panties. And him complying with shaking hands, his fingers sliding over her molten heat, before entering her with a hunger so all-consuming that it had completely blown his mind. He swallowed. All his legendary self-control had deserted him the moment he'd laid a finger on her. The powerful head of Barberi associates thrusting hungrily into one of his lowly employees, with his trousers around his ankles like a teenager!

He swallowed before shaking his head. 'On the contrary, *tesoro*—I'm deadly serious. This petition could not have come at a worse time for me.'

'Really?'

'Yes, really. I'm in the middle of a deal, which is balancing on a knife-edge right now.'

'Gosh. I thought you had a hundred per cent success rate where business was concerned. You must be slipping, Rocco.'

He gave an impatient flicker of a smile. 'This deal is a big one,' he said softly. 'The biggest in a long time. I'm attempting a hostile takeover bid of a European company, which will increase my stock to make Barberi the biggest pharmaceutical business in the world.'

'So what's the problem?'

His eyes narrowed as he met her gaze. 'The problem is that there has been some opposition to my involvement. Several of the shareholders have hired a PR agency to see what dirt they can dig up on me and a complicated personal life could provide fuel for their stories. Plus, one of the biggest shareholders is a man named Marcel Dupois who's known for being extremely conservative, particularly around family matters.' He shifted his weight slightly. 'The last thing I need is an estranged wife coming out of the woodwork seeking a divorce at such a sensitive time.'

'So drop your business bid.'

'But I don't want to drop it.' His voice hardened. 'It's too important to me.'

Nicole nodded. Of course it was. Business had always been important to Rocco. The only thing which really mattered in his life. His go-to activity which took precedence over everything else, even his wife. Especially his wife. 'So what are you expecting me to do— call off the divorce?'

'Only temporarily.'

'I wasn't being serious, Rocco.'

'But I am.' His sapphire eyes flattened. 'Deadly serious.'

'You want me to delay the petition.'

'I want you to play a role. You were always very good at role-play, weren't you, Nicole? It's easy. All you have to do is pretend to be my wife for a couple of days.'

'Pretend to be your wife,' she repeated slowly.

'Sure. I have a high-profile weekend coming up and having you by my side as my loving spouse could be extremely useful.'

'Useful?'

'You don't like the word?'

Nicole bristled. Of course she didn't like the word, which seemed to emphasise the only thing she'd ever been to him. Someone who was convenient. Who could be picked up and put down like a commodity. She wanted to push him towards the door. To tell him to get out and never come back—until she remembered what her lawyer had said just before he'd filed the papers.

'Your husband is a powerful man, Mrs Barberi. Not a man you'd want to get into a protracted legal battle with. Not under any circumstances. My advice to you is to keep proceedings as amicable as possible.'

She got that, but even so.

Masquerade as his *wife*?

Open herself up to all that pain and frustration and make even more of a mockery of their doomed marriage?

No way.

She shook her head.

'It's a crazy suggestion. You must realise that. I'm sorry you've come all this way for nothing, Rocco, but I can't do it.'

He looked around the small scruffy room before returning his gaze to her. 'I meant what I said, Nicole,' he said. 'Unless you were prepared to cooperate, I might not let you have your divorce.'

She shook her head. 'You can't stop me.'

'Oh, but I can,' he argued softly. 'We've been separated for two years but you still need my agreement.' There was a pause. 'I've spoken to my lawyers and I can easily defend the petition by saying I don't believe the marriage has broken down irretrievably.'

'You wouldn't…' she breathed.

'Wouldn't I? I would do whatever it takes to make this deal, Nicole.' His eyes gleamed. 'The choice is yours, *tesoro*.'

Nicole heard the steely determination behind his words and thought about his power and influence. Her lawyer had been right—Rocco could do exactly what he wanted because he had limitless funds to support him, and she didn't. Simple as that. In theory she *could* wait for her divorce—but she didn't want to. Three more years of being tied to Rocco Barberi with all the memories that brought with it? Of feeling that something was always holding her back from living her life? Of being unable to stop those rugged features and sapphire eyes from invading her dreams every night? No way.

Slowly, she lifted her eyes to his. 'And if I agreed? What would it entail?'

He didn't react. There was no triumph on his face. His expression was as coolly impassive as ever it had been. Of course it was, Nicole told herself bitterly. Rocco didn't change. He was still the same cold-hearted control freak he'd ever been.

'You will accompany me to a film screening, a dinner and a cocktail party over the course of a couple of days, that's all.'

'That's all,' she repeated slowly.

'*Se*. We pretend we're giving our marriage another go. We become yet another couple who've come unstuck and are trying to solve our "issues". Everyone likes a love story and it will show a more *sympathetic* side to my character.' His eyes gleamed mockingly. 'You get a weekend in Monaco and I get my deal.'

'Monaco?'

'That's where I live now.'

She stared at him in surprise. 'Not Sicily?'

'Not any more.'

She wondered whether she had imagined the sudden bleakness in his voice, but Nicole's head was too full to wonder why he had left his beloved homeland. She tried sifting through her options as he stared at her and wondered if she could go through with his crazy plan.

Yet how ironic was it that she needed to put on a convincing performance as his reconciling wife, in order to gain her freedom from that very role?

Could she pull it off?

In public, maybe—but in private… Her tongue slid over the sudden parchment-dry surface of her lower lip. Because yes, they might still be at war but things were never that simple. They never were with Rocco. He'd been the only man she'd ever really wanted and she was fast discovering that he still was.

And even though he hadn't given a single indication that he might feel the same way about her, there was no knowing what was going on in that unfathomable mind of his. If Rocco still felt a flicker of the desire she was feeling right now—what then? If he should turn all that blazing Sicilian charm on her, would she be capable of resisting it?

Resisting *him*?

She had no choice. She didn't want her heart broken all over again and therefore she mustn't allow her sexy husband anywhere near her. All she needed to do was remember just how bad the pain had been and how much it had hurt to walk away.

She shook her head. 'I can't do it, Rocco,' she said, swallowing down the emotion which was threatening to make her voice tremble. 'You must be able to see that.'

But if she was hoping for understanding or for a modicum of consideration then she was about to be disappointed, because his features darkened into a look of determination she recognised only too well. He nodded and glanced at his watch as if he was late for a meeting, before giving a careless shrug of his shoulders.

'Then it looks like I'll see you in court, Nicole,' he said softly.

And she believed him. Rocco wasn't a man who said things he didn't mean. He was a man who had the power to do exactly what he wanted and if that involved using a wife he had never loved to further his business ambitions, then he would do it. He had her in a corner. He knew it and she knew it, too. Nicole's heart was racing as she met his brilliant gaze, unable to keep the anger from her voice. 'Very well,' she said. 'Since you leave me no choice… I'll do it.'

Rocco nodded, his senses on alert as he registered her reluctant agreement. He had achieved what he had set out to achieve but now he found himself wondering why she was prepared to do something she clearly detested, just to get her damned divorce.

'So why the rush to the lawyers?' he questioned silkily. He cast a disdainful eye around the room. 'Can't wait to get your hands on my money? Did you wake up one morning and decide that this shabby little place simply wasn't for you? Did you think your wealthy husband ought to provide you with a settlement which would enable you to get out of here—is that what this is all about, Nicole?'

She shook her head. 'It's not about the money, Rocco. I'm not planning to bleed you dry, if that's what you're hinting at.'

'No?' And then something else suddenly occurred to him—and Rocco was startled by the powerful streak of jealousy which flooded through him like dark poison. Because he had thought he was over her. He had decided that from the moment he had arrived back from the States and discovered she'd left him. 'Then maybe it's something else, something rather more common in these situations.'

'What are you talking about?'

'Perhaps there's a new man on the horizon and you want to be free for him. Is that what it is, my little temptress?' His voice hardened as he allowed the thought to grow and suddenly he could see yet another benefit to making her work for her divorce. Because if Nicole *did* have a new lover, then wouldn't that lover be outraged to learn she was spending the weekend with Rocco Barberi? He felt a sudden punch of sadistic pleasure. 'Perhaps you've already started a relationship and he's telling you to get rid of your Sicilian husband pretty damned quick.'

If Nicole had been feeling more genial she might have laughed in his face. For a start, no other man had even looked at her since she'd left her husband, mainly, she suspected, because she was giving out such negative vibes. But even if they had—even in the unlikely event of some gorgeous man sashaying into her little art shop and asking her on a date—it would have left her completely cold. Because no other man could ever be Rocco and he was the only man she'd ever wanted and sometimes she worried that was never going to change. Was that going to be another lasting legacy from her failed marriage—an inability to forget him?

But he doesn't need to know that, she told herself

fiercely. *He doesn't need to know anything about you.*

Defiantly, she met his questioning gaze.

'My reasons are mine and mine alone,' she said coolly. 'And they are none of your business, Rocco.'

CHAPTER THREE

So this was Monaco.

Stepping from the private jet, Nicole felt the warmth of the sun beating down on her head as she looked around, narrowing her eyes behind her sunglasses. In the distance she could see the bright blue blaze of the Mediterranean with fancy white and silver yachts bobbing on the glittering sapphire water.

She'd never been here before but she knew all about the sun-drenched principality at the tip of southern France, which was home to some of the richest people in the world. A place of luxury and excess and glamour. Her heart gave a funny twist. And now it was Rocco's home, too. She pushed her sunglasses further up her nose. Strange to think of him living in this billionaires' playground when he'd always been so fiercely loyal to his homeland and its rustic values. When he'd insisted that simple pleasures were what turned him on, not the lure of the gaming tables, or restaurants which were all about show instead of serving real food. Not for the first time, she wondered what had made him leave Sicily.

She walked towards the shiny black car which was

waiting on the Tarmac, glad she'd insisted on a few days to herself before coming here. She'd told Rocco she needed to organise someone to take her place at the shop and water her plants for her and that much was true, but really she'd needed time to compose herself. To strengthen her resolve not to do anything she might later regret and try to achieve a state of impartiality before she faced her estranged husband again. She'd told herself that whatever happened, she couldn't afford to let desire cloud her judgement and on the plane journey here she'd convinced herself that she had succeeded. But as she looked around in vain for Rocco's dark head and spectacular body, she realised her heart was racing and her skin was clammy—and if *that* wasn't desire then what was?

The uniformed chauffeur stepped forward to open the car door for her.

'Welcome to Monaco, Signora Barberi,' he said in perfect English, with a marked French accent. 'Unfortunately, your husband has been delayed and was unable to meet your flight. He asked me to say he will see you at the house.'

Nicole opened her mouth to tell the driver that she actually preferred to be called Ms Watson these days, until she remembered. *None of this was real.* She wasn't a feisty singleton who was forging a new and independent life for herself. She was supposed to be a woman fighting tooth and nail to hang onto her marriage. So be that woman.

Giving what she hoped was a suitably disappointed expression, she slid onto the back seat of the limousine, pressing her knees together and trying not to think how scruffy the faded denim of her jeans looked against the opulence of the car.

The seat was deliciously soft and the vehicle was coolly air-conditioned, but even so it was difficult to relax. As they drove through the pristine streets of Monaco, Nicole sat as stiffly as someone on their way to a job interview. She'd barely slept a wink since Rocco had turned up at her shop and sent her thoughts and her senses into disarray. Suddenly it hadn't been so easy to put him into that forbidden box where he'd been locked away for so long. Suddenly she'd found herself wondering how on earth she was going to pretend to be reconciling a marriage which had barely got off the ground in the first place. When they'd been nothing but a pair of mismatched strangers with nothing in common other than twin tragedies in their young lives.

They were both orphans: Nicole had been dumped outside a snowy hospital in a shopping bag and Rocco's parents had been killed outright in a speedboat accident when he'd been fourteen. Nicole had thought their dual losses might have provided some kind of bond, but Rocco had adamantly refused to discuss the past. Whenever she'd tried to bring up the subject he would shake his head and tell her it had happened a long time ago and he was over it. And she should be over it, too. He'd told her they should list their blessings instead. She had found herself a kind adoptive mother—and he and his grandfather had helped rear his two heartbroken younger siblings.

They were both over it, he'd insisted.

Nicole stared out of the car window as they passed the fancy stores with designer clothes and jewellery which made you feel you'd been transplanted into the centre of Paris. This was real high-end living, she thought, and once again found it difficult to reconcile Rocco living in such a glitzy place. But what did she really know about him? She was hardly qualified to cast judgement on a man so far out of her league, who had never really allowed her to get close to him. A billionaire who would never have married her if she hadn't been carrying his baby. Nicole felt a brief spear of pain as she pushed her fingers back through her curls. Even now she couldn't believe how two people from opposite ends of the social spectrum should have become lovers—something which had caused outrage at the Barberi family's swanky Mayfair offices, where Nicole been employed as an office cleaner and Rocco was the big boss.

Not that she'd ever intended to be a cleaner. She'd been about to take up a scholarship at one of London's most prestigious art schools when her adoptive mother had been struck down by a virulent form of cancer. Fired by fear and devotion, Nicole had nursed the kindly woman who had taken in the abandoned little girl. The lonely child who had passed through streams of foster parents before Peggy Watson had appeared in her life as a saviour. Nicole hadn't been able to imagine a life without her but, despite her frightened prayers, Peggy had died a painful death. And something in Nicole had died along with her.

Grief had left her barely able to lift a paintbrush, let

alone have any ideas worth putting down on paper. Ignoring the pleadings of her teachers, she had deferred
her place at art school. Suddenly, she'd felt *old*—as
if she'd had nothing in common with the whacky art
students and their garish clothes. How could she possibly behave in a carefree way when inside she'd felt
so numb? All she'd wanted was a well-paid job she
didn't have to think about—and cleaning the Barberi
offices had provided the ideal solution. She'd told herself it was just a case of recovering her confidence and
clawing together some savings until she felt ready to
continue with her art. And that had been her intended
path, until the night she'd bumped into the Sicilian billionaire who, against all the odds, had been destined to
become her husband.

She'd known who he was because he'd had a reputation for staying late and burning the midnight oil. And
like all her co-workers, she'd agreed that the workaholic
billionaire was the hunkiest man she'd ever seen. But
Nicole had regarded Rocco Barberi in the same way
you might regard the leading man in your favourite
TV box-set—easy to fantasise about, but totally out of
reach. Until the evening they had collided—literally.
When Nicole had been carrying her mop and bucket
along the corridor and seen the Sicilian heading towards
her and they'd been so busy staring at each other that
their paths had crossed. The metal bucket had caught
the edge of the tycoon's ankle and Nicole had looked
down in horror to see soapy water sloshing all over his
pristine suit trousers and handmade shoes.

'Oh, my gosh. I'm so sorry,' she'd stumbled, looking up to find herself transfixed by the bluest pair of eyes she'd ever seen. 'I... I wasn't looking where I was going.'

'And neither was I. *Non importa.*' He had made a careless movement with his hand. 'They will clean.'

He'd still been staring at her, staring at her as if he'd known her, or as if he hadn't been able to quite believe what he'd been seeing. And Nicole had felt exactly the same. She might have been a virgin and naïve in the ways of men, but she'd been unable to deny the powerful attraction which had temporarily incapacitated them both. It hadn't seemed to matter that she'd been wearing a blue uniform which had been straining across her breasts, nor that her flyaway curls had been tugged back with a single strand of the green velvet ribbon she always wore, because it matched her eyes. Or that the man in front of her had exuded a power and status which was many lofty rungs above her own. She'd just felt as if she knew him. As if they'd met in a previous life. Or something.

When she'd analysed it afterwards, she'd realised just how dumb she'd been. All that had happened was that she'd been captivated by a man who any painter in a life class would drool over and he had obviously felt something very similar. Their connection had been purely physical. Or chemical. A freak of nature which shouldn't have gone anywhere else, except that it had.

She'd felt apologetic the next day but she'd also felt intensely *alive*—as if he'd woken her from a long sleep. She'd painted him a little postcard—the first time she'd picked up a brush since Peggy's death—and on it she'd depicted a cartoon of Rocco standing in a sea of soapy water on which floated an empty bucket and the single word, *sorry*, at the bottom of the card.

Maybe Rocco had been frustrated at the time and that was why he'd thrown caution to the wind and told her how much the postcard had made him laugh, before asking her out for a drink. And maybe Nicole had just wanted something joyful to happen after the two bleak years since Peggy's death. Either way, their drinks had lain untouched, and the dazzling skyline outside the fancy rooftop bar had gone unnoticed. He'd asked her to dinner and she'd said yes, and it had been the most wonderful evening of her life. But he hadn't touched her, even though she had desperately wanted him to.

A week later they'd had dinner again and then, over a drink following a trip to Milan, he'd asked if she'd ever been on the London Eye. She hadn't as it happened, and as the giant wheel had circled London's imposing monuments Nicole had realised that she was completely smitten by her billionaire boss. Smitten enough to find herself at his apartment later that day with Rocco breaking through her hymen with a groan of hunger followed by disbelief.

Apparently, it was a big thing in Sicily for a man to take a woman's virginity and Rocco had alternately stormed at her, before hugging her tightly to his chest and then lowering his head to suck on her nipples. It had gone on like that for days. Snatched moments of bliss—even at work. That time on the desk would be scorched in her memory for ever. She'd never known that sex could be so *addictive* and Rocco had told her he felt exactly the same.

But then something had changed.

When Rocco had started buying her gradually more daring items of underwear and asking her to wear them Nicole had been eager to try out his sexy commands, yet on some deeper level—she'd been a bit wary, too. Had instinct warned her that the more outrageous his demands, the more he'd seemed to be distancing himself from her? Had he already decided her humble status meant he should end their liaison—and the provocative items of lingerie had been helping highlight her unsuitability? She'd been about to tell him he was making her feel like an object, when she'd missed her period, and her newly tender breasts had told her what the pregnancy test had quickly confirmed—that she was carrying Rocco Barberi's baby.

Telling him had been nothing like the rose-tinted version she'd secretly longed for—a version as far away as possible from her own bleak beginnings on the snowy steps of a wintry hospital. She'd wanted to give him the news somewhere neutral, but he'd told her he was expecting a call and maybe they should take a rain check on the date they'd planned—and had he mentioned that he was planning a trip to the States the following week and wouldn't be around for some time? And that was when it had all come blurting out, there in his penthouse office—with her untouched mop and bucket standing on the floor beside her feet.

'Rocco, I'm pregnant.'

She would never forget his expression as he'd looked

up from his computer. A brief shuttering followed by a shadowed caution.

'You're certain?'

'Positive.'

'And it's...'

His words had faded but a sudden chill had washed over Nicole's skin.

'Yours?' she'd questioned with a perception which had made her suddenly feel quite sick. 'Is that what you were going to say, Rocco?'

He had shaken his head. 'Of course not.'

She hadn't believed him and had started to cry when he'd 'jokingly' suggested she might have deliberately sabotaged the condom in order to trap him. Had her woeful, red-eyed face tugged at his conscience? Was that why he'd risen from his desk and walked across the office towards her? His unkind words had been blotted out by the deep sense of gratitude she'd felt when he'd taken her in his arms and told her that of course she must marry him. He was going to stand by her and that meant a lot to someone who had been abandoned as a baby. And of course, she had thought herself in love with him. Yet all the time she had been acutely aware of the dutiful way he went about preparing for their marriage—as if he was being forced into something he'd never intended.

If she'd been an independent woman instead of a broke cleaner with hardly any qualifications, might her answer have been different? Would she have tried to go it alone to bring up her baby and told him he was very welcome to have access visits whenever he wanted? She thought not. Even if she *had* been inclined to embrace single parenthood, she recognised that Rocco would never have allowed that to happen. She had been carrying *his* child and therefore she had been *his* possession. That was something else she understood. It was something to do with being Sicilian and something to do with being a Barberi.

Their unlikely union had excited a flurry of interest in the European gossip but the Cinderella slant of the newspaper articles had made her feel somehow...*less than*—and that wasn't a good way to start a marriage. And anyway—the whole thing had been a waste of time, hadn't it? Rocco had only gone through with the wedding because she'd been pregnant—but her body had been unable to hold onto the baby she'd wanted so much. She had failed the baby, just as she had failed Rocco. She had let everyone down. She felt the sting of tears at the backs of her eyes and dabbed at them furiously with a curled-up fist.

She wasn't going to think about that.

She wasn't going to let herself go there.

But Nicole's hands were trembling as the powerful car suddenly turned off the main drag and began to ascend a steep and curving street before eventually coming to a halt at the top, outside a deep rose-hued house with its amazing view over Monaco's harbour. She looked up at it in surprise. Somehow she hadn't imagined Rocco living somewhere like this—in a house on a street—not when he had grown up amid roaming acres of olive groves and vineyards in beautiful rural Sicily.

The front door was opened immediately, almost as if

someone had been watching out for the car. But it wasn't Rocco who stood on the doorstep, but a chic woman in a black and white uniform, which made Nicole realise why so many women wore French maid outfits to fancy-dress parties when they were trying to look sexy.

'Welcome, *signora*,' the woman said, with a coral-tinted smile. 'I'm Veronique and I'm the housekeeper. Signor Barberi's assistant, Michele, is waiting upstairs for you in his office and I will take you there.'

Slightly disorientated by the size of the entrance hall, Nicole turned to stare out of the still-open front door where the limousine was parked. 'But my suitcase—'

'The driver will bring it in and leave it in your room,' said Veronique. 'Do not concern yourself. Please. Come with me.'

Nicole followed the housekeeper along a gleaming marble corridor and into a huge room whose only concessions to being an office were a giant desk and a row of clocks on the wall depicting different time zones around the world. For the most part it just looked like an amazing room with an equally amazing view. A tall blonde was waiting for them, her high-heeled shoes matching her fitted pink dress, and Nicole wondered just how many beautiful women Rocco surrounded himself with and whether any of them provided any additional extras.

But that's none of your business, she told herself fiercely trying to downplay the savage little kick of jealousy which flared up inside her. If he wants to sleep with the staff, that's up to him.

The blonde stepped forward and extended her hand.

'Hi! I'm Michele, Rocco's assistant, and I'm delighted to be able to welcome you to Monaco, Signora Barberi.'

'Please—call me Nicole.'

Michele smiled. 'Nicole it is. I'm afraid he's a bit tied up at the moment.' She gave an apologetic shrug which suggested she was no stranger to conveying this message. 'His last meeting went on longer than anticipated and he's taking a conference call right now. He said to tell you he'll be with you as soon as he can and that I should show you around.'

Unsure if Rocco's assistant was aware of the make-believe nature of their reconciliation, Nicole forced herself to adopt an expression of lively curiosity. 'That would be great.'

'So why don't we start down here?'

Nicole followed Rocco's shapely assistant through the most luxurious house she had ever seen. High-ceilinged reception rooms were studded with modern furniture and once again, she couldn't help comparing it to Rocco's Sicilian home. There was no dark wood, or furniture which had been worn down by previous generations who were now unsmiling faces in framed sepia photographs. Everything looked so new and so…bright. She found herself liking it because it had no obvious history and an unexpected smile curved the edges of her mouth. A bit like her, really.

Briefly, she looked around the well-stocked library, peered into an imposing gym and gazed wistfully at the infinity pool which overlooked the Mediterranean, wishing she'd remembered to bring a swimsuit. There were six bedrooms in all, the largest of which was obviously Rocco's, and Nicole's heart flipped when she saw *her* suitcase sitting in the centre of the floor.

'And this is the master suite,' Michele was saying. 'I think you'll find everything you need, but please let me know if there's anything else I can get you. The fundraiser doesn't start until eight tonight so you have plenty of time to acclimatise yourself. Would you like me to leave you to unpack? I expect you want to hang up your dresses.' Michele glanced diplomatically at Nicole's battered little suitcase as she indicated a section of inbuilt wardrobe doors. 'Rocco has left plenty of space for your belongings. Or perhaps you would rather have something to drink first?'

Nicole wasn't planning on putting her belongings anywhere near Rocco's, but she didn't want to embarrass his assistant by telling her that. And there was no way she could ever sleep in here—it was too unsettling on too many levels. She could sense Rocco's presence everywhere. That tantalising scent which was all his—a subtle mix of sandalwood and bergamot. The well-thumbed crime novel which lay open on the bedside table which was probably on exactly the same page as it had been since his last holiday. She could see a pair of gold and lapis lazuli cufflinks lying on the dressing table—and the intimacy of being inside his bedroom again was causing her heart to contract with a flurry of emotions which was making her feel dizzy.

'Actually, I'd love something to drink,' she said weakly.

'In that case, come and I'll have someone bring it up

to the terrace, which I think you might like.' Michele's smile widened. 'You see, I saved the best for last.'

As soon as Nicole stepped out onto the terrace she realised Michele hadn't been exaggerating. Pursing her lips into a silent whistle of appreciation, she looked out over the balcony. This was the kind of view which only wads of money could buy and Nicole's first thought was how much she would like to recreate these colours on clay. The deep azure of the sea lay before her in an endless dazzle and above it was the paler hue of the sky. How incredible it would be to make a collection in all these different shades of blue and maybe to hint at the greens and greys of the distant mountains. It was opulent and stunning and it felt unreal. In fact, *she* felt unreal. But hadn't she always felt out of place in this wealthy world she'd left behind?

'Would you like water, or tea?' Michele was asking. 'Or we have champagne, if you prefer.'

Nicole shook her head. 'No, honestly. Water would be perfect. Thanks.'

After Michele had gone, Nicole leaned over the railings and gazed ahead but this time she wasn't really focussing on the view. She thought about the child she'd once been—the insecure little outcast who had been pushed from pillar to post until Peggy Watson had taken her in. Could that orphaned little girl ever have imagined standing somewhere like this, about to draw a line under her marriage? And despite everything, she felt a pang of pain that she hadn't been able to make it work. It made her start wondering if there had been anything she could have done to have saved it. If her own grief had made her keep Rocco at arm's length. Perhaps it had. Perhaps she might handle it very differently now.

But you can't keep going back over the past. It's too late to do anything about it now. It's over.

'Beautiful, isn't it?' A rich voice washed over her skin like dark silk and Nicole turned round, her heart clenching. Because Rocco was walking towards her, a glass in his hand-the darkness of his hair almost blue-black in the bright sunshine.

'Very beautiful,' she said breathlessly.

'That's Cap Ferrat directly opposite—and the land you can see over there is Italy.' He moved directly in front of her and held out the glass. 'I believe you told Michele you wanted something to drink.'

Nicole's heart was pounding and suddenly her senses were going crazy because she couldn't seem to think straight when he was standing this close. Her body seemed programmed to react in a way she couldn't prevent—no matter how hard she tried. For a split-second she wanted to put her arms around his neck. To melt into the hardness of his body while he began to stroke her in that way which had always made her shiver with longing...

Until she forced herself to remember that this was Rocco. Heartless Rocco who didn't give a damn about her. Who had ridden roughshod over her feelings and brought her out here to help further his ruthless business ambitions. With a tight smile she took the water from him and sipped from the crystal glass. 'Thanks,' she said.

'You're welcome.' His blue eyes were mocking. 'Made yourself at home?'

'Easier said than done,' she quipped. 'This place is so big it reminds me of one of those stately homes in London. I suppose if your business deal falls through you could always charge an entrance fee and make a little extra money on the side.'

'A novel suggestion,' he murmured.

'I'm nothing if not enterprising, Rocco. And I've been running my own shop for the past year so I'm pretty much up to speed with running a small business.'

Reluctantly, Rocco smiled. He'd forgotten that her very different upbringing gave her a sometimes irreverent take on his world, and how it had once enchanted him. Just as he'd forgotten how fresh and vibrant she could look, without even trying. He narrowed his eyes. Compared to the manufactured glamour of most of the women he mixed with, her natural beauty seemed to shine through—and the suddenly powerful throb of his groin was an indication of just how instinctively his body responded to that.

'Did Michele show you where everything was?' he questioned unevenly.

'She did.' She put the glass down. 'Though I thought you might have turned up at the airport to meet me.'

'And were you disappointed?'

She shrugged. 'I don't know that I would describe it as *disappointment*. I just thought that after all the fuss you made about me coming out here, you might have made the effort to meet me from the plane. If you're supposed to be playing the spouse eager to get his marriage back on track, ignoring my arrival isn't really the way to go about it.'

'I'd planned to be there but I'm afraid it didn't work out that way,' he said smoothly. 'I was snowed under with work.'

'So I gather.'

Her thick curls were gleaming darkly in the bright sunshine and suddenly Rocco found himself wanting to tangle his fingers in them, the way he used to do. 'What can I say?' he said, with a shrug. 'It was a call I needed to take.'

'But mightn't it have occurred to you to postpone it?' she continued coolly. 'Rather than dumping me on your assistant, who clearly isn't quite sure what to do with me?'

'Nobody was dumping you, Nicole. It was urgent.'

'It's always urgent with you, isn't it, Rocco? Work always takes precedence.'

He raised his eyebrows. 'You think organisations like the Barberi Foundation just run themselves?'

'No, I don't think that. But I do think work can become an addiction and a substitute.'

'A substitute for what?'

'You tell me. When was the last time you had a holiday?'

'You know I don't like holidays.' He frowned. 'Anyway, what difference does it make who shows you around?'

And that was the trouble, Nicole reminded herself. He really couldn't see it. He had no understanding of the way he treated the people in his life—as if they were mere accessories, to be brought out if and when it suited him. Wasn't it time someone told him? Pointed out a few home-truths which were long overdue? She pushed back her curls, aware that she might be about to become the cliché of a nagging wife—but also aware there were things she'd never dared say to him while they'd been together and maybe she had nothing to lose now. 'Didn't you think it might have been awkward for me when your assistant mistakenly assumed we'd be sharing a bedroom?'

'That was no mistake, *tesoro*,' he said softly. 'We're supposed to be giving our marriage another go and naturally we will need to share a bedroom.'

She shook her head. 'But that's where you're wrong. It's only a game, Rocco,' she reminded him. 'Remember?'

It was only a game, Rocco repeated to himself silently—but right then it was hard to think of anything other than how much he desired her, despite the cheap jewellery and faded jeans. She was far more assertive than she'd ever been in the past and this unaccustomed display of spirit from his once passive wife was doing peculiar things to his pulse-rate. He swallowed. He thought about other women he had dated before his marriage. Classy women, who wore designer clothes instead of jeans and a shirt. With subtle diamonds glinting in their earlobes, not big silver hoops which dangled amid the wild tangle of curls.

Yet Nicole was the one who did it for him. Still did, if he was being honest. Who powered his heart so that it hammered against his chest like a piston. Who made him feel about sixteen again. Rocco felt a sudden rush of lust which wiped out every thought other than the blindingly obvious. He thought about the way her body convulsed and spasmed around him when she was coming—and the erection which was currently throbbing hotly at his groin became almost unbearable.

Sucking in a deep breath, he tried to assert the self-control which had become his default at the age of fourteen, when he had been forced to grow up overnight, but for once it was proving elusive. Was she feeling it too—this attraction which was almost tangible as it sizzled in the air around them? He looked into her eyes as all kinds of new possibilities began to open up in his mind. 'It may only be a game,' he stated softly, 'but I think we need to make it as convincing a game as possible, don't you?'

'Not by sharing a space,' she argued. 'And before you try telling me that your staff will notice we're not in the same room—I don't care. I'm assuming everyone who works for you is loyal, since loyalty is something you've always demanded from the people around you.'

'And were you loyal to me, Nicole?' he said suddenly.

The question took her by surprise. 'Yes, I was. Completely. More than you'll ever know. 'She gave a short laugh. 'Or maybe you aren't aware of the offers I got to tell my story when our marriage broke down?'

He leaned back against the railing and studied her, his blue eyes thoughtful. 'What kind of offers?'

She shrugged. 'Oh, you know. Big ones. Journalists who tracked me down wondering why a Barberi ex-wife was living such a shabby existence when she'd

been married to one of the richest men on the planet.
Why I was working in a puny little art shop instead of
living in a luxury flat and giving your credit card a bat-
tering. I don't know why you're looking so surprised,
Rocco—you can see how much they might have wanted
the story. Isn't that what newspaper readers love to read
about? The fairy-tale marriage which came to such an
abrupt ending.'

His sapphire eyes had become shuttered by the thick
curtain of his dark lashes. 'But you didn't talk to them?'

'Of course I didn't.' Frustratedly, Nicole shook her
head. How could he even *ask* that? The raw pain of losing their baby had been replaced by a kind of numbness
that her marriage was over—they had pushed each other
so far away that there was nothing left between them.
She'd forced herself into a zombified state of acceptance
as she had stumbled through the days without realising
what was going on, only knowing she needed to start
over. She'd convinced herself that Sicily had been nothing but a strange interlude and she needed to reconnect
with England, but it hadn't been easy. She'd felt like a
tiny craft thrown into a raging sea, not knowing which
direction life would take her. One minute she'd been
a cleaner and then a billionaire's wife. One minute a
mother-to-be and the next…nothing. There was no word
in the English language to describe a mother who had
lost her child, was there? Nicole swallowed. Only someone who was seriously deluded would have wanted to
relive that pain and disruption and see it printed in a
newspaper. 'Did you really think I would ever talk to a
journalist?' she demanded. 'Did you?'

He shrugged as his mouth flattened into its habitual uncompromising line. 'The financial rewards might have tempted some people.'

'But I'm not *some people*, Rocco! When will you ever believe that I was never interested in the money? That wasn't what attracted me to you. What you've never had—you never miss.'

He was still studying her, still with that same intense scrutiny. 'Is that why you left without taking anything?'

Nicole hesitated. Maybe this was what it all boiled down to for him. Because for Rocco, everyone had their price, didn't they? He'd told her about the women who had been bewitched by the Barberi fortune and were eager to get themselves a slice of it for themselves. Just as he'd told her about the people who tried to muscle in when they found out who he was. He didn't really trust people and never let them close. Much easier for him to believe that everyone had an ulterior motive where he was concerned because that gave him a legitimate reason to keep people at a distance. She wondered how honest she could afford to be—yet surely it was a waste of time trying to conceal the truth from him now, in these dying days of their relationship. Because her answers were academic. Whatever Rocco wanted, it wasn't her.

She stared at him. 'I didn't take anything because I wanted to cut all ties between us. In fact, I never wanted to see you again.'

She met his eyes with a steady challenge and Rocco stilled. How *dared* she be so dismissive? It was an insult to his pride, yes—but it struck at something darker, too. Something deep inside which made him want to lash out at her blatant rejection. Yet there was no need to fight, not when there were different ways for him to vent his frustration or show her just what a mistake she had made. Things which had been on his mind all day—all week—ever since he'd walked into her little art shop in Cornwall and seen her bite her lip so that it took on a deep, rosy glow. And despite having told himself this was not going to happen, he found himself taking a step towards her.

'So you never wanted to see me again?' he mused silkily. 'In which case it didn't work very well for you, did it? Seeing as you're here with me now.'

She continued to hold his gaze with a look of pure defiance. 'And I can walk away whenever I choose,' she said. 'Divorce or no divorce. Either you accept that I'm not sharing a room with you, or I'm out of here. Because I'm not interested in you that way, Rocco, if that's what you're thinking.'

'You're saying you don't want to have sex with me?'

She nodded. 'That's exactly what I'm saying.'

He saw her green eyes widen as he reached out to pull her into his arms, her luscious curves instantly pliable beneath his fingers. 'Then perhaps you'd like to put that to the test, my defiant wife,' he murmured as he lowered his head towards hers.

CHAPTER FOUR

HE WAS GOING to kiss her and after everything she'd just said, Nicole knew she needed to stop him . But suddenly she found herself governed by a much deeper need than preserving her sanity, or her pride. A need and a hunger which swept over her with the speed of a bush fire. As Rocco's shadowed face lowered towards her she found past and present fusing, so that for a disconcerting moment she forgot everything except the urgent hunger in her body. Because hadn't her Sicilian husband always been able to do this—to captivate her with the lightest touch and to tantalise her with that smouldering look of promise? And hadn't there been many nights since they'd separated when she'd woken up, still half fuddled with sleep, and found herself yearning for the taste of his lips on hers just one more time? And now she had it.

One more time.

She opened her mouth and Rocco used the opportunity to fasten his mouth over hers in the most perfects of fits. And instantly Nicole felt helpless—caught up in the powerful snare of a sexual mastery which wiped out everything else. She gave a moan of pleasure because it had been so long since she had done this. She'd forgotten what it was like to kiss him because kissing was one of the first casualties of a failing marriage. You stopped kissing and touching and all too soon it was difficult to contemplate anything other than the icy barrier you had created between you.

And Nicole had felt like a living statue since they'd been apart. As if she were made from marble. As if the flesh and blood part of her were some kind of half-forgotten dream. Slowly but surely she had withdrawn from the sensual side of her nature until she'd convinced herself she was dead and unfeeling inside. But here came Rocco to wake her dormant sexuality with nothing more than a single kiss. It was like some stupid fairy story. It was scary and powerful. She didn't *want* to want him, and yet...

She wanted him.

Her lips opened wider as his tongue slid inside her mouth—eagerly granting him that early intimacy as if preparing the way for another. She began to shiver as his hands started to explore her—rediscovering her body with an impatient hunger, as if it were the first time he'd ever touched her. His fingers skated over her breasts, palms massaging the swollen contours until each taut and aching nipple was in an exquisite state of arousal. Instinctively she writhed against him and felt the hard cradle of his desire. And now the moaning sound she could hear was *his* as he deepened the kiss—underpinning it with a sudden sense of urgency.

'Nicole,' he said unevenly and she'd never heard him say her name like that before.

Her arms were locked behind his neck as again he circled his hips against hers in unmistakable invitation and, somewhere in the back of her mind, Nicole could hear the small voice of reason imploring her to take control of the situation. It was urging her to call a halt to what they were doing and to do it now, before it was too late. But once again she ignored it. Against the powerful tide of passion, that little voice was drowned out and she allowed pleasure to shimmer over her skin.

She drew back a little to pull some air into her lungs—and the expression on his face both shocked and thrilled her. Because she'd never seen Rocco look like this before. The tension had turned his features into a taut mask. His eyes were blackened with lust, their sapphire brilliance almost concealed by the dilated pupils. Two lines of colour flared along the edges of his high cheekbones and contrasted with the hue of his olive skin.

'So, *tesoro*.' His murmured words were provocative as his circling groin gave yet another candid demonstration of just how aroused he was. 'Is this what you've been missing?'

Nicole swallowed. She should tell him not to be so arrogant. She should tell him a lot of things which were long overdue. But she was in no fit state to give a coherent answer because he was idly whispering his middle finger down over her midriff and somehow the barrier of her filmy shirt was making what was happening doubly provocative. So that instead of telling him to stop, she found herself whispering, 'Yes.'

He gave a little groan of satisfaction as he slid his

hand up beneath her shirt to cup the breast which was straining madly against her bra. So close to the skin, she thought frustratedly—and yet much too far away. Her mouth dried as he began to circle a nipple with his thumb and her eyelids fluttered to a close as she felt it puckering beneath the lace. How could a touch which was barely there feel so *incredible*? 'Oh,' she said, her voice sounding slurred against the seeking pressure of his kiss.

He gave a low laugh as his hand moved from her breast down to the waistband of her jeans and Nicole held her breath. Would he dare go further? Surely she shouldn't allow *this*? She knew she ought to break the spell yet she was so in thrall to what was happening that she was powerless to move. She heard the rasp of her zip as he began to slide it down and she held her breath, praying he would continue even though she knew he ought to stop. And now he was slipping his hand into the space provided by the open denim, and was easing one finger on a downward path over the warm surface of her belly. She swallowed.

'Is there something else you would prefer me to do?' he murmured. 'In which case, you'd better tell me, because although I have many skills where women are concerned, I'm afraid mind-reading isn't one of them.'

His teasing incited her—it made the heat raging inside her intensify to such a pitch that the idea of calling a halt to this madness seemed unbearable. Yet it angered her, too. How dared he bring up the subject of *other women* at a time like this? Did he think she didn't care about stuff like that? With a yelp of rage she kissed him hard and she could feel his mouth curving into a smile, because by now he was slipping his fingers inside her panties. And didn't the molten wetness he encountered there seem like a kind of betrayal? A physical demonstration of just how much she still wanted him, no matter how much she wished she didn't. Her head fell back as he began to circle the tip of her clitoris with a feather-light touch.

'Oh, my,' he said softly as she quivered uncontrollably beneath the rhythmic caress of his finger. He gave a soft laugh. 'Oh, Nicole. Just like old times. So wet and so *hot*. I think we'd better do something about this, hadn't we, *mio tesoro*?'

She opened her mouth to tell him he'd got it all wrong but her desire was so great that she couldn't speak. And even if she could, what the hell could she say?

Stop what you're doing because it's wrong. It's making me feel weak and vulnerable and I vowed never to let myself feel that way again.

Because right now she didn't care about any of that. All she cared about was the way he was making her feel. So she stayed silent as layer upon layer of pleasure began to build—so sweet and so achingly familiar. It took her to such a pitch of sexual hunger that she found herself wanting to whisper his name over and over again, like some life-affirming mantra. She was going to come—she knew she was—when the sudden memory of his mocking words crashed into her mind and shattered the magic spell he was weaving.

Just like old times, he'd said.

But it wasn't, was it? It was nothing like old times,

when she'd still been naïve and foolish enough to think there was some connection between them, which could get deeper if they worked on it. They weren't those star-crossed lovers she'd imagined them to be and nor were they the unlikely newlyweds with no idea how to communicate with each other. The past was gone and this was not how she intended her future to be.

Nicole clamped her hand over Rocco's wrist, halting the finger still poised with tantalising precision over the engorged bud as she summoned up all the willpower she possessed. And although her body was screaming out its objections, she blocked them. Because she'd been through a lot to get to where she was today. She'd worked hard and built her little business up from scratch—and it might not be very much, but it was all *hers*. She was beginning to establish herself as the artist she'd always wanted to be before life and Rocco had sucked her up and wrung her out to dry. She'd even started to convince herself that one day she would be properly over him. Was she really prepared to jeopardise everything—including her precious self-respect—just because her hormones had been reactivated by Rocco Barberi's overt sexuality?

Heart pounding, she yanked his hand out of her panties and stepped away to turn her back on him while she readjusted her clothing. Her cheeks were burning as she zipped up her jeans and smoothed down her white shirt while the silver chains around her neck jangled like wind chimes. Slowly she came back to reality, blinking as she took in her surroundings to realise that they'd been making out on a penthouse terrace not far from

Monaco's picture-book harbour. And while they weren't exactly being overlooked, what was to stop someone on one of those fancy yachts from peering through a pair of binoculars and seeing them? Some paparazzi photographer taking a few candid snaps to earn himself some unexpected money? Or one of Rocco's staff turning up with papers for him to sign? She gave a violent shudder of remorse as she turned on him.

'How dare you try to have sex with me?' she hissed.

Unabashed, he shrugged. 'That isn't the message I was just getting. And isn't it a little late in the day for such an outraged reaction? I thought only teenagers played games like that.'

'I wasn't *playing games*!'

'Letting me go only so far and no further?' He raised his eyebrows. 'You don't consider that an adolescent game?'

'Not in the circumstances, no. You were making me feel like...like an *object*.'

'I was making you feel pleasure,' he corrected. 'What's wrong with that?'

She shook her head. 'And now you're insulting me by asking such a dumb question. Having sex with you would complicate an already complicated situation— we both know that. And that's not the reason I'm here.'

'But you wanted me,' he said slowly, his bright sapphire gaze taking in the breasts which were still heaving beneath her filmy shirt. 'You want me now. Your body is crying out for me to touch you again. Surely even you wouldn't deny that, Nicole.'

Nicole bit her lip, angry that he could look so cool

and controlled when she felt so hot and bothered. Hating the fact that if she denied his accusation, she could rightly be accused of hypocrisy. And she didn't *have* to answer him. She could flounce off this terrace any time she wanted except that wouldn't be a very mature response, and she was supposed to be all about maturity these days. Wasn't that one of the benefits of getting older, that you learnt from the knocks you experienced along the way? You learnt that what didn't kill you made you stronger, even if at the time you wanted to just curl up and die.

She smoothed her hands down over her ruffled curls in a vain attempt to smooth them. 'Of course I *want* you,' she said carefully. 'Or rather, my body does. You are a very charismatic man, as I'm sure many women must have told you in the past—'

'You were always one of the most vociferous advocates,' he reminded her softly.

'I know. But I was young. And I don't think talking about the way we felt back then is particularly helpful,' she said. Because she was starting to realise how dangerous it could be. It was feeding those feelings she'd forced herself to repress. Dangerous feelings about love and longing, which had been pointless then and were even more pointless now.

'Let's just chalk it up to experience,' she continued, swallowing down the lump in her throat. 'We were just two people trying to do the right thing. It just didn't work out.'

A thoughtful look shadowed his face. 'But there's no reason why that should stop us having sex right now, since it's what we both want,' he murmured. 'Isn't that so?'

Nicole shook her head, trying to fight the sudden desire provoked by the velvety caress of his words. 'That's not going to happen, Rocco.'

'Do you want to tell me why?'

'You know why. Because it would feel…wrong. And I'm pretty certain it would invalidate our two years of separation and take even longer to get a divorce.'

'Ah, yes. Your precious divorce,' he mused.

'My ticket to freedom, you mean? Yours, too.'

His smile was mocking. 'At least you've answered one question for me,' he observed.

She looked at him. 'Oh? What question is that?'

'Back in England, I asked if there was another man waiting in the wings and you didn't give me a satisfactory answer. But now I'd be prepared to bet my entire fortune there isn't.'

'I thought you said mind-reading wasn't one of your skills.'

'It's not. It doesn't need to be. It's written all over your face, Nicole.'

'What is?' she said, even though on some level she was aware she might be walking straight into a trap.

'You're so horny,' he answered throatily. 'Hornier than any woman would be if she'd been having sex on a regular basis. Yet you were able to pull back, despite being so close to coming. Such steely resolve.' He gave a soft laugh. 'And I admire that quality in you, Nicole— even if I'm the one who ultimately missed out.'

His words wrong-footed her because they sounded

like a compliment and just like the next woman, Nicole was a sucker for a compliment. Had he said it to lull her into a false sense of complacency before moving in for the big seduction? She wondered how many other women had stood here, like this, their clothes all rumpled and their blood pulsing as they went willingly to the Sicilian billionaire's bed. Well, she wasn't going to be one of them.

'I'm ending this conversation as of now,' she said. 'And now I need to find myself a separate bedroom because this is a *pretend* reconciliation, not a real one. We don't share rooms and we don't make out.'

Rocco saw the determined way she pulled back her shoulders and recognised she was serious. A flicker of disquiet edged his growing frustration. If it had been any other woman he could have persuaded her with a kiss. A kiss which this time she would find impossible to stop, because if Rocco Barberi was hell-bent on something, or someone, he always got it. But the steadfast expression flattening his estranged wife's soft lips was unfamiliar and suddenly he realised he didn't know this new Nicole at all.

When he'd gone to see her in England sex had been the last thing on his mind. He'd gone there to punish her and to use her, not to make love to her, yet something had changed his mind. That kiss they'd just shared had started out as nothing more than a challenge—a demonstration of his own power in the light of her resistance—and yet she had responded in a way which had sent his desire soaring.

And yet she had pushed him away.

His heart pounded, because now he was determined to have her one last time and nothing was going to stop him. But for once he realised that he was going to have to work for it. Maybe he should give her enough space to realise what she was missing, instead of pushing his own agenda. How long before she decided that denying her hunger for him was simply not sustainable—and slipped into his arms again?

So he nodded his head and gave her a cool smile. 'If that's what you want, then that's what you shall have. Take any bedroom you want—there are plenty to choose from,' he said, enjoying the confusion which had suddenly clouded her emerald eyes. 'Just make sure you're ready for the screening and dinner tonight. The car will be here just before eight.'

He ran his gaze over the unruly dark curls and the mismatched silver necklaces and a rogue glimmer of amusement found its way into his voice. 'No doubt you've brought something deeply unsuitable to wear?'

Unexpectedly, her eyes danced in response. 'You think I'm going to turn up looking like this?'

He shrugged. 'I have no idea. I offered to buy you some suitable clothes for this trip but you turned down my offer.'

'Because we tried that once before and it didn't work. Remember? You were so eager to make me into what you thought a Barberi wife should be that I felt like some kind of dress-up doll.'

He frowned. 'I was trying to make you feel more comfortable.'

'What, by employing that expensive stylist who put

me in those horrible starchy dresses which didn't suit me? Or the fancy hairdresser who decided to chop off all my hair so I ended up looking like a shorn lion?'

'That *was* a mistake,' he conceded.

She looked at him uncertainly, clearly taken aback by what for him almost passed as an apology, and the fleeting vulnerability on her face stirred something deep inside him, reminding him what had attracted him to her in the first place. Well, that and her killer body.

'But not any more. Tonight I'm going to wear my hair and clothes exactly as I like them,' she continued airily. 'And if you're worried I'm going to disgrace you with my appearance, Rocco—you shouldn't be.'

'Oh?' He was curious now.

'If people criticise my less than conventional appearance at least it will reinforce why our last-minute attempt at reconciliation didn't work. If they see us together and think "chalk and cheese", they'll wonder why we ever got married in the first place.' She slanted him a challenging look. 'Because although opposites attract—they can also repel. We both know that.'

With that she turned her back on him and left the terrace with a sway of her denim-covered bottom, which Rocco found almost unbearably provocative.

And after she'd gone, he felt restless—a feeling kick-started by the echo of her final words. *Were* they better off without each other? Not right now they weren't. The fingertip he ran over his dry lips only added to his frustration as he breathed in the earthy aroma of her sex. By now she should have been in his bed—eagerly opening her legs so they could lose themselves in sweet oblivion, not leaving him here aching and frustrated.

Looking out to sea, he scowled. When his PA had called to say Nicole had arrived at his Monaco home he had been unprepared for the primitive rush of satisfaction he'd experienced, knowing she was here. Back in the marriage she had walked away from. It had never happened to him before—a woman telling him she was going, and meaning it. Only the stark note lying on top of an unmade bed had made clear her wishes.

Please don't follow me, or try to contact me. It's better this way, Rocco. I'm sorry.

And that had been it. A few words signalling the end. Yet he hadn't seen it coming and shock was something he didn't handle well. Maybe the only thing he didn't handle well—not surprising given his history. He remembered the blood draining from his face as he'd crumpled the note in his fist and had proceeded to do something completely alien. Taking himself off to the bar in the nearby village, he had got himself very, very drunk. Groups of the local Sicilian men had looked surprised because Rocco Barberi was not known as a drinker. He remembered smashing his fist down hard on the counter and shattering a glass and hearing the old men's voices raised in alarm. Someone must have made a phone call because he vaguely recalled his oldest friend arriving and getting him back to the complex, and Salvatore telling him that women were capricious creatures and she would be back before he knew it.

But she hadn't come back and Rocco had told himself he didn't *want* her back. Why would he want a wife who had deserted him—who had given up at the first hurdle? Yet despite her behaviour, his sense of duty went deep and his tenacity even deeper. He didn't like failure and a shattered marriage fell very firmly into that category. So he had written to her, reminding her of the solemn vows they had made in church and suggesting they give their marriage another go.

She hadn't even bothered to reply and Rocco had geared himself up to resist the demands for money he was certain would follow. He remembered his growing anticipation of the forthcoming battle—a battle he would certainly win—and his determination to bring her to her knees in court. It was the first moment of pleasure he had experienced in a long time. If she wanted his money then she was damned well going to have to fight him for it.

But...*niente*.

Nothing.

There had been no demands for alimony. Even the recent letter from her lawyers had simply requested that the marriage be formally ended. She had asked for nothing and somehow that had only intensified his rage.

His features were set as he undressed and stepped into the shower, but the powerful jets of cold water did little to ease his aching body as he pictured Nicole on the balcony, her rosy lips parted with pleasure as his fingers flicked over her heated flesh and brought her so tantalisingly close to orgasm.

As he towelled the icy droplets from his skin a renewed determination crept over him.

He would have her, he vowed silently as he willed his erection to subside. Because sex was the only thing which would rid him of her enduring memory.

And he would not wait much longer.

CHAPTER FIVE

'So. How do I look? Does my appearance confirm your worst fears, Rocco, or will I pass the test?'

Nicole kept her words deliberately light as she walked into the vast sitting room where Rocco was standing with his back to her, staring through the open windows which overlooked the sea. Because what she was *not* going to do was beat herself up or crumple with shame when she allowed herself to remember how nearly she had succumbed to him earlier. It had happened. She hadn't been expecting it to happen because she'd thought those kind of feelings had left her. But they hadn't, had they? Rocco had melted the icy wall which had surrounded her for so long, and her image of herself as someone who could no longer feel desire had been shattered. Heart pounding, she had left him on the terrace and gone to find herself a bedroom in this vast house of his—glad to escape from his disturbing proximity. But she had lain down on the bed for a long time afterwards, her body trembling with frustrated desire, unable to get him out of her mind.

She let her gaze drift over him, wishing she could

acquire some kind of immunity against him. Dressed in an immaculate dinner suit, his powerful body was silhouetted against the bright light of the Mediterranean but at the sound of her voice he turned round. And even though she tried to fight it, the brief, unguarded expression on his face filled her with pleasure. She'd seen that look of appreciation before—but usually when she was naked. Not when she was wearing a long dress which, apart from a scooped neck and bare arms, covered her body all the way down to her ankles. Fashioned from fine, black jersey it clung to her curves like a second skin and she had teamed it with black pumps and a black bag onto which she'd sewn lots of glittery sequins. The green of the sequins matched her dramatic green necklace and chandelier earrings, which gleamed whenever her wavy hair swayed.

His eyes narrowed as, slowly, they took in her appearance. 'What happened?' he questioned softly. 'Did you rob a bank?'

'I bought this dress from a market stall, as it happens.'

'I wasn't talking about the dress,' he growled. 'I meant the jewels.'

It was a small victory and Nicole couldn't quite hold back her smile of triumph. 'These? They're fake, Rocco. Paste,' she added. 'I told you—nobody can tell the difference these days. And these were cheap enough for it not to matter if I lose one of the stones—not like the time that big diamond fell out of the bracelet you gave me on our wedding day and caused so much trouble with everyone having to hunt round for it.' She was aware that she had started to babble, but maybe that was something to do with the fact that he was still looking at her as a lion might look at a lump of flesh, just before devouring it. And even worse—that she *liked* him looking at her like that. In her current state of frustrated arousal she could have let him look at her like that all day. She resumed her inane monologue about the wedding bracelet. 'Still, at least we were able to get the money back on the insurance and I—'

'Was that why you left behind all the jewellery I gave you?' he interrupted suddenly. 'Because you didn't like it?'

There was a short silence and she shrugged her shoulders. 'It was a joint asset,' she said. 'And as such, wasn't really mine to take. And I wanted...'

'What did you want, Nicole?'

She met his gaze, uneasy at this sudden line of questioning from a man who had never cared about such things before. 'A clean break, I think they call it.'

'A clean break,' he echoed, his mouth twisting into a bitter smile. 'Yes, of course. The modern, disposable marriage. If you try hard enough you can pretend it never happened.'

She opened her mouth to ask him what *he* had done to help save it but the sudden pain spearing through her made the words die in her throat. It didn't matter what either of them had done or failed to do. Bottom line was that they'd messed up so and it still had the power to hurt. 'Why rake up all this now, Rocco?' she questioned, trying hard to keep her voice steady. 'I thought the whole idea was for us to appear tonight as a couple who are trying to get it together—and we won't convince anyone if we've been fighting. People can always tell if a couple have been rowing. So why don't you tell me about what kind of event it is, so I can be fully briefed?'

For a moment Rocco didn't answer, unwilling to be placated by this newly assertive Nicole who looked so damned gorgeous that all he wanted to do was to pull her into his arms and get intimate with her, despite the market dress and fake jewels. But maybe she was right. What was the point of sparring when they had a whole evening to get through—a necessary preliminary before he got down to the more important business of seducing her. And when he seduced her... His mouth hardened. His anger and his resentment would disappear with one fell stroke. He would enjoy her matchless body one last time. He would take his pleasure and pleasure her in return.

And she would spend the rest of her life remembering it.

'Some of the major shareholders from the drug company I'm trying to buy are in town,' he said evenly. 'They've financed an art-house film which looks as if it's going to be a commercial success.'

She blinked. 'You mean they invest in films *and* drug companies?'

He walked over to the mirror which hung over an ornate marble fireplace and adjusted his tie. 'Why not? They like to spread their investments around. It's how you make the big bucks.'

'And where do I fit in?'

He turned back to face her, his expression unreadable. 'You'll accompany me to the screening and afterwards we're having dinner with the stars of the film, who are over here promoting it. All you have to do is gaze at me adoringly, *tesoro*. You play the young wife eager to get back with her husband. Do you think you can manage that?'

His words were wry but Nicole wondered what he would do if he knew the truth. That behind her nonchalant air, her senses were on fire. That every time he even looked at her she wanted to melt. She dug her fingernails into the sequins on her handbag. And he *mustn't* find out because then he might start touching her again. And she *wanted* him to do it to her again—that was the most dangerous thing of all. Next time she might not be strong enough to resist him.

'Oh, I think I can just about manage to maintain the façade of adoring you for a few hours—just so long as we're back before midnight strikes,' she said coolly. 'Just give me a couple of minutes and I'll go and fetch my wrap.'

But that sense of unreality she'd felt earlier swept over her again as she climbed into the back of Rocco's car—this time with the brooding billionaire by her side. She tried to make conversation but sensed that Rocco could see right through her attempts at chit-chat. Was he aware that it was all she could do not to reach out her hand and caress the honed hardness of his taut thigh, or run her fingertips through the ebony ruffle of his hair? Could he guess she was fantasising about him pressing the button which would bring down the screen shielding them from the driver, before lying her on the back seat and pulling her panties down. Little beads of sweat spring out on her forehead as she started imagining his tongue exploring her heated flesh and Nicole was relieved when finally they reached the venue.

The place where the screening was fancier than anywhere he'd ever taken her and she was amazed he could seem so relaxed in such a high-profile setting, for the Rocco of old would have curled his sensual mouth with derision. Flashbulbs popped as they walked up the flower-decked red carpet, his guiding hand placed unnervingly in the small of her back and making her shiver, despite the warmth of the evening.

The lights went down and the big screen lit up and Nicole watched a film which didn't really do it for her, even though everyone else seemed to love it. She'd never been a big fan of black and white movies and, besides, she was distracted by what was going on in the semi-darkness. She noticed that the American actress who was starring in the picture and seated on Rocco's other side was spending an awful lot of time cupping her hand over his ear to whisper into it. And suddenly all Nicole's defiant words about nobody being able to tell the difference between real and fake jewellery seemed like so much hot air, because Anna Rivers looked a class act in her waterfall of diamonds, with the burly man from security who was guarding them never far from her side. Nicole shot her a glance, aware that the beautiful actress was flirting outrageously with her husband and that she didn't like it. She didn't like it one bit.

Afterwards, they ate dinner in the Café de Monaco,

an award-winning restaurant which overlooked the harbour. Yet despite not having eaten anywhere this grand for a long time, the experience was wasted on Nicole. She seemed to have lost her appetite and the glass of champagne she'd drunk at the beginning of the evening had left her with nothing but a raging thirst. But she was determined to honour her side of this crazy bargain and did her best to chat as agreeably as she could to the various shareholders. She treated them as if they were prospective customers in her little Cornish pottery shop and tried not to be offended by their obvious surprise when they learned who she was. Even the star of the film gaped like a stranded fish when she overheard Nicole talking.

'You are Rocco's *wife*?' clarified Anna Rivers slowly.

'I am,' agreed Nicole.

The actress frowned. 'But I didn't even know he was married.'

'Well, there you go,' said Nicole weakly, feeling a total fraud—although she was unable to deny her satisfaction when the actress spent the rest of the evening talking to her leading man instead of trying to monopolise Rocco.

Nicole stood there in her plain black dress, flashing a friendly smile whenever anyone looked in her direction. At one point she was targeted by an Argentinian ex-polo player, Javier Estrada—a flirtatious man with flashing black eyes who frankly left her cold. As the evening drew to a close, she found herself in animated conversation with Annelise, the wife of Marcel Dupois—the conservative shareholder Rocco had warned her about.

The Frenchwoman turned out to have a passion for pottery so they had lots to talk about and when Nicole lifted her head it was to meet Rocco's questioning gaze burning into her like bright blue fire.

Gaze back at him adoringly, she told herself. Act like a wife who wants to make up with arguably the best-looking man in the room. She managed a passable imitation of adulation and her cheeks flared in response to the answering intensity in his eyes. He didn't look away and neither did she and for a few extraordinary seconds the make-believe felt almost real. Her chest tightened and suddenly she was having difficulty breathing. How was it possible to want a man yet hate him at the same time? To wish he were close, yet want to push him as far away as possible? Quickly, she turned away and stared out at the lights which were glittering in the harbour, trying to drink in a view which would soon be nothing more than a fast-fading memory.

'Nicole?'

The sound of Rocco's voice made her tremble and silently Nicole cursed it. She found herself remembering the way he'd purred her name like that when he had been unzipping her jeans on the terrace—and wasn't she now in danger of playing out the memory in a little too much detail? Composing her face into a smile, she turned round, trying very hard not to react to the wicked gleam in his eyes.

'Rocco!' she said brightly. 'Hi.'

His eyes mocked her. 'Hi.'

'Are you—' she swallowed '—having a good time?'

He shrugged. 'Tolerable. But I think we've had

enough partying for one night, don't you? We should think about going.'

It was an unequivocal statement intended to terminate the evening and Nicole wanted to protest. To say she was enjoying herself and could they please stay. But that was only delaying the inevitable—and why was she suddenly feeling so *nervous*? Just because she wanted him didn't mean anything was going to happen, did it? Women wanted men all the time but they didn't act on those desires. She certainly wasn't going to jeopardise everything she'd worked for by falling into the arms of a man who spelled nothing but danger.

Her smile didn't slip as she tucked her clutch bag under her arm. 'Sure. Why not?'

In the limousine Rocco was silent, staring out at the principality's glitzy shops as they drove by, as if he'd never really noticed them before. And Nicole did the same—concentrating on the steep roads and the breathtaking views of the harbour as the powerful car gained height. She told herself she was glad he didn't want to engage in meaningless chatter but in truth the silence was unsettling her. At least talking would have been a distraction from the growing awareness inside her body—the unwanted tingling of her breasts and the heat pooling low in her belly, which was making her feel like a victim of her own desire. It was all she could do not to squirm impatiently on the seat beside him and beg him to put her out of her misery with the hard pressure of his kiss.

'You did very well tonight,' he said when at last the car drew up outside his house. 'I could see how well you connected with Annelise Dupois. She obviously thought you were very engaging.'

'Thanks.'

'Our Argentinian friend certainly thought so, too,' he added drily. 'You seem to have won yourself a new fan.'

'As did you,' she said sweetly. 'Why, Anna Rivers could barely contain her dismay when she discovered I was your wife.'

In the semi-darkness his eyes gleamed like a jungle predator who had suddenly appeared from behind thick foliage. 'So we have discovered that we are both attractive to the opposite sex,' he observed.

'Hardly ground-breaking news where you're concerned, Rocco.'

'And that we can both be somewhat...*territorial* about each other.'

The lightness in her voice didn't quite come off. 'Speak for yourself.'

'Oh, I am. But you can hardly deny your own irritation whenever Anna whispered in my ear,' he said wryly. 'Since it was written all over your face.'

Had she been that transparent? 'I noticed you didn't try to stop her. Were you enjoying her warm breath on your earlobe and the way she was giggling hysterically at practically everything you said?'

He shrugged. 'Not really. I was more interested in your reaction.'

'I was acting, Rocco—that was all. Trying to play the part of the reconciling wife who would have been jealous at such an interaction. You really shouldn't read anything more into it than that.'

She reached for the door handle and the waiting chauffeur must have been watching because immediately he jumped out to open the door and Nicole stepped from the claustrophobic atmosphere of the car. As she felt the warm Mediterranean air wash over her skin, she knew she needed to get a grip. To ask herself why she was feeling so possessive about a man who only ever tolerated her. And then to stop it.

Veronique must have been off duty because Rocco unlocked the door himself and the absence of servants made their homecoming seem curiously normal. Only it wasn't normal, Nicole reminded herself fiercely. That was just another figment of her overactive imagination.

'I'm tired,' she said. 'I'm going to bed. Goodnight, Rocco.'

'Goodnight, Nicole.' He didn't try to stop her.

Had she thought he might?

Of course she had. Her body was in such a heightened state of desire that she felt almost deflated when she pushed open the door to the bedroom suite she had chosen—as far away from Rocco as possible—and clicked it shut behind her.

Stripping off the black jersey dress and letting the worthless gems spool into a green heap on one of the modern glass tables, Nicole gathered her hair up beneath a voluminous plastic cap and went to stand beneath the gushing shower. But rubbing soap over breasts which were already aroused and imagining it was Rocco's dark fingers sliding between her thighs instead of her own was not the relaxing experience she'd been anticipating. In fact, when she turned off the jets of water, she felt even more churned up than she had done in the limousine.

She dried her skin and raked a wide-toothed comb through her curls but she was feeling much too edgy to think about sleeping. The moon was so bright that it was flooding the room with silver light and, pulling on a baggy T-shirt and slipping on a clean pair of panties, she walked across the room towards the terrace and stepped outside, the tiles cool beneath her bare feet. Above her the dark sky was punctured by the bright glitter of stars and the moon was huge as she leaned her elbows against the wrought-iron railings and stared out at the inky gleam of the sea.

Had she been crazy to come here?

Probably.

She realised it was going to be hard to forget Rocco after this and it had nothing to do with the fancy house, or cars, or the yacht he'd casually mentioned was moored in the harbour. It was being in his company again. She'd forgotten how charismatic he was and what a powerful magnetism he exerted over everyone, but especially over her. She'd forgotten because it had been in her best interests to forget and she had been trying to move on. But now she was confused and aching. He hadn't kissed her tonight—he hadn't even *touched* her—and yet it was as if he'd started a slow blaze inside her. A drift of wind lifted the curls from the back of her neck and she sighed, realising that sleep wasn't going to come easily. Still, nobody ever died from a lack of sleep, did they? She would just stand there and watch the moonlight glinting on the water and wait until her eyelids started growing heavy.

She heard the click of the bedroom door as it opened but she didn't turn round. She didn't need to. Nobody else would walk into her bedroom uninvited. Nobody else would dare. But even if a hundred people had pushed open that door, she would have known it was Rocco from a hundred paces. Was she so sensitive to his presence that she could detect him—like some animal who had sniffed out her natural mate in the wild? Was that why her nipples had started puckering so that she wanted to open her mouth to cry out that they were craving his touch?

He was moving across the room and the only other sound she could hear was the amplified pounding of her heart above his approaching footsteps.

Tell him to go, she thought.

Beg him to stay.

'Nicole?'

Like rich velvet, his voice filtered through the warm air and Nicole shivered as he stepped out onto the terrace behind her. Had she thought the spoken word would shatter the spell he'd managed to weave without even being in her eyeline? Because if so, she had completely misread the situation.

'What?' she said, in what was surely the most pointless question of all time.

'Turn around,' he said.

She told herself she was going to resist—but how could she? She felt herself turning in response to his sultry command and suddenly realised it wasn't resentment she felt, but *relief.* Yes, relief. Because wasn't this shimmering feeling of excitement better than the half-dead way she'd felt at the end of their marriage? Wasn't it good to feel properly *alive* again in a way she hadn't felt for a long time? 'What do you want, Rocco?'

'You know damned well what I want.' His lips twisted into a predatory smile. 'I want you.'

And, oh, the feeling was mutual. She wanted him to take away this terrible aching and the deep well of loneliness inside her but it was a risk—and a big one. What if having sex only increased her desire for him instead of killing it? Restlessly she shifted beneath his shadowed gaze, knowing it was a risk she was prepared to take because the thought of sending him away was intolerable. One more night, that was all. One night to finally rid herself of these lingering demons. All she needed to remember was to be on her guard against unwanted emotion because it had no place in what was about to happen. Rocco was programmed to want sex and she was programmed to want something deeper—because that was what women did. And love was something she would never get from Rocco Barberi.

So she stood beneath the silver spotlight of the moon and wondered if her expression gave away the hunger which was snaring her with its silken tendrils. He was wearing nothing but jeans—the top button undone so that dark hair arrowed down towards the ridge-like bulge pushing against his crotch. His chest was glowing and an arrogant smile was curving his lips as if he was already anticipating her surrender. And Nicole knew then that if she did this, it was going to have to be on her own terms.

She needed to remember they were equals. He wasn't her boss and soon he wouldn't even be her husband. This was physical, that was all. It was what grown-ups did. They had carefully considered sex which they could walk away from with nothing but a glow of satisfaction. She tried to iron out the emotion from her voice but she could hear an underlying tremble as she answered him. 'So what are we going to do about it?'

'I think you know the answer to that.' In the moonlight his eyes glittered. 'Get undressed,' he said softly.

CHAPTER SIX

THE CONTROL IN Rocco's voice threatened to destroy the sensual mood which had ensnared her and Nicole stared at him resentfully. Did he think she was the same grateful virgin he'd first seduced, who would do whatever it was he demanded?

She held his gaze, her chin tilting as he studied her with cool calculation. 'What did you say?'

He gave a soft laugh. 'You heard.'

'I want you to repeat it, Rocco.'

There was a pause. 'I told you to get undressed.'

'To perform a striptease for you, you mean?'

He shrugged. 'If you like.'

'Well, I don't like,' she said. 'Not any more. I've changed, Rocco—haven't you?'

His eyes gleamed but he didn't answer her question directly. 'So why don't you tell me what you *do* like?'

And despite everything she knew and everything she had learnt, Nicole found herself wishing for the impossible. Wanting him to say something romantic. To tell her he'd missed her and his life hadn't been the same since she'd gone. Wouldn't a few tender words enhance what was about to happen, even if he didn't mean them? So that for a while she could pretend he cared, as she'd pretended so often in the past. But that would be a pointless thing to do because grown-ups didn't demand hypocritical words. They accepted things exactly the way they were. And this was sex—farewell sex or break-up sex, whatever you wanted to call it. One last taste of Rocco Barberi's magnificent body—and hadn't she better make the most of it?

Raking her fingers back through her still-damp curls, she was aware that her hardened nipples were thrusting against her T-shirt and his eyes were following the movement, like a man hypnotised. Briefly she revelled in a feeling of power as she met the smoky hunger of his gaze. 'I want you to take off my clothes for me,' she said huskily. 'And to do it as slowly as possible. I want you to test your own patience—so we're both so turned on that we can't bear it a second longer. That's what I'd *like*, Rocco.'

His eyes narrowed, suspicion shadowing them. 'Since when did you start having fantasies like that?' he demanded, in a low voice. '*Has* there been another man?'

'You think I don't have any kind of imagination? Or that I'm incapable of articulating my own desires unless a man shows me how? Oh, wow.' She shook her head. 'Thanks for reminding me how unspeakably arrogant you can be, Rocco—and for making me realise that this would be a very bad idea.'

She went to walk past him, her hair swaying in the breeze from the terrace, but he caught hold of her and pulled her up hard against him. She could feel her breasts flattening against his bare chest through her T-shirt and hear the wild patter of her heart.

'I don't think you want to go anywhere, do you, Nicole? Not really. You just want to play provocative and you want me to do the same.' His finger traced down the side of her face, before coming to rest against the throbbing pulse at her neck. 'Have I got that right?'

She attempted a shrug which didn't quite come off because showing bravado was one thing—but not quite so easy when his face was just inches away and all his hard, honed flesh was this close. 'I'm not slipping into old patterns,' she said huskily. 'I'm not stripping for you just because you've snapped your fingers. I don't want to play those games any more. If you want me naked, then you'll have to undress me yourself.'

A smile touched his lips. 'Is that so?'

She nodded, unable to speak because now his hand was drifting from her face down her body and she wished her T-shirt weren't so baggy. What had possessed her to wear such an unflattering garment? As if he'd read her thoughts, he rucked up the material to slip his hand underneath so that his fingertips were on her bare skin and her nerve-endings were instantly fired as she felt that first light touch.

'So how slow would you like me to go?' he questioned almost conversationally as he cupped one of her breasts luxuriously in the palm of his hand and began to massage the underside of it with the edge of his thumb. 'How long shall I take before I remove this delightful piece of clothing you're wearing?'

Nicole's knees sagged. 'Oh,' she said breathlessly.

'You're not making yourself very clear, Nicole. Oh, what?'

'I don't...' She closed her eyes. 'I don't remember.'

'Sudden memory lapse, *tesoro*?' he murmured, his Sicilian accent a velvety caress. 'I wonder what might be causing it?'

Nicole couldn't answer because now his thumb was flicking across her thrusting nipple, sending little ripples of pleasure criss-crossing over her skin. He stroked tiny circles over the engorged flesh before turning his attention to the other breast and Nicole could feel her frustration begin to mount. Squirming beneath his touch, she wondered why on earth she'd told him she wanted this done slowly when already her desire was so intense that she could feel a honeyed heat between her thighs. She wanted—no, *needed*—to get horizontal but he showed no sign of moving and she realised that, in order to stop her knees from buckling, she was going to have to cling onto his shoulders to anchor herself. He gave a soft laugh as her fingers dug into his flesh and he buried his mouth in her neck, his lips becoming entangled with the wild spill of curls as he drifted the tip of his tongue over her skin.

'R-Rocco,' she whispered.

'What?'

'Take...take off my T-shirt.'

'I thought you told me to take my time. To stretch my own patience were the words I think you used. And believe me, *tesoro*—I haven't even started yet. I'll show you just how patient I can be.'

It was both a promise and a threat—as well as a boastful demonstration of just how controlled he could be—and Nicole closed her eyes as he ran the flat of his hand over her belly, taking care to avoid the place where she most wanted to be touched. She bit her lip. Had she really been so sure of herself to think she could wait when she so desperately wanted to feel him inside her? She squirmed as deliberately he inched his way along the lacy edge of her panties, praying for him to slip his finger inside so that he could feel how much she wanted him, but he didn't. She had wanted to control what was happening by setting the pace, but she had done the exact opposite and given him all the power. She wondered what the hell she'd been playing at.

So what was she waiting for?

She was his equal—remember?

Reaching between them, she tugged down the zipper of his jeans, feeling his hard length spring against her palm as she freed him, and his words were a muffled moan as she began to stroke him.

'I thought you said—'

'I changed my mind,' she whispered. 'It's a woman's prerogative, Rocco—hadn't you heard?'

With her thumb and her forefinger she began to tease his taut erection but he halted her fingers with the firm clamp of his own and she heard him give an unsteady laugh.

She stared at him indignantly. 'What's so funny?'

'You are. I had no idea you could be so…mercurial. I like it.'

A prick of sadness threatened to puncture Nicole's

blissful state. Of course he hadn't known what she was capable of and had never bothered finding out *because he hadn't really cared*. To Rocco she would always be the office cleaner in the too small uniform with the mop and bucket in her hand—the last woman in the world he should have married.

But she wasn't going to think about that.

Not now.

She was going to think how good this felt and to enjoy every single second of it.

And then she was going to kiss him goodbye.

'I'm pleased you like it but you'd better not get used to it,' she warned softly.

'To what?'

'The sex.'

He raised his eyebrows. 'Oh?'

'Since we both know this is only going to happen once.'

'Is that so?' He seemed to recover himself then and Nicole saw the light of challenge in his eyes as he peeled off her T-shirt with a fluid movement and carried her over to the bed. 'In that case maybe we should stop wasting so much time talking and get down to business.'

'You're obsessed with business,' she said faintly as he put her down on the bed, and he laughed. Nicole watched him fishing around in the pocket of his jeans before kicking them off and joining her. And suddenly he was towering over her, one knee pressed on either side of her hips as she lay there naked, except for her brief pair of lacy black panties.

'So how do you want it?' he murmured. 'Fast? Slow? Lights on? Off?'

She wanted to tell him not to be so flippant until she realised that too would be wasting time. He was right. What was the point of talking when she wanted him so badly that her heart was threatening to burst right out of her chest? Why bother trying to score points when none of this meant anything? She looked up into the unfathomable gleam of his eyes and spoke from the heart. 'Make love to me,' she said.

She saw his features tense as he stroked her hair away from her face and for a moment she thought he was going to kiss her. But he didn't. Instead, he began to explore her—his fingers drifting erotic pathways over her body as he reacquainted himself with skin which wouldn't seem to stop shivering. He hooked his fingers into the sides of her panties and she thought he might rip them off as he'd done so many times before but he didn't—though she noticed his hand was unsteady as he slid them down over her knees. Greedily, her lips pressed against the silken flesh of his shoulder as she parted her thighs for him.

'Mmm… So responsive,' he breathed as she arched up towards him. 'That much never changes, does it, Nicole?'

But Nicole didn't want comparisons. She didn't want a then-and-now scenario, which might alert all those little indicators of pain which she'd blocked but which were just waiting to spring out if she wasn't careful. And this was supposed to be about pleasure, not pain. So take what you want and give him something in return. Wipe the slate clean so you can walk away from each other and leave the past where it belongs.

Exploring each of his nipples with a feather-light touch, she enjoyed the muffled groan he gave in response, watching his eyes flutter to a close as she drifted her fingertips down over the taut dip of his belly. She smoothed the symmetrical ridges of his ribs and thought, not for the first time, how magnificent his naked body was, the olive skin glowing invitingly against the whiteness of the sheet. This was a feast for all the senses, she thought. She could taste him and feel him and she could smell him, too—that beguiling scent of bergamot underpinned with a raw masculinity, which she breathed in with each unsteady intake of air.

Did he hear how erratic her breathing had become? Was that what prompted him to push her back against the pillows so he could bend his head to her breasts, his tongue cleaving a moist path over each tender mound until they were so acutely aroused that she began to writhe impatiently? His teeth grazed over her hardened nipples as his hand moved between her thighs—and Nicole gave a yelp of pleasure as he moved his finger against her moist slickness. And, oh, she had missed this—she was only just realising how much. She could feel the inexorable build of heat and remembered the way she'd almost come apart in his arms when they'd been outside on the terrace earlier that day and, dazedly, she opened her eyes. 'No,' she whispered.

'No?' he echoed incredulously, his accent growing deeper as it always did during moments of intense pleasure. 'You choose this moment to change your mind?'

'I meant not…not like that,' she amended breath-lessly.

He understood immediately and in the moonlight she saw hunger darkening his rugged features as he reached for the condom he had taken from his jeans. She watched while he ripped the foil open and stroked the rubber over his aroused length and the intimacy of the simple action was almost her undoing. Because hadn't he taught her how to do that and to turn it into a kind of erotic foreplay, a task she had happily undertaken? And hadn't he turned on her that time and asked her if she'd punctured the condom with her fingernails—de-manded to know if she'd deliberately tried to get herself pregnant? He'd retracted the accusation immediately but the memory had lingered for a long time afterwards.

Yet all those dark thoughts vanished the moment he entered her and were replaced by a feeling of such com-pletion that it took Nicole's breath away. How easily plea-sure could conquer pain, she thought. Could make you so helpless that you barely knew who you were any more. Suddenly you forgot you were a wife who was seeking a divorce and became that same blown-away creature who had given her innocence to him so willingly.

'Rocco,' she said, brokenly.

He didn't answer. He was too busy doing all the things he knew she loved best. Hooking her quivering thighs around his hips to angle himself just right. Cup-ping her buttocks and bringing them towards him—the slick action making his penetration all the deeper. And despite knowing that for him this was nothing more than physical, Nicole was lost. Lost in sensation as one thrust followed another and the sweet and familiar layers began to build. She wanted it to last all night but that was never going to happen—not when she was in such a heightened state of arousal. She'd almost dissolved from the moment he entered her and now she couldn't hold it back any longer.

'I'm coming,' she whispered.

'I know you are, *tesoro*,' he whispered back, his voice deep and husky.

The murmured intimacy of that comment broke through the last of her resistance and Nicole felt herself dissolve around him. Through shuddered little gasps she could feel her legs splaying and her back arching. He gave a low growl of appreciation as she began to convulse around him and rogue tears pricked at her eyes as Rocco's own movements became more urgent. She knew from the tension in his body just how close he was to the edge and she gripped his shoulders as he drove into her like a man possessed. And didn't she revel in the fact that she could still do this to him? Could still make him moan like that as his body jerked with his own powerful orgasm?

There was silence in the room afterwards as his dark head lay pressed against her neck. Staring over his shoulder at the moon-dappled ceiling, Nicole wanted to say something reassuring. To make some cool and clever remark which would make him realise this meant nothing to her. Something to reassure him that she wasn't reading too much into what had been just sex. But instead she found herself whispering the only thing which was on her mind. 'Rocco.'

Rocco grew still as he heard her murmur his name like that, trying to regain the control he'd lost from the moment he'd entered her voluptuous body. The way she touched him unsettled him and the way she said his name unsettled him even more because she sounded confused. And wasn't the truth that he was feeling pretty confused himself? Tangling his fingers in the curls which flowed down her back, he told himself this was all he had wanted. Having her underneath him and hearing her gasp out his name one last time had been the whole point of the exercise. He'd wanted her and now he'd had her—which meant he could just walk away. Could give her the divorce she so desperately wanted and set them both free.

But suddenly it didn't seem that simple and walking away no longer looked such an attractive prospect. Instead he found his hand straying to her breast and his fingers teasing a pouting nipple into life all over again as he waited for her little murmur of assent. For the silent wriggle of her curvy hips to indicate that she'd acknowledged his hardness growing inside her and wanted it to happen all over again. Only this time she wasn't so accommodating and instead of wrapping her luscious thighs around his back, she was pulling out from under him and wriggling away, until she was lying on the far side of the mattress—so far away that she might have been on a different planet. He turned his head to see the set of her profile as she stared up at the ceiling, where the moon shadows were dancing in an undulating display of light and shade.

'Is that it?' he questioned.

The slight nod of her head was the only indication she'd heard him and when she spoke it was in a voice he didn't recognise. 'What were you anticipating, Rocco? Another bout of wild sex? Round number two?'

'Why not?' His gaze settled on her hardened nipples, dark against the silver wash of her breasts, and he thought how her body was contradicting the conviction of her feisty words. 'The first time is simply the appetiser—the second time is the feast. Surely you remember that, Nicole?'

He watched her throat constrict as she swallowed and he could hear the stiffness in her voice as she answered.

'The circumstances are rather different this time around.'

'In what way?' he drawled.

She shrugged. 'We obviously both enjoyed that—in a physical sense, certainly. Perhaps it's better not to tempt fate by doing it again.'

'And if I don't agree?'

'I'm afraid you don't have any choice but to agree, Rocco.'

There was a pause and when he spoke his voice was very calm. It was the same kind of thoughtful response he might have used if someone had raised an awkward question in a board meeting. 'I thought you wanted me to be accommodating about the forthcoming divorce.'

Slowly, she turned her head to meet his eyes and he thought how beautiful she looked with her dark curls all wild and free and the faint flush which had spread from her cheeks to her breasts.

'Is that a threat?' she demanded. 'Are you saying

that if I don't agree to have sex with you again, you'll block the petition?'

'Please, Nicole. Do not insult me. I would not dream of asking you to do anything you don't want to do.' He reached across the bed to place his palm over her thigh, pleased but unsurprised by the instinctive quiver of her flesh in response. 'I'm merely pointing out that it seems a waste for us not to capitalise on our remarkable chemistry while we have the opportunity to do so.'

She pushed his hand away even though he could sense her reluctance.

'You mean the chemistry which got us into so much trouble in the first place?'

'Is that how you see it?'

'Of course it is. Because it's the truth, Rocco, and one I made myself accept a long time ago. I was just another body. Just another face. Just another one of the long list of women you seduced. The only difference between me and the others was that I was a virgin.' She reached for the rumpled duvet which lay at the foot of the bed before yanking it up, though he noticed she didn't include him in the protective cover she gathered round herself. With only her face visible, she stared at him and her bottom lip was jutting out stubbornly. 'And you felt differently about that. Perhaps you were jaded because you'd had so many experienced women throwing themselves at you. Wasn't that the way of it, Rocco?'

His answering smile was hard. 'That first night with you blew my mind.'

'The thrill of breaking through my hymen, I suppose? That unique tightness which you can never get back.'

He stiffened, unfamiliar with the sudden steel which had entered her voice. 'You have become very cynical, Nicole.'

Shivering violently despite the warm cloud of duvet which enveloped her, Nicole wanted to ask what on earth he expected. Had he thought she'd just walked away from him without having learned anything? Because if you didn't learn from your mistakes then what hope was there? She'd realised that in order to survive she needed to view what had happened dispassionately, and there was nothing to be gained from trying to put a sentimental slant on her failed marriage. The giddy virgin who'd fallen for the powerful Sicilian was now just a distant memory and she'd worked hard on gaining a whole load of perspective in the interim. She didn't fabricate myths or believe impossible things any more, just to make herself feel better. And a single bout of fantastic sex with the man she had married was not going to make her change her opinion.

She realised there was something else they hadn't talked about—something far bigger than a young women being introduced to sex for the first time—but she couldn't face bringing up the subject of their baby. Her fingers tightened around the duvet. Not tonight. Maybe not ever. He hadn't wanted to talk about it at the time, had he?

And neither had she, she realised, with a sudden flash of insight. *Rocco's reluctance to communicate had suited her very well. He hadn't wanted to talk about what had happened to them, while she had simply been unable to articulate her pain. Had that made the void even deeper?*

She sucked in a deep breath, resolutely bringing her thoughts back to the present. 'Maybe I needed a touch of cynicism. Maybe I was too much of an innocent in all senses of the word,' she said, aware of the sudden prick of tears at the backs of her eyes and terrified he might see them. 'And now I think it's time you went back to your own bed.'

He shifted his weight slightly on the mattress. 'Or I could stay here and spend the night making love to you. Since that is what we both want.'

And despite everything which was wrong between them, Nicole was tempted. Who wouldn't be tempted by such a man? He looked like a lion lying there, so certain of his own strength as the moon coated his powerful body with silver. A quick glance told her that the faint arousal she'd felt while he was still inside her was now fully grown, and didn't the irrational side of her nature—the hungry, yearning side—make her long to put her arms around him and have him do it all over again?

But that way lay a madness which would blur her shaky hold on reality. Already she felt weakened by the realisation of how deeply he could still affect her. She wondered what had happened to the woman who was supposed to be over him—but deep down she knew the answer. That woman didn't—maybe couldn't—exist when Rocco held her in his arms. Why make herself vulnerable to him by having more sex when she still had the rest of the weekend to get through?

'I think I'll pass on that,' she said, the surprise on his rugged features only increasing her resolve. She gave him a thin smile. 'And now I want to go to sleep. Alone.'

He made no attempt to persuade her, rising from the bed in a display of muscular grace—his buttocks pale against the dark olive of his powerful thighs. But as he bent to pick up his jeans Nicole turned onto her stomach and buried her face in the soft pillow, trying to block out the rasping sound of his zip. She heard the door click quietly shut behind him but her emotions were too jangled to even think of sleep.

And she realised that not once during that entire episode had he kissed her.

CHAPTER SEVEN

'WHAT CAN I bring you for *le petit dejeuner, madame*?'

Her eyelids feeling as heavy as lead, Nicole sat down at the table which had been laid up for breakfast on the terrace, momentarily dazzled by the crystal and silver which gleamed in the early morning sunshine. The air was warm with the combined scent of jasmine and strong coffee and Veronique was gazing at her expectantly.

'We have bread and croissants, *madame*,' the housekeeper continued. 'Though Signor Barberi has reminded chef that it is the English way to eat a cooked breakfast—should you wish for bacon and eggs.'

Nicole smiled, even though smiling was the last thing she felt like doing. Pulling a face full of remorse would surely be more appropriate in the circumstances. After a restless night haunted by disturbing dreams she had woken up amid sex-scented sheets, revelling in the delicious glow of her body until the heart-sinking moment when she'd remembered exactly what had made it feel that way. Or rather, who.

An image of her unzipping Rocco's jeans and caressing him intimately rushed into her head and her cheeks burned as, hastily, she put on a pair of sunglasses and pulled her coffee towards her, wishing that last night wouldn't keep flooding back in a conflicting rush of hungry and humiliating memories. Her cheeks burned as she recalled the way she had welcomed her husband into her body with an urgency which had taken her by surprise—startled her in the discovery that her desire for him was stronger than ever. And that had puzzled her. Because at the tail end of their marriage, hadn't she resigned herself to the fact that she no longer wanted Rocco anywhere near her?

And he hadn't wanted her either, had he? They had pushed each other away in every sense of the word. She watched the breeze tugging at the pink petals of the roses at the centrepiece of the table and tucked her hair behind her ears. Last night shouldn't have happened but there was nothing she could do about it now. She couldn't wind back the clock and wish she'd suggested Rocco take a hike when he'd wandered into her bedroom—*uninvited*—and told her to undress.

But her sexual gymnastics had left her with a ravenous appetite and hungrily Nicole eyed the dish of iced peaches before looking up at the housekeeper. 'I'd love some poached eggs,' she said. 'With wholemeal toast, if that's possible.'

'*D'accord, madame.*'

After Veronique had gone, Nicole ate some fruit and watched the expensive yachts bobbing in the exclusive harbour until the housekeeper returned with the rest of her breakfast. She was busy dipping a rectangle of toast into the runny yolk of an egg and oblivious to the presence of anything else when a shadow fell over the table and she looked up to see Rocco standing there, obviously fresh from the shower. His black hair was curling in shiny tendrils around his neck and his jaw looked newly shaved. Unjacketed, his ice-blue shirt contrasted with the much darker hue of his eyes and those exquisitely cut trousers emphasised his long legs. Her breakfast forgotten, Nicole stared up at him and all that blatant masculinity so early in the morning began to do worrying things to her pulse-rate.

'Rocco!' she accused. 'Do you always make a habit of creeping up on people like that?'

'I move quietly, *tesoro*. It is in my nature. It's only because you're so damned jumpy that you react like that,' he drawled, drawing out a chair opposite her and lowering himself onto it.

Nicole put her toast back on the plate because eating had suddenly lost its allure. Those thighs, she thought with unwilling hunger, unable to forget their tensile power as he'd driven into her last night. She grabbed her napkin and blotted it over her lips. 'Maybe it's just you who has that effect on me.'

He leaned across the table to pour himself a cup of coffee. 'Should I be flattered?'

She met his gaze. 'What do you think?'

He shrugged. 'I never know what to think where you're concerned, Nicole. Take last night, for example. One minute you're hot for me and the next as cold as ice. You are something of an…enigma.'

She gave a short laugh. 'That's rich, coming from you. The man who never talks about his feelings.'

'Because that is not my way,' he said, lifting the cup to his lips and sipping from it. 'You know that. It has never been the way of Barberi men.'

Nicole pushed her plate away. That much was true. She thought about his grandfather, the man who had helped bring up Rocco and his siblings after their parents had been killed in the dramatic speedboat accident which had been splashed across the front pages of the world's press. She remembered the day she had arrived at the family complex just outside Palermo, fresh from her honeymoon and slightly daunted at meeting the patriarch of Sicily's most powerful clan for only the second time since her wedding. Very quickly she'd discovered that the revered elder was as uptight as Rocco about expressing his feelings. She'd thought his lack of warmth was because Turi was an old-fashioned man who would have preferred his golden-boy heir to have married a Sicilian woman with an equally elevated status.

Yet despite the barriers she'd encountered, Nicole had been determined to overcome them and make a good impression. She'd wanted to fit in, no matter what it took, because she'd wanted to make a proper family home for her new husband and their baby. She had spent most of her American honeymoon—when she wasn't being sick—trying to learn as much Italian as possible in order to impress her new family and especially Rocco's grandfather. But everything had seemed so new and strange and different when she'd arrived in Sicily. She had felt like a lonely outsider in the huge and sprawling house with nothing much to do all day and nobody to talk to. Rocco had buried himself in work and Turi had spoken only in dialect so that they had barely been able to communicate with each other. Like grandfather, like grandson, she remembered thinking. Maybe her mistake had been to expect anything different. To think that the orphaned nobody who had mopped floors could ever have been considered *suitable*.

And it was weird. Rocco spoke of *her* inability to discuss her feelings as if it were a character flaw, while for him it was simply something he accepted as a natural trait of Barberi men. Meanwhile, he showed no inclination to change. He was still concealing his feelings—if he had any—behind the weapons of blame and possession. He was a hugely successful man with a massive global influence, who examined business opportunities in the most minute of detail. He was prepared to bring her out here in order to facilitate a deal, yet he was able to ignore the deep, dark hole at the centre of their marriage and make as if it had never happened.

He was acting as if they had never created a baby together. As if that brief little life had never existed.

Her heart contracted with pain and suddenly Nicole knew that she couldn't carry on not knowing. Maybe that was why this whole relationship felt so…*unfinished*. She recognised now that she must shoulder some of the blame, because she had run away rather than face up to their issues. But she was here now, wasn't she? Maybe it needed to be resolved once and for all before either of them could have true peace. Was it that which gave her the courage to come right out and say it? The sense that she would never get the answers she sought unless she pushed for them, no matter how painful that might be?

She removed her dark glasses and looked at him. 'Okay,' she said, sitting back in the chair. 'We've both accused the other of never discussing our true feelings—'

'I don't remember putting it exactly like that,' he said.

'You called me an enigma,' she pointed out. 'So why don't we agree to ask each other a question and then answer it truthfully? No excuses—and no getting out of it.'

'You're proposing some kind of party game?'

'Don't deliberately misunderstand me, Rocco. That's not what it's about.'

His flattened lips indicated a lack of enthusiasm which bordered on contempt. 'No? And the purpose of this interrogation is…what?'

It was a bad sign he even had to ask but Nicole wasn't going to back down now. She leaned across the table towards him. 'Couldn't you just do it, Rocco? Just this once. Just to humour me?'

'Very well.' He gave an impatient sigh. 'As long as you are prepared to ask first.'

How typical of him to say that! Nicole took a deep breath and started to speak and the words came rushing out before she had a chance to question the wisdom of saying them. 'You only married me because I was pregnant, didn't you?'

There was a pause. 'Yes,' he said at last.

She felt her heart twist as if someone were turning a corkscrew in her chest. She'd known that all along—so why did it hurt so much? Did hearing him say it mean she could no longer pretend that her brief marriage had been anything more than a sham?

She was tempted to abandon the conversation but forced herself to continue. After all, they'd come this far—which was further than they'd ever come before. Why stop now? 'Now you,' she said, praying for him to address the subject they'd both shied away from for so long. She'd given him a lead by talking about her pregnancy—all he had to do was take it from there and confront the dark space which linked them both. 'Your turn.'

He took a sip of coffee before turning the full brilliance of his sapphire gaze on her. 'That's easy.' His voice dipped into a seductive caress. 'Did you enjoy last night?'

Nicole blinked and stared at him in dismay, unable to believe he'd come out with something so…so…*superficial*. Was that the only thing which mattered to him? *Sex?* She swallowed. Maybe it was. Sex had been the thing which had brought them together and remained the only thing which united them.

'You mean, was I satisfied?' she demanded, her temper suddenly flaring. 'Yes, of course I was. You're very good at satisfying a woman, Rocco—but you don't need me to tell you that.'

It had been a mockery of a question and she suspected he'd asked it simply to even the score. To make him an equal player in this 'game'—or maybe warn her against ever trying to do something like this in future. But his attitude infuriated her. Couldn't he have done the bigger thing and asked her about something which mattered? No, of course he couldn't—because Rocco Barberi didn't *do* feelings. He acted like a machine and expected everyone else to do the same. And suddenly she knew she couldn't let this opportunity go. She was going to say it, no matter how much it angered him, or how much it brought back the pain. *Because she needed to say it.*

'You never talk about our child, Rocco.'

She saw a shadow briefly cloud his face but if she'd been expecting heartache, or anger, or pain, or longing, or any of the dark stream of emotions which had dragged her down into the depths of despair so many times, then she was about to be disappointed. Because Rocco was putting his cup down on the saucer as calmly as if she'd just asked him how often it rained in Monaco, his rugged features as impassive as she'd ever seen them, his blue eyes their habitual shade of cold.

'What is there to talk about?' he questioned tonelessly. 'It happened and there's nothing we can do to change it. We both wish it hadn't, but there you go.' He shrugged. 'I don't think there's anything more I can add to that and neither do I intend to.'

She wanted to shake him. To rail at him. To accuse him of being unfeeling and heartless—but how could she do that when he'd never pretended to be otherwise? Everything she'd ever wanted from Rocco Barberi, he was incapable of giving her. She had been determined to somehow win his love if only she tried hard enough. But love wasn't a competition you could win, she realised— and even if it was, surely having a winner would imply there had to be a loser.

And she didn't want to be that loser.

She didn't want to be anchored by the past. She wanted to be free of heartache and regret. Of him.

Briefly she thought about getting up from the table and telling Rocco she was going back to England and if he wanted to make her wait for her divorce, then she would just have to suck it up. But she had run away once before and where had that got her? It had left her with an underlying feeling of failure, no matter how many modest achievements she'd managed to chalk up along the way. Wasn't facing up to the truth like this—in a way they had never done in their marriage—a therapy of some kind, even if it hurt like hell?

But Rocco didn't hurt, did he? Rocco didn't give anything away. Not then and certainly not now.

Pushing back her chair, she rose to her feet and flung her napkin over her uneaten toast. 'Oh, what's the point of trying to talk to you?' she said. 'So why don't I make it easy for you, Rocco? Let's just spend the day apart and I'll join you for your cocktail party later. That way neither of us will have to endure a second more of each other's company than we need to. I'll be there for you in public and that's what matters. That was the deal, wasn't it?'

Rocco's eyes narrowed. He was aware that he had hurt her and wondered if that had been deliberate. Part of him had suspected that his blunt answers to her unwanted questions would have her running for the hills again—and wouldn't that have been simpler? Things were certainly less complicated when Nicole wasn't around, because she was turning into a constant stream of surprises. For a start, she wasn't intimidated by him. Not any more. She had the courage to ask him stuff and had been surprisingly calm when he'd given her the brutal truth.

At times during that uncomfortable conversation, she had clearly been trying to hold back her own feelings. There had been anger on her face and bitterness, too. And pain, of course—plenty of that. But no tears. He found himself wondering if it was a struggle for her to maintain that politely enquiring expression and from somewhere he felt the unfamiliar stab of his conscience. Had he been unnecessarily harsh with her?

'Yes, that was the deal,' he agreed slowly. 'But maybe we could amend it.'

'Really?' Their eyes locked. 'And just what did you have in mind, Rocco?'

It was unlike Rocco to search for the unspoken but he did so now. He saw the expression of resignation which had flattened her green eyes—as if sex was all he was capable of offering her. And even though up until a few minutes ago he might have echoed those very sentiments, now his ego rebelled against such an assumption. He would not tolerate being regarded as a stud, but it was more than that. Their conversation had left him feeling *disquieted*. He could see how vulnerable it had left his estranged wife, no matter how hard she tried to disguise it. And vulnerability was always a danger where women were concerned. It made them capable of misinterpreting an act of physical intimacy and loading it with imaginary significance. If they had sex right now, wouldn't it be asking for trouble?

He let his gaze drift over the simple white sundress which flattered her curvy body. She looked as sweet as on that first evening he'd met her, when she'd stood in front of him in her cleaner's uniform, looking guilty for having splashed him with soapy water. The fabric of his trousers had been warm and wet against his ankle but all he could remember was the emerald blaze of her eyes—and Rocco was unprepared for the sudden jolt of nostalgia he experienced.

His jaw clenched.

No. Sex would be a bad idea. He needed to get them as far away from the vicinity of a bedroom as possible and, for once, the idea of leaving her to sun herself by the pool while he buried himself in work was leaving him cold. 'Why don't I take you walking?' he said.

'Walking?' she echoed.

'I meant around the Rock.'

'The Rock?'

'That's what everyone calls Monaco. Because it's built on a rock,' he added.

'I'd kind of worked that one out for myself, Rocco.'

He gave a reluctant laugh as his gaze travelled to her feet—currently encased in a pair of high, strappy wedges which defined her shapely ankles and briefly made him regret his impetuous decision. 'Do you have anything more suitable you could wear?'

'Like trainers?'

'Trainers would be fine,' he said evenly. 'Why don't you go and put them on?'

Glad to escape the disturbing scrutiny of his gaze, Nicole sped upstairs, her heart pounding as she pushed open her bedroom door. She'd straightened the rumpled bedding before going down to breakfast but someone had obviously been in and changed the linen because now the bed looked so pristine that last night might never have happened. But it had. She could feel her cheeks heating as she located her sneakers, trying to forget their explosive passion and to remember instead what he'd just told her.

He had only married her because of the baby.

She remembered the doctor telling her that early miscarriage was very common. That she should go home to her husband and get pregnant again as soon as possible. But how could that be *possible* when Rocco had resolutely stayed away from her after she'd lost the baby? When he'd seemed almost *relieved* to have a legitimate reason not to resume marital relations. Was that how he'd felt only been afraid to admit it? Had some part of him recognised that the terrible thing which had happened was probably best in the long run, if it freed him from a marriage he had never intended?

But she had never asked him, had she? Had never sat him down or confronted him and not just because she was feeling out of her depth as the billionaire's new bride. She hadn't talked about stuff because, in a way, she hadn't known how. Those years in foster homes hadn't exactly been warm and although Peggy Watson had loved her like a mother, she had come from a fierce generation of practical Irishwomen who got on with things, rather than discussing how they made them *feel*.

Wasn't she as much to blame as Rocco for the lack of

communication between them at the time—which had speeded up the end of their forced marriage?

Tying her shoelaces, she grabbed a canvas tote bag and went back to the terrace to find him waiting, blue eyes gleaming as he quickly appraised her change of footwear.

'Much better,' he murmured.

Nicole's eyebrows shot up. 'Strange coming from the man who once insisted I parade about his office in a pair of sky-high stilettos. What happened, Rocco? Did your tastes undergo a dramatic change?'

His face was impassive. 'You are no longer my mistress, Nicole—that's what happened.'

But she'd felt like his mistress last night. He had treated her with that same raw hunger he'd displayed at the beginning of their relationship, before they were married. And that was something else which had always puzzled her, something else she had felt unable to ask him in the past. But now she had nothing left to lose and she looked unflinchingly into his bright eyes. 'Those things you used to get me to dress up in. The packages you used to buy from that shop in Soho—'

'You're going to tell me now that you didn't like them?' he questioned roughly.

'No,' she said slowly. 'I'm not going to say that. I wore them because you *did* like them. But the more outrageous the outfits, the more...*disapproving* you seemed to be, even though they clearly turned you on. It was as if you were trying to turn me into someone you could ultimately despise. Is that what you were doing, Rocco?'

Rocco felt his mouth dry. She was far more perceptive than he'd given her credit for, or maybe he'd just never stopped to notice it before. He'd been horrified to discover that the beautiful cleaner had been a virgin, because he hadn't wanted an innocent, he had wanted a *mistress*. Turning her onto the more colourful sexual practices enjoyed by his previous lovers had been an attempt to place her firmly into the latter category. Because the alternative was admitting he was captivated by having straightforward vanilla sex with his eager young lover. And that admission had made him uneasy because what then would she want from him—and could he ever be that man?

His mouth tightened. And then she'd fallen pregnant and once again he had been cast into the role which had haunted him all his life.

Responsible adult.

Ask Rocco.

See how Rocco does it.

Well, not any more.

He was free now and that was the way he liked it.

'Maybe I *was* trying to get you to despise me,' he admitted eventually.

Confusion fired in the leafy depths of her eyes. 'But why would you do that?'

He saw the colour which had risen to her cheeks and somehow he knew he couldn't duck out of this. 'Because I knew I was the type of man who could hurt you,' he said, in as candid an admission as he'd ever made. 'And I didn't want to do that. Not when I discovered just how sweet and innocent you really were.'

'Could you...elaborate, please?'

Rocco scowled, wondering why she was being so persistent when this was only going to hurt her. 'I thought that if I tried to objectify you, it would drive a wedge between us.'

'And it did,' she said dully.

'It did,' he agreed.

Her teeth were biting into the cushioned pinkness of her bottom lip but she said nothing more. She didn't have to. Her face gave it all away. That he'd ended up hurting her anyway. Because that was what he did. She'd tried to get close and he'd pushed her away. He didn't know any other way. *He didn't want it any other way.*

His gaze swept over her. 'So, have you changed your mind about sightseeing?'

She hesitated for a moment before shaking her head. 'Actually, I'm looking forward to it.'

He looked at her curiously. 'Despite the things I've just said?'

'Maybe *because* of the things you've just said,' she agreed then gave a shaky laugh. 'I've found this discussion very...useful.'

'I thought you didn't like that word.'

'That depends on the context.' She shrugged and wound a curl around her finger. 'Understanding what makes someone tick is always useful, Rocco. It helps me make some kind of sense out of what happened.'

And then she smiled and inexplicably Rocco felt his heart pound and for a moment he found himself wishing he'd kept his mouth shut and that they could just have spent the day in bed. 'Let's go,' he said abruptly.

CHAPTER EIGHT

THEY SAT BENEATH a canopy of tangled green leaves as the Mediterranean sea glittered in a blue haze in front of them. The waiter had just brushed away the remains of the seafood platter but Nicole could see a shiny pink piece of prawn shell he must have missed, which sat on the tablecloth like a picked-off piece of nail varnish. She leaned back in her chair, knowing she couldn't keep staring at the table or distracting herself with the amazing view for much longer. Wishing there were somewhere else to look than at Rocco's ruggedly handsome face.

Yet there was nowhere else she would rather look. She could have feasted her eyes on him all day—on those fiercely intelligent eyes and lips which smiled so rarely, but, when they did, it was like the sun coming out from behind dark cloud. She wondered what he was trying to do to her. To beguile her with a glimpse of how life could have been as his wife, if he'd loved her rather than being programmed to hurt her?

Today they had played tourist in his adopted city where he'd shown her the Monaco which was hidden behind the façade of glitzy shops, exploring narrow streets which felt as if they were full of secrets. They walked through the beautiful Saint Martin gardens and the Byzantine cathedral and the Place du Palais, where they joined all the other sightseers watching the daily changing of the guard. Side by side they stood, their bodies close but never quite touching while Nicole's skin tingled with unwilling frustration.

And they'd ended up in this beautiful restaurant where the waiter had just placed two leather menus in front of them and Rocco was still studying her with those mesmerising eyes, which spoke of his distant Greek ancestry.

'Would you like dessert?'

She shook her head. 'Not really. How about you?'

His gaze became speculative. 'What I want isn't on the menu.'

'You want them to make you something special?'

'Like what?'

She opened her eyes very wide because suddenly she realised they were flirting. 'Oh, I don't know—a soufflé maybe, or some *crepes suzette*?'

He leaned forward and lowered his voice, even though nobody could possibly overhear them. 'After what we were doing last night, I'm amazed you can ask those questions with such an innocent look on your face,' he said. 'Which makes me wonder whether it's real or whether it's feigned. Or whether it's an invitation for me to acknowledge the heat which has been building between us all morning and won't seem to go away. Is that what you'd really like me to do, Nicole?'

She met his gaze before turning her head away, afraid of what he might be able to read in her eyes, when she didn't even want to admit it herself. 'I don't know what I want,' she confessed.

'Then perhaps I will make the decision for us. I think we ought to discuss this matter further, only in private.' His words filtered over her skin. 'So why don't we leave the table and do just that?'

The sudden tightness in Nicole's chest was making it very difficult to breathe. 'You mean…you want to go back to the house?' she croaked.

He shook his head. 'No. That's not what I mean. Who wants to waste time trailing back through the city?'

'Well, what, then?'

'We could get a room.'

'Where?'

'Right here. This restaurant serves some of the best food in the city, but it also has rooms.' He paused as he looked at her. 'But you might not want that.'

Nicole shifted uncomfortably beneath his searching expression. Of course she *wanted* to. She'd wanted nothing else since they'd left his house that morning when the world had seemed to blur so that Rocco had become her only real focus, no matter how detached she had been when studying the architecture of the city or how many paintings she'd looked at. When just having him that near had been like electricity firing over her skin—making her long for them to get properly close. She'd told herself sex wasn't going to happen again. That she'd emerged from that passionate bout last night with her heart just about intact and she wasn't sure she'd be so lucky if there was a next time.

But her body was hungry and her desire was strong—and maybe Rocco had picked up on that. She licked her lips, trying not to be affected by his raven-dark glint of his hair in the sunshine, or the pure muscular power of his body. If she was being sensible she would say no. She would suggest he call for the bill and take her back to the house while she whiled away a few blameless hours by the pool, before getting ready for cocktails on his yacht. She would play at being his wife in public and for the rest of the time she would do her best to avoid him, just as she'd originally planned.

But being sensible wasn't all it was cracked up to be. When was the last time she'd been *reckless*? When she'd thought about what she really *wanted* rather than what she needed? Next week she would be back in Cornwall with damp clay underneath her fingernails and bills to pay, but today she was on a sunny Mediterranean terrace and the only man she had ever really wanted was asking her to go to bed with him. Surely only a fool would turn down an opportunity like that.

'They might not have a room,' she said.

His eyes gleamed. 'We could try.'

Of course, they *did* have a room and Nicole felt like a naughty schoolgirl as Rocco handed over his credit card and was given a key. And crazily, she found herself wishing she were wearing her wedding band, which was the only piece of jewellery she'd kept from her marriage. She wondered what the staff thought of customers who came for lunch, then booked themselves a room. Did they think she was Rocco's mistress and he was about to spend an illicit afternoon with a woman who wasn't his wife? And wasn't it ironic that somehow she seemed to fit that role much better? She'd made a much better mistress than she had a wife, she reflected.

The ride in the elevator was conducted in a breathless kind of silence, mainly because of the presence of a middle-aged woman who was decked in diamonds and carrying a small white dog in her handbag. But Nicole honestly didn't think she would have dared go anywhere near Rocco even if the elevator had been empty. She was in such a heightened state of excitement that she suspected a single touch would have had her clawing at him like a wildcat. Greedily taking what she could from him in the certain knowledge that after Sunday she would be saying goodbye for ever.

After what felt like an eternity, the lift came to a halt and Rocco swiped the key card with a hand which wasn't quite steady. Their room was opulent, with silken drapes and Persian rugs. The walls were decorated in soft shades of grey and the air heavily scented with freshly cut crimson roses. But the décor was nothing but a secondary feature because the moment the door closed behind them, they started pulling at each other's clothes.

'Rocco...be careful,' she breathed as he tugged impatiently at the zip of her sundress. 'If you tear it, I don't have anything else to wear—'

'Then I'll send out for a replacement,' he drawled as the white dress pooled to her ankles and he briefly lifted her up so she was free of it. 'There are plenty of shops close by.'

It was an arrogant assertion and Nicole's heart sank as she acknowledged that this was the way he operated. You ripped a woman's dress off and then you bought another. And she realised something else, too. That whatever his love-life had been since their marriage ended—Rocco wouldn't stay celibate forever. Of course he wouldn't. One day he would be renting a post-lunch room with someone else like this and ripping off *her* dress.

But that uncomfortable realisation was banished by the practised touch of his fingers as they skated over her quivering flesh. With one-handed dexterity he unclipped her bra and let the lacy garment fall to the ground, his lips immediately locking around her nipple and making her moan softly. He was undoing the belt of his trousers as Nicole began unbuttoning his shirt, her fingers sliding eagerly over the silken warmth of his bare chest. The only sound she could hear was the growing intensity of their laboured breathing until the final piece of clothing was removed and they were both naked.

Impatiently, he threw aside the silken cushions and laid her on top of the bed, stretching her arms above her head as if she were some kind of ancient sacrifice. And didn't it feel a bit like that, as he licked at her nipples before turning his attention to the hollow of her navel? It felt primitive and exciting and somehow *inevitable*. Nicole held her breath as his tongue traced a sinuous path to her parted thighs, at last flickering over the gloriously aroused bud until she was brokenly pleading for him to stop teasing her. She wanted him. All of him. She wanted him *inside* her.

'Can't you wait, *piccolo*?'

'No!' she gasped.

'So I see.' His laugh was low and exultant as he stroked on a condom and his hard body came down on top of hers.

'Rocco!' she moaned, tilting her hips towards him, and suddenly he was making that first deep thrust which filled her and the lips she'd opened to cry out her pleasure were being silenced by the hungry pressure of his kiss.

Nicole had never experienced anything quite so intense. Was that because for the first time she *really* felt like his equal—a lover who knew how to please him? Who could meet him on his own terms instead of being the unlikely mistress or the doormat wife? Her head thrashed wildly against the pillow as he drove into her and very quickly tipped her over the edge. Her body started convulsing and almost immediately she felt Rocco bucking inside her as he gave that shuddered groan she recognised so well. His body warm and spent, he collapsed against her, his heart pounding against her damp breasts, and her fingertips automatically moved up to stroke the ruffled tendrils of his hair.

In silence they lay there and must have fallen asleep, because when Nicole's eyes eventually flickered open it was to find her lips pressed against Rocco's neck. The tip of her tongue edged out so that she could taste the saltiness of his damp skin. If only they could stay like this for ever, she thought dreamily. If only all the stuff which had kept them apart didn't exist. But it did. Because this was sex. Nothing but sex. He hadn't dressed it up or cloaked it in promises. He'd booked a room and she'd gone there willingly. And if at this moment they were equals—then maybe she should capitalise on that. Because they hadn't quite finished that conversation of earlier, had they?

'Rocco,' she said, her finger tracing a slow path along the darkened stubble at his jaw.

'Mmm?'

'Can I ask you something else?'

There was a trace of post-coital indulgence in his voice but also the merest note of warning. 'If I say no, will that stop you?'

'No.'

'I didn't think so.' He rolled away from her. 'So what is it now, Nicole?'

If only she'd had time to prepare—like when you went to see the doctor and were supposed to write down all your symptoms on a piece of paper in case you forgot them. As it was, the words came stumbling out in an unplanned rush. 'When you told me earlier that you are the kind of man who hurts women, I wondered... well...' She stared at the stillness of his profile. 'Do you know why?'

'I don't hurt *them*,' he corrected, his voice growing cool. 'I am simply unable to meet their expectations, which are always predictable.'

She arched her brows but deep down she knew what was coming. 'Oh?'

'Women want love,' he said softly. 'And I don't do love.'

'Why not?'

He flexed and unflexed his fingers, the burnished skin looking very dark against the rumpled white sheet.

'Because I can't,' he said at last. 'I'm like someone who was born with no sense of smell—wave a rose underneath my nose and you'd be wasting your time. I don't feel the stuff which other people claim to feel. That's just the way it is. Blame it on the way I was brought up, if you like. Perhaps you have to witness something in order to experience it and there was no real love in our house—at least, not between my parents. Their marriage was based on duty, rather than joy.'

'I see,' said Nicole slowly, trying to absorb what he'd told her. Had he fallen into a familiar pattern when he'd married her, because that too was based on duty? Was that why he'd written her those letters insisting she came back—because he'd felt he *had* to? 'So they weren't happy?'

'Not with each other, no.'

'But they never considered divorce?'

'With three children to consider?' Rocco's mouth hardened. 'No way. And divorce at that time would have been frowned on, especially in that part of Sicily. I guess all their simmering resentment had nowhere to go and was one of the reasons why they lived life so dangerously.'

She shifted her weight slightly, so that she was propping herself up on her elbow. 'What do you mean, *dangerously*?'

He turned to look at her and Nicole thought she caught a flash of vulnerability in his eyes, but it was gone so quickly she might have imagined it.

'They got their kicks out of high-risk stuff,' he said. 'I gather it's a guilt-free way of getting your adrenal buzz, rather than breaking your marriage vows. They opted for dangerous sports rather than infidelity. You know, the kind of activities which make your insurance premiums shoot up. Sky-diving, heli-skiing, free-diving—you name it, they did it. When my father crashed the speedboat it was profoundly shocking but, on some level, I realised I'd been waiting for something like that to happen for a long time.'

Nicole held her breath, unwilling to say anything which might shatter the fragile atmosphere. She wondered why he'd never told her any of this before. *Because they'd never had that kind of relationship.* They'd been about to split up when she'd discovered she was pregnant—and after that, everything had been about the baby. Even after their marriage they'd never confided in one another because their compartmentalised lives had never seemed to overlap. It was only now, when their relationship was almost over, that Rocco seemed prepared to reveal something of the real man behind the successful mask he presented to the world. Too little, too late, she thought—but that didn't stop Nicole's heart from going out to him.

'Oh, Rocco,' she whispered. 'I'm so sorry.'

His voice was dismissive. 'I don't want your pity.'

'It isn't *pity.* It's compassion.'

'Whatever you call it, I don't want it. It all happened a long time ago and I think we've done this subject to death, don't you?' He stifled a yawn and glanced at his watch. 'We'd better order a car to pick us up.'

Nicole registered the dismissive note in his voice and realised what he was trying to do. He was deliberately changing the subject. Telling her in no uncertain terms to keep her pity and her comfort to herself, but Nicole wasn't done. Not yet. She licked her lips. 'Just one more question.'

This time he made no attempt to hide his impatience. 'This is getting tedious, Nicole.'

'I need to know something else, Rocco, and this may be the last chance I get to ask it. Was salvaging your personal reputation the real reason you brought me out here?'

In the muted grey light of the upmarket room, his sapphire eyes looked very startling. 'I could probably swing the deal without you by my side,' he said slowly. 'Let's just say your presence was a precautionary measure.'

'And that's all?'

His eyes met hers. 'Originally.'

'And then?'

He shrugged. 'Once you got out here I realised there was something unfinished between us.'

Her heart pounded. 'You mean sex?'

There was a pause before he nodded. '*Se*. That's exactly what I mean. It has been a long time since I've been intimate with a woman.' He met the question in her eyes. 'Not since the last time I had sex with you, if you're interested.'

'I'm not,' she said breathlessly, and wondered if he could read the lie in her voice.

'It seemed a pity to deny something we both wanted,'

he continued thoughtfully. 'You were always the best lover I'd ever had and I wanted to know if you were as good as I remembered.' He gave an odd kind of laugh. 'And you are. But that's all it was—lust, fired by curiosity.'

'You certainly don't pull your punches, do you, Rocco?'

'Don't ask questions if you can't deal with the answers,' he said as she got out of bed and turned her back on him.

But as he watched her getting dressed, Rocco was aware of a sudden feeling of frustration. He'd thought sex would mean closure—a satisfying finale to their doomed marriage. Yet somehow it hadn't worked out like that. It had ended up being about more than the physical. It had given her the courage to ask him stuff and her questions had made him open up. Made him tell her things. *Feel* things. Things he didn't want to feel. His mouth hardened as he reached down the side of the bed for his phone, closing his eyes to blot out the sight of Nicole pulling a pair of white panties up over her smooth, pale thighs.

Nicole hooked her bra in place, trying very hard to stop her hands from trembling and trying to ignore the fact that Rocco was speaking in rapid French on his phone and acting as if she wasn't even there. She felt like some kind of hooker he'd brought to an anonymous hotel room, and even the revelation that there had been no other woman since their split wasn't enough to calm her ruffled senses. She had been a fool. No two ways about it. She had been there for the taking and he had taken her. His *unfinished business*, as he had described it.

But for her?

For her it felt as if he'd picked her apart and left all the ends unravelled, so that she was left aching and wanting more. Pulling on her white sundress, she tried to smooth out some of the creases. More of him. Why hadn't she realised that physical intimacy would take her to a place where it wasn't safe to go? All that hard work she'd done on herself to try and forget him was all for nothing because right now she felt as vulnerable around Rocco as she'd ever been.

And she still had to endure some wretched cocktail party on his fancy yacht.

Nicole's cheeks were burning as she walked through the lobby in her crumpled white sundress, aware of the doorman's faint and knowing smile. And as she stepped out onto the sun-drenched pavement she realised that Rocco still hadn't kissed her.

CHAPTER NINE

SMALL WAVES SLAPPED rhythmically against the side of the craft and, on the shoreline, distant lights glittered like scattered diamonds. Standing on the deck of his luxury yacht, Rocco Barberi surveyed the guests who were drinking champagne and chattering, wondering why he felt like a spectator at his own party. Fresh oysters and tiny blinis heaped with caviar were doing the rounds, and below deck one of the dealers from the famous nearby casino was demonstrating card tricks to accompanying squeals of disbelief. The party had the indefinable buzz of being a success—and Rocco had just been presented with the succulent cherry which would sit on top of the cake.

A short while ago, Marcel Dupois had taken him aside to say they were satisfied with his offer for the company, and saw no reason for any further delay. Rocco sensed that a deal could be concluded as early as next week and he should have been toasting his own success and looking hungrily to the future, just as he always did.

So why was he feeling a distinct lack of enthusiasm about putting together a new deal?

Why the hell was his temper feeling so damned *frayed*?

He knew why. The evidence was right there before his eyes. Nicole, wearing a close-fitting scarlet dress—a colour he'd never seen her in before—which apparently she'd made herself, just as she'd made the white sundress he'd torn from her body earlier that day. A Nicole who once again had everyone eating out of her hand with a sunny display which was in marked contrast to her distinctly cool mood once they'd left their hotel room.

Had she been angry with him for being so frank with her this afternoon? Her chilly attitude towards him had seemed to suggest as much. As soon as they'd arrived back at his house she had excused herself, saying she needed to get ready—and during the drive here she'd spent the whole time playing with her mobile phone, and acting as if he weren't there.

Yet the moment they'd set foot on his yacht she had blossomed into the vivacious beauty who was drawing the eye of everyone at the party. Heads turned as she walked by and he found himself wondering if people could detect her natural sensuality, as if what they'd been doing straight after lunch was manifesting itself in her glowing appearance. His fingers tightened around the rail, because now he was bitterly regretting having told her things. Things about his parents. About not knowing about love. Things she didn't need to know.

Annelise Dupois was tapping him on the arm. 'Oh, but she is so *charmant*,' she said, her gaze following the direction of his to where Nicole was standing, her mahogany curls illuminated by a soft golden light overhead so that she looked like a dark angel. 'My husband and I were just saying what a lucky man you are, Rocco.'

And for once in his life, Rocco couldn't think of a thing to say. Was it *lucky* that Nicole had somehow acquired the power to make him feel stuff he had no desire to feel? His mouth hardened.

'I understand you and your wife have been estranged?' Javier Estrada chose just that moment to break into his thoughts—the Argentine's apparently innocent question belied by the spark of interest in his black eyes, which was setting Rocco's teeth on edge. He knew the South American tycoon's reputation as a ruthless womaniser and had no intention of giving him the green light where Nicole was concerned. Things might be almost over for them, but he was damned if he would stand by and let a man like Estrada salivate all over her.

'Not any more. We are in the process of reconciliation,' Rocco answered coldly, not caring that it was a lie.

'Pity,' murmured Estrada, and it was as much as Rocco could do not to have him ejected from the boat. Better still, to heave him into the dark waters himself!

But he strode away from him just as a pretty waitress extended her tray of champagne and Rocco waved an impatient hand. He didn't want food, or drink, or to dance to the sound of the string quartet which was entertaining people at the far end of the vast deck. All he seemed capable of doing was thinking about the woman he had married and wondering if he'd taken a temporary leave of his senses when he'd demanded she accompany him this weekend.

He hadn't expected her to be so…

He shook his head. That was the trouble. He had entertained zero expectations where Nicole was concerned. Even when he'd discovered that his desire for her was as potent as before, he'd thought some long-overdue sex was all he needed. It had seemed a simple solution to vent his frustration and get the wife who had deserted him out of his system—all in one neat swoop. His mouth twisted. It just didn't seem to be working out that way. He wondered how he could have made such a bad call and how this whole weekend could have turned into something else. Something he hadn't bargained for. He felt as if Nicole was stripping away layers of himself, leaving him raw and revealing a side he'd always kept hidden. How had that even happened? he asked himself furiously. But really, he knew.

He stared at the dark rippling waves of the sea. It was because Nicole had changed. She was no longer that uncertain woman who gazed at him with reproachful eyes and was prepared to take whatever he dished out. This new version was more sure of herself. Confident and self-assured, she was behaving as if leaving their marriage had given her the courage to be herself. As if *he* had been holding her back.

His mouth hardened. Well, let her think whatever she wanted to think. Soon she would be gone and out of his mind. In the morning he would put her on a flight back to England and sign the divorce papers and that would be it.

The end.

He watched as Anna Rivers walked by in a strappy

little silver gown—the actress slanting him a slow and lazy smile over her shoulder as she passed. Despite having discovered his marital status, the invitation in her eyes was unmistakable but Rocco wasn't interested. He scowled. He'd had enough of women for the time being. Once Nicole had gone and the dust had settled he would resume the life he'd had before she'd tumbled into it. He would operate on a level he was comfortable with. Casual affairs with women who knew the score. Women with careers and lives of their own, who he could take or leave as it suited him. Not women who tried to burrow underneath his skin and stay there.

As soon as they left the cocktail party he would say goodnight and in the morning he would have left for the office long before she awoke. And despite the fact that she was undoubtedly the sexiest woman at the party, he would not share her bed or her body tonight. It was too disquieting. Too...*intense*. That way she had of cooing in his ear when he was deep inside her. The soft wrap of her thighs around his back while he rode her. He felt the warm wash of hunger heating his blood but, deliberately, he dampened it down. Bringing her here had been a mistake, he conceded grimly. A mistake he would not compound by being intimate with her again.

The phone in his pocket began to vibrate and he glanced at it, his senses instantly on alert when he saw it was a missed call from Sicily. And it was late. Was it his grandfather? he wondered, his heart clenching with instinctive dread as he followed the sway of Anna River's bottom towards the lower deck. But once there, he bypassed the actress's footsteps to turn left, heading for the sanctuary of his on-board office before putting a call through to the Barberi complex, just outside Palermo.

Maria answered the phone on the first ring—not a good sign—and Rocco automatically slipped into dialect to speak to the family's housekeeper.

'Nonno?' he demanded.

'Your grandfather is sick,' said Maria.

'How sick?'

'He has a fever. Some kind of infection, the doctor says. We called him straight away.'

Rocco's fingers tightened around the phone. 'And what's happening now?'

'He is on medication and we have hired a nurse. She's with him now. So am I.' There was a pause. 'Are you coming home, Rocco?'

'Of course I'm coming home!'

There was another pause and this time Rocco was certain he could hear the voice of his grandfather in the background—weaker than he'd ever heard him speak before. 'Is that Nonno?' he demanded. 'What's he saying?'

Maria's next words were tentative. 'He wants to know if you are reconciled with your wife.'

Rocco narrowed his eyes. *'What?'*

'Michele mentioned that Nicole has been staying with you in Monaco,' said Maria.

Silently, Rocco swore. What right did his assistant have to go informing on him to his family, like some sort of amateur spy? He would have words with her, he thought grimly—but that would have to wait.

'He wants you to answer his question,' Maria said. 'And you know he will not rest until you do so.'

Rocco stared around his on-board office without really seeing it. If it had been anyone other than his grandfather he would have told them to go to hell. But Nonno was different. He had a place in Rocco's life which nobody else could ever occupy. He had been there for him and his siblings when their world had imploded. He had been the one true rock in their world. And he might be dying. Pain shot through him and Rocco's eyes refocussed as slowly he became aware of his surroundings—the fancy office from which he had conducted some of his most audacious deals. Yet all the gleaming wood and brass might as well have been muddy pieces of driftwood. Suddenly all the awards and commendations counted for nothing.

Niente.

Because these were not the things which mattered.

'No,' said Rocco, aware that his voice was husky with fear. 'We are not reconciled.'

His words were now being conveyed to Nonno but Rocco didn't need Maria to come back on the line to tell him what he could hear for himself.

'He wants to see her, Rocco. He wants you to bring her to Sicily.'

The party was in full swing and Nicole was trying very hard to listen to what the tall Frenchman with the purple bow tie was saying. She knew he was a shareholder and that they viewed Rocco's bid very favourably. She knew that because he'd told her, even though he probably shouldn't have done—but he, like everyone else, seemed to be knocking back the expensive champagne which was being served as freely as water. But it was difficult to concentrate on his words. Difficult to think about anything other than the fact that Anna Rivers had just left the deck with Rocco following the beautiful actress, and that he had been gone for some time.

Nicole told herself it didn't matter where he went or who he went with, but that wasn't quite true. She was suddenly finding that it mattered a lot more than it should have done, yet that was stupid. Just because she'd had hot sex with him that afternoon didn't mean she had any rights over him. Hot sex when he *hadn't even kissed her*. That told her pretty much what he really felt about her, didn't it?

Her cheeks were flushed as she walked to the far end of the deck where it was much quieter. Did Rocco realise that the takeover bid was pretty much a done deal? Had he now decided she was surplus to requirements and he could safely ignore her for most of the party? Probably. What did she expect? That he would treat her with respect when she'd behaved that way—falling into his arms as if none of the bad stuff had happened?

There was a buzz behind her and Nicole turned to see Rocco reappear, looking dramatically handsome in his dinner suit, his black hair gleaming beneath the coloured fairy lights which were strung around the deck. He was looking around, as if trying to locate someone, and then he saw her and began to walk towards her. But the instinctive leap of her heart was replaced by a distinct sense of foreboding as she saw the ravaged look which was darkening his features.

'What's wrong?' she said as soon as he'd reached her.

'I've just had a call from Sicily.' His jaw clenched. 'My grandfather is sick.'

Nicole sucked in a breath, her shock much greater than it should have been because Turi was very old and so such news could never be described as unexpected. But some people seemed indestructible and the elderly patriarch was one of them. She tried to imagine the Barberi complex without the larger-than-life figure at its helm and couldn't. She wondered how it would be for Rocco and his siblings if they lost the man who had always been there for them. The lynchpin of their lives. She looked up into Rocco's empty eyes. 'I'm so sorry,' she said. 'How...how bad is it?'

He shrugged. 'They don't know. My brother is in South America and my sister has been in Los Angeles, so everyone is away. They're both on their way home, but the flights are long and he needs someone with him now. I'm going to Sicily as soon as air traffic control have approved my flight plans. Michele is sorting that out for me now.'

'Yes, of course.' Briefly, Nicole closed her eyes, praying that Rocco would reach his grandfather in time, but she couldn't prevent the other thought which came rushing through her mind. That this really was the last time she would ever see him. She opened her eyes, unprepared for the cold wash of heartache which followed in the wake of this realisation. This really *was* goodbye, she thought, and was just working out how best to say it, when Rocco spoke again.

'He wants to see you, Nicole.'

She blinked, aware that his shadowed eyes had grown flinty and a muscle was working insistently at his temple. 'Who does?' she said.

'Nonno. I spoke with Maria. He's been asking for you.'

'For me?' She didn't make any attempt to hide her bewilderment because there had been no real closeness between her and the octogenarian patriarch, no matter how hard she had tried. 'But why?'

'Who knows?' he growled, tugging impatiently at his tie as if it were strangling him. 'Turi is a law unto himself and always has been.' There was a pause. 'Will you come, Nic?'

'Do you want me to come?' she questioned quietly, trying not to react to a nickname he hadn't used in a long, long time.

He seemed to steel himself before shaking his head. 'Not really,' he said. 'I think we both know that you and I have reached the end of the line. But my grandfather could die at any moment—and who am I to deny a dying man his wish?' He looked her straight in the eyes and they might as well have been alone in a room, rather than on a crowded yacht in the middle of a cocktail party.

Nicole met his questioning gaze. Nobody could accuse Rocco of lying—or caring how much his words could hurt. Yet behind his blunt statement she could sense a vulnerability which for once he wasn't bothering to hide. Maybe he couldn't hide it. Suddenly it occurred to her that right now Rocco needed her as she'd always wanted to be needed by him, but like everything else it had come too late.

And she was scared. Going back to Sicily had the potential to reopen painful wounds—but what choice did she have? If she had any kind of conscience she couldn't refuse what he was asking of her. She was doing this for a sick man, yes, but she was also doing it for Rocco—because she could never live with herself if she let him down. And how crazy was that? 'Of course I'll come,' she said quietly.

'*Grazie.*' He nodded, before glancing down at her red dress. 'We need to go straight from here to the airfield. There won't be time to return to the house but I can get Michele to pack your clothes and have them sent straight to the plane.'

'That's fine,' she said.

'Then let's get going,' he said roughly.

Silently, they slipped away from the party and Nicole could see people smiling as they passed. Were they assuming that she and the Sicilian were sneaking away to celebrate the impending deal, or maybe the renewal of their own relationship?

And for one brief moment, didn't some rogue part of her wish it *had* been a real reconciliation instead of a cold-blooded arrangement to settle some *unfinished business*? Instead, she risked getting herself in even deeper than before, by agreeing to return to a place full of difficult memories—a place where she had been nothing more than an outsider. Would Rocco remember that and look out for her or would he simply throw her to the lions, the way he'd done before?

A hundred questions were bubbling up inside her and she stole a glance at Rocco as his private jet soared up into the starlit skies over Monaco, wondering if she should just be upfront and ask them. But his profile was hard and uncompromising and, sensing he had little appetite for conversation, or any more of her unwanted questions, Nicole spent the flight in an uneasy silence.

CHAPTER TEN

IT WAS DARK when Rocco's jet landed in Sicily and the air was as deeply scented as Nicole remembered. She breathed it in with remembered clarity, her senses saturated by the fragrance of lemon and jasmine, and earth baked warm by the sun. She thought how peculiar it was that the stars on this island always seemed brighter than they did anywhere else, or maybe it was just that the sky was darker.

Suddenly a whole shoal of memories began to bombard her. Memories which had the power to make her heart twist with regret. The way she'd felt about Rocco when he'd brought her here. The way he'd kissed her and told her that he would try to be the best father he could. The way she'd lain in his arms and imagined a future for them with their baby. She shook her head a little, surprised by the sudden yearning which washed over her. Was it self-protection which had made her forget all the positive stuff about their marriage, hoping that would make it easier to forget him?

She walked down the aircraft steps where a car was waiting, with a driver Nicole recognised sitting behind the wheel. He gave her a brief nod of acknowledgment, and as he and Rocco slipped naturally into dialect Nicole turned to look out of the window as they drove through the darkened Sicilian countryside.

She stared at the olive trees which lined the roads, their leaves metallic as they glinted beneath the moonlight, their fruits tiny and as yet unripened. The countryside looked unfamiliar in the darkness but the sprawling Barberi residence was exactly as she remembered. As the electronic gates swung open Nicole could see the various residences laid out before her, and the lateness of the hour would have normally ensured that the main house was dark and silent. But the lights blazing from the windows indicated that things were far from 'normal'.

Rocco turned to her as soundlessly the car slid to a halt in the forecourt, his features shadowed. 'Why don't you make your way to our house and get settled in?'

She nodded. 'Okay.'

''I'll go straight to Turi. If you want anything to eat or drink, Maria will still be up.'

Was that a flash of fear she could read in his eyes as he pushed open the car door? The fear of confronting the mortality of someone you loved? Impulsively, she reached across for his hand and squeezed it and for a moment Rocco stilled before squeezing hers back. And Nicole thought how strange it was that such a small gesture could somehow seem more intimate than sex itself.

'Send Turi my love,' she said huskily.

'I will.'

Carrying her small suitcase, Nicole made her way

across the terrace towards the house where she and Rocco had begun and ended their married life. Security lights flickered on and illuminated the imposing building in a golden halo of light. *Our house*, Rocco had said, but it had never really been her house, had it? And it had certainly never felt like home. It had been filled with dark antique furniture which had been in the Barberi family for many decades, and she'd found the style heavy and oppressive but had been too timid to suggest any changes. Too timid to do anything really, except feel eternally grateful that Rocco hadn't kicked her out on the street when she'd fallen pregnant.

Pushing open the door, she clicked on the lights and began to reacquaint herself with the place, trying to get herself into a state of calm to face whatever lay ahead. It was all exactly as she remembered. Only the room they'd designated as a nursery had altered. The crib had gone and so had that swirly animal mobile which she'd brought with her from England. Everything gone. The walls were painted a neutral colour instead of that sunny yellow, and, although it was furnished with a couple of comfortable armchairs and a sophisticated sound system, it didn't look like a room anyone had ever used. Because Rocco didn't live here any more, she reminded herself fiercely. And he'd never even told her why he'd left.

She went to the bathroom, stripped off her red dress and took a long shower—the soapy water sluicing off her heated skin making her feel relatively human again. Afterwards she raided her suitcase for the T-shirt which doubled as a nightshirt and slipped it on. She found some cold water in the fridge and drank it and thought maybe she should stay awake in case Rocco came back. But she was tired. Bone-tired. So much had happened in such a short time. Perhaps she would just lie down and wait.

Unable to face the master bedroom, she grabbed a blanket and lay on one of the sofas in the sitting room, yawning heavily and trying to keep her heavy eyelids open. But Rocco didn't return and the minutes ticked by—and next thing she knew she could feel the warmth of the morning sun on her face. Blinking, she scrambled off the sofa. She'd left the shutters open and she gazed out at the Sicilian morning. Already, the sky was a deep and cloudless blue and in the distance she could hear the sound of church bells. The birds were singing like crazy and the sheer beauty of the morning inexplicably bolstered her spirits. She found her case and she put on jeans and a T-shirt. As she brushed her curls she thought about Turi and offered up a silent prayer that he'd made it through the night.

It would have been easier to go into the kitchen to see if there was any coffee but Nicole knew she couldn't keep putting off going into the room she'd never thought she would see again. Her pulse was skittering against her wrists as she walked into the bedroom she'd shared with Rocco—an elegant room dominated by a huge antique bed. She remembered how gentle he'd been with her. So protective of the new life inside her. Only now could she understand the reason for the exaggerated delicacy with which he'd handled her, when at the time she'd feared he now longer found her attractive. It was strange the perspective which distance gave you.

Swallowing down the sudden lump in her throat, she looked around. On one of the walls was her only contribution to the décor—a black and white photograph of New York, which she'd admired on their honeymoon and which Rocco had secretly bought and had shipped here, so it was waiting for her on their return. She remembered being overwhelmed by the gesture, thinking it symbolised a romantic future which hadn't ever materialised. And it twisted her heart with nostalgia as she stared at it. Why was it still hanging there?

She wasn't sure what made her open the closet but what she found inside unsettled her even more than the picture had done. Because all her clothes were there— exactly as she'd left them. Neat lines of colour-coordinated outfits which had been chosen by the expensive London stylist. Shirtdresses and neat trousers—all with toning shoes and accessories. Yet looking at them now she could see that, although they weren't her style, they were in no way offensive. Why had she made such a fuss about them?

She sighed. The problem hadn't been in the choice of clothes, but in her. If you let people treat you like a doll then you couldn't really complain when they did, could you? She wondered, if she could do it all again, whether she would have behaved differently, but really she knew the answer. Of course she would—but the outcome would probably have been the same. Because a marriage could only work if it was based on love and Rocco didn't have the ability to love—he'd told her that himself.

As if thinking about him had somehow conjured him

up, Rocco chose that moment to walk into the bedroom and Nicole's questions were forgotten as she searched his face, registering eyes which were shadowed from lack of sleep and a hard and unsmiling mouth.

Her heart squeezed. 'Turi?' she questioned, her voice squeaky with anxiety.

His jaw tightened but he nodded. 'He's hanging on in there. He's in some kind of deep sleep. He didn't seem to know I was there.' He paused and a muscle began to work at his temple. 'I don't know if he's well enough to see you right now and—'

'Honestly, Rocco—it doesn't matter.' Her words tumbled over themselves. 'He may not have been himself when he suggested seeing me—and there's your brother and sister to consider. I don't want him exhausted when they arrive and maybe I'd better not—'

'Shh,' he said, and his voice was unexpectedly gentle. 'It's okay. The doctor says that, physically, he's as strong as an ox—and he's been defying the odds all his life. Let's just see how he goes. He wants to see you, Nic—and as far as I'm concerned, that's what's going to happen.'

Nicole nodded, thinking that the things they were saying to each other were polite and functional but there was a whole different conversation going on underneath the surface. At least, for her there was. She looked into Rocco's eyes and wondered what he thought when he saw them both standing here in this bedroom, like ghosts of the people they used to be. Did he find it as poignant as she did? Were the memories flying out of nowhere to remind him that it hadn't been all bad? But these were questions she would never ask because she had no right to.

'I'm going to take a shower,' he said, his hand reaching up to undo the buttons of his shirt. 'And then we'll go over to the main house and have some breakfast. Maria is waiting for us.'

The sight of her husband about to start undressing was enough to have Nicole scuttling from the bedroom and thirty minutes later they were sitting in the kitchen of the main farmhouse, with Maria bustling around them. The housekeeper had been with the Barberi family since Rocco was a baby and greeted Nicole with a surprising affection, enveloping her in a fierce hug which left her breathless. Afterwards she turned and said something in rapid dialect to which Rocco made a drawling response which had Nicole looking at him questioningly.

'She says that Turi's fate is in God's hands now,' Rocco interpreted. 'That he is very frail but she is certain he will recover now that I have returned. And I told her that if she was trying to make me feel guilty about moving to Monaco—then it wasn't going to work.' Unexpectedly, his eyes flashed with humour. 'She also wants to know if you'd like some *granita* with your coffee?'

'I'd love some,' said Nicole, sitting down at the table and taking the bowl which was being pushed towards her.

Rocco watched as Nicole began spooning up the famous Sicilian *granita* which Maria had made using lemons taken from the estate. His grandfather had made it through the night, his brother and sister were on their way and the coffee he was drinking was strong and dark. There were many reasons to count his blessings, but the tension in his body remained as tight as ever. Was it having Nicole here which was disturbing him so much? Sitting across the table from him with her dark curls tumbling over her shoulders and her rosy lips looking so kissable. He put his cup down with a bang, resenting the sudden shafting of his body because surely he shouldn't be feeling desire when his grandfather lay upstairs, so sick.

But it *was* desire, that was the trouble. It was there, ever-present—as much a part of him as the blood which pulsed through his veins. He watched as his wife popped a piece of deep-fried *ciambella* into her mouth and tried not to be distracted by the luscious curves of her breasts pushing against her simple T-shirt. She was simply… captivating and suddenly he found himself wondering what the hell he was going to do with her all day while she was here—if you discounted the very obvious.

A pulse flickered at his temple. Occupying himself wouldn't normally be a problem but this was different. For once Rocco realised he couldn't escape into the endless refuge of work, or allow himself to be consumed by its constant demands. He could hardly leave Nicole to amuse herself while he locked himself in the office, could he? He glanced across at her, mentally sifting through all his options. If he took her to the nearby village or even into Palermo itself—by evening it would be all round the island that Rocco Barberi was back with his wife. And that was not going to happen – because it wasn't true.

'Why don't we go for a walk round the estate?' he said, watching as her benign expression changed into one of wariness. Was she remembering how their walk around the Rock of Monaco had ended, with him hiring a room after lunch—a room blatantly intended for sex? Was that why she produced a distinctly cool smile in response?

'Sure. Why not?'

This time he didn't need to suggest she change her shoes, because her footwear was sensible, and this time there was no sense of showing her somewhere new. Because she knew this place. He didn't have to point out the way when he suggested going to the orchards—she turned left automatically. It had been easy to forget that she'd lived here. Too easy, perhaps.

To Rocco's surprise, the morning unfolded with a surprising sense of effortlessness as Nicole reacquainted herself with the Barberi estate. Her enthusiasm seemed genuine as she admired the terracotta and green landscape and she even remembered the word for goat as she surveyed the rangy-looking creatures who were gnawing away in one of the scrubby meadows. It was when they reached the olive groves and he was congratulating himself on managing to kill a few hours without any kind of drama, when she asked the question he guessed he should have been expecting all along.

'So why exactly did you move to Monaco, Rocco?' she said, her English voice sounding very clear and steady. 'Why leave Sicily when it's clear you love the place so much?'

Rocco took his time before answering, bending down to study one of the rose bushes planted at the end of each line of olive trees, to discourage insects away from the precious fruit. Satisfied with the gardener's efforts, he straightened up, brushing his hands down over his thighs. 'Because most of my work is in mainland Europe and it cut my commuting time right down.'

'And your grandfather didn't...' She lifted her shoulders. 'Didn't he miss you?'

'I'm sure he did,' he drawled. 'But he soon got used to it. People migrate all the time. And my sister lives here. The last thing Turi would want would be for me to stay here out of some kind of duty.'

Rocco's mouth hardened. Because he'd been absolved of duty. He'd done more than his fair share of it and Turi understood that. He glanced at his watch, wanting to put an end to this. To stop the introspection which always seemed to affect him whenever Nicole was around. 'The nurse said you could go in before lunch, even if Nonno's asleep. Shall we go back to the house to get something to drink first?'

She nodded. 'Yes, please. And I'd like to freshen up.'

Back at the house, Rocco took the opportunity to check his emails while Nicole went to change and he was just passing the partially open door of the spare room when a movement from inside made him glance in.

He had automatically thought she'd be using their old bedroom even though he'd noticed earlier that the bed hadn't been slept in last night. But she hadn't. Yet again she had chosen a room away from him, and as he looked in he could see she was struggling with her dress. He saw her hand angling awkwardly down her back as she struggled to pull up the zip and even though he knew it was the wrong thing to do, he found himself standing in the doorway, as if somebody had wound the clock back and he were her husband again. As if he had a right to take part in all those small domestic rituals which were a part of every marriage.

'Can I help?'

She looked up and a flurry of emotions crossed her face. She screwed her nose up, as if something inside her was hurting—and then suddenly she gave an almost efficient nod of agreement. As if she would be a fool to struggle with her own zip when someone was willing to take over the troublesome task for her.

Only it didn't quite happen that way.

Rocco honestly didn't think he had intended seduction at that moment but the instant his fingers connected with her silky flesh, he was lost. Maybe she was, too, because he heard a shuddered sigh escape from her lips. So that suddenly, instead of doing the zip up, he was sliding it down. All the way down to where her back curved inwards and then beyond even that, so that all it needed was the slightest tug of his fingers to let the garment slide to the ground. But he paused before he did that. Long enough to allow her to move away or chastise him and ask him what the hell he thought he was playing at.

But she didn't. Her sigh became a quickened breath

and still she said nothing as he slid his hands around her back to cup her straining breasts. He could feel his erection hard and almost painful as it pressed against her lacy lingerie and he thought maybe it would be better if he did this almost...*anonymously*. He could push her up against that wall and pull her panties down before freeing himself. He could slip inside her from behind. He could take her quickly and efficiently and give them both pleasure and not a single word need be exchanged. They didn't even have to look at one another. And afterwards they could make as if it had never happened. They would never speak of it again. He'd done that with other women before, but never with Nicole.

And he didn't want to do that now. Not with her. Never with her. He gave a little groan as he turned her round to find her eyes as darkened and as full of sensual promise as he'd hoped they would be. He bent to slide his arm beneath her knees and carried her over to the bed.

'I want you,' he said unsteadily as he laid her down on top of the embroidered cover, before ripping the shirt from his body, uncaring of the buttons which broke free.

'And I want you,' she echoed chokingly.

'Nicole—'

But she silenced him with a fierce shake of her wild curls. 'I don't want analysis or promises neither of us can keep,' she said. 'I just want you, Rocco. Now. That's all.'

And wasn't it ironic that by taking *his* line—by removing all the emotion from what was about to happen—

she somehow increased her power over him? So that, for the first time in all the time he'd known her, it felt as if it was *Nic* who was taking charge. As if everything he'd ever taught her had crystallised into this one, single act. It felt as if they were doing it in slow motion. As if their bodies were glued together, with no space between them. He kissed her. And kissed her. His lips brushed over hers in a tantalising graze until hers eagerly parted and he licked his way over their trembling surface.

She gave a gasp as he entered her and he blotted out the sound with the slow caress of his lips. She wrapped her soft thighs around his bare back and he thrust. And thrust again. He made it last for as long as he could, until the little cry she gave sounded as if she might be in some sort of pain, and then he came too and all thought was temporarily banished from his mind.

But her smile was dreamy when he studied her afterwards and he could instantly feel himself hardening again. He leaned over her, his lips automatically seeking hers, but she wriggled away from him with a decisive shake of her head.

'No,' she said.

'Really?'

'Really.'

'Why not?'

'You know exactly why not, Rocco. We shouldn't have done it once—and we're certainly not going to do it twice.'

'Because?'

'Because… There are a million reasons, which you really don't need me to articulate for you, but mainly because I have to go and see your grandfather and the nurse will be expecting me.'

He nodded. 'Okay. Go and take a shower. I'll use one of the other bathrooms and wait for you downstairs.'

Her words echoed round in his mind as Rocco stood beneath the jets of the gushing shower, and he reluctantly realised Nicole had been right. They shouldn't have done it. Because what purpose had it served? Okay, it had fed his desire—and hers—but they were supposed to be over, and divorcing couples didn't keep having sex.

He turned off the shower and towelled himself dry but once he'd dressed and gone downstairs he was surprised by a wave of emotion. He found himself thinking about the future and about what might happen when Turi died. Even if he survived this bout of illness, he couldn't go on for ever. Nobody could. Rocco found himself asking what it was going to be like here once Turi had gone and why he'd never stopped to think about it before.

Because Turi had always been there. A man who was larger than life—and you imagined that those kinds of men never died.

But they did.

He wondered if his siblings would turn to him and expect him to slip into the replacement role of patriarch? What if he told them he wasn't interested in such a role? That he had already given as much as he was prepared to give to ensure the survival of the family?

Was he in danger of overthinking matters because he'd been stirred up by Nicole's presence here? And wasn't he in danger of allowing her to skew his vision? Just because the sex had been dynamite, didn't mean it couldn't be as good with somebody else. His lips hardened with renewed resolve as he heard her light footstep on the stairs.

Once she had returned to England everything would shake down. He could stop looking at his life and questioning it. He could start bedding women who didn't mess with his head.

He clenched his fists.

Once she had gone.

CHAPTER ELEVEN

'Do you want me to stay ?' Rocco questioned as he pushed open the door of the sickroom.

Nicole wasn't sure what she wanted as she stepped into the shuttered room and gazed over at the inert body in the bed. Would Rocco be a comforting presence at her side, or a distraction? The latter, probably—especially after what had just happened back at the house. The sex which had just sort of *happened* and which had blown her away. Not because of his amazing technique, which had never been in question, but because of his unexpected tenderness which had made her heart want to burst with pleasure and break with sorrow, all at the same time. She was just about to politely tell him she'd be fine on her own when the figure in the bed spoke.

'Leave us, Rocco.'

Turi's voice wasn't as strong as Nicole remembered but it still wasn't the kind of voice you ignored and she watched as his grandson gave a terse nod.

'The nurse will be in the room next door, if you need anything,' Rocco said. 'Don't wear yourself out, Nonno.'

Turi lifted a wavering hand to indicate that he should cut short the lecture and leave. 'Come,' the old man said to Nicole, once the door had closed.

Nicole approached the bed. The quietness and the dimness of the room reminded her of nursing her adoptive mother and at that moment she missed Peggy Watson very much. As she grew closer she could see that although age and sickness had diminished him, the faded blue eyes, which must once have been so like Rocco's, were unexpectedly bright as the elderly patriarch gestured for her to sit down.

'Turi,' she whispered as she perched on a chair next to the bed and squeezed his gnarled old hand in hers. 'I wish I could say *I hope you're feeling better*, in dialect.'

'I think we had better speak in English,' he said. 'Don't you?'

Nicole couldn't hide her surprise and something in the way he said it made her suddenly want to get honest with him. Because if you couldn't say what was really on your mind at times like this, then what was the point of anything? She remembered his refusal to use her native tongue when she'd arrived at the house—even rejecting her faltering attempts in Italian as he'd insisted on conversing in Sicilian dialect. 'Unlike before,' she said quietly.

He nodded in agreement. 'That was foolish of me. I recognise that now. I wanted you to integrate fully with life here and I thought that imposing a tough regime from the beginning was the way to do it.' He gave a croaky little sigh. 'I wanted so much, but none of it happened the way it was supposed to. I handled it wrong. Just like I handled Rocco all wrong.'

Nicole felt a frown pleating her brow. 'What do you mean, Nonno? What did you do wrong with Rocco?'

His voice gained more strength as he began to speak. 'Did he ever speak to you of his childhood?'

She shook her head. 'Never. He used to shut all my questions right down and make me feel bad about asking them. It was only very recently that he talked about his parents.'

Turi's eyes were inquisitive. 'You know he was only fourteen when they died?'

She nodded. 'Yes, I knew that much.'

'His brother was nine, his sister only five and the little ones, they were…' The old man blinked his rheumy eyes rapidly. 'They were broken,' he said at last, clearing his throat. 'I was trying to do it all. My wife was no longer alive and I had the business to run—as well as the younger children to cope with. I leaned on Rocco too much. I see that now. I told him…'

Nicole leaned forward as his words faded away. 'What, Nonno? What did you tell him?'

He indicated she should plump up the bank of pillows behind his head, and once she'd done so he lay back on them and continued. 'I told him that the younger children would look to him for strength and that was what he needed to show them. To keep his head down and work hard and carry on, no matter what—because that would hold the family together. To follow my example and never cry or show his feelings. And he didn't. He learned his lesson well. Too well, perhaps.'

To never show his feelings. A painful breath escaped Nicole's lips because didn't Turi's words explain so much about the man she had married? Why he could appear so *distant.* Why he had the ability to bury himself in his work, no matter what was going on around him. Was that why he hadn't reacted as she'd thought he might when she'd had the miscarriage? Why he'd never really talked about it—not even when they'd been having that heart-to-heart in Monaco, when she'd given him every opportunity to do so. 'Yes, he did,' she said slowly. 'But then, I imagine that Rocco must have been an exemplary student in everything he undertook.'

'Not once did I see a tear fall,' Turi added shakily. 'At least, not then.'

Nicole narrowed her eyes as he held her gaze. 'What do you mean?' she whispered. 'Not then?'

There was a pause. 'When *you* left, he was heart-broken.'

Angrily, Nicole shook her head. Turi might be old and sick but even he couldn't convince her of *that.* Heartbroken? Never in a million years. Rocco had pushed her away and no mistake. She remembered him taking a trip to the States when she'd most needed him, weeks after it had happened, when she'd still been mired in her own sense of misery.

But she hadn't told him that, had she? She hadn't really known how and he hadn't seemed to want her to.

She'd put his emotional distance down to the fact that he'd been forced to marry her and once there wasn't going to be a baby, there was no reason for the relationship to continue. Yet what Turi had told her made her look at it differently. Wouldn't Rocco's behaviour be more understandable if he'd been schooled in the art of concealing his true emotions?

No, she told herself fiercely. It wasn't like that. Turi was an old man sentimentalising his past in a clumsy attempt to achieve some sort of peace towards the end of a long life. And she wasn't going to buy into it—because hadn't she already dealt with her own pain? She'd done that and come out the other side and nothing could be gained by dwelling on what could never be. She could allow herself to feel an aching sympathy for the hardships Rocco must have been forced to endure, but she should never start making the mistake of thinking he was capable of loving her, because that way lay madness. He was capable of having fantastic sex with her, as he'd very recently proved—but nothing more than that. 'No,' she said. 'I don't believe you.'

'Yes,' Turi argued, with a sudden vehemence which belied his frail physique. 'What benefit would it bring if I started lying at this stage of my life? Didn't you ask him why he left Sicily? Why he couldn't bear to live in the house once you'd gone? Why he refused to give away any of your things?'

Fear washed over her—a fear which was motivated by stupid, stubborn hope. And hope was futile where Rocco was concerned. Nicole knew that better than anyone. She could see that Turi was looking tired now, as if the exertion of all he'd just told her had exhausted him, and quickly she stood up and poured out a glass of water before holding it to his lips.

'I'm going to go and let you get some rest now,' she said softly.

'Promise me,' he croaked as he took another small sip, then waved the glass away, 'that you will ask him why? Just promise me that, Nicole, even though I have no right to demand such a promise.'

What could she say? How could she possibly refuse a sick man this simple request?

'I promise,' she said, putting the glass down and dropping a light kiss on his forehead, and the old man smiled before his eyes closed.

The nurse must have heard the sound of Nicole's chair scraping against the floor, because the door to the adjoining room opened and she appeared, looking crisp and fresh in her white uniform as she glanced enquiringly at Nicole.

'*Tutto bene, signora?*' she questioned.

Nicole's Italian might have been basic, but even she could understand this simple query. '*Sì. Grazie,*' she said and left the room.

But her head was spinning once she stepped out of Turi's residence with no real idea of what to do or where to go. Buying herself time, she took off to a quiet section of the estate in an attempt to get her thoughts in order, but that proved impossible. She didn't believe Turi because she didn't *want* to believe him. She didn't dare. Because even if what he said was true, what good would come of raking it up now?

Just suppose that Rocco *had* cared for her at the time—he had certainly grown out of it, hadn't he? He'd told her that the only reason he had taken her to Monaco was to have sex with her and get her out of his system and he had done just that. Even an hour ago he had done that. Maybe he would continue having sex with her for as long as she allowed him to and if she did that, wasn't it cheapening what she'd once felt for him?

But she had promised Turi. She'd promised a sick man she would ask Rocco that question. And you couldn't make promises like that and not follow through...

She went to search for him and when Maria informed her he was down among the lemon trees it struck an instant chord. Nicole knew he sometimes liked to take his work there and it had always been one of the prettiest places to sit on the Barberi estate, with its wooden bench placed beneath the sweet scent of the creamy lemon blossom. He had taken her there sometimes when they had returned from their honeymoon, when they would sit quietly listening to the drowsy buzzing of the bees in the lavender bushes, while she'd tried to get her queasy stomach to settle. It had been this place she'd been thinking of when she'd made her bestselling pottery collection.

Her mouth was dry as she approached the lemon grove and saw Rocco sitting beneath the shade of a tree, a weighty-looking sheaf of papers on his lap. The warm sun was beating down on his black hair and he had rolled up the arms of his shirt to reveal his strong forearms. She remembered the way those arms had been holding her just a short while ago. The way his hands had cupped her face as he had kissed her over and over again—as if he couldn't get enough of her kisses.

And hadn't that made her realise…?

No. Not *realise*. That was the wrong word. It had made her *think* she might still be in love with him.

And she wasn't.

She definitely wasn't.

'Rocco?'

He glanced up as she approached, his features darkening as he pushed the papers aside.

'Turi's fine,' she said, in answer to the unspoken question in his eyes. 'The nurse is with him now.' She walked over to the bench and indicated the space beside him. 'Mind if I sit down?'

There was a pause. *'Certo,'* he said, raising his shoulders in a non-committal shrug.

His momentary hesitation jarred, as did the less than welcoming look on his face and Nicole wanted to forget about her promise, but she couldn't. Deliberately choosing the far end of the seat, she sat down, her heart racing as she watched a butterfly hovering over some little white flowers and tried to work out how she could possibly phrase this without looking a complete…

No.

She'd been there and done that. It didn't matter what this did to her reputation or how it made her look. And besides, caring about that kind of thing was shallow. What mattered was getting to the truth, no matter what that might be.

'Turi had some interesting things to say,' she said slowly.

Was there something in her tone which made his face grow guarded? Was that why he slanted her a thoughtful look which was followed by one of slight *boredom*? 'Do I really want to hear them?' he drawled.

She suspected not, but he was going to hear them anyway. 'He told me to ask you why you left Sicily. So I'm asking.'

It was not what Rocco had been expecting and Nicole's words hit him like bullets from a gun. He could feel his body tensing as every instinct urged him to shut this topic down. To tell her it was none of her damned business—nor Turi's either. His laugh was short and, infuriatingly, his curiosity stirred. 'No doubt he had a few ideas himself—a few explanations why that might be?'

She drew in a breath which wasn't quite steady and he could see the doubt written on her face. 'He did, but I'm not sure I believed them. He told me lots of things. He seemed to feel guilty about the way he treated you.'

At this Rocco held up his palm to silence her, wanting her to know that she was in danger of crossing a forbidden line. 'My grandfather stepped in when my parents were killed,' he said coldly. 'How could he possibly feel guilty about something like that?'

'That wasn't what I meant,' she persisted. 'He told me he'd insisted you never show your feelings or emotions after they died. That because you were the oldest he forced you to be strong for the sake of Olivio and Romina.'

'And I was damaged as a result? Is that it?' he questioned, before giving a dismissive flick of his hand. '*Madonna mia*, I had no idea that Turi had taken such an interest in amateur psychology in his advancing years.'

But Nicole doggedly ignored his sarcasm and kept

her gaze fixed firmly on his. 'So why *did* you leave Sicily?'

He could feel a muscle beginning to work at his temple and once again he wondered how she had the ability to make him feel so damned *angry.* 'Maybe I found it intolerable to stay once my darling wife had disappeared without any warning, leaving the whole of Sicily buzzing and the international press camped out on my doorstep. You can't blame me for wanting to escape all the speculation after you'd gone. And since we're on the subject of raking up the past—just why *did* you go, Nicole?'

'I thought it was what you wanted,' she said dully.

'You thought it was what I wanted?' he repeated. 'Then that just shows how little you really knew me, doesn't it?' He picked up the sheaf of papers as if she were keeping him from something very important and raised his eyebrows. 'Look, I'm grateful to you for coming here and seeing Turi, and I'm glad he's been able to get what was clearly bothering him off his chest since undoubtedly that will aid his recovery, but there isn't any reason for you to stay any longer. We're done here, aren't we? I'll sign the papers and you can have your divorce. My plane will take you back to England as soon as you're ready—and since you're pretty much packed, I don't think there's any reason for you to hang around. *Capisce?*'

The words rolled smoothly from his tongue as if he couldn't wait to get rid of them. To get rid of *her.* Nicole met the sapphire glitter of his eyes. This was her cue to make a dignified exit. To go back to the house and gather her few things together. She would say a rather awkward goodbye to Maria and then be whisked away from here in Rocco's private jet—one last taste of luxury before she returned to her newly single life in England.

Wasn't that what she'd wanted all along?

She could feel the painful pounding of her heart.

No.

It might have been what she'd thought she wanted when she'd first filed those papers, but not any more. Because being with Rocco made her world come alive in a way it didn't do with anyone else, whether she liked it or not. Didn't matter that logic was urging her to get out while she still could, because all the logic in the world couldn't change the fact that her heart ached whenever she was with him. She'd loved him from the start and she loved him still—and love was an emotion which defied logic. She had never known what had made Rocco Barberi the unfathomable man he was, but she did now. She thought how lonely and bewildered he must have been as a bereaved teenager—unable to show his own grief because he was too busy being strong for his siblings. Couldn't she help break down the wall he had built around his heart? Couldn't she try? She'd learnt to articulate her own emotions—maybe she could help him do the same.

Because she didn't want a divorce. She really didn't. She wanted a reconciliation—a real one this time, not one which was just for show. One which might or might not work, but surely they could give it a try.

But only if he wanted it, too.

She sat up very straight, the wooden slats of the bench pressing into her back. 'I don't want to fly back in your private jet, Rocco,' she said in a low voice. 'I want to stay here, with you. Or go back with you to Monaco—whichever you prefer.'

His features darkened. 'What the hell are you talking about?'

He snarled the question rather than asking it and, stupidly, that gave Nicole a glimmer of hope. Because Rocco was cool and measured and controlled, wasn't he? He didn't *snarl*. 'I want to give our marriage another go,' she said calmly. 'And I'm hoping you might feel the same.'

'Are you insane?'

The snarl was even more pronounced now and that gave Nicole the courage to carry on, because now she had nothing left to lose. She was laying it all on the line and pride was pointless. She was fighting for her future, she realised—a future which suddenly seemed empty without Rocco. 'Perhaps a little,' she admitted huskily. 'But I want to tell you a few things I've discovered since you came back into my life.'

'Nicole—'

'Please, Rocco. At least do me the courtesy of hearing me out. Because I've discovered I am as much to blame for what happened as you were,' she said, cutting across his words in a way she would never have dared do before. 'I can see that now. I was just so...*grateful*... that you'd married me. Relieved that I wouldn't end up like my own natural mother—so desperate for money and support that I'd dump my own baby and leave them

crying feebly on a snowy hospital step. Only I would
never have let that happen,' she added fiercely, flaring
her nostrils to suck in a shaky breath. 'No matter what
happened, I would have kept our baby...'

Her words tailed off and as she struggled to contain
herself, Rocco shifted awkwardly on the seat. 'Nicole,'
he said again, only this time his voice sounded almost
gentle—like a doctor trying to placate an hysterical patient. 'Please. Don't do this.'

'But I *need* to do it!' she burst out. 'Don't you understand? I wanted you to comfort me after the miscarriage, to tell me that it was all going to be okay and
we could try again. After all, lots of women go through
that experience. It's not the end of the world, even if it
feels like it at the time. But you wouldn't let me near
you, Rocco—and I didn't tell you what I wanted. What
I needed. I had grown up in so many different foster
homes that I never learnt the art of true communication.
I learnt to hide my true feelings away because it was
safer that way. And like you said, you aren't a mind-
reader—how could you have been expected to know
what I needed? You were too busy protecting yourself
from your own pain. Trying not to show it and succeed-
ing in doing that—as you had been taught to do and
have been doing all your life.'

'I don't have to sit here and listen to this,' he said,
his blue eyes furious now.

'Oh, I think you do, Rocco. I think this needs to be
said, no matter what happens.' She drew in another
breath because while this was the hardest thing of all
to say, somehow it was the easiest too. 'And I'm telling

you that I love you. That I never really stopped loving you. That I'd like the chance to start over. To give our marriage another go—only a real one this time.'

'And you think—what?' He stared at her incredulously. 'That I will magically start to love you, too?'

'Who knows what could happen if you dared let me close?' she whispered. 'Why did you keep all my things if you didn't care about me a little bit? Why didn't you just get rid of them?'

'Did my grandfather tell you to ask me that as well?' he demanded.

Nicole saw his face darken and she realised that she might have pushed him too far. 'He might have mentioned it,' she admitted and then swallowed. 'Look, you don't have to say anything right now. Just think about it, that's all.'

'How confident you sound, Nicole,' he said, and now his words were icy-cold. 'Whatever happened to that wide-eyed amenable woman who first bewitched me?'

'She grew up,' Nicole answered simply. 'And the confidence is just a veneer, Rocco. Inside I'm shaking with nerves because something in my heart is telling me not to just give up on this marriage. So this is what I'm going to do.' For a moment she stared up at the deep blue sky behind the fretwork of leaves and lemon blossom and inhaled the warm, sweet scent of the flowers. 'I'm going to Palermo to find myself a hotel room and to look into the availability of cheap flights back to the UK—'

'And I just told you—'

'I know what you told me and it's a very kind offer

to let me use your plane, but if we're splitting up then I'd rather do it under my own steam. Start as I mean to go on. I'll text you to let you know where I am and which flight I'm booked on, and if you want me to stay…if you're prepared to open up your heart to me, then…' she drew in another breath '…all you have to do is come and get me.'

He rose to his feet, his face darkening as he tucked the sheaf of papers under his arm, his sapphire eyes blazing and brilliant. 'You can have your answer right now, Nicole, and it's very simple. I don't want that kind of relationship. I never did. I'm sorry about everything that's happened but we just have to live with that. Perhaps you were right all along and we need to move on.' One of the sheets of paper he'd been working on fluttered to the ground like an oversized piece of confetti, but he didn't even appear to notice. 'My offer to fly you home remains—but I'm not going to force you onto my plane. It's up to you. Let me know if you change your mind, but that's all you're going to get from me.' His mouth hardened. 'You're on your own from now on.'

CHAPTER TWELVE

THE HOTEL ROOM was small, clean and perfectly functional. It had plain walls, a dark-beamed ceiling and a bed with a mattress so hard it might have been made of stone.

Just like Rocco's heart, Nicole thought before forcing herself to stem *that* particular tide of thought. She couldn't blame him for being the man he was. She couldn't force him to feel emotions he wasn't capable of feeling or make him want to try again. Because that wasn't what he wanted. She'd been honest enough to put her feelings for him on the line and he'd been honest enough to tell her he wasn't interested. All she needed to do now was be grown-up enough to accept the situation *as it was*, not how she wanted it to be.

But, oh, it hurt.

How could it hurt so much?

Because she had allowed him back into her heart, that was why. She'd broken every single promise she'd ever made to herself and now she was paying the price. All those weeks and months and years of trying to forget about her Sicilian tycoon might as well not have happened.

Opening her computer, she went online and booked an early-morning flight for England, then changed and went down to the nearby pizzeria for supper. But despite the delicious smell of the *capricciosa*, she merely prodded at the pizza aimlessly and ate barely any of it. She sat there for a while, drinking coffee, and when at last she left the small restaurant she found herself going into the little church she'd seen at the far end of the street. Stepping into the dimly lit and cool interior, she gazed up at the brightness of the stained glass above the altar and thought about Peggy, and about Rocco's parents, too. She thought of the baby she'd never had, and she lit a candle for all of them. And something in that ageless symbolism gave her a new strength—as if in the flicker of those four flames she saw what she needed to do.

And that was to forget Rocco. To collect her pride and set him free. Her heart pounded. She wasn't going to send him a text telling him which flight she'd be on or which hotel she was staying in because that would be the behaviour of someone desperate, and needy. *And she wasn't that person any more.* She'd told him how she felt but you shouldn't say something just to get something back. Rocco didn't want her—he couldn't have made it any plainer and she needed to get that simple fact into her thick skull. She still had a life and a future—it was just one which didn't involve him. She would go back to Cornwall and make her pots and she wouldn't hide away from what had happened. She would embrace the experience—with all its accompanying pleasure and pain—and produce a new collection based on the things she had seen in Monaco. Who knew? One day she might even be able to think about the man she had married without an aching deep in her heart.

Back in the hotel room she lay beneath the thin sheet, listening to the sounds of people in the street below, as the minutes ticked slowly towards midnight. Her eyes were shadowed from lack of sleep when she woke the next day and she despised the eager way she instantly reached for her phone. But the screen was blank. There was no missed call or message from Rocco asking where the hell she was.

Of course there wasn't. She hadn't told him where she was staying but he did have her mobile number.

How long would it take her to accept that he just didn't want her?

The taxi which took her to the airport next morning was stuffy and smelt of cigarettes and Nicole was glad when she reached the terminal, even though she recognised she was leaving Sicily for ever. And that hurt, too. Wasn't it stupid how everything seemed to hurt today? Half-heartedly she removed her shoes and belt but for once the security process seemed speedy and her progress onto the fully booked flight relatively smooth. She had just snapped on her seat belt when some kind of commotion started happening on the opposite side of the aeroplane. People were pointing out of the windows and exclaiming in voices of rising excitement.

Nicole leaned over to see what they were looking at and her heart gave a lurch of disbelief. Because there, running across the Tarmac like a champion sprinter, was Rocco. Rocco as she'd never seen him before, suddenly appearing breathlessly on the plane, his face filled with dark intensity and something else...something she didn't recognise. He spotted her straight away and began to walk down the central aisle towards her. People's necks were craning and women were turning to watch him as he moved, their voices instinctively murmuring their appreciation.

Sitting bolt upright in her seat, Nicole ignored the loud pounding of her heart and glared at him. How *dared* he do this? Cause some kind of major disruption, which was probably going to get them both into all kinds of trouble. And for *what*? Especially when he'd already rejected her and she'd been coming to terms with that, and now she was going to have to do the same thing all over again.

'What are you doing here?' she bit out.

'You told me you were going to let me know where you were, and you didn't,' he accused. 'I searched every damned hotel in Palermo!'

'Tough. I changed my mind. It's a woman's prerogative—remember? And anyway—you had my number if you wanted me.'

'And if I'd phoned, you probably would have hung up on me.'

How convenient of him to think that. Nicole's lips tightened. 'I probably would,' she agreed steadily, as if she didn't care. 'So what are you doing here? You made your feelings very clear yesterday. Why don't you just leave me alone to get on with my life independently, Rocco?'

He was crouching down beside her and his face was

very close—those bright eyes burning into her like twin blue lasers. 'I'm here to tell you something you need to hear, which is that I love you, Nicole. Very, very much.'

His words were like a red rag to a bull. How dared he say such things so carelessly? Furiously, Nicole shook her head, pulling back from him so that she couldn't be influenced by the warmth of his breath or his proximity. 'You don't love me. You don't love anyone except yourself and your wretched business.'

'I love you,' he repeated fiercely. 'And I want to do all those things you suggested in the lemon grove. To start over. To be with you. And to spend the rest of my life making up for everything I've done, or failed to do.'

Nicole shook her head, trying to cling onto some sense of normality, despite the fact that one of the air stewards was now speaking into the intercom and any minute now he was going to get kicked off the plane—and so, probably, would she. Didn't he realise she didn't have the kind of funds to keep buying more tickets? Did he even *care*? 'It's too late for all that, Rocco. Don't you understand? It's just too late.'

'It can't be,' he said stubbornly.

'It can be whatever I want it to be,' she said, with equal stubbornness.

After a moment he nodded, as if he'd come to some kind of decision, and then he began to talk in a low voice. 'In Monaco you asked whether I had married you because you were pregnant and I said yes.' He voice became more fervent. 'But the main reason I was willing to marry you wasn't just because of duty or the life you carried inside you, but because with you, for the first and only time in my life, I had experienced the *colpe di fulmine*—'

Nicole frowned because for some reason all the passengers within earshot—far from seeming irritated at their delayed take-off—were now cheering wildly.

'What are you talking about?' she snapped.

'The thunderclap,' he interpreted, punching his fist hard against his heart. 'When love strikes like lightning—so intense and powerful that it cannot be denied.'

Nicole blinked at him in sheer amazement. Was this really Rocco—cold, emotionless Rocco Barberi—declaring his feelings and his love for her in front of a *plane-load of people*? 'Why are people cheering?' she questioned suspiciously.

'Because Sicilians are by nature romantic and they enjoy a love story.'

'Well, it's still too late. And now the captain has appeared and is putting on his cap and walking towards us and you really *are* going to get into trouble.'

'Please, *tesoro*.' He cast a wry glance over his shoulder. 'Can we at least go somewhere else and talk about this? I may own the airline but I really don't want the plane to miss its take-off slot.'

He owned the airline?

Nicole blinked.

Was there really no escaping the influence of Rocco Barberi on this infernal island?

She told herself to say no. To tell him she didn't need him—and maybe she didn't. But deep down she wanted him and something told her that was never going to change.

'Very well,' she said grudgingly. 'I will hear you out—just as long as you understand that I'm not making any promises.'

'I understand,' he said gravely.

But despite the clapping which accompanied them as they made their way off the plane, Nicole refused to give the laughing passengers the fairy-tale ending she suspected they wanted. A prolonged kiss in slo-mo and the big clinch on the Tarmac. Because life wasn't a fairy tale and she still didn't believe she had any kind of future with Rocco.

He ushered her towards an unmarked door and before she knew it they were in some sort of private lounge, with huge potted palms, squishy sofas and panoramic views over the runway. But instead of feeling overwhelmed or joyous—or any of the emotions she might have felt if he'd said these things just eighteen hours earlier—Nicole felt flat. More than that, she was angry with herself for allowing herself to be led off a flight which *she* had paid for—like some docile little mouse. Wasn't she supposed to have shed her mouse-like skin?

'So hurry up and say whatever it is you want to say, Rocco.'

It wasn't the most promising of beginnings. In fact, Rocco would go so far as to say that he had never seen Nicole look so angry. And he knew then that he needed to go further than he'd planned. Further than he'd ever been before. That she would not be willing to accept half-measures—and why should she? He'd pushed her away so many times—why would she believe he had changed unless he was prepared to show her? Unless he opened up a heart which had remained locked and bolted for so many years.

He sucked in a deep breath. 'You accused me of pushing you away once we were married and maybe I did—but not for the reasons you imagined. It wasn't because I didn't want you, Nicole—there hasn't been a second of my life since we first met that I didn't want you—but because I was being cautious.'

'Cautious?' She fixed him with an enquiring look.

Restlessly, he shrugged. 'I had no idea how to deal with a pregnant woman—and you were sick. So very sick. I thought you would prefer a nurse rather than a husband who was out of his depth, and then...' He swallowed. 'Then you lost the baby...'

'And *that* was when you pushed me away—'

'I was giving you space,' he argued. 'I thought that's what you needed. I could see how broken you were and I couldn't get near you.'

'You didn't want to get near me,' she said slowly.

'It wasn't that. You wouldn't talk. You wouldn't even look at me. I thought if I went to the States to work that you would have the chance to come to terms with it in your own time.' He sighed. 'And maybe deep down I was relieved that you didn't want to talk about it.'

She tilted her chin to meet his gaze full on. 'Why?'

There was a pause. 'Because I was afraid,' he admitted. 'Afraid of facing my feelings about losing our baby. Afraid of where it might take me.'

The husky choke of his voice made Nicole's heart twist and she wanted to wrap her arms around him and hold him tight. But not yet. Because he needed to do this. To say it and feel it, no matter how much it hurt.

'I was afraid that it would bring up all that stuff from the past when my parents were killed. Stuff I had suppressed and didn't want to look at. Naively, I thought that if I went away—everything would have calmed down by the time I got back.'

'You went to America,' she said woodenly.

He nodded. 'Yes, I did. Which only made it worse. And then I came back to Sicily and—'

'I had gone,' she finished.

'Se.' His features looked like a tight mask. 'I tried telling myself it was all for the best. That I'd never planned for this marriage to happen. I knew I could never make you the kind of husband you wanted. The kind of husband you richly deserved.'

'And that's why you never came after me?'

He nodded. 'That's why I never came after you. Until that divorce petition landed on my desk and suddenly my lifelong ability to suppress my emotions was blown out of the water. I felt anger—and indignation, too. I convinced myself that I was going to get you to come to Monaco with me, because that would be the last thing you wanted. I intended to punish you by making you jump through hoops to get your divorce. I even convinced myself that my desire for you was no more— mainly because my ego had been wounded by having a woman leave me, the way you did.'

He paused. 'And then I saw you... I saw you and the thunderclap happened all over again and there didn't seem to be a thing I could do about it, no matter how

much I fought it. I told myself that having sex with you
would rid me of my hunger, but it only increased it. Just
as being with you reminded me of all the things I love
about you. Your creativity. Your irreverence. The way
you make me laugh. All those things reinforced what I
was reluctant to admit—even to myself.' There was a
pause. 'That I love you and want to be with you. Now
and always.'

She didn't say anything but her gaze was very steady
as she looked at him.

'Could we start again, Nicole?' he said huskily. 'Or
continue where we left off? Is spending the rest of your
life with me something you would ever consider?'

Her lips seemed to be closing in on themselves and
as he saw her struggling to contain her emotions, Rocco
desperately ached to hold her, but he knew he must not.
Because the answer to his question had to come of its
own accord. Not because he was stroking her or kissing her. It needed to come from the mind and the heart,
not the body.

Say yes, he prayed silently. *Say yes, my love.*

It seemed to take an eternity but eventually she
nodded. 'Yes, I would,' she said, in a rush. 'Of course
I would. For all my life if you want it. Oh, Rocco…
Rocco,' she said falteringly.

'Let it out, *tesoro,*' he prompted shakily, though he
knew he had no right to tell her to connect with *her*
emotions when he'd been so cut off from his own for so
long. But Nicole's emotions had been repressed too—
and wasn't she as much of a novice in all this stuff as
he was? 'Just let it out.'

His soft entreaty must have worked because that was when she started to cry—great big tears welling up from those beautiful green eyes and sliding down her cheeks like rain. He held out his arms and she went into them, burying her head against his shoulder while he smoothed down the wild tumble of her curls. She cried until there were no tears left and he suspected she was crying for their lost baby as well as for the wasted years apart. And when he had dried her cheeks with his fingertips, he touched his lips very gently to hers.

'Where we live and how we live is up to you. Tell me what you want and where you want to go,' he said unevenly. 'And I will do everything in my power to make that happen.'

Her eyes were very bright and for the first time a smile lifted the corners of her lips. 'I don't care where we go or what we do,' she said simply. 'The places or the trappings aren't important. I only want to be with you, Rocco. That's all I've ever really wanted.'

EPILOGUE

ROCCO'S VOICE WAS thick with emotion. '*Tesoro*, he is... *bello*.'

'Isn't he?' Nicole looked down into the crib at the sleeping baby, then gazed up into the proud eyes of his doting papa. 'And the image of his father.'

'Then let us hope he has his mother's good heart and sense,' responded her husband drily as he pulled her into his arms, smoothing his hand over the crown of her head. 'I thought today went well, didn't you?'

Brushing her lips against his neck in a drifting kiss, Nicole smiled. Today had been their son's baptism—a joyous day, celebrated first in the Sicilian church where she and Rocco had been married all those years ago, and then afterwards at a champagne reception outside, in the fragrant lemon grove on the Barberi complex. They had named their son Turi in honour of the patriarch who had died peacefully last year—contented to see Rocco and Nicole reunited at last and taking great pleasure in the role he had played to help bring that about.

Turi hadn't lived to see his great-grandson, but he had doted on the twin girls who had been born exactly a year after Nicole and Rocco had decided to make their permanent home in Sicily, albeit with trips to Cornwall whenever their schedules allowed. With their raven corkscrew curls and bright blue eyes, little Lucia and Sofia would have melted the heart of any statue, but they had adored Rocco's grandfather, who had been their biggest fan.

'It was a perfect day,' Nicole said softly. '*Perfetto*. I liked your brother's latest girlfriend and I thought your sister looked very well.'

So much had happened since that day when Rocco had walked onto the aircraft and declared his love for her in front of a planeload of passengers. Approaching their future in an orderly way, her husband had accompanied her back to Cornwall, to help her find someone to take over her little shop—someone who would cherish it as much as she had done.

They had returned to resume their married life in Sicily—not just because Turi was old and frail, but because Nicole found herself valuing the simplicity of life there. And this time she felt she belonged. This time she was no longer the outsider with no legitimate place. Rocco had sold the Monaco apartment and started delegating as much work as possible, in order to spend as much time with the people who really mattered.

His family. The twin daughters who had him wrapped around their little fingers, and now his new son. And Nicole, of course. A day didn't pass without him telling her that she was key to his happiness and none of this could have happened without her.

He had built her a studio with a kiln where, whenever Lucia and Sofia allowed her a rare spare moment, Nicole would craft the vases and the bowls which were gaining her something of a reputation. She had already exhibited in Palermo and Rocco had spoken about buying her a shop there, but she'd told him not to rush anything. That there was a time and a place for ambition and she wanted to enjoy the gifts she had been given. She wanted to give silent thanks that three children had now worn a little romper suit which had lain unused in a drawer for so long...

'Are you sleepy, *tesoro*?' Rocco's softly accented voice broke into her thoughts.

She shook her head. 'Not in the slightest.'

'Then shall we sit outside? Drink some *limonata* on the terrace and watch the stars unfold?'

The complex was quiet after the excitement of the party, which had included most of the villagers and gone on throughout the afternoon and well into the evening. Nicole had listened to smatterings of conversation and had understood most of them, because she had quickly realised that becoming fluent in her husband's language was a necessity and not a hobby. She recognised that communication was key, so she had knuckled down to regular one-to-one lessons with a local schoolteacher and was growing more confident with each day. It amused Rocco no end to hear his English wife calling to him in dialect!

The ice was chinking in her glass and the sweet-sharp *limonata* made from the estate's lemons was cool and refreshing. Above them the darkening indigo sky had begun to glimmer with the promise of the brightest stars Nicole had ever seen and she sighed.

Did Rocco hear her? Was that why his head turned towards her.

'*Felici?*' he questioned softly.

'Oh, yes. Totally happy,' she said.

Rocco smiled. Who would have realised he could find everything he wanted here, in the arms of his beautiful wife, amid his rapidly expanding family? Sometimes he thought about how much Nicole had taught him. How to face up to your feelings, even if they brought you pain—because with pain came understanding and, from that, true contentment. She had taught him how to love and in so doing had taught him how to live.

He glanced over at her, where she had kicked off her sandals and was wiggling toes which were painted a violent shade of orange. She tied her hair back much more frequently these days because the twins tended to use the thick strands like ropes—but tonight she had shaken the curls free so that they flowed down her back in a dark cascade. Her ankle-length dress in filmy pink chiffon was still more Boho than classic, but that was okay. She looked beautiful in whatever she wore—and she was an artist, after all.

She glanced up to find his gaze trained on her and raised her eyebrows.

'What?' she said.

He moved his shoulders a little restlessly as the heat in his body began to rise. 'I was just wondering if perhaps we might have an early night…'

The answering glint in her eyes answered his question and as he rose from his chair she held up her hands so that he could pull her to her feet.

'You must have read my mind,' she whispered.

'I wonder if you can read mine?' came his answering growl.

She giggled. 'Rocco Barberi, you are a terrible man.'

'I know,' he said, lacing his fingers in hers and leading her towards their house. 'And that's one of the reasons why you love me.'

* * * * *

CONTRACTED FOR THE PETRAKIS HEIR

ANNIE WEST

With smiles and thanks to
Anna C for both prodding and cheering
and Efthalia P for the Greek!

CHAPTER ONE

ADONI PETRAKIS SURVEYED the crowd filling the ballroom of his flagship London hotel. Initially the guests had been on their best behaviour for the wedding ceremony, partly from finding themselves in such a prestigious venue. There had been open-mouthed stares at the soaring antique glass domed ceiling, the recently refurbished hand-blown chandeliers and the other elegant furnishings.

Now the mood bordered on raucous. His school friend Leo's new English in-laws were letting down their hair with abandon.

Adoni's gaze cut to Leo and his bride, now changed out of their church clothes, surrounded by a phalanx of groomsmen playing a drinking game. There was a flurry of bridesmaids in ostentatiously frilled dresses that ranged from pale lemon to a particularly bilious shade of mustard. A braying laugh from one of them scraped like fingernails across a blackboard and Adoni shuddered.

Now the formalities were over, the cake cut, photos taken and speeches delivered, there was nothing keeping him. He'd done his bit, offering Leo the premises for the event and attending in person, even dancing with the bride.

He lifted one shoulder, easing the old stiffness in his collarbone. It had been a long week. A long month for that matter, and while he wasn't ready for bed, nor was he inclined to stay for an increasingly rowdy party. This group had little in common with a man whose life was devoted to business.

If there'd been a woman here he found attractive he might have invited her up to his suite for a private celebration. There wasn't. The only really pretty women were either attached or looked at him with dollar signs in their eyes.

He'd learned his lesson long ago with that breed.

Instead he crossed the room, wished the happy couple all the best, kissed the flushed bride on both cheeks then left. A nod to the hotel events coordinator who was keeping an eye on the evening, then Adoni was in the blessed peace of the atrium.

Since he didn't have company for the night, he'd look over that new contract. Or maybe use the gym.

He was restless, his thoughts on the couple who'd just pledged their lives to each other. And, inevitably, on his own hastily cancelled wedding years ago. His mouth firmed.

He sure as hell didn't carry a torch for Chryssa. Yet it was strange how, all evening, his mind had backtracked to that half-forgotten past, when life had seemed straightforward and he'd believed in love.

A lifetime ago.

He keyed in the code for his private lift to the owner's suite. The doors slid open and he stepped inside. Seconds later a figure catapulted into the small space, slamming against him in a slither of satin and a cloud of pungent hairspray.

Adoni's nostrils pinched and a sneeze escaped.

'I'm sorry. Did I hurt you?' a husky voice whispered near his chin. 'But please, don't give me away.' Instead of moving back the girl pressed closer, hip to his thigh, hand clawing his sleeve.

'Give you away?'

'Please. He'll hear.' She reached out a pale hand and jabbed the button to make the door close. As soon as it did she released her grip and sank back into the corner.

'Are you okay?' Adoni's voice sharpened. Her head was downcast but the tension in her shoulders and the frenetic pulse at the base of her throat spoke of fear. 'Has someone hurt you?'

'Hurt me?' She shook her head and straightened away from the wall, swaying a little. 'No, though I'm sure he'd like to strangle me if he could. He hates me and he's a vicious little toad.'

With a gasp she clapped a hand over her mouth and looked up. Unfocused eyes of slate blue met his. Eyes that might have been pretty if it weren't for the huge swathe of too-bright azure eye shadow and the most enormous pair of false eyelashes weighting her lids. She looked like a startled trollop.

'I didn't mean to say that out loud.' She frowned up at him suspiciously as if he'd coaxed the words from her.

'He sounds like a man to avoid.'

'Oh, he is.' The girl nodded so emphatically another acrid wave of hairspray assaulted him. She *was* a girl. Eighteen maybe, twenty max, and trying to look older with that brash make-up. 'If I'd known he was going to be here I'd never have said yes to Emily. Discretion is the better part of valour, after all.'

'Emily?' Adoni crossed his arms and settled his shoulders against the wall, intrigued. Why this unprepossessing female caught his curiosity, he couldn't say. But he was in no hurry. There was nothing waiting in his suite except work and a good brandy.

'The bride.' The frown became a scowl. 'Weren't you at the wedding? I thought I saw you on the other side of the room looking all dark and brooding.' She leaned closer, her gaze intent, and beneath the sharp hairspray smell he caught a hint of something delicate.

She swayed back again. 'I'm *sure* it was you. The silly sisters were tittering with excitement, egging each other on to ask you to dance.'

'Silly sisters?'

'The other bridesmaids.'

'Ah.' No wonder she looked vaguely familiar. This was the bridesmaid who'd sat on the end of the long table, her dress of dark yellow tinged with green making her look slightly nauseous. Or maybe she *was* nauseous.

'Are you sick?'

'Only of the company in there.' Again those eyes grew huge and her hand hovered over her mouth.

Adoni watched, fascinated despite himself, as she blinked and stood straighter, the top of her head reaching the level of his mouth.

'It must be the champagne,' she murmured, her hand dropping. 'Who'd have thought it? I only had two glasses. Would that do it?' She tilted her head, surveying him owl-ishly.

'Do what?' Adoni repressed a smile.

'Make me so loqua…' Her brows knotted in concentration. 'Talkative. Normally I think before I speak. Always.'

He folded his arms over his chest. 'It depends how much you usually drink.'

'I don't. Tonight was my first taste of champagne.'

'Then yes, it probably is.' Diverted as he was, her friends would be looking for her. 'Isn't it time you went back?'

She shuddered and clutched his sleeve. 'No! Not till he's gone.' She looked at the controls. 'Why aren't we moving?' She slammed her hand onto the up button. 'I'm sorry. I hope you want to go up. I'll go anywhere so long as it's away from him.'

'The toad?'

'Yes! How did you know?' Her face broke into a wide smile that hit him in the solar plexus. When she smiled he saw something that even the plastered-on make-up couldn't conceal. 'Dark and brooding and clever too! I like you, Mr…?'

'Petrakis. Adoni Petrakis.'

Again those eyes rounded. 'Adoni?'

He nodded, waiting for the usual gushing excitement. He'd never had trouble attracting women but since he'd built his fortune…

'As in Adonis?'

'It's a Greek name.'

'Of course it is, but it's all wrong for you.' She squinted up at him, her lips pursed in a moue of concentration that looked surprisingly sexy, despite the bright shade of coral lipstick that clashed horribly with her pale skin. 'You're no Adoni.'

Adoni stared down at her. He was accustomed to flattery from women, not disappointment.

'You know who Adonis was?'

She waved a dismissive hand as if he interrupted her thought processes. 'In Greek mythology he was a gorgeous young man, loved by Aphrodite and later killed by a boar.' She bit her lip. 'Or maybe by someone else, I can't remember. But you're *not* an Adonis.'

Adoni couldn't keep his smile back. Had he ever met a woman who spoke to him like this? Not flattering and eager? 'Not pretty enough?'

Again that disparaging wave of her hand. 'No one could call you pretty.' Her voice rang with certainty. 'Handsome yes, but in a tough, dangerous sort of way. And those wicked eyebrows.' She lifted a hand towards his face but stopped short of touching him. 'More like Ares, god of war. Sexy but hard.'

The doors slid open behind her and she turned while Adoni was still trying to work out if he'd just been insulted or complimented.

'Oh, this is nice.' She drifted out of the lift into the foyer of his private suite, peering through the open door to the vast sitting room. 'Do you think it would be okay for me to stay here for a bit till he's gone?'

She moved forward, catching her shoe on the hand-knotted rug. Arms windmilling, she swayed till Adoni strode over and caught her upper arm. Her flesh was cool and smooth as silk.

'Are you sure you only had two glasses of champagne?'

She sagged against him, one hand planted on his chest. 'Absolutely. But I don't think I'd better have any more. I feel a little…different.' She blinked hazily up at him. 'Do *you* think I'm behaving oddly?'

What he thought was that, beneath the harsh make-up and the unflattering dress, this young woman was surprisingly appealing. And potentially vulnerable.

'Your friends will be missing you.'

She shook her head. 'Not my friends and they won't miss me. I don't know anyone there, except Emily—she's my cousin. And her parents. But they don't have time for me. They never did. I'm just a ring-in because bridesmaid number seven had to bail at the last minute. Oh, and the toad—I know him.' She grimaced. 'But I don't want to see him. Couldn't I just sit quietly for a bit? I could sneak out and catch a train home but I do feel a bit wobbly.'

Adoni scrutinised her. Clearly she couldn't make her way home alone yet. She was far too trusting to be let out without someone to keep an eye on her.

'Very well. Stay here and I'll make us coffee.'

'Lovely! I never thought of Ares being so domesticated. I think of him being all passion and fire.' She beamed again, that huge, beatific smile, and to his astonishment Adoni found himself smiling back. She was talking nonsense but her sense of humour appealed. As did the fact she didn't walk on eggshells around him.

'Do you think I could use the bathroom?'

'Of course. Down the corridor on the left.'

The sitting room was empty when Adoni came back. He set the tray of coffee and sweet shortbread on a table, telling himself he'd been a fool to let her in. He didn't know anything about her. Except that she couldn't hold her champagne and did know a surprising amount of Greek mythology. He didn't even know her name.

He stalked from the room, doubt rising. Where was she?

'Are you okay?' He pounded on the bathroom door.

'Sorry. I won't be long.'

'Are you sick?' She'd seemed tipsy, not drunk, but perhaps he was wrong.

'No. Not sick. Just sticky.'

Sticky? Adoni scowled. That made no sense.

The door opened and his visitor stepped out. She looked completely different. Shorter for a start, her shoes dangling from her hand.

'I used the shower. I feel much better now.' She stepped out into the corridor and tripped over the hem of her long dress, straight into his arms. Automatically Adoni caught her, but not before her soft breasts collided with his torso and her slim frame came to rest against him.

'Oops. Sorry.' She pulled back and smiled vaguely. 'This dress is too long. It was made for someone else.'

'Someone wearing shoes,' he murmured, trying to shove the thought of her lithe body from his mind.

'Ah.' She nodded. 'That explains it.' She sniffed. 'Is that coffee I smell?' Before he could answer she lifted her trailing skirt so high he caught a tantalising amount of shapely, bare legs before she turned and, hand on the wall, made her way to the sitting room.

Adoni took his time following. He'd been rocked by his response to the woman who'd emerged from the guest bathroom. Gone were the thick make-up and fake lashes. Without them he discovered a clear peaches and cream complexion that suited those dark blue eyes. Then there was a heart-shaped face and a pink mouth that looked too much like a cupid's bow for comfort.

Gone too was the elaborately curled and rigid hairstyle, threaded with mustard-yellow ribbon. Instead her dark hair lay straight and long around her shoulders. It was still wet, dripping at the ends, making the bodice of her dress water-stained and clingy.

He swallowed as he watched her turn and sink abruptly onto the sofa, the lamplight caressing the unexpectedly sweet tilt of her breast beneath the wet fabric. Heat stirred in his groin at the astounding sexual allure of her gentle curves and bare face.

Adoni frowned. His sex drive was healthy but such an instant, urgent response was rare. Especially as she wasn't even trying to attract him.

Was she?

He'd met some devious women in his time, going to extraordinary lengths to snare him, but instinct told him this one was exactly what she seemed.

'What's your name?' His voice emerged thick and abrupt but she didn't seem to notice.

'Alice. Alice Trehearn.' She looked over her shoulder at him and, to his astonishment, the line of her throat, the angle of her neat chin and the curve of her smile fanned the fire in his belly to a needy, urgent blast of heat.

'Don't frown, though I have to say you look very sexy when you do, all macho and...' Her words petered out and she squeezed her eyes shut. 'Remind me never to drink champagne again.'

Despite himself Adoni laughed. There was something so refreshing about a woman who spoke her mind.

'How old are you, Alice?' Suddenly it was important he find out.

'Twenty-three next week.' She turned away and poured milk into one of the coffees. 'How old are you?'

Relief filled him. With her unguarded behaviour he'd wondered if perhaps she was far younger. 'Thirty-one.'

A lifetime apart from her in experience, but, he realised in shock, that didn't dim his interest. His burgeoning interest. His trousers were too tight as he sat down opposite her.

'You look older.' She tilted her head as she surveyed him. 'Except when you smile. I like your smile. You should smile more often.' Carefully she put the milk jug down on the table.

Adoni's lips twitched. Had he really preferred candour? The answer was a definite yes.

'I thought you liked my…er…dark, brooding looks.'

'Oh, I do.' She stopped abruptly, her mouth sagging a little as if she realised what she'd said, then she focused on the mug of coffee, cautiously taking a sip. 'But your smile makes you look less like some bossy Greek god.'

'Ares?'

She nodded emphatically. 'Yes.' She paused. 'Or the one who threw thunderbolts.'

'Zeus?' Was he really so fearsome? Adoni preferred to think of himself as controlled and focused, a man who didn't suffer fools in business or gold-diggers in his personal life.

'That's the one.' Her brow furrowed. 'Except they always show him with a beard and you don't have one.'

Adoni suppressed a smile. 'I could grow one.'

'No.' She shook her head. 'That would be a waste. You've got a nice chin. Maybe a bit on the obstinate side but very nice.' She took another sip of coffee and smiled vaguely.

'Thank you. So do you.' It was a little pointed perhaps but just the right counterpoint for that lush mouth he found himself staring at.

Adoni leaned in and grabbed his mug, gulping hot coffee. When he lowered it, she was staring, her mouth slightly open and her breathing quick.

'Is everything all right?' He told himself he was behaving impeccably, pretending he didn't recognise her response for what it was—feminine interest. An answering interest quickened his pulse as he took in her delicate features and slim body.

'Fine. You just look so…'

Maybe she was sobering up, for she thought better of finishing her comment.

'So…?' Adoni didn't fish for compliments but he found himself wondering what she'd been about to say.

Dark lashes veiled her eyes as she took another sip of coffee. 'Nice. You look nice.'

He'd bet his last dollar that wasn't what she'd been going to say. 'You do too.'

'There's no need to lie.' She lifted her head, viewing him from under regally arched eyebrows. 'I look dreadful. Why Emily chose this colour I don't know. Honestly, it's the colour of baby poo.'

Adoni laughed. She was right; it was reminiscent of a rather nasty stain. 'It's fair to say it's not a good match for your colouring.'

'That's what *I* said, but it was too late to change it. Too late even to alter the fit.' Her mouth turned down in a sulky pout Adoni found far too seductive.

'At least it's only for one night.'

She nodded. 'That's what I keep telling myself. It's a day of firsts.'

'Firsts?'

Another nod. 'Absolutely. First time wearing yellow, for one thing. Never again.' She shuddered. 'First time in London. First time as a bridesmaid. I thought it would be a lot more fun but the other bridesmaids kept tittering and gossiping amongst themselves. And the groomsmen…'

'Not your type?'

She shrugged hugely and one pillowy puffed sleeve slid off her shoulder. 'I don't really know. But I think not.' She lifted her legs and tucked them under her then wriggled back on the sofa.

There shouldn't have been anything remotely seductive about the action yet Adoni found himself fixated on that luscious little shimmy of hips and breasts.

'You don't know?' His voice sounded unfamiliar.

She shook her head. 'I need to research more.' She blinked back at him and smiled. 'I have some firsts.' She looked down at her dress and scowled. 'But there are a lot of nevers too.'

'Nevers?' Adoni's English was excellent but he'd never heard of that before.

'Absolutely.' She lifted one finger. 'Never had luck with the opposite sex.' Then a second finger. 'Never had a kiss that blew my socks off.' Her gaze narrowed. 'You look like a man who could blow a girl's socks off with a kiss.'

Adoni choked on his coffee. 'Is that a proposition?' He was torn between amusement and a dark, fast-running channel of temptation.

Devoid of that tacky lipstick, Alice Trehearn had the most alluring mouth he'd ever seen. He swallowed hard and reminded himself this was the drink talking.

'As if a man like you would kiss a girl like me.' She leaned her head back against the sofa, her eyelids drooping. She lapsed into silence and he wondered if she was falling asleep.

'Never driven a car either.' She sighed. 'I bet you have a *lovely* car.'

'Yes, I do.' And there was no way he was letting this inebriated woman near it, despite her eager smile. 'But I'm not letting you drive it.'

She looked so ridiculously disappointed, her mouth turning down at the edges, that he almost wished he could bring back that sunny smile of hers and the twinkle in her fine eyes.

'Is there anything else on your never list?'

Alice opened her mouth then closed it again. A flush of pink rose to her cheeks. Instantly his interest piqued.

'Alice?'

She shook her head. 'It's nothing.' She leaned forward, reached for her coffee and, seeing the mug empty, sank back.

'You might as well tell me what it is you haven't done. I promise to keep it to myself.'

Was he really so curious about her?

To his surprise, Adoni discovered he was.

She fidgeted. 'I'm doing all the talking. Shouldn't you tell *me* something?' Just as if she hadn't barged uninvited into his private suite. Yet Adoni hadn't enjoyed a woman's conversation so much in a long time.

What did that say about the women he dated?

'What do you want me to say?'

She shrugged, melting even further into the sofa. 'Anything you like. Tell me something you haven't told anyone else. I promise to keep it to myself.'

The idea was absurd. Why share with a complete stranger? Yet as he sat in the mellow lamplight, watching Alice Trehearn's easy smile and expectant look, he found himself tempted.

Because he wasn't accustomed to sharing anything truly personal?

Because she was a stranger he'd never see again?

That, and the surprising tug of attraction, must be why he even considered playing along. And why he'd allowed her into his space when he was notoriously private.

His mood had been odd all evening. Restlessness had kept him on edge. Remarkably, it was only since she'd inserted herself into his presence that he'd begun to relax.

'I don't like weddings.' The words came suddenly. Adoni was surprised how good it felt to admit it.

'Really?' One fine eyebrow arched. 'Any particular reason?'

He took another mouthful of coffee. It didn't taste as rich this time. 'I was nearly married once. I suppose weddings bring back memories.'

Of rejection, disbelief and disappointment. But he'd been young enough to learn his lesson well. These days, apart from his hand-picked managers, he didn't put his trust in anyone but himself. It was safer that way. When those closest to you could turn so viciously against you, trust was the first casualty, along with love.

Absently he rolled his shoulder, releasing a stiffness along the collarbone.

'I'm so sorry.' She leaned forward, her hand lifted towards him as if to smooth away the frown he felt settle on his brow. Then she sank back, regarding him seriously.

He waited for the inevitable, a question about why his marriage hadn't proceeded, but again Alice Trehearn surprised him. Even inebriated she had enough delicacy not to trespass further. 'Tonight must have been a trial.'

He shook his head, automatically rejecting sympathy. 'It was fine. It was no big deal.' Time to change the subject. 'So what is the other thing you've never done? I told you my secret. It's time for you to share too.'

She blinked, staring back at him with a look he couldn't interpret. Annoyance? Embarrassment? Certainly the colour in her cheeks warmed to rose madder.

'Alice?'

Her mouth tightened and then the words tumbled out. 'Never had an orgasm, if you must know.' For an instant she looked as regal as a young swan, stretching her neck higher and tilting her chin, trying to hide what he guessed was embarrassment.

Then something unexpected flashed in her eyes. 'I don't suppose you'd like to help me with that?'

CHAPTER TWO

HELP HER HAVE her first orgasm? Adoni tried and failed over the next hour to put Alice Trehearn's words from his mind.

The idea was so outrageous it was laughable.

A woman, clearly the worse for drink, propositioning him so clumsily.

A woman without glamour or any of the usual seductive skills he expected in a lover.

A woman in an ill-fitting dress the colour of bile, with her hair hanging damp around her shoulders and not a scrap of make-up. She didn't belong in his world and shouldn't be in the least attractive.

Yet Adoni couldn't banish the provocative idea of giving Alice her first orgasm.

Was it the idea of initiating her to pleasure that snared his imagination and wouldn't let go? Or was it Alice herself?

The rose-pink colour of her cheeks would spread across her breasts. Those dark eyes would glitter and that decadent mouth would open on a gasp, or perhaps a scream as he toppled her over the edge into rapture.

The image of her naked beneath him, trembling with satiation, was so vivid it had him rock-hard in an instant.

The chirp of his phone, an urgent call from his North American manager, had saved both him and Alice from the embarrassment of a response. Then, when he'd ended the call and turned to tell her she needed to leave since he had work to do, Adoni had found her asleep.

Suspicious, he'd initially wondered if it was a ploy, especially as she looked ridiculously cute curled up, hands beneath her cheek and bare feet pale against the cushions.

But her occasional tiny snuffles proved him wrong. They were too close to dainty snores for any would-be seductress to countenance.

Now, sitting at his desk on the other side of the room, reviewing the contract his manager had just sent, Adoni directed a darkling stare towards the woman lying on his sofa.

How dare she make such an invitation then go to sleep? She rolled onto her back, the too-big bodice pulling askew to reveal the gentle curve of one pale breast.

The pulse in Adoni's groin pounded hard and fast as his gaze traced her slender figure. His mouth dried as she shifted and the edge of the fabric strained, close to revealing one nipple. Her skirt was rucked up above her knees from the way she'd twisted. Even so, most of her was covered by that appalling bridesmaid's dress.

She shouldn't look attractive, much less seductive. Yet Adoni registered the heaviness in his lower body, the restlessness, the powerful hunger.

Maybe it was that sultry mouth, those lush, slightly downturned lips, surely designed for sin. He looked at her and thought of those lips on his body and it was no wonder he couldn't concentrate on the document before him.

Perhaps it was the novelty of not knowing what she was going to say next. Her cheerfully frank assessment of how she looked in that dreadful dress, or the apparently artless combination of guilelessness and insight.

Or was it the shy hints that she wanted him? The blush, the spark in her eye when she'd asked about him giving her an orgasm.

Of all the preposterous pick-up lines, that was the best he'd heard.

Except it hadn't been a pick-up line. She hadn't wanted to admit her inexperience. That probably explained her flippant question about him helping her rid herself of that particular lack in her life. She'd been bluffing. Of course she had.

Adoni turned back to the screen. Yet it wasn't the legal document he saw, but the rosy blush that coloured her creamy skin and her haughty, challenging glare.

Give her an orgasm? The trouble was how much the idea enticed.

What had she said? She'd never had luck with men, never had a kiss that knocked her socks off. Never had an orgasm. Clearly she *was* unlucky if none of her lovers had bothered to take care of that when they sought their own pleasure.

Adoni's heart might no longer be engaged when he had sex, but he prided himself on being a generous lover. His partner's satisfaction added to his own pleasure, and he'd no more bed a woman and leave her wanting than he'd renege on a business contract.

The contract. He ploughed his fingers through his hair, sinking his head into his hands and forcing his attention back to the computer.

He'd finish the contract then wake Ms Trouble-on-Two-Legs Trehearn and send her off in a taxi. Then he'd get a decent night's sleep ready for work tomorrow, despite it being Sunday.

Adoni ground his teeth at the sly voice telling him his life was lacking if that was the best he could do on a Saturday night. Send home the female he lusted after then get an early night ready for work.

Was this what all those years of toil had been for? He'd scraped himself up from the gutter when Vassili Petrakis, the man he'd believed to be his father, disowned him. He'd risen above the pain of his fiancée's rejection and poured his anger and determination into building his company from nothing.

He'd let his drive to succeed fill the void where his personal life used to be. He had no family to distract him now.

Fleetingly, he thought of his younger brothers, a pang of regret piercing his chest. But they belonged to another life, one barred to him for ever.

Now he was CEO of a company worth billions. He had homes in Greece and the UK, plus a ski chalet in Colorado and a yacht that shared its time between the Med and the Caribbean. Not that he managed much downtime to enjoy them.

Adoni sighed and raked his hand through his hair again. Maybe that was the problem. He needed a vacation.

Or an affair. Intense, enjoyable and short—just the way he liked them. He had no inclination for long-term now he'd taught himself never to trust a woman's intentions, despite protests of undying love.

Rubbing his temples, he hunched over the screen, re-reading clauses he'd skimmed half a dozen times.

He was just sending his response to his New York manager when the back of his neck prickled. He stiffened, instantly aware that his guest was awake. He felt her eyes on him. Worse, that needy throb in his groin was back full force, reminding him he'd been celibate longer than usual.

Even so his reaction to this woman was unprecedented.

Adoni didn't turn to look at her. That would, for reasons he couldn't identify, be a sign of weakness. Instead he finished his message, sent it, then closed the computer. Only then did he deign to swivel round in his seat.

She was standing, half turned from him. The satin of her dress slid over svelte, sinuous curves and delectably long legs as she raised her hands to fix her hair in a tight knot.

'Don't.' The sound of his voice surprised him and made her swing round, eyes wide. 'I like it down.'

He couldn't read her expressive eyes from this distance but the sudden clamp of her jaw made him expect some dismissive response.

Adoni was surprised when, instead, she paused, arms still raised. 'Do you?'

When he nodded she dropped her arms and a dark curtain of hair fell to cloak her shoulders. Now it was dry he saw rich hints of auburn in the dark brown. He curled his hands closed against the impulse to get up and stroke those shimmering tresses.

Her breasts rose with her deep breath and Adoni's gaze trailed from her bare shoulder where one sleeve drooped down her arm, across the upper slope of her breasts then up via her slender throat to her lips.

Damn! That sulky, sexy mouth would be the death of common sense. Why hadn't he fully appreciated it till she wiped the horrible lipstick away?

'I'm sorry. I didn't mean to fall asleep on your sofa.' Had she misinterpreted his shudder of arousal for one of disdain? 'I apologise for...' she faltered and gestured wide '...for inviting myself in here.' She looked around the vast executive suite as if she'd never seen it. Presumably she hadn't taken in her surroundings earlier.

That, and the way she spoke, plus the shadow of tension where before there'd been nothing but a lack of inhibition, told Adoni the effects of the alcohol were wearing off.

He was torn between relief that she was obviously recovered enough to go home, and regret.

As if he wanted her to stay.

For her amusing conversation, or something else?

White teeth bit that plump bottom lip. Did she read the sexual interest he couldn't douse?

'No need to apologise. It's been an interesting evening.'

She shut her eyes for a moment. 'I'm sure it has. You've been very forbearing. Thank you for...' again that wave of one hand '...for the coffee and for letting me sleep.' Once again, soft colour stained her pale cheeks. Adoni found himself wondering how long it had been since he'd met a woman who still blushed.

'My pleasure.' He stood and again her eyes rounded as they traced him, as if she hadn't realised how tall he was. Or perhaps he looked different now he'd shed his jacket and tie, undone a couple of buttons and rolled up his sleeves.

Neither moved. Did he imagine the heavy chug of energy thickening the atmosphere? Adoni wasn't prone to flights of fancy, yet it seemed all the air in the room was being sucked away, making it hard to breathe.

He watched her swallow, her slender throat pale and alluring, especially when compared with that mustard horror of a dress. It was as if someone had taken something pure and hidden it beneath layers of camouflage.

Pure? An old-fashioned word for a woman who'd blatantly invited him to be sexually intimate. Yet it seemed apt. Alice Trehearn was surely the most honest woman he'd ever met. In Adoni's world, where people pretended affection in return for material comforts, honesty was the purest quality he knew.

He took a step closer and Alice's insides twisted like a riot of butterflies dipping and fluttering over a spring meadow.

Now the effects of the wine had worn off she was stunned to find herself alone with such a man.

That he was wealthy and powerful went without saying. It was obvious from the casual way he wore his hand-tailored clothes and the equally nonchalant way he took this exquisite, ultra-expensive suite for granted.

But it wasn't the fact he came from a world far removed from her own that made her stare. It was the man himself. Tall, with a hard, chiselled face that had more than a trace of arrogance in those winged black eyebrows and high cheekbones. His mouth looked as if it didn't smile enough, as if his world was too serious. Yet when he did smile his eyes, an amazing colour somewhere between blue and green, danced. The tight curve of his lips undid her as if he reached out and loosened a ribbon deep inside her.

What on earth had she said to him? She remembered some of their conversation, not all. She vividly recalled his laugh, rich and warm, enfolding her.

He hadn't laughed *at* her, despite her appearance and the way the wine affected her. He'd laughed *with* her, sharing whatever joke she'd made. That sense of humour undercut her common sense. It was too appealing.

How she'd missed laughter lately.

She felt a link to this man she'd never experienced before, except to David, her godfather, who'd been her best friend despite the age difference. But her feelings for David had been a far cry from *this*. She swallowed hard, simultaneously shocked and intrigued by the way her body came alive under the Greek's sea-bright stare. Tiny shivers prickled her skin and her nipples budded against the loose bodice of her dress.

When he noticed, his gaze dropping to her breasts, Alice's breath clogged and excitement danced in her blood. To her amazement her breasts seemed to both tighten and swell. She'd never felt anything like it. But then her experience of men, and of sexual arousal, was almost zero.

She blinked, lifting her hands to rub her bare arms.

Was she trying to invite his attention? As if he'd be interested in a woman so ordinary and unsophisticated!

Yet her feet seemed welded to the floor.

'Well, thank you again for your hospitality.' She moistened her bottom lip with her tongue and was shocked when his eyes zeroed in on the movement. A hot wire of sensation tugged between her mouth and her breasts, then down to the achy spot between her legs. 'I should be going.'

She made herself turn, looking for her handbag on the sofa. When she turned back he was closer—much closer.

She had to tilt her head back to keep eye contact. Dimly she realised she was barefoot, that she'd need to search for her shoes. Her toes curled into the thick pile of the rug at the look in his eyes.

'Is someone waiting for you at home?'

Alice frowned, feeling the sudden gnaw of anxiety that had become so familiar. She'd lost her home when David died and, though she'd known that day would come, she'd been so caught up in looking after him, making his final days comfortable, she hadn't focused enough on where she'd live afterwards. Her little nest egg hadn't gone nearly as far as she'd hoped. Nest egg! It had been barely enough to keep a roof over her head until she got a job.

'I live alone.'

'Then there's no rush to leave.' Those sleek dark eyebrows rose as his expression turned wickedly seductive.

Alice's heart banged her ribs and her breath stalled. 'Are you...' She paused, hardly crediting what she read in his face. 'Are you suggesting I stay here?'

'You weren't so hesitant earlier.' His smile was slow and intense and it superheated her blood.

'I wasn't?'

He frowned. 'You don't remember?'

'I...' She frowned as snippets of conversation came back to her in vivid clarity. 'I asked if you were a good kisser.' Part of her shrank at the memory of such champagne-induced frankness, but now she was here, toe to toe with this fascinating man, excitement overrode bashfulness.

'Would you still like to find out?' His voice dropped to a low note that wound its way through her belly and down to her knees, making them wobble.

Impossible that he should affect her so intensely, this man whose name she couldn't even recall. Adoni something. She knew so little about him.

Sensible Alice Trehearn, the one who'd spent years being

dependable, devoted and reliable, knew this was her cue to leave. Yet another Alice Trehearn, the one who secretly yearned for *life*, and who'd only surfaced previously in her hell-for-leather gallops across the moor, shivered in excitement.

'Yes.' The word was out before she thought about it. Because if she thought about it she'd never say it.

'Good,' he murmured. 'Your mouth has been driving me crazy.'

Her mouth? Alice lifted a hand to her lips but instead met his chin as his head lowered. He stopped a breath away. She felt his exhalation on her lips, scented with coffee and brandy and something indefinable. The pads of her fingers trembled against the solid plane of his jaw, then spread, testing warm skin with a hint of stubble that grazed her flesh as she settled her whole palm across his chin.

She'd shaved both her father and later her godfather, David, when each grew too ill to do it themselves. Neither had been like this. Adoni radiated heat and vigour and a sensuality she felt right down to the marrow in her bones. He was strong, his flesh taut and so vitally *alive*.

Alice drew a shuddering breath filled with the alien, delicious scent of man in his prime. She stared up into eyes as bright as she imagined the Aegean Sea to be. She read a question there. He was giving her time to change her mind.

In answer, Alice slid her hand around into his thick, short dark hair, surprised at its softness. She rose on tiptoe and pressed her lips to his.

For a moment he didn't move and she cringed inside. This was a mistake. Hadn't she known he couldn't really be interested?

Then his mouth moved on hers, gently persuading her lips apart. His warm tongue slicked her lips then delved within and everything inside her melted and swayed at the eroticism of that sweet invasion. Her belly liquefied, her knees loosened and it was only the firm loop of his arm around her waist that kept her high against him.

His other hand eased the hair back from her face in a gesture so tender her heart rolled over.

Alice slipped her other hand up over his chest. The feel of hard, lean muscle sent a sizzle of excitement through her. She leaned closer, a willing pupil as he delved deeper, drawing out the kiss into something that sent shivery hot darts of flame through her blood.

She didn't know which was better—the way Adoni kissed, making her feel treasured, or the feel of their bodies locked tight. The arm at her waist slid lower, drawing her hips against him.

Her breath stilled as she came in contact with a hard length against her belly.

Instantly he lifted his mouth and Alice almost wailed with disappointment at her loss, her face instantly tilting higher as if to tempt him back. Instead he pressed his lips to her forehead.

A shudder racked his tall frame and it hit her that she wasn't the only one swept away in the moment. Surprise and satisfaction filled her. Even if this had started as a one-sided favour it had become something else.

'Adoni?' Her voice was husky and uneven.

He drew back just far enough to meet her eyes. What did he see? She felt flushed and wanton, not like herself.

'This is your chance to change your mind.' Gone was the slightly teasing gleam she'd seen in his face when he'd talked of kissing her. Now he looked solemn to the point of grimness.

'About kissing you?'

'And the rest of what you wanted.'

The rest? Her brow furrowed as she tried to recall their earlier conversation but her foggy memory couldn't compete with the heady sensations bombarding her. That delicious spicy scent of his skin, the rich flavour of him still on her tongue. The heat of his large body surrounding her and that strange mix of vulnerability and power she felt at the differences in their closely aligned bodies.

'You wanted an orgasm.'

Fire flooded her face as she met his steady scrutiny.

'Please, tell me I didn't say that.'

One corner of that thin mouth tipped up and fire trailed through her middle right down to her womb.

'Apparently the men you've known haven't been very obliging.'

Alice closed her eyes and dropped her forehead against his collarbone. Maybe if she wished hard enough she'd wake up in her own bed and discover this was a dream.

An intense, remarkably erotic dream. One large palm circled her lower back and instinctively her pelvis tilted forward, right to that hard column of masculine arousal.

Should she tell him there'd been no men in her life, not the way he thought? Admit that her previous experience of kissing had been once in her early teens and once again a couple of years ago, neither of them memorable except for her disappointment. Clearly her expectations had been too high.

But this man blasted those expectations to smithereens. She'd never thought a kiss could make her feel so...

'Alice?'

She lifted her head. 'I'd like to kiss you again.' Her voice was rough, unrecognisable, and she swiped her tongue over her bottom lip. A shudder ripped through her at the way his eyes narrowed on the movement.

'Is that all you want?'

She opened her mouth but didn't know what to say. She'd never had a conversation like this. She'd assumed that when the time was right and she'd finally found a man with whom she wanted to lose her virginity, it would just...happen.

Stupid to be shy now when she'd apparently already propositioned the guy. But now she was sober. Her head as clear as it was possible to be when wrapped in the arms of an impossibly gorgeous Greek God of a man.

'Couldn't we just kiss and see what happens?'

Again that tiny uptilt to the corner of his mouth, only this time Alice read tension there as much as humour. 'I already know what will happen. We'll have sex and we won't stop till we're both utterly sated.'

Her heart gave a wild flutter and something tugged hard inside her. She felt moisture at her core and wriggled, hyper-aware that the ribbon of fabric between her legs was damp.

'You need to decide.'

He gave her the choice to step away and behave like sensible, sane Alice Trehearn.

Yet how could she when the tips of his fingers traced a pattern of temptation across her back? They roved from one hip to the other, dipping and swirling and making desire course through her.

'I…' She closed her eyes, trying to gather her wits. But all she could summon was the realisation she wanted this man as she'd never wanted before. It didn't matter that she'd always imagined sex as part of a loving, committed relationship. Life had taught her that you never knew what was around the corner and happiness had to be grabbed with both hands.

Maybe it was partly the champagne but she sensed it was Adoni himself who tempted her to take a step she'd never taken before.

Surely he was the perfect man to initiate her into sexual pleasure?

What did she have to lose except her inexperience?

And wouldn't a night in his bed be the perfect antidote to loneliness? Loneliness had compounded the sharp ache of grief since she'd been forced to leave David's estate and all the people she cared for.

Firm hands gripped her shoulders and he stepped back, shocking Alice with the sudden, urgent distress she felt.

'No! Don't!' She looked up into those dazzling eyes and knew there was only one answer she could give if she was to be true to herself. 'I can't guarantee orgasms but I'd like to stay with you.' The words came out in a breathless tumble.

A warm hand cupped her chin, his thumb stroking rhythmically over her mouth till her bottom lip dropped open and Adoni traced her mouth. Alice shivered at the heavy weight of desire filling her belly and the decadent promise of pleasure in his remarkable eyes.

'I'd like you to stay too, Alice.' The way he said her name, with the slightest of accents, sent a shiver of pleasure through her. 'As for the orgasms—' he smiled, a slow, sexy smile '—let me worry about those.'

CHAPTER THREE

ADONI ROLLED ONTO his back, his blood thundering, after-shocks of rapture echoing through him. Light flashed in the blackness of his closed eyes and he struggled for breath, his chest rising mightily as he sucked in air.

Finally he found the strength to open his eyes and stare at the ceiling of his bedroom. It looked unfamiliar, as if the events of the evening had changed his perspective, even on something as mundane as cream paint.

Certainly he felt different. Not just sated but as if he'd tapped into an energy source that both drained and renewed him at the same time.

'They didn't do it right,' he said finally, his voice raw.

'Sorry?' Alice's voice was a wisp of sound. It shivered across pleasure points on his body that were still remark-ably receptive to that sweet cadence.

'The guys you had sex with. The ones who didn't give you an orgasm. They had no idea what they were doing.'

For Alice Trehearn had to be one of the most sensual women he'd met. Her responsiveness, her passion, had sol-dered a connection between them that felt rare, almost pre-cious, even if her limited experience had been glaringly obvious. She hadn't been able to conceal her shock at some of his caresses.

At one stage, when he'd finally allowed himself to thrust deep within her, he'd even imagined for a moment that he was her first. She was so incredibly taut and close around him she might have been a virgin. Except virgins didn't offer themselves to strangers and talk so casually of or-gasms.

He'd half wondered if, despite her frank talking, she

might be reticent and cold with a man. Instead she'd been like a live wire just waiting to explode in a shower of sparks.

Aware that she'd never before had an orgasm, Adoni had taken his time exploring her body, lavishing caresses all over till she was trembling and gasping against him, sobbing for release. Her throaty pleas had been sweet as wild honey and had prolonged her sensual torture. For he'd lingered, experimenting, revelling in each gasped exclamation.

By the time he'd slipped his fingers across that nub at the centre of her need, it had taken barely a caress for her to lift off the bed, shuddering as she gasped out her release. And again when he'd nuzzled her there...

Adoni closed his eyes at the vivid memory of musk and sweet femininity, of silky thighs clamping round him and her choked little cries of disbelief as rapture took her.

He'd almost come undone there and then, so aroused was he by this woman. Yet she'd been worth the wait. Finding his own completion, deep-seated within her velvet heat, watching her slate-blue eyes blaze in wonder as her body reached that pinnacle a third time. That was a pleasure that would stay with him well into the future. He couldn't remember another climax so intense it felt as if he'd lost a part of himself.

But he'd eagerly lose himself again and again with a lover like Alice Trehearn. Even now, gasping for breath as they fought their way down from that incredible high, her fingers splayed possessively across his thigh.

If this was how it was when they barely knew each other's bodies, what would it be like when they were even better attuned?

How would it feel if she did for him some of the things he'd done for her?

Adrenaline slammed into his blood, hurtling around his body at dangerous speeds.

'Well, I'm glad *you* know what you're doing.' Her voice was an uneven whisper. 'That was amazing.'

Something about the hoarse strain in her tone made Adoni open his eyes and turn his head.

She too lay on her back, staring at the ceiling, her pert breasts rising and falling with her rapid breathing. The sight of them, the memory of their sweetness on his tongue, sent a charge of energy back to his groin.

Again? So soon?

Adoni smiled, his nostrils flaring as he inhaled the scent of sex underlain with the orange blossom fragrance of her hair. There was something overwhelmingly attractive about a woman who made a man feel all man.

He opened his mouth to murmur something suggestive when his gaze rose to her face and his mouth snapped shut.

Her pale brow was furrowed in thought and those full lips pursed as if something other than bliss occupied her brain. His gaze moved to a reddened patch of skin on her slender throat. Razor burn. He'd kissed her there as he powered into her, stifling the need to yell his triumphant pleasure with a ravaging caress of her tender flesh.

'Alice?'

She blinked rapidly and to Adoni's consternation he saw fat tears spike her dark lashes.

He didn't do emotion. Not with lovers. Sex was about pleasure, scratching an itch, not—

Her tongue slipped out to swipe her reddened lips and, despite his sudden tension, Adoni's sex stirred.

'Sorry.' She swiped her cheeks with the heel of her palm. 'I'm feeling a little…overwhelmed. It will pass, I'm sure.' Her laugh sounded strained. 'It was just so much more than I expected.'

She turned her head and snared him with her brilliant eyes. Adoni's heart knocked his ribs in a rough, unfamiliar rhythm.

'Thank you.' Her mouth turned up into a crooked smile that did something devastating to his internal organs.

'My pleasure.' What a weird conversation. They were so…polite when just seconds ago he'd been deep within her, pulsing out his climax and revelling in her broken gasps of wonderment and the close embrace of her body.

He wanted to kiss her again, see if the promising stirrings of his lower body would strengthen. But that mouth was so solemn. That puckered brow so serious. Above all, there were those crystal teardrops clinging to her thick, bunched lashes. Those made him pause and rethink.

'I need to see to the condom.' Even as he said it, an inner voice rose in protest, telling him he could have her again, find easy satisfaction with this unlikely siren.

But a lifetime's caution came to his aid. He refused to get involved with feminine tears and…feelings.

He levered himself from the bed and strode across to the bathroom. Strange how, with every step, he felt the weight of her gaze. It was as if she touched him, a light caress that strayed from his shoulders, down the sweep of his spine to his buttocks and thighs, then back up to the bunching muscles of his glutes. A shiver of awareness rippled through him.

Again, temptation rose to turn back to Alice and take more of what they'd already shared. Instead Adoni kept walking. It was only when he closed the bathroom door behind him that the tension pushing at his shoulders eased.

In the end he decided on a cold shower, sluicing water off his face and relying on the chill to douse his libido. It would be too easy to fall back into sex with Alice Trehearn. Her combination of naivety and forthright ways attracted as he couldn't recall being attracted before. She was different, possibly unique, and something about her cut straight through his hard-won caution to the instinctive risk-taker deep within.

Which was why Adoni would take stock before having sex with her again.

That they *would* have sex again was a certainty. He might be cautious but he wasn't a self-denying fool.

He grabbed a towel, roughly drying his hair, then leaned forward, considering the shadow darkening his jaw. He should shave, out of consideration for Alice's delicate skin. Yet he hesitated. He'd gone blindly into sex with a stranger and got more than he'd bargained for, in satisfaction and pleasure. But in tears too, and that made the hackles of caution rise.

For a second he hesitated. That in itself piqued his anger. He prided himself on his quick decisions, yet with this woman he was second guessing. Frowning, he reached for a towel and wrapped it around his hips. They had some talking to do.

After that there'd be time for shaving and for more sex. Lots more sex.

Adoni repressed the urge to smile as he crossed the vast bathroom. Already he was fantasising about where the next time would be. The whole time he'd showered he'd been picturing Alice naked with him under the icy spray. Or naked on the sofa by the fire. Or up against the big picture window that gave his owner's suite its multi-million-dollar views of central London.

He swallowed, his mouth drying as he thought of those delectable legs wrapped around his waist, her sultry mouth open as she gasped her pleasure and—

Adoni slammed to a stop. The sheets were a riotous tumble on the vast, empty bed but Alice wasn't beneath them. He frowned.

Was that a door he heard closing down the corridor?

'Alice?' He cast about, expecting to see her in some dim corner of the room, but she wasn't there. Nor was that abomination of a dress.

A niggling sensation started up in his belly. He couldn't place it but it reminded him of the nerves he'd felt the first time he'd gone, virtually penniless, to beg for a loan to start his business. When he'd had nothing to recommend him but his bright ideas and determination to succeed or die trying. Anything to prove to Vassili Petrakis that the son he'd disinherited was a man to be reckoned with.

The memory of that day halted him, mid-stride. His frown became a scowl. Nothing could compare to the way he'd felt that day.

Yet that curious, unsettled feeling persisted.

His stride lengthened as he headed down the corridor, checking out each room as he went. She was nowhere to be found. He paced the sitting room. Hadn't she left her shoes beside the couch? Hadn't her purse been there too?

'Alice?' He swung round, taking in the unmistakable emptiness.

She'd gone. Not just gone, but run away without a word.

Unbelievable! No woman had ever done that before.

He didn't like it.

Adoni retraced his steps, his brow furrowed as he tried to work out why she'd run.

Embarrassment? It seemed unlikely, given the conversation they'd had and her enthusiasm for sex. Heat stirred anew at the memory of Alice, abandoned with rapture. It had felt like the first *real* moment in this long, trying day. He'd even had someone trying to sell him real estate over the wedding dinner.

Adoni stood in the bedroom doorway, scanning the room as if it could provide a clue to her bizarre behaviour. In his experience women were far more likely to hang around long after you wished they'd left than go too early. Most had that greedy look in their eyes. The one that said they lusted after his body or his money or probably both.

Unease filled him. Was Alice capable of looking after

herself alone in London late at night? Should he follow her? She wasn't drunk any more, he'd never have taken her to bed if she was, but—

His thoughts halted as he spied his wallet on the floor. When he'd shed his clothes it had still been in the pocket of his trousers. Now it lay, splayed open, beside the bed. The side of the bed where Alice had lain, exhausted and emotional.

Apparently exhausted and emotional. For now he stepped closer Adoni saw that not only was his wallet open but one of his credit cards was tugged out of its slot.

He blinked, mind cataloguing the implication of the open wallet. Yet something, a part of him that hankered after the illusion of an honest woman, protested he couldn't be seeing what he thought.

Adoni picked up the wallet and sank onto the bed. How much cash had been in there earlier? He flicked through the notes. Nothing was obviously missing. But that didn't mean she hadn't helped herself to some.

Of more concern was that she'd obviously been rifling his credit cards. They were all there; she hadn't stolen them.

But maybe she'd made a note of the numbers and security data to use later? She could even have taken an imprint. Who knew what she carried in her bag?

Adoni leaned back against the bedhead, torn between disbelief and anger at himself for being so easily gulled. Women had tried to inveigle their way into his life in so many ways, he'd thought himself awake to them all. Yet he'd allowed Alice Trehearn to slip under his guard.

If that was even her name. Now he thought about it, it sounded a little too sweet and old-fashioned. Made up to allay suspicion?

He raked a hand through his hair. What a bloody fool he'd been! Thinking with his penis while she'd been busy scheming to get her grimy fingers on his money.

You'd think, by thirty-one, he'd be awake to such schemes. Especially given his history. A mother who'd lied shamelessly to both her husband and her son. A fiancée who'd fooled Adoni into believing she loved him then dropped him the moment he was disinherited.

As for the man he'd once called Father...

Truly, it was remarkable Adoni had allowed himself to be conned. He'd learned the hard way not to take people at face value.

Until tonight when a slip of a girl with an endearing smile, an owlish stare and a voracious sensuality had blindsided him.

His mind clicked back to that heady rush of primal, masculine possessiveness. That first slow thrust to Alice's silken core, when she'd felt as tight and untried as he imagined a virgin would be. Then she'd looked up with wonder in her glazed eyes and something had beaten hard and insistent in his chest. Pleasure and a primitive satisfaction that made him feel as sophisticated as a caveman.

He'd even believed, when her breath caught and her whole body stilled, that perhaps she *was* a complete innocent. Until her fingers dug into his buttocks and she demanded 'More!' in that husky little voice that was the most potent aphrodisiac he knew. That had banished the strange moment of fantasy.

Adoni's jaw set. He supposed he should be thankful he hadn't taken longer in the bathroom. If he had he was sure his wallet and his credit cards would have been exactly where he'd left them and he wouldn't have realised Alice was a thief till large sums disappeared from his accounts.

Alice Trehearn was just another gold-digger who'd set her sights on his fortune.

He breathed out hard, shoulders rising and falling in self-disgust that he'd actually fallen for her scam. She'd better look out if their paths crossed again. He wouldn't fall for her wiles a second time.

He reached for the phone. It was time to cancel his credit cards.

'Sensitive breasts. That was the first sign.' The woman's whisper penetrated the hum of the crowded café. 'Even when I just crossed my arms.'

Alice paused, feeling her eyes widen at the empty cups and plates she was clearing from a nearby table. Her own breasts had felt sensitive for the last couple of days.

Out of all the customer conversations in the room, her tired brain *would* snag on that one. Any minute now she'd hear that the woman had since been diagnosed with a weird flu or some horrible life-threatening illness. Alice did *not* need to hear that. She couldn't afford time off with illness. She had enough trouble making ends meet.

She blinked and tried to focus on her task, wrinkling her nose at the half-drunk coffee she loaded onto her tray. For some reason the scent of coffee, one she usually adored, seemed downright unpleasant today.

'I didn't have that at all.' Another woman spoke. 'My first sign was cigarette smoke. Every time Jake lit up I gagged. I made him quit smoking, which is just as well when you think about it. But it wasn't just cigarettes. Coffee too. I couldn't bear the smell.'

Alice froze, her arm outstretched towards a cake plate.

Was this some hoax? Was she being set up in an elaborate joke?

She shook her head. Tiredness was confusing her. She'd spoken to no one about either of those strange symptoms. It was just coincidence.

Briskly, telling herself she wasn't listening, she finished stacking the tray.

'And of course that led to morning sickness.' It was the

second voice again. 'You don't know how lucky you were to miss out on that.'

Alice felt the hairs on her nape lift, one by one, till her flesh drew tight. She took a slow, calming breath, its effect spoiled as another waitress walked by with a load of coffees. Alice inhaled the fumes and swallowed convulsively.

She felt clammy now, as if her skin was too tight for her body. Perspiration popped out on her hairline and she swayed.

It took an enormous effort to straighten, supporting the laden tray, and turn towards the kitchen. As she did her gaze turned to the pair who'd been speaking. Both were young and healthy-looking. Both smiling. One had a baby on her knee and the other was so pregnant it was a wonder she managed to fit in the alcove seat.

A tremor racked Alice and she almost dropped the tray. Pregnancy!

That was what they were talking about?

But Alice couldn't be. It wasn't possible.

He'd used a condom!

Of course she wasn't pregnant. She was only twenty-three. She was just starting to live life for herself. She had no plans for a baby.

It was just coincidence.

A strange, scary coincidence.

But as the morning wore on Alice became more and more conscious of the way her breasts tingled whenever her arm pressed in as she reached for something. She found herself avoiding the coffee machine as much as possible.

By her break, despite some stern self-talk about not leaping to conclusions, Alice found herself in a pharmacy, handing over hard-earned cash for a pregnancy kit.

It couldn't be. Of *course* it couldn't be.

But it was.

Alice stood in the cramped staff washroom and stared at the indicator that told her she was pregnant.

She didn't slump against the counter. She didn't squeal with excitement or cry. She didn't do anything but stare as the implications worked their way into her brain.

She'd experienced so many life-changing events. Alice had learned railing against fate or trying to avoid reality didn't work.

Her mother had died in a car crash when Alice was twelve. Her father's injuries in the same smash left him in a wheelchair, needing constant support until he'd died of complications when she was seventeen. At least her godfather, David, had given them a roof over their heads when their money dried up and the house had to go. Then David, as close as family, had been diagnosed with a terminal condition. Alice had been the one to look after him through the prolonged illness till last year when—

Alice shook her head. At least, for a change, the latest crisis in her life wasn't about death, but about life. Maybe when she got her head around it she'd even be happy.

She stared into the mirror at the wan-faced young woman whose eyes seemed too big for her face.

Fear stirred.

Fear of the unknown. She knew nothing about babies!

Fear about how she'd support a child when she could barely support herself.

And, yes, a blinding moment of frustration and self-pity. Because, as she'd lost the people she loved, she could find only one positive—that now she could begin experiencing those things her peers took for granted. Parties and carefree weekends. Dating. Starting a career. Going to art school, if she could scrape enough money to support herself.

Now art school would be on hold again, perhaps permanently. She'd have to find a way to support her child, plus a career that earned well and had family-friendly hours.

Alice's mouth twisted at the impossibility of it all.

She grabbed at the counter as another thought struck and her knees gave way.

She'd have to tell *him*. Adoni Petrakis.

For, she realised, she *was* having this baby. She didn't know anything about babies but she was sure she didn't want a termination.

That was one thing sorted at least.

She tried to smile at her reflection and failed. For she cringed at the idea of confronting Adoni. They were from different worlds. It was a miracle they'd ended up in bed together. He was rich, sophisticated and urbane. She was ordinary and embarrassingly inexperienced. More, she'd been downright gauche that night.

The memory always left her torn between horror at what she'd done and a wish that it had never ended. She could get used to a handsome, sexy man with a sense of humour and an appreciative glint in his eyes. A man who was kind and generous and awakened all sorts of unfamiliar desires.

Just as well she'd peeked into his wallet to check his surname. At the time shame had pushed her to spy because in her alcoholic haze she'd forgotten his last name. She'd been determined to know the full name of the man she'd given her virginity to.

Her crooked smile became a rictus grin, her cheeks aching at the pull of taut flesh.

At least she had a name to put on the birth certificate!

CHAPTER FOUR

'MR PETRAKIS?'

'Yes?' Adoni paused on the way into his London office. He smiled at the temporary assistant filling in for his trusted PA, and watched the young woman blush. He repressed a sigh. The sooner his PA returned the better.

'I'm sorry to interrupt.' She glanced to the man beside him. 'But a woman has been ringing quite a lot, wanting an appointment.' Adoni heard what might have been a snicker from Miles Dawlish and the temp blushed even more. 'But her name isn't on the approved list.'

'Then she doesn't get an appointment.' Adoni turned and gestured for Dawlish to precede him into the office. He didn't like the man but the deal he offered was interesting enough to warrant Adoni's personal attention.

'It's just that…' He swung round to find the temp biting her lip. He waited, reining in impatience. She leaned forward, her voice dropping. 'She said it was *personal*. And that it was vital she see you.'

Adoni felt his eyebrows wing up. How difficult was it to get a competent replacement for his sick PA? Surely any assistant worth the name understood the meaning of 'no unapproved meetings'?

The woman's gaze dropped and she fiddled with the notebook on her desk, the picture of guilt. She looked so nervous he almost felt sorry for her.

'What name did she give?' he asked, determined not to scare off another temp.

'Alice Trehearn. She was very insistent. It sounded… important.' The woman looked up, relief in her eyes, but Adoni barely noticed.

Alice Trehearn?

Unbidden, memory unfolded like a bud bursting into bloom. Skin as pale as ivory. A lithe body that responded to him like an instrument tuned to his touch. Lips like crushed berries, sweet and reddened from his kisses.

A mouth that lied. A woman who'd targeted him and played him for a fool.

Yet, even as he opened his mouth to say there'd be no meeting, curiosity rose. What did Alice hope to gain from seeing him? She must have tried his card numbers without success. Was she hoping to seduce him into giving her something else?

The idea of Alice Trehearn trying to seduce him again was undeniably titillating. Especially as Adoni had no intention of letting her get her greedy claws on anything of his. It might be amusing to have sex with her again, purely to finalise unfinished business. Ever since that night a month and a half ago he'd been plagued by the realisation that he still wanted her, despite the fact she was on the make.

Sex with Alice Trehearn still appealed. Almost as much as wiping the smile off her face afterwards when he told her he was awake to her schemes and she'd never get a penny of his.

Adoni smiled at his temp and didn't even mind when the woman blushed and smiled dazedly back.

'Tell her I'll see her. As soon as possible. Here in my office.'

'Oh, but she wondered if you could meet—'

'Here.' Adoni paused, his smile fading. 'Tomorrow. Or not at all.' Then he strode into his office where Miles Dawlish stood. Adoni gestured for him to take a seat.

'I couldn't help but overhear,' the Englishman began. 'I know an Alice Trehearn too. She was at the wedding reception where you and I met. I wondered if it could be the same woman.'

Adoni didn't respond, but took a seat opposite. He had no intention of sharing his personal life. If it weren't for Dawlish's property, Adoni wouldn't waste time with the man. Adoni knew his sort—convinced the world owed him a living. Ready to sell off his inheritance, a truly superb estate, for ready cash.

Even in the days when Adoni had been the favoured elder son of Vassili Petrakis, the billionaire shipping magnate, he'd had to work. He'd learned the ropes in the family company, developing the skills needed to run the enterprise. He'd never have countenanced selling off the family estate.

Those days were long gone. He had no family. His business he'd built by the sweat of his brow. And he wouldn't let anyone, either competitor or thief, take any part of it.

'If it *is* her, the same woman, I mean, you need to be careful.' Dawlish leaned forward. 'Skinny girl, big eyes, smart mouth. Does that ring a bell? She was one of the bridesmaids. Got invited to take part at the last minute. A charitable act by the bride, I understand.'

'I'm afraid I didn't pay much attention to the bridesmaids.' It wasn't a lie. Adoni had barely looked at them, till Alice had pushed her way into his presence and started babbling so artfully about kisses and orgasms. 'But I don't understand. How is an invitation to be bridesmaid charity?'

Dawlish shook his head. 'Not charity precisely. But there was a long-standing rift between the cousins, probably because Alice is such a scheming little...'

'Please. Do go on. I'm fascinated.'

For a moment the other man looked discomfited, as if he realised he'd strayed from the purpose of the meeting. But his hatred of Alice Trehearn needed an outlet. 'Not to put too fine a point on it, she's a conniving bitch.'

'She sounds like a woman to be wary of.'

'Oh, *you'd* see through her in a moment, I'm sure.'

Adoni's answering smile was tight. He'd been furious when he realised Alice had duped him. But learning he was just one of those she'd fooled...

Had he been this incensed when his fiancée Chryssa dumped him and revealed her true colours? It didn't seem possible.

'She tried to deceive you?'

Dawlish shook his head. 'No, I saw her for what she was. It was my uncle she conned. David Bannister.'

'Bannister. The name is familiar.'

'From the documents I sent. He was my uncle by marriage. My aunt, his wife, left the family estate to me but only after David's death. They didn't have children and I was her closest relative. David had free run of the estate while he was alive.' Dawlish clamped his jaw as if grinding his teeth. 'Miss Butter-Wouldn't-Melt-in-Her-Mouth Trehearn moved into his house years ago. She was in her teens, you know, but David was besotted. She could do no wrong in his eyes.'

Adoni frowned. Theft was one thing. But a teenager seducing a much, much older man? Such things happened. Adoni had seen it. Yet it left a nasty taste in the mouth.

'How old was your uncle?'

'In his sixties. Old enough to know better. But they say there's no fool like an old fool, eh?' Dawlish settled back in his seat, stretching out his legs. 'He even let her handle his money, would you believe? And she had the hide to bar my calls and visits, saying David didn't want to see me.'

He sneered. 'But she got her comeuppance. I bet David didn't tell her the estate wasn't his. She probably thought she was sitting on a goldmine and he'd leave it all to her instead of putting it towards running the estate or leaving anything for me to inherit. But she got her hands on everything she could.'

'And was it? Put towards the estate, I mean?'

Dawlish nodded. 'Don't worry on that score. The place is flourishing. David might have been besotted but he'd never let the place go to rack and ruin. He and my aunt even started up an artists' colony a decade or more ago in some of the old estate buildings. You'll see from the material I sent you there are some quite prestigious artists living there. That's in addition to the house and farmlands.'

'It sounds fascinating.' And indeed it was. Adoni and his most trusted staff had been over the details of the place with a fine-tooth comb. It was just what he was looking for. The ancient house would be perfect for a luxury country hotel.

Adoni's fortune was founded on innovative software but he believed in spreading his investments. The upmarket London hotel, another in Santorini and potentially one in the country were part of a plan to ring-fence his wealth.

But of all the things Dawlish told him, Alice Trehearn was most fascinating.

She really was something. She'd almost convinced him he'd taken a virgin to bed, yet she'd been living with a man old enough to be her father, or maybe her grandfather, for years.

Adoni was torn between disgust and curiosity about why she'd show her face again. Did she believe they could take up where they'd left off?

If so, she was in for a short, sharp lesson.

Alice tugged at her cropped black jacket then smoothed unsteady hands down the matching straight skirt as she walked the London street to the address she'd been given. She'd worn this outfit to her father's funeral, then David's. She hated the colour and the memories it evoked, but it seemed the most suitable for today.

It was her going-to-job-interviews outfit. Before David's death she'd worn it again and again while dealing with strangers over estate business. As his illness progressed and he retreated into art and books, David had entrusted her with the day-to-day running of his much-loved property. And while those who lived there knew her capabilities, outsiders saw only her youth and decided she was a pushover to be dismissed or even duped.

Her lips twitched with wry humour. They'd learned. You didn't have to be old to be competent and organised.

Was stark black an improvement on bilious yellow?

Compressing her lips, Alice reminded herself it didn't matter what Adoni Petrakis thought of her appearance. What mattered was delivering her news and discovering if she'd been right about him. She'd been drawn not just to his sexy looks and take-charge air but by the glimmer of humour in his eyes, his tenderness and his patience with a woman who was clearly not at her best.

Surely that boded well? If he were a decent guy, and she had no reason to suspect he wasn't, maybe they could come to an amicable arrangement so their child didn't grow up without knowing its father.

Remarkable how important this tiny baby had become in just a few short days. What would it be like when she held it in her arms? When it was no longer a baby but a toddler, able to run and laugh and hug her back?

A rush of warmth drenched her at the thought of loving and being loved again. This wasn't at all the life she'd planned, but she was determined to look on this pregnancy as a positive, not a burden.

No matter how terrified she was.

Alice swallowed hard, pushing down doubts and fears, reminding herself she was determined and capable. She'd had to be.

What she didn't know she'd learn. And if she was poor—well, that was nothing new. With hard work and maybe some assistance she'd be able to provide for the child.

She reached the glass doors of a sleek building, checked

the address and strode in, not giving herself time to hesitate. Soon after, she arrived at one of the top floors.

The doors opened onto a beautifully appointed reception room. All muted tones, expensive furniture and just a touch of flamboyance in the artful arrangement of exotic orchids and the vast seascape that dominated one charcoal wall.

Maybe it was the art, maybe the quiet air of comfort, but Alice felt the jitters in her stomach ease. She drew her first full breath since she'd begun the five block walk from the underground.

'Ms Trehearn?' A neatly dressed woman approached.

Alice nodded. 'That's me.'

'Won't you take a seat? Mr Petrakis will see you soon. In the meantime would you like tea or coffee?'

'Nothing, thanks.' Nausea had dogged her since she'd got out of bed in the early hours, for the long train trip from the West Country to London. She'd wait till this was over then find somewhere for a nice, refreshing cup of tea.

By the time the receptionist approached again Alice had skimmed four magazines and memorised the painted scene before her.

Had Adoni deliberately kept her waiting? But why? He didn't need to prove a point. She already knew he was powerful and wealthy. She'd done some homework on him. What she'd learned had made it seem as if that evening in his hotel suite was an illusion. What did she have in common with one of Europe's most eligible self-made billionaires?

Sex. That was all.

And now a baby.

The thought calmed the drifts of butterflies in her middle and she smiled at the receptionist's apologies over her long wait.

It didn't matter that Adoni had been heir to one of the world's wealthiest ship owners. Or that he'd been estranged from his family in circumstances no one quite understood. Or that he'd since made his fortune with a software company that grew above market expectations.

Adoni was just a man. Together they'd made a baby. That made them equals in the ways that counted.

If she kept telling herself that she might just get through the next half-hour!

Her first thought on entering his spacious office was that he looked as scrumptious by daylight as he did at night. Though stern, as if he'd just received bad news.

Alice felt a pang of regret. She remembered the conspiratorial smile that had turned his face from sombre and a little haughty to blindingly attractive and beckoningly approachable.

Approachable he was not.

Adoni Petrakis was back to being Ares, god of war. He stood by the window, light slanting across proud, arrogantly handsome features. His thin lips were flat and his nostrils pinched as if against some unpleasant odour.

Alice refused to be intimidated, even though it meant squashing the urge to spin round on her heel and head back out the way she'd come.

This wasn't about her. This was about her child. Their child. She had an obligation to the baby and to Adoni, even if he looked at her as if he'd never seen her before.

Or as if he didn't *want* to see her.

That thought was acid, eating at her composure.

Deliberately she pushed her shoulders back. She'd learned that if she pretended to be strong, even when she was falling apart inside, she could get through most things, one step at a time.

Keep telling yourself that, Alice.

She made herself pace across the room in her freshly polished and only pair of high heels. She ignored the visitor's chair in front of the vast, almost bare desk. She wasn't an employee, here to receive instructions from on high. Instead she skirted the desk and walked right up to him.

Was that surprise flickering in his ocean-bright eyes?

Tucked up in her narrow bed in Devon, she'd told herself she'd embellished his good looks. But, staring up into those remarkable eyes, she realised she'd embellished nothing, except perhaps his friendliness.

'You're not pleased to see me.' She stopped before him, linking her hands to stop them fidgeting under his steady regard.

Had she really hoped he'd be thrilled to have her turn up? All they'd shared was a one-night stand. Not even a night. An evening. A casual sexual encounter.

'I confess I'm intrigued.' His deep voice, at least, was familiar. Too familiar. Heat swept her skin and, in its wake, wave after wave of goose bumps. She'd dreamed of that voice with its suede caress. 'Won't you take a seat?'

'Thank you.' Alice turned, again ignored the straight-backed chair near the desk, and instead crossed to a cluster of lounge chairs. They were grouped beneath an eye-catching work in oils, a wintry city street scene, daring in its use of colour.

The painting eased her nerves. No man with such taste in art could be as ice-cold as he seemed now.

The man she'd made love to—no, had sex with—hadn't been cold at all. He'd been warm and generous and passionate. Where had he gone?

Gratefully she sank into a leather armchair. Stress made her knees wobble and her stomach churn. 'I like your artwork.'

One dark eyebrow rose, a questioning slash on his olive forehead. 'You didn't come here to talk art.'

Alice waited for him to cross and take a seat too, but he remained standing. His cool stare chilled and she fought the impulse to rub her hands up and down her arms.

Okay, he definitely wasn't happy to see her.

Alice pushed aside stupid regret and the even more foolish daydream she'd had that maybe, just maybe, he'd welcome her with open arms, literally. That he'd smile and hold her close and tell her he was pleased to see her. That he'd make everything okay. Even that he'd been searching for her.

She huffed in a little breath of self-disgust. Since when had she believed in such pathetic twaddle?

The answer was easy. Since the man before her, or perhaps his amiable, generous, friendly twin, had seduced her so thoroughly she was more than half in love with someone who existed only in her head. Someone with humour, tenderness, strength and passion.

Alice bit back a sigh and met his guarded stare head-on. 'You're right. I didn't come to discuss art.'

Adoni was stunned at the depth of his response to the slim woman in the sober suit, her dark hair pulled back in an uncompromising arrangement. He had perfect recall of every sinuous centimetre of creamy skin she hid beneath stark black. So perfect he found himself breathing quickly as she sauntered across the room to stare provocatively up at him.

Or was that simply the natural effect of her sulkily sexy mouth and wide eyes beneath long, silky lashes?

No, definitely provocative. Was she annoyed that he'd kept her waiting? He felt his forehead pinch into a frown at the touch of sass he detected in her attitude.

If she'd come to cajole him into an affair so she could part him from his cash she was a little too...deliberate, ignoring the chair before his desk and appraising him so frankly.

He'd expected her to be more conciliatory, more charming. Yet though Adoni felt the impact of her stare like a punch to the ribs, she wasn't conforming to any of the scenarios he'd considered. Neither the vamp nor the tease, nor even the frail female in need of protection.

But then Alice Trehearn hadn't conformed to any stereotypes the first time they'd met either.

Amusement brushed through him as he remembered the outrageous things she'd said that night and her shock as she realised what she'd let slip. Until he recalled it had all been a clever tactic to win his trust and sneak under his guard.

He watched her sashay across to a lounge chair, his gaze roving her tidy, beautifully curved rear as she sank into a seat, her attention apparently on his picture. Beneath the down-lights her hair glowed with a warm hint of auburn.

She was good, he'd give her that. Not even a hint of discomfort on that pale face, though she must know he'd cancelled his credit cards.

Adoni strolled across, drawn despite himself.

Curiosity, that was all.

'You're right. I didn't come to discuss art.' Her voice was husky, as if she wasn't as confident as she appeared. The flickering pulse at the base of her throat drew his eyes and he recalled how he'd kissed her there as she came down from a rapturous high, her whole body quaking. She'd tasted sweet as honey and—

'What did you come for?' His voice was harsh, fuelled by annoyance that the memory of her was indelibly branded on his brain.

She started and her hands clasped tighter in her lap.

'I needed to see you…' She paused and swallowed.

If he didn't know better, he might have been taken in by her sudden show of nerves. She looked paler than before, frail even. But that was an illusion. This woman was tough as tempered steel.

'Yes?' He didn't bother to hide his impatience.

Something flashed in her eyes as she looked up at him. Anger? That surprised him. Surely she was better able to contain her impatience when trying to pull the wool over the eyes of a man she'd targeted?

'You don't want to sit?' No sooner were the words out than she bit the corner of her mouth, as if regretting the question. Because it revealed that he had the upper hand? Or was it some double bluff, designed to make her appear defenceless?

Adoni found his attention lingering on those ripe, dusky pink lips.

Suddenly he lost patience. He'd been curious about her. But now, feeling himself respond to her mixed signals, he'd had enough. He was no one's fool. Not any more.

'No, I don't want to sit. I want you to tell me why you're here. My time is valuable.' Deliberately he crossed his arms.

Something happened to the slate blue of her eyes, as if, just for a moment, they darkened in temper. Then she uncurled herself from the low seat as if electrified.

'Fine. Far be it from me to take up your valuable time.'

She took a step away towards the painting she'd admired, then swung round to face him. Her face looked drawn and that pulse was going crazy, but Alice Trehearn looked anything but vulnerable. She looked defiant.

'The night we had sex.' She seemed to falter and her mouth tightened. 'It had consequences.' Her chest rose and fell as she took a quick breath. 'I've just discovered I'm pregnant.'

Adoni stared at those pretty pink lips, as if, by staring long enough, he could force them to say something else.

Pregnant?

Not likely. He was meticulously careful about protection.

Yet, to his amazement, his belly tightened at the thought of his seed in Alice Trehearn. Of her carrying his child. Some emotion he refused to identify thrummed through him.

Possessiveness?

Absurd. He had no interest in a family. At least not yet. When he did it would be on *his* terms. And not with some grasping thief who saw him as a meal ticket.

The audacity of the woman stunned him. He supposed he should have been ready for this. Instead he'd expected her to try inveigling him into an affair. When she'd arrived, dressed for a business interview rather than a passionate interlude, she'd confounded him.

'Nothing to say? Nothing at all?' That mouth he'd seen tilt down at the corners in a smile he'd found both unique and intriguing turned down again, but not in amusement. She looked indignant as she crossed her arms, plumping up her breasts beneath her dark suit.

'I see.' She bit out the words as if she'd like to take a chunk of his flesh. 'If you think of anything to say about it, anything at all, your secretary has my number.'

She pivoted and strode towards the door, every centimetre vibrating with suppressed energy. It reminded him of the night they'd met, the sensation that she gave off sparks, or that she was likely to detonate with the right trigger.

Oh, she'd detonated all right.

Adoni reached her in two strides, his hand curling round her upper arm, drawing her inexorably back towards him.

'Not so fast, Ms Trehearn.'

CHAPTER FIVE

His voice was a snarl and his big hand was brutally hard.

And, to her absolute horror, Alice felt, muddled in with her indignation, a tremor of excitement at finally getting a reaction from Mr Superior.

No, no, no.

She was not going to let him get to her.

Or play those man-woman games she was sure to lose.

She was a novice and Adoni Petrakis was too adept.

Alice drew herself up as tall as she could, doing her best to ignore her body's mixed signals—jaw clenched in anger, knees shaky with something close to fear and, worst of all, that snaking coil of sexual response drawing her belly tight.

Though she hated his aggressive attitude, Alice's body responded as if expecting more of that sensual bliss he'd bestowed. As if he'd imprinted himself on her psyche and she associated him with amazing sex and the euphoric sense of well-being that had stunned her when he'd held her close.

The thought appalled.

Deliberately she looked at his big hand on her arm, then up into that beautiful dark face with its infuriatingly condescending expression.

'There's no need to get physical, *Mr* Petrakis. I'm happy to stay and discuss this now you've found your voice at last.'

Was he grinding his teeth? A muscle jumped in his jaw and her chin hiked higher. *She* had nothing to apologise for. He'd been in a bad mood since the moment she'd arrived.

With a slight shake of his head he released her. 'Sit down, Alice. We need to sort this out.' He turned his back and strode to the desk, murmuring something into the phone, presumably to his secretary.

Alice sank back into an armchair, surprised at how shaky she felt. She hadn't expected this to be easy but nor had she expected outright animosity.

'You say you're pregnant?' Adoni lowered himself into a chair opposite, his long legs stretched out as if he hadn't a care in the world. Yet his face looked as hard as if it was cast in bronze.

'I *am* pregnant. I saw a doctor yesterday.'

'And you'd have me believe the baby is mine?'

Alice bit back the instinctive retort that rose to her tongue, ignoring the flicker of hurt that he'd think she'd lie about something so fundamental.

He didn't know her, after all. Just as it was becoming clearer by the moment that she didn't know him either. She'd thought him…nice, caring and tender, funny and—

'Having second thoughts about your story, are you?' He leaned forward, his scrutiny so keen Alice swore she felt it scrape over her features like a blade.

'It's no *story*. I wouldn't be here if it wasn't true.'

His eyes narrowed to gleaming slits. 'How convenient that none of your other lovers, before or after me, was so… potent. Incredibly potent, since I took the precaution of using a condom.'

It took enormous willpower not to respond to the snarky innuendo in his tone. Alice refused to lower herself to his level. 'Condoms aren't foolproof, as any medical practitioner will confirm. And as for other lovers…' She paused, feeling heat rise in her cheeks.

'You were saying?' Adoni steepled his hands under his chin as if weighing every word.

Damn. Alice hadn't wanted to admit this, but it seemed she had no choice. 'There haven't been other lovers. Either before or after.' Sheer willpower kept her staring into his narrowed eyes, despite the embarrassment curdling her insides.

Adoni's expression didn't alter, other than a slight puckering of his forehead.

The silence thickened and Alice felt a horrible sensation creeping up her spine to tighten the back of her neck, as if gnarled fingers fastened round her nape.

'You expect me to believe you were a *virgin*?'

Alice tore her gaze away, down to her knuckles, clenched in her lap. 'I know it's probably unusual these days, but yes. I was.'

When she looked up Adoni had tilted his head to one side as if to view her better. 'And what about your long-term lover? Or doesn't he count?'

'Long-term lover? I don't have a lover.'

He leaned forward, teeth bared in what might have passed for a smile if it didn't make Alice think of a ravening wolf. Even his teeth were white and almost perfectly straight!

'That's not what I hear. In fact I'm informed you're a *femme fatale*, living off gullible men.'

Alice shook her head, bemused. 'You've got me confused with someone else.'

'No. *You've* got *me* confused with someone who'd fall for your lies.'

'I'm not lying! I never had a lover before…you.'

Where had all this animosity come from? She'd shared things with Adoni Petrakis that she'd never shared with anyone. She wouldn't have known him for the same man who'd laughed with her and made love so wonderfully.

'Really? What about David Bannister? I hear you lived with him for years.'

'David?' She frowned, sitting back in her seat. 'How did you…?' Alice shook her head. It didn't matter how he knew, just that he'd misunderstood. 'You've got it wrong. David was a friend.'

'A very dear friend. Much older and very wealthy.' Cynicism dripped from every syllable.

'That had nothing to do with—'

'It seems to be a habit of yours, making *friends* with older, wealthy men. Like when you barged into my private space.' He leaned nearer, his gaze needle-sharp. 'Did someone tell you that night that I owned the hotel? Or had you been planning your approach for some time?'

'No!' Alice threw up one hand, trying to stem the flow of accusations. 'You've got it all wrong. I'm not like that.' Her breath came in short, hard gasps. If it weren't so appallingly horrible, it would have been absurd. Her, as a gold-digger! 'Whoever told you about David made a mistake.'

Adoni's lip curled. 'Which is what I'd expect you to say.'

The feral light in his eyes, the cruel twist of his mouth and the furious rasp of that deep-pitched voice cut through Alice's composure. Suddenly she felt not indignant but anxious. It was clear mere words wouldn't convince him.

Once, maybe, she'd have stood her ground and made him eat his words. But she'd changed. Maybe it was exhaustion from her first ever bout of full-blown morning sickness on the train this morning. Or the primal need to remove her unborn child from the vicinity of danger. But suddenly she was on her feet, putting the chair between her and the man giving off such waves of aggression.

The door opened and his secretary came in, carrying a tray with cups and a cafetière. The woman slanted a surprised look at Alice, then placed the tray on a low table, said something to her boss and left.

Alice pried her fingers off the back of the chair and turned to follow her, feeling as if every move took far too much effort. Stress, she assured herself.

She'd only taken a few steps when the scent of coffee hit her. Good strong, aromatic coffee. The sort she'd once loved.

Bile rose in her throat and she gagged. She froze, one

hand going to her stomach and the other to her mouth. Time splintered as she fought against the indignity of vomiting here, in front of this inimical stranger.

Then Adoni was standing before her, those winged eyebrows scrunched in concern. 'What is it? You look grey.'

'Coffee,' she whispered. 'The smell.'

For a second he stood, uncomprehending, then he whipped round, grabbed the tray and carried it out.

When he got back Alice had found his private bathroom. Her hands were braced on the edge of the black marble basin and she was shaking. She hadn't been ill this time but it had been a close call. Nausea still hovered and her mouth tasted of acid.

Studiously she avoided her image in the mirror. Instead she took slow breaths, willing the nausea to subside.

'Alice?' His voice was deep and soft. If she closed her eyes she could almost believe herself back in his luxury hotel suite when he'd been charming and gentle.

She sucked in a hiss of air then croaked, 'I'll be okay in a minute.'

Silence extended, then she heard running water. A moment later damp towelling settled on the nape of her neck, cool and surprisingly refreshing. Without hesitation she let her head droop forward, accepting his ministrations.

After a couple of minutes he murmured, 'Turn,' and it seemed natural to comply. Still with eyes shut, she leant back against the basin while the damp cloth traced her cheeks and mouth, her forehead and throat.

Alice swallowed, surprised to find herself reviving now the pungent aroma of coffee was gone.

'Sip this.'

She opened her eyes, locking onto his serious greeny-blue stare. Something shuddered inside. Not fear or indignation but something vital that even nausea hadn't dimmed.

She looked down to the glass of water he held to her

mouth and took it from him, careful not to touch his hand. Obediently she took a tiny sip, then another, relief settling around her shoulders as her stomach didn't revolt.

'Thank you.'

He surveyed her, unblinking, from under hooded lids. Dully, Alice wondered what he saw, or thought he saw. She'd be distressed by his distrust when the nausea passed. Right now she didn't have the strength to be anything other than grateful for this ceasefire in his antagonism.

'Can you walk?'

She nodded, stifling the urge to ask whether he'd carry her if she couldn't. It was crazy the way she craved his tenderness. His solicitude changed nothing. He thought her a liar.

Alice took a deep breath and looked towards the door to the office. It seemed a mile away. But she hated appearing weak, especially to someone with such a low opinion of her.

Setting her jaw, she took a careful step forward. The room pitched then settled. She took another step. Only a few score more to get out of here.

Except Adoni moved, swooping down to tuck an arm beneath her knees and wrap another around her back. He held her high against his chest, her head against his shoulder as he carried her into his office.

'This is unnecessary,' she whispered, her throat raspy. 'My legs work fine. It's just morning sickness.'

Adoni didn't answer. Instead he settled on a long sofa with her on his lap. Water spilled from her glass onto her skirt with the movement but she said nothing. It felt so good to be held against his powerful body. That intense heat of solid muscle was soothing and he was surprisingly comfortable to a woman who felt as powerful as a blossom in a strong wind.

If she rested just a moment to regroup she'd be ready to go another round or three with him.

'Try one of these.' His voice rumbled up from somewhere below her ear as he leaned forward, reaching for the coffee table. The movement folded her closer into his body so she was enveloped by him, breathing in the elusive scent of cedar and spice that had entranced her that night in his bed. Her nose wrinkled. Strange how this scent didn't seem to disrupt her upset stomach.

He cradled a small bowl of pistachios.

'I don't want to eat anything.'

'It might help. When my stepmother had morning sickness she used to nibble salted wafers and nuts.'

Alice looked down at the broad, bronzed hand cupping a silver bowl. Surprise burrowed through her at the intimacy of that revelation. Tentatively she took a nut, its shell half open.

'Bite gently on the shell and it will open completely.'

Alice complied, relishing the salty dusting on the outside and the soft nuttiness inside. She slipped the shell into her hand and swallowed the pistachio.

Hesitant, she waited, but her stomach didn't heave.

'Try another.' Adoni proffered the bowl again.

'Thanks, I will. But I'd rather sit alone.'

It was a lie. Alice had never felt more comfortable than slumped, half-boneless, against Adoni's strong form. Which was unbelievable, given his earlier animosity.

After the shock and anxiety of this week his powerful masculinity propping her up felt ridiculously reassuring. Except that was a temporary illusion. He didn't trust her. Worse, he despised her. And even if he didn't she couldn't afford to get accustomed to the idea of anyone else looking out for her. The news of her pregnancy had reinforced the fact that she had no one to rely on. It would be up to her to look after herself and her child.

He stiffened. Then, without a word, he lifted her and put her down on the seat beside him.

Fleetingly Alice thought about how much upper body strength it took to manage that. Till her brain kicked into gear, reminding her she had other things to concern her than Adoni Petrakis's muscles.

'Eat.'

She nodded and tried another pistachio, sucking the salt from the shell, then methodically chewing the nut. She'd never had pistachios before. 'Are these Greek?'

'They are,' he murmured.

'I like them.' Strange how easily the words came. Almost as easily as that first night. The memory of her unguarded, downright outrageous behaviour drenched her in sudden heat and she pushed the bowl away.

'You feel sick again?' His voice came from near her ear as if he leaned closer. Alice wondered at the concern in his voice.

'No. I'm okay.' She took another sip of water and shut her eyes, willing herself to concentrate. It was difficult to whip up indignation against the man who'd just tended to her so carefully. She didn't know where she was with him.

Finally she leaned forward and put her glass down on the coffee table with a decisive click. Then she swivelled to face him.

Troubled eyes met his. Adoni couldn't see any hint of the woman he'd expected, the woman who'd set him up to bleed him dry. Yet looks deceived.

He felt a pang of regret. He was torn between that and ingrained caution. There was no doubt that physically Alice Trehearn was weak. Feeling the tremors running through her slim frame and seeing her distress at almost being sick evoked long-dormant instincts to protect. He'd gathered her to him and almost *wanted* to believe in her. Just as he'd been drawn to her the night of the wedding, charmed by what seemed a uniquely refreshing woman.

Yet there was nothing unique about a woman scamming a rich man.

'You still don't believe the baby is yours.' Her voice was flat but her eyes pleaded for understanding. Did she really think his unwilling sympathy over her nausea would blind him to the bigger picture?

'No, I don't.' He ignored the flare of apparent hurt in her eyes. He knew how well a woman on the make could pretend.

'So where does that leave us?'

'Simple.' His voice was harsh. Yet to his amazement what should have been simple—getting to the bottom of Alice Trehearn's allegation—was mired in unexpected emotion. 'Have a paternity test. If the child is mine, then we'll talk.'

Her eyes darkened and she looked away, but not before he read hurt there. Again, Adoni found himself torn. His silent applause at her dramatic skills warred with a sliver of guilt that perhaps he had this wrong and she was, against the odds, an innocent.

'Of course.' She seemed to gather herself. 'I'll be in contact when it's arranged.' Then she shifted to the edge of the seat and made to rise.

Adoni's hand shot out, grasping her arm, holding her where she was.

'What?' Her dark gaze met his before sliding away.

'Where are you going?' Surely she wasn't well enough to leave? She still looked parchment-white. Besides, she hadn't yet broached the all-important issue of money.

'Home. If I leave now I can be back in Devon in time for my evening shift.'

'Evening shift?' Even now she trembled beneath his hand and the fragility of her slim body struck him. Surely she wasn't well enough for work?

'I'm a waitress.' She looked pointedly at his hand on her sleeve, as if waiting for him to remove it.

'A waitress who can't stand the smell of coffee?'

Her lips tugged into a crooked smile for just a second before she saw him watching and pursed that lovely mouth. 'Ridiculous, isn't it? But hopefully it won't last long. Now, if you'll let me go I'll be on my way.'

With deliberate slowness Adoni released his hold and sat back, crossing his arms. The gesture masked his reluctance to release her. It had been like that the night they'd met—that urge to touch, to caress, to connect.

'Surely not,' he drawled, watching her like a hawk. 'Didn't you come here for money?'

Her head whipped round, hectic spots of pink colouring her cheeks. She drew herself high, perching on the very edge of the sofa, and surveyed him down the length of her not very impressive nose.

'No. I came here because I felt you deserved to know you're going to be a father.'

'So getting rid of the child didn't occur to you? You're definitely having it?'

She nodded and Adoni felt the old distrust spike. Of course she'd have the child if she thought there was benefit in it.

'Ah, but would you have made the same decision if I weren't rich?'

Instantly the pink drained from her cheeks and her skin took on the greenish pallor she'd worn when she battled nausea.

'That's a foul thing to say.' Her eyes looked huge and wounded.

Adoni met her stare unblinking. 'It's a cruel world. There are plenty of women who'd barter a rich man's child for an easy life, or dispose of an inconvenient one.'

Her nostrils flared and her mouth tightened. 'I'm not one of them. And if that's the only sort of women you know, I pity you.'

'It's not pity I need. Just the truth.' His jaw clenched and his chest rose as he dragged in a calming breath.

How dare she take that attitude with him? Just because he faced facts. It was true, the women who'd figured largest in his life had been devious and disloyal, but he was the last person to need pity. Especially from this slip of a girl.

'So tell me, *Alice*.' He leaned close, pinioning her with his eyes, daring her to lie barefaced. 'Didn't you come hoping I'd give you money?'

She blinked, her gaze dropping for a tell-tale moment. Strangely, Adoni didn't feel triumphant but disappointed.

Slowly she nodded. 'Well, yes. I thought you'd probably want to know our child and build a relationship with her or him. And I hoped...' She swallowed and stared straight back at him. 'I thought you might contribute later. You know, for school costs and that sort of thing.'

'Not now?' His lips curled derisively.

'Now?' Fine vertical lines appeared on her forehead. 'It hasn't even been born.'

It was Adoni's turn to be surprised. Was she for real?

'Surely there are expenses?' He let the words hang. Given the chance, she'd no doubt fill it with a wish list of comforts.

She shook her head. 'Not so far.' She paused. 'I was going to buy some pregnancy books but the local library had some excellent ones.'

When he remained silent she continued. 'One of the other waitresses has a pram and cot and other bits and pieces in good condition. She swears three boys are enough and she won't have more children, so she'll let me have what I need.' Alice's hint of a smile died as she registered his expression. 'What? What's wrong?'

What's wrong? Either Alice was the most convincing actress he'd ever met or his baby was going to grow up in the wilds of Devon, surrounded by second-hand furniture and reliant on the goodwill of others.

There are worse ways to grow up.

What did luxury and money matter when there was no honesty, much less genuine love from those closest to you?

'Adoni?'

Get a grip, man. You don't even know if it's your child.

'Nothing is wrong. I was just thinking.'

Since when had he been unable to think and speak at the same time? Adoni found himself reacting viscerally to this situation, instead of logically. Betrayal by a woman he'd trusted, however fleetingly, cut too close to the bone.

For a decade he'd guarded his heart. Hell, he probably didn't have a heart to guard. He liked women physically, but he allowed none close emotionally. Casual and mutually pleasing was how he kept his relationships. He'd learned distrust in a hard school and would have bet his fortune that no woman would ever unsettle him again.

Alice Trehearn did it with just a look.

Yet, unaccountably, he discovered within himself an unexpected yearning for the very thing life had taught him he couldn't have—an honest, caring woman. A family.

Adoni hated to acknowledge it, but the prospect of fatherhood ignited a firestorm of emotions and memories. Of blissful happiness, trauma and finally abandonment.

Alice eyed him doubtfully. 'So, I'll ask my doctor about a paternity test and—'

'No. I'll arrange it. You'll be contacted.' Adoni had no intention of taking the word of someone Alice lined up to advise on the baby.

She nodded and got to her feet.

Adoni repressed the urge to bar her way. She was pale and he registered smudges of tiredness beneath her fine eyes that he hadn't noticed before. But she didn't need him to care for her, even if that was what she was ultimately angling for.

He rose, noting how her chin reflexively notched higher as if she was determined not to let down her guard around him. That made two of them.

'My PA has your contact details?'

Alice nodded, then paused as if waiting for something. A kiss? An offer of lunch? Or something more? The stormy light in her eyes told him something was going on in that pretty head of hers. It infuriated him that he couldn't interpret her expression.

'Goodbye, Adoni.' Without waiting for a response, she turned and walked straight-backed out of the room.

Adoni noted the finality of her tone. Because he'd called her bluff and he'd never see her again?

He wished it were that simple but, in his experience, life rarely was.

CHAPTER SIX

ALICE SMILED AT the elderly couple. 'Of course it's okay to change your order.' Again. 'I'll just nip into the kitchen and sort that out.' But she'd have to be quick.

Turning, she threaded her way between the tables, pushing exhausted muscles to hurry, though it felt as if she were wading through treacle, her feet ridiculously heavy. She glanced at her watch. Another hour. Could she make it to the end of her shift?

She'd been grateful for the additional work when one of the other girls hadn't been able to come in, knowing it meant a little extra in the bank for when the baby came. Yet now she felt worn too thin. Exhausted as she was, she couldn't sleep properly.

Was she doing the right thing, severing contact with Adoni? Not taking the paternity test he'd demanded?

It was a major step, one she couldn't take lightly. Yet the things he'd said in London, his ultra-cynical attitude... She wasn't sure she wanted him helping bring up their child.

Not that he would. His idea of involvement was probably throwing money at the kid. Paid nursemaids and posh boarding schools, rather than love and caring.

He'd made it clear he had no interest in the baby, other than as a financial burden or a tool for blackmail. She shivered, wondering what sort of world he inhabited where distrust and deceit were the natural order.

Wearily she pushed open the door to the kitchen and relayed the change of order. Then she grabbed a glass of water and slumped against the wall. She needed to catch her breath long enough to get through the next hour.

Alice closed her eyes, taking another slow drink. Had

she done right, telling Adoni's PA when she'd rung to arrange the paternity test that she'd changed her mind? She wasn't going through with the test.

He'd think it was because the child wasn't his.

The trouble was, this way she'd deny her baby the chance to know its father. If she had the test, Adoni would be involved in their baby's upbringing. Yet Alice feared what that meant for the child.

And for her. Because even while he'd been spouting the most abhorrent accusations, she'd found herself craving the physical comfort she remembered from Adoni's embrace. When she was nauseous and, instead of walking away, he'd cared for her, she'd felt almost ready to forgive him his doubts.

How dangerous was that?

She refused to become a woman who made excuses for a man's bad behaviour. Who knew where that would end?

'Alice, there you are.' It was Viv, her boss. 'Hey, are you okay?'

Alice straightened and opened her eyes. 'Just grabbing some water. I'm running on empty today, but don't worry, I'll go and—'

Viv waved her hand. 'That's what I came to talk to you about. You look done in. I've called Chrissie and she's coming straight over. She'll be here in five so you can grab your stuff and go.'

Alice stared. She couldn't help it. Viv was a decent boss, but she'd never before noticed when Alice felt on the verge of collapse, which had been several times lately. Even when the morning sickness was at its height, fortunately only for a short time, Viv had been almost oblivious, concentrating on her booming business.

'Go on, what are you waiting for?' Viv smiled. 'I'd be hurrying if I had such a good-looking escort to take me home.'

'Escort? I don't have an escort.'

Viv's blonde eyebrows rose and her smile was positively girlish as she nudged Alice. 'Keeping him quiet, are you? That's fine, love, so long as no one else sees him. But even in that tucked-away corner he's attracting a lot of attention. If I were you I'd get my skates on.'

'But—'

'No buts.' Viv pushed her towards the cupboard that served as a locker for staff belongings. 'You don't keep a man like that waiting.' The older woman gave a slow wink. 'Especially since he persuaded your boss to let you leave early. Now, get going before he comes in here to see what's taking so long. He looks the sort to do just that.'

To Alice's astonishment she heard a rasp of approval in Viv's husky voice. Viv who, as far as she knew, cared for nothing but her café and her two cats.

Dazed, Alice relinquished her order pad, put on her jacket and shoulder bag and walked back into the café.

Instantly her gaze turned to the far side of the room from the tables she'd been serving, to the dark corner couples often chose for its intimacy.

Her eyes bulged. Her breath was a sharp indrawn hiss.

She almost backed into the kitchen, thinking of the rear exit into a deserted lane.

But it was too late. Adoni Petrakis had seen her.

He got to his feet, apparently oblivious to the stares of every woman in the room. His gaze was fixed unerringly on Alice. She felt it like the stroke of one large hand sliding across her cheek, down her throat and settling like a warm weight around her.

His face was impassive, utterly unreadable, yet her heart thrummed impossibly fast as she met that penetrating stare.

He wore a crisp white shirt, golden cufflinks at his wrists. His black hair gleamed in its perfect cut. Against the rich olive skin, his eyes were bright as the Mediterranean on a hot summer day. Or maybe that was Alice, her temperature rising as he prowled towards her with the lithe, concentrated grace of a natural predator.

She swallowed and backed a step, only to find her heels rapping the kitchen door. Another staff member was trying to come out and Alice stumbled forward.

Hard hands caught her. Hands that felt appallingly familiar. Her dreams were peppered with vignettes of those hands, and that amazing body, doing the most wondrous things to her.

'Alice.' His low voice was a wash of heat across her skin. 'We need to talk.'

'Not here.' She was conscious of the curious stares, not only from customers. The back of her neck prickled and she guessed the other staff were craning for a view of the Greek god who'd descended into their midst. He looked as out of place amongst the farmhouse chic and cream teas as a lynx in a litter of tabby cats.

'No, not here.'

Two minutes later they were on the narrow pavement and his hand was still on her elbow as he led her towards a classic vintage sports car.

Alice stopped short, her sensible shoes gripping the cobblestones. 'No. I don't want to go in your car.'

He arched one jet eyebrow, his face impassive. 'You'd rather have our discussion here?'

Other pedestrians brushed past, hurrying as the damp, fog-laden air pressed down on them. From the corner of her eye she saw faces in the bow windows of the café turned towards them. Adoni Petrakis was the biggest thing to hit town in a century or two. No doubt everyone was wondering what he was doing with someone as ordinary as Alice.

'There's no need for a discussion. We can agree to go our separate ways.' Even as she said it, Alice knew it wouldn't work. Adoni looked as immovable as the tors on Dartmoor.

He didn't bother to reply, merely raised that other winged brow in silent query.

Alice shivered and pulled her thin jacket tight round her. The weather had changed for the worse since she'd arrived this morning, taking her by surprise. Which showed how distracted she was. Normally she was far more organised.

Alice suspected the chill she felt owed little to the gloomy weather and more to nerves.

Adoni moved abruptly, swinging his jacket around her shoulders, enveloping her in cashmere warmth and a tantalising aroma of cedar wood and male skin. She shivered again and this time she feared it was with sheer sensual delight.

'You look exhausted. I'll take you home.' Then he was opening the car door and ushering her in and Alice found any inclination to object had fled. Was she so easily seduced by the promise of physical comfort? Or, worse, by this man who viewed her as a gold-digger?

Maybe exhaustion had overcome caution.

She should have realised she couldn't just walk away from him. He'd want absolute certainty the child wasn't his. Even though he clearly didn't want a child, Adoni Petrakis was too definite, too emphatic to leave anything to chance, especially the possibility he'd fathered a baby.

He got into the car, filling the space with his long body and her senses with his presence. The air seemed to crackle with an excess of energy and the fine hairs on her body stood to attention. Alice bit her lip and looked out of the window as he switched on the ignition and pulled the purring vehicle out onto the street.

Faces slid by, hurrying pedestrians. She heard the swish of tyres on rain-slicked streets and watched the buildings pass till finally, as they drew up to the kerb, her mind processed what had happened.

'You know where I live?'

He said nothing, just switched off the engine and got out. Alice was still fumbling with her seat belt when her door opened and he leaned in, unfastening the buckle. Her fingers were all thumbs.

'How do you know where I live?'

She should have waited till he stepped back to ask. Instead he leaned into the car, his face mere inches from hers, those polished eyes so close she could make out the rays of green mixed with the blue. It was like staring at some exotic sea and feeling the undertow drag her down. Beautiful but dangerous.

'I know much more about you than that, Alice.'

She watched his mouth form her name, heard the faint, delicious foreignness of it on his tongue, and felt something shudder to life deep inside. She moistened her lips with her tongue and was surprised at the flare of interest she read in his eyes.

How could that be? He thought her a lying tart. He couldn't be attracted to her.

And she should be completely indifferent. He'd insulted her in the worst possible way. Pride dictated that she feel nothing but contempt for him.

Yet it wasn't contempt trailing lazily through her body. The realisation scared her.

'What do you mean, you know more about me?' Realisation struck and with it her laggard indignation. 'You had me investigated?' Her voice rose to a ragged screech. Suddenly the close confines of the car were too claustrophobic. She put her hand to his shoulder and pushed.

Finally he withdrew and Alice stumbled out onto the pavement.

'You had me investigated.' She couldn't quite believe it. It sounded like something in a movie.

Alice shivered at the thought of paid investigators digging into her past, maybe interviewing friends and acquaintances, prying into her personal affairs. Not that there was anything to hide, but the idea made her feel grimy.

Apparently this too was the norm in his world for he shrugged those straight shoulders and spread his hands.

'Why not? Surely I have a right to know about the woman who claims to be carrying my baby.' His voice rang out in the quiet street and Alice found herself looking around, but they were alone.

Adoni had no such qualms about being overheard. 'Before that all I knew for sure was that you can't hold your liquor and that you have an interesting chat-up line.' His eyebrows lifted in that superior way of his. 'About orgasms, as I remember.'

Heat scorched her cheeks and she squirmed inside. His face was solemn as a judge but she knew he was smirking at her. 'That wasn't a chat-up line.' He made her sound like a cross between a lush and a vamp.

Or maybe just a fool for ever thinking she had anything in common with Adoni Petrakis.

'If you say so.' That casual shrug was supremely annoying, as if it didn't really matter what she thought or said.

Alice grabbed the luxuriously warm jacket engulfing her and shoved it against his chest. He was the most infuriating man she'd met. Right up there with David's nephew, Miles Dawlish. How come the only nice guys were a generation older than her?

'Thank you for the lift.' The words shot out. 'But I'm feeling unwell. I need to rest. If there's anything else, I suggest we sort it out over the phone.'

It wasn't gracious of her. She sounded downright waspish, but he deserved it. Besides, it wouldn't do him any harm to learn the world didn't dance to his tune.

Without waiting for goodbyes, Alice swung away, grabbing the key from her bag as she stalked up the cracked path to her ground-floor bedsit. Through the front door, then her own door and—

A large form crowded her from behind as she tugged the key from the lock.

'Hey, I—'

'Allow me.' Adoni's hand covered hers. Before she knew it he had her key and her door had firmly shut behind him.

Alice opened her mouth to blast his impudence, but—

'Here. You need to sit.' Quick, deft hands undid her jacket and tugged it from her shoulders as he pushed her into the room's one ancient armchair. 'A cup of tea? That's what you English have as a restorative.'

Without waiting for a response he was investigating the couple of white-painted cupboards in her tiny kitchen corner, pulling out a mug and a canister of tea bags.

'Leave it. I can do that.' Alice levered herself up, vaguely surprised at how heavy her arms and legs felt after that marathon shift. But then Adoni loomed over her again.

His brows pinched down. 'Stop fussing. I'm not going to steal the family silver, I promise.' He paused and she watched, fascinated, as he drew in a deep breath that hefted that impressive chest high, almost as if he found this situation as difficult as she did.

'I'm not leaving till we've had our chat, Alice, so you might as well make yourself comfortable and rest up. You look like hell.'

CHAPTER SEVEN

IT WAS A LIE. She looked weary but her dark blue eyes glittered bright as jewels and the spots of blush pink on her cheeks emphasised the delicacy of her features and her pale, fine-grained skin. The indignant jut of her chin drew attention to that memorable mouth, and as for her supple body…

Adoni was stunned by the wave of hunger that swept him, remembering how good they'd been together.

But he was here for answers, nothing more.

'You might as well sit, Alice. I'm not going anywhere.'

'Give me my key.' Her jaw tilted higher.

Slowly Adoni withdrew it from his pocket. He took her hand and raised it, palm up. She was trembling, ever so slightly. Sensation sparked where they touched and an answering resonance, low down in his belly, heralded the reawakening of that desire he'd never quite banished when he was with her.

He pressed the metal into her palm and closed her fingers over it, his eyes locked with hers, reading her confusion and turmoil. It was as if she didn't understand or couldn't accept the quick, hard pull of attraction between them. As if it frightened her.

He'd almost feel sorry for her, except he still wasn't sure about her. She could be as honest as she appeared or a talented liar. He resented the games she played. First that surprise announcement of a pregnancy, then a complete withdrawal.

Why?

Second thoughts about trying to con him?

A miscarriage?

Adoni's mouth settled into a grim fold at the sharp slicing sensation through his middle.

The kettle boiled and he swung round. 'Milk? Sugar?'

'Milk, please.'

He opened the tiny fridge, taking time to peruse the contents. Milk, butter, two eggs. A pot of yoghurt. And on the tiny kitchen counter a bowl with a couple of pieces of fruit. She was eating sensibly but there didn't seem to be much of anything.

Adoni frowned. The whole place, what little there was of it, was sparse. The bed pushed up against the wall was a single, the table was tiny and the wardrobe meagre. The only signs of bounty in the place were the bookshelves bulging with paperbacks and a collection of exquisitely executed botanical studies on one wall.

He opened another cupboard. Rice and dry pasta. A tin of fish. Plain cracker biscuits.

'What are you looking for? I don't take sugar.'

He swung round, his eyes roving her slender form. Had she lost weight since he'd seen her? Shouldn't she be putting on weight?

He took two paces across to her chair and passed her the mug. She took it slowly, careful not to let her fingers brush his.

Adoni found himself staring at the milky paleness of her flesh so close to his deep olive skin. That night in his bed her pink and white softness against his bronzed flesh had added to the potent eroticism of the experience. Just looking at her had wildly aroused him.

Even now…

Then he noted how she cradled the hot drink in both hands as if she were cold.

'Have you seen a doctor?'

'I told you, I saw one to confirm the pregnancy.'

'I mean since then. You've lost weight.'

She shrugged and took a tiny sip of tea, her shoulders easing down a fraction. 'The joys of morning sickness. I'm sure I'll put on weight soon enough now that seems to be passing.'

It was on the tip of Adoni's tongue to question further, till he caught himself. He needed to get back to the main agenda.

'You agreed to a paternity test. Why change your mind? If you're scared of the risk to the baby, I'm informed there's a newer non-invasive test that doesn't affect the child at all.'

She looked down at her tea, avoiding his eyes. Was that guilt he read?

Abruptly her head lifted. 'First, answer a question for me. If it *were* your child, what would you expect?'

'Expect?' Adoni frowned.

'Would you expect to be involved in his or her life? Or would you…' she waved one hand '…just offer some financial support and stay out of the picture?'

Was she serious?

The idea of his child growing up without him sent a shudder of revulsion through Adoni. The very idea tapped into the vein of unresolved emotions that eddied like a dark, poisonous current within him.

He felt his blood thicken, his pulse grow heavy, as anger simmered. 'No child of mine will grow up unacknowledged.'

He barely recognised the voice as his own. Before him Alice blinked hard and sat further back in her chair, looking at him as if she'd never seen him before.

'Every child deserves to know its parents.' Adoni paused, swallowing the bitter taste of outrage.

His child—if it *was* his child—would be not only acknowledged but loved, and accepted always.

'When I have children I will be an intrinsic part of their

lives.' Anything else was unacceptable. 'Now, answer *my* question. Why change your mind about the paternity test?'

Here was her chance to admit the child wasn't his.

Strange he didn't feel more relieved at the prospect.

After reading the short dossier on her, he'd almost come to accept that the pregnancy had been a result of their evening together. According to the investigator, Alice Trehearn had spent the last six months living here very quietly. No reports of men in her life at all.

As for the couple of years she'd lived with David Bannister in his historic property near Dartmoor, there'd been very little detail on those. The locals, when questioned, had been surprisingly unwilling to gossip about the young woman who'd shacked up with a wealthy man so many years her senior. But this baby couldn't be Bannister's. Alice was still in the early phase of pregnancy and Bannister had died too long ago.

Eyes as dark and bleak as the evening sky met Adoni's. 'I didn't follow through because once you had confirmation the baby was yours there'd be no going back.'

'Sorry?' He folded his arms over his chest. She was talking in riddles.

She pursed her lips and turned away, staring out of that small, bare window. 'I went to see you in London because I believed a man should know if he's going to be a father. But after the things you said, the accusations you made...' She shook her head and wisps of rich, glossy hair framed her face. 'I don't want my child to grow up in a world where cynicism and money are more important than trust and love. I don't want my baby growing up tainted by that.'

She turned back, her eyes locking on his, and Adoni read, not calculation as he'd expected, or even nerves, but disdain.

Alice Trehearn had judged him and found him wanting?
Preposterous!

Of course he'd been doubtful. Only a fool would take such a statement at face value, especially given his history. Adoni was no fool. He'd learned his life lessons. Caution, hard work, reliance on self rather than others, distrust of emotions and of the motives of beautiful women. All had served him well. He saw no reason to change now.

It was outrageous that she'd judge him on his initial response to her news. She couldn't seriously demur at his involvement with the child.

Adoni's brain circled her words. 'You mean it really *is* mine?'

Slowly—reluctantly, if he was any judge—she nodded.

Instantly sensation exploded in his belly. Not desire. Not anger. Excitement. Tiny ripples of it rayed out like aftershocks from an earthquake. Adoni sank onto the hard little bed opposite her, hands knotted on his thighs.

Her word was no proof. But teamed with the investigator's report...

He leaned forward and she shrank back, clutching the mug. 'You were going to let me believe the child was someone else's? Is that why you withdrew from the paternity test?' His voice bit like bullets, shattering the silence. 'Because you, in your infinite wisdom, decided I wasn't fit to be a father?'

The nerve of the woman!

Adoni had thought he'd known anger. He *had* known it. He'd dredged the depths of fury and despair in his time.

But nothing prepared him for the surge of adrenaline that pumped through his blood, hearing she'd considered having his child in secret. Or perhaps not having it at all!

To be deprived of his own flesh and blood?

He who had no family at all?

Adoni shot to his feet, paced to the window then spun to march back to the door.

Damn this tiny room. There wasn't space to breathe, much less think.

He turned and strode to the window, planting his fists on the sill and watching rain stream down the glass.

'I don't honestly know.' Her voice was muted as if it came from far away. Perhaps the thunderous pulse in his ears blocked his hearing. 'I needed time to think. What you said, the way you were in London, scared me.'

Adoni swung round, stunned. 'I would *never* hurt a woman. Or a child.'

Yet there was a brittle quality about Alice as she watched him that told him she wasn't ready to trust.

Adoni scraped a hand across his collarbone, rubbing hard. The situation was laughable. It hadn't been confirmed that the child was his. Yet there she sat staring down her nose at him as if he were the one who didn't measure up.

A maelstrom of emotions warred inside him.

Adoni, with his usual single-mindedness, ignored them. Emotions didn't help. They made you weak and you had to be strong to survive in this world.

First, he had to establish if the child was his.

Second, if it *was* his, he and Alice needed to discuss the future. There would be arrangements to make, legalities to finalise.

He glanced around the sad little bedsit. Not here. His brain wouldn't even let him picture his child here.

He breathed deep, considering his options.

If the paternity test confirmed her statement, there was one obvious path that would ensure the child's future.

Marriage. It would cement his absolute right to bring up the child as he saw fit.

Except his distaste for marriage was all but insuperable, given Chryssa's betrayal and that of his mother. Just the thought of it made his skin crawl. To be tied to a woman he barely knew, when those he'd thought he'd known absolutely had betrayed him utterly?

No, that wasn't the answer. Which meant any other arrangement they made had to be completely watertight.

As the child's mother, Alice could be an ally or a formidable opponent, with rights under the law that couldn't be ignored. It was imperative they forge an understanding. Imperative she trust him.

Instead of looking at him as if he were the Prince of Darkness himself.

Adoni forced himself to take a seat on the narrow bed, composing his features. 'I'll have my PA reschedule the paternity test for tomorrow.'

Slowly, she nodded. 'If that's what it takes to convince you.'

He told himself things would be so much simpler if the baby were someone else's. Yet already he was working on the basis Alice carried his child. His gaze dropped to her flat belly. Instantly she stiffened.

How different she was from the uninhibited, passionate woman he'd met in London. That inner fire and her cheeky attitude had attracted him. Along with that sexy, streamlined body and a mouth so delectable it made his head spin just looking at it.

Adoni spread his hands in a posture of openness. 'In the circumstances my reaction to your news was reasonable.' Alice opened her mouth but he lifted a hand, stopping her. 'I can understand why you thought it wasn't, but our experiences have been different. I know you had a close-knit family.'

'I have nothing to hide. Anything you wanted to know you could just have asked, instead of paying an investigator to pry.'

At least now she looked haughty rather than spooked.

Adoni preferred that. Alice's spirit had appealed from the start.

'Only a very little prying,' he murmured. 'I know you were born in Cornwall, only child to artistic parents, and that apparently you were all very happy together.' Until her mother died in a car crash that put her father into a wheelchair.

Adoni was tempted to probe about what came more recently, her years as David Bannister's live-in mistress. But that wasn't the point. The point was this child and securing the future Adoni wanted for it.

'You didn't have a happy childhood?' Her expression softened though she still looked wary.

'It was okay, with a workaholic father and a mother whose passion was shopping rather than family.' He shrugged. 'After she died my father married again and my stepmother was pleasant enough.'

Alice frowned. Clearly she deemed 'pleasant enough' unsatisfactory. Which was a good thing, he decided. If he was seeing the real Alice, then surely it meant she'd aim to do far better for their child.

Their child. The idea, so outlandish still, unnerved him. He, Adoni Petrakis, a father!

His actions now would set the tone for their relationship and, most importantly, his child's future.

It was time to win Alice's trust, even if it meant breaching the barricades of his reserve. For trust didn't come easily to him any more. Not since he was nineteen.

Not even Chryssa, his ex-fiancée, knew the reason he'd been disinherited. But after years of reticence Adoni no longer cared who knew this particular truth. It was no reflection on the man he was. The only one whose pride would be punctured if the revelation became public was Vassili Petrakis.

Adoni's lips curved. It would be almost fitting if Alice

Trehearn took the story to the media. But he doubted she would. He was beginning to suspect she wasn't the woman on the make he'd accused her of being.

He wanted to believe in her. That, in itself, rang warning bells. For there was no empirical evidence he was wrong about her. Why would Dawlish tell outright lies about her? Adoni didn't like the man but that didn't negate his claims. Besides, Adoni had learned enough to know extreme wealth attracted clever, unscrupulous women.

'Tell me then.' Alice put down her mug and folded her arms across her chest, presumably unaware of the way it plumped her breasts against her shirt. 'What do you think excuses your attitude to me in your office? Or, for that matter, your arrogance in having me investigated?'

Instead of being annoyed by her questions, Adoni nodded, as if acknowledging her right to ask. The hard stare, guaranteed to shrivel impertinence, had disappeared. Yet Alice was sure she read tension in the set of his jaw and the fast tic of his pulse at the base of that strong, bronzed throat.

'How about the fact that's exactly what my mother did?'

Alice frowned. 'Sorry? I don't understand.'

He leaned back on hands splayed wide on her bed. He looked far too at home on the thin mattress. Alice was distracted by the realisation she'd be haunted by the memory of him there when she tried to sleep later.

He'd stalked into her home and completely filled it with his presence. Even the air smelled different, spiced with an exotic tang that lingered in the nostrils, teasing with the hint of warm male skin and testosterone.

Adoni shrugged, the movement dragging her attention to those powerful shoulders then back to that lean, sculpted face. 'My mother got pregnant. She then went to a very rich man, the sort of man who could provide for her and her baby multiple times over, and seduced him, persuaded him the baby was his. He married her and brought up the baby, believing it was his.'

Alice felt her mouth sag in astonishment. She didn't know what she'd expected but it wasn't this. It sounded so callous, so ruthless. So scheming.

That was why he'd accused her of being a *femme fatale* who lived off men? Because his own mother—?

'For years no one knew the truth. Till one day the old man had a hospital procedure. In the process he discovered from his blood type that his eldest son couldn't possibly be his son.'

Alice's eyes felt round as saucers. Adoni was talking about himself, not a sibling. She knew from her recent research that he was the eldest son in the family, his younger half-siblings being around a decade younger.

She tried and failed to imagine what it would be like, having that bombshell dropped on you. To discover everything you knew about yourself and your family was a lie.

'Your mother? Did she explain?'

Adoni shook his head. 'We only discovered the truth when I was nineteen. My mother was dead by then and no, she never told me the truth. So, you see, all we know for sure is Vassili Petrakis *isn't* my father. She lied to us both and took my real father's identity to the grave. I have no idea whose bastard I am. It's too late to revisit history and try to discover who she slept with.'

Adoni's thin lips stretched up in a smile that looked as affable as a hangman's noose. 'In the circumstances, I think it quite reasonable I'm wary of a woman I barely know telling me I'm about to become a father.'

Alice's breath was an indrawn hiss. Of course he was wary. Her revelation must have seemed like history repeating itself or, judging from his eyes, like blows to an unhealed bruise. For, despite the adamantine strength of his jaw and the assured tilt of his head, Alice saw a flash of something else in his expression. Something akin to pain. It was gone in a second and she'd never have noticed it except she'd seen its echo in the mirror from time to time when her resilience cracked and grief welled.

Looking at Adoni now, she read only assurance. No hint of distress.

'I'm so sorry,' she whispered. 'I don't know what to say.'

He shrugged. 'Nothing. It was all a long time ago.'

'But to do that to you, and your father...' She shook her head. 'It must have been...'

'It's water under the bridge.' Adoni slashed the air with a dismissive gesture. 'At the time I thought it vital I discover who fathered and abandoned me. But I realised it was a waste of energy. My identity isn't about my parents. It's about what I make of my life. Who I've become.'

He paused, and Alice saw he was watching her absorb his words. Yet he wasn't looking for sympathy. The stern set of his lips and the arrogant tilt of his head reminded her he was no longer the bereft teenager he must once have been. This was a powerful man in control of his life and his world.

Until you sashayed in and told him he was going to be a father.

Was that why he'd been so furious? Because this was something he had no control over?

Or was it that the situation cut too close to the bone? Because it required him to overcome his prejudice and trust her.

'I'm not like your mother, Adoni. I didn't plan this.' Surely he realised that? He'd seduced *her.*

He regarded her without comment and Alice felt a little twist of distress as she realised that, given his history, he couldn't possibly take her word for that. He couldn't trust her.

'I'll take the paternity test tomorrow.'

He nodded, abruptly. '*Efharisto.* Thank you.'

Adoni took one of her hands in his. His were large and capable. There was a dusting of silky black hair across his olive skin and Alice had sudden, intimate recall of his naked body, the same lovely burnished colour all over. Heat bloomed and she swallowed hard.

'I may have reacted badly, Alice, but don't judge me on that.' Absently he stroked her thumb. 'Just as I won't judge you on the fact you got drunk and put the hard word on a total stranger.'

She stiffened, yanking her hand back, but he merely tightened his grip. 'I didn't—'

'Shh. That doesn't matter.' This time he stroked his thumb across her palm and she shuddered. To her horror she realised it wasn't indignation rippling through her, but arousal. 'What matters is the baby.'

'Exactly. The baby.' Alice nodded, her head moving jerkily as if pulled by a string. It was difficult concentrating on his words when her body responded so flagrantly.

Her *pregnant* body. Surely sexual arousal should dim with pregnancy, shouldn't it? She knew so little about this stuff!

Looking into those mesmerising eyes, feeling the evocative tug of his deep voice right at her very core, Alice didn't *feel* pregnant. She felt hot and bothered, tense and aware and…interested.

'There's no need to worry, Alice.' Did he misread her distraction? She was just giving thanks that he'd misconstrued her reaction for nerves when he continued.

'If the child is mine I'll be there every step of the way.' His gaze dropped to her abdomen in a provocative, assessing stare.

Just as before, Alice felt a shudder of elemental response tear through her. It started as embarrassment but that was eclipsed by a jagged gouge of physical arousal and a bone-deep thrill of power.

Because there was something like possessiveness in his unwavering gaze and warm grasp. As if, despite himself, he too approved and wanted. Not just the baby, but *her*.

Pride, logic and modern morals told her she should require far more from a man than *want*. But in her state of heightened awareness, Alice had never known anything as powerful as the urge to reach out and test the boundaries in the most primitive way possible. To push a little and rediscover the heady sense of oneness she'd discovered with Adoni, the sheer carnal pleasure of melding with his beautiful body.

He leaned closer, his fresh breath soft on her cheeks. 'If this child is my flesh and blood, my *only* flesh and blood, I'd never abandon it. I'll do whatever it takes to keep and care for it. To guide and protect it. I'll be part of its life every day.'

Alice met his unwavering gaze as his words penetrated. Abruptly that swell of arousal faded.

By admitting the baby was his she'd removed the safety net she'd craved—time to consider whether she really wanted Adoni Petrakis and his sophisticated, cynical world to impinge on her baby's life, and hers.

The dynamic between them had shifted irrevocably.

Adoni had money, prestige and authority. He was her baby's father and, it was now clear, he had every intention of being a hands-on father.

How far would he go to ensure that?

She knew nothing about the legalities. She told herself firmly that there was no way he could have the baby taken from her so he got sole custody. Was there?

Another tremor racked her, yet this time it wasn't the heated rush of excitement but the chill cascade of fear.

CHAPTER EIGHT

'THE CHILD IS MINE? You're absolutely sure?' Adoni planted a hand on the gleaming desktop, the phone clamped to his ear.

'Yes. It's yours.' The voice kept talking about DNA and percentages but Adoni didn't take the words in. 'Yes' was all he needed.

His heart hit an unfamiliar rhythm. Quick and—could it be—triumphant?

It didn't seem possible. His life was meticulously planned. An unexpected child hadn't been in his schedule.

That changed now. Everything changed now.

He'd thought he'd prepared himself for the possibility that Alice carried his child. But nothing could have prepared him for the deeply visceral response welling in his taut body.

His child.

His flesh and blood.

His family.

The words thrummed with each pulse of blood in his arteries. They carved themselves into his bones and shuddered through his cramped lungs.

'Thank you—' he cut across the speaker '—and yes, I want the report in writing.'

Adoni hung up and stared across his office at the view of central London, the sky a mix of pale blue and grey cloud that still felt alien, even after years using this country as his base.

Suddenly, unaccountably, he found himself longing for the endless bright skies of his childhood summers in Greece. The scent of wild herbs crushed underfoot, the salt tang of the sea, sharp and beckoning as he clambered down the track to the coast. The freedom to run wild whenever they left Athens for their country estate.

Abruptly Adoni shoved his chair back and strode to the window.

Was that what he wanted for this baby?

He had a country retreat there, in the final stages of completion. But it was a retreat, not a permanent home. His business was in the city.

Yet even as he thought it, Adoni acknowledged he could run his business from wherever he wanted.

What came first was his child—what was best for it. One thing was certain. His child wouldn't live in a dismal bedsit. It would have the best of care, as of now.

His baby would be protected and nurtured. Loved as Adoni had never been, with his mother intent on pleasure and his supposed father engrossed in money-making.

Adoni picked up his phone.

'Greece? You can't be serious!'

'It's an excellent idea.'

Alice digested the cool certainty in Adoni's voice and stifled a bubble of hysteria.

Her? Go to Greece?

She took a slow breath, then another. She stood hunched in the overhang of a shop roof, sheltering from the persistent rain that had already soaked the bottom of her trousers as she walked to work.

She'd got a passport years ago but never had a chance to use it. Never gone further than London.

An image she'd once seen filled her mind. Brightly coloured boats bobbing in the crystal waters of a sun-drenched harbour. In the foreground, under the shade of a spreading tree, were tables and rush-bottomed chairs of vibrant blue. The elegant townhouses crammed around the cove were a wash of pastel colours that invited you to forget your cares and drink in the scene.

A cold, fat drop of rain hit her cheek and slithered down her neck. Alice rubbed her chilled flesh.

'I can't drop everything and go to Greece. I have a job and—'

'That's no problem.'

The soft burr of Adoni's deep voice made her shiver, but not from cold. She didn't even like him, did she? Yet she responded to him every time. As if they shared some secret link, some affinity. 'Sorry? I missed that.'

'I spoke to your employer.'

'You did *what*?' Her voice rose and a woman bustling down the narrow pavement gave her a wide berth.

'I explained you needed rest to regain your strength—'

'You told her I was pregnant?' Alice's temper soared. Usually she was slow to anger, her emotions under control.

Adoni Petrakis, however, had a knack for igniting her fuse.

'Of course not. I just mentioned I was concerned for your health.'

'That isn't something you should discuss with my boss.' Severely, Alice repressed the idea of a holiday. It was a luxury she couldn't afford. 'If I want to ask for leave *I'll* do it. But I can't. I haven't been there long enough and it's busy—'

'But you can.'

'Pardon?' Alice drew her collar closer and scowled into the rain that had graduated from a miserable drizzle to solid sheets of icy water.

'She is happy for you to go.'

Alice frowned. It sounded unlikely. They were rushed off their feet. One waitress was off with a broken leg and another on compassionate leave to care for her sick mother.

'I can't leave my job.' Because chances were there'd be no job to return to.

'Are you always this obstinate?'

'Are you always such a bulldozer?'

His laugh, a rich, baritone chuckle, was like liquid chocolate, warming her chilled bones. 'Touché.' He paused. 'If it's the income you're thinking of, I'll cover your expenses while you're away. And your rent.'

Was the man a mind-reader?

Yet it wasn't just the money; it was the way he'd dealt direct with Viv, interfering outrageously now he was sure Alice carried his child.

She tried to whip up fury but instead sagged back against the wall of the shop.

Adoni was right. The long hours she was working, taking extra shifts in the scramble to save as much as she could, were getting too much.

Nor could she really blame him for needing proof of paternity. They were strangers. Despite the quickening she felt whenever he came close, or like now, when his treacle-rich voice was soft in her ear.

'Think of the baby,' he purred. 'It needs you to be healthy and well-rested.'

'Lots of women work during pregnancy.' If he tried to make her feel guilty...

'Of course, but I'm sure most would appreciate some extra rest. Besides, we have decisions to make for the future. Wouldn't you rather do that when you're refreshed and on vacation?'

Alice's nerves twitched at the determination she heard on the word *decisions*. As if he had very definite views on their child's future and intended to have his say.

I'll be there every step of the way.

I'll be part of its life every day.

'I can't talk now. I'm late.' She lifted her head and more windblown drops spattered her cheeks.

'We *do* need to talk. To work out the details.'

It was on the tip of her tongue to say they'd got this far without working out any details. But he was right. She just wished she didn't feel so hemmed in, by him and the pregnancy.

'I'll call you later, Adoni.'

But switching off her phone didn't banish his words. Especially when she arrived at the café to find Viv talking about *when* she went to Greece with that delectable man. How *nice* he'd been. How *considerate*. He'd even arranged an interview with someone from his London hotel who wanted to relocate to the country. Viv was excited about the new waitress with her experience in a top London hotel but adamant there'd be a job for Alice on her return.

Then Alice's landlord confirmed that next month's rent had already been paid.

In the end Alice found, to her chagrin, she had no excuses left.

She was going to Greece with the father of her unborn child. The only man who'd tempted her into letting go and living for the moment. The one man who still tempted her in ways she refused to think about.

Typically, Alice refused to make things easy for him. Any other woman would leap at the idea of lounging in luxury by the Aegean. Not Alice.

Because she was determined to prove she wasn't a gold-digger? Or because she genuinely had other priorities? What could they be?

Adoni set his jaw as he left the elegant Georgian mansion he'd just inspected and followed a path through the woods that he'd been assured led to a cluster of estate houses.

He'd planned to be in Greece by now. Instead he was in

rural England, collecting Alice from an engagement she'd insisted she couldn't miss. She'd promised to catch the train to London when it was over, but Adoni had no intention of kicking his heels at the airport, perhaps receiving a message that she'd been delayed.

He'd rearranged his schedule to take another look at the property he planned to purchase. The very property where Alice had lived with David Bannister. The property Bannister's nephew, Miles Dawlish, had approached Adoni about buying.

The manor house was perfect for the exclusive country hotel retreat Adoni envisaged. As for Dawlish's plans to get the adjoining swathe of land rezoned for housing, that didn't bother Adoni. The manor would be secure in its landscaped valley, surrounded by woods on three sides and the moor behind it. Besides, his contacts advised the rezoning application was doomed to fail.

Dawlish had done Adoni a favour, bringing the place to his attention. The man was greedy, his asking price inflated; he was desperate for a quick sale to cover escalating gambling debts. The sale would proceed on Adoni's terms, not Dawlish's. The sting in the tale was that, while the sale would make Dawlish solvent again, the man would have to change his lifestyle and work for a living if he wanted to keep his head above water.

As for Dawlish's warning about Alice being a conniving slut—

Adoni frowned. Had Dawlish feared she'd seduce David Bannister into leaving more of his personal funds to her? That she'd somehow break the inheritance? Had that tainted his view of her?

Yet Alice had openly lived here, with a man old enough to be her father, supported by him. Adoni had prowled the vast, elegant house with the agent, assuring himself it would suit his purposes. Yet all the time he'd thought of

Alice there with her much older lover. Seen them sprawled across the vast four-poster bed in the master suite. Envisaged Alice, her moonlight-pale skin bare as she stretched over the shining ebony of the grand piano in one of the salons, her ripe mouth curled in an inviting smile.

His pace quickened as he passed a dappled glade of bluebells, their sweet scent at odds with the acid in his throat.

She'd lied about her sexual experience. She must have. She'd been thoroughly debauched by the time she reached Adoni's bed.

Debauched? He sounded like someone from another century, full of double standards. He didn't give a damn how many men she'd been with. All that mattered was securing the child she carried. *His* child.

His thoughts were an unsatisfactory whirl of conjecture when he stepped out of the woods and discovered a cluster of picturesque cottages. They lined a narrow lane, half of them thatched and white-washed and the other half stonebuilt and equally attractive with quaint windows and roses around the doors.

Adoni had expected a ramshackle collection, ready for the bulldozers that would clear the farmland beyond if Dawlish's plans proceeded. Instead, they appeared in excellent condition.

Laughter drew his attention, husky and low-pitched. The skin at his nape pinched in anticipation.

Alice. His belly tightened and so did his groin at the memory of that throaty laugh in his bed that memorable night. Of the caress of her sweet breath on his bare skin and the taste of her luscious mouth.

Adoni quickened his step and saw her outside a cottage with two men, one grey-haired and smiling down at her. The other, with an unkempt shock of white hair, had his arm around her shoulders.

Something dark and chill engulfed Adoni.

Maybe she was genuinely attracted to old men. The idea made Adoni grimace.

Or perhaps they were simply easier to dupe, eager for a pretty young woman's company.

He strode closer and the trio turned.

'Adoni.' Alice sounded breathless and her chest rose quickly as if in agitation. In her short-sleeved floral dress she looked fresh, young and innocent. Then her smile solidified. Adoni took in her flushed cheeks and the glitter of her eyes and thought he'd never seen her look lovelier.

The knowledge didn't improve his mood.

The shaggy-haired man at her side narrowed his eyes under tangled white eyebrows. 'I hear you're taking Alice to Greece.' His deep voice boomed like the sea thundering into a cave. 'I expect you to look after her.'

'Jasper!' She turned, breaking his hold and frowning.

'I am and I will.' Adoni held his gaze. 'She'll be better off with me than working herself to exhaustion.'

The older man stared a moment longer, then nodded abruptly. 'That's what she said.' He turned to Alice. 'But don't forget, there's always a place for you here. Maureen and I have missed you.'

Alice's smile this time was wide and genuine. 'Maybe Maureen has, though how you'd fit another person in your cottage I'm not sure. And I know you, Jasper. You've probably been so busy in the studio you don't even know what month it is.'

She turned to Adoni. 'Let me introduce you. Adoni, this is Jasper Hyde, an old friend of my family, and—' she gestured to the other man, silent beside them '—Felix Christow, down from London for the day. Felix, Jasper, this is Adoni Petrakis.'

Adoni shook hands, amused by Hyde's punishing grip, as if he sought to deter Adoni with a show of strength.

'A family friend?' Adoni queried.

'Yes.' It was Alice who answered. 'My father and I moved into the end cottage after...' she paused '...when I was twelve. Jasper and Maureen were our neighbours. They looked after us.'

'No more than you did for us, Missy, these last years when David got sick.'

'David?' The name shot out. Were they talking of her ex-lover?

'David Bannister,' Jasper said. 'Our friend and landlord. He lived in the big house I hear you're planning to buy. He created the artists' colony here with his wife, years ago. A good man.' He shook his head. 'Unlike his obnoxious nephew.'

The third member of their party spoke up. 'Well, it's time I headed back to London. Thank you for your help, Alice, Jasper.' He shook hands with each in turn. 'I'll send invitations to the opening.'

'I'll look forward to it.' Did Adoni imagine it or did Alice's eyes glow more brightly?

'Nice to meet you, Mr Petrakis. Perhaps I'll see you at the opening too.'

As his car drew away Adoni turned to Alice. 'Opening?'

'Felix is curating an art exhibition in London of my mother's work.' She sounded proud and excited. 'I promised to meet him to provide some background information for the exhibition.'

Jasper Hyde scowled. 'He doesn't even know? Yet you're haring off to Greece with him?' The old man's disapproval showed in his mottled features.

Alice shrugged, obviously uncomfortable. 'It's not like that. We're not...'

Jasper raised abundant white eyebrows and Adoni was fascinated to see colour wash Alice's cheeks. He had no idea what was going on, but if he didn't know better he'd believe Alice was nervous about telling the old man exactly what linked them. Sex and an unborn baby.

A strange attitude for a woman who'd openly lived with her previous lover on this estate.

'It's time we left,' Alice said quickly. 'It's a long way to London. Give Maureen a hug for me and—'

'Don't forget that jam she made. I'll never hear the end of it if you go without it.'

Alice nodded and, with one wary look at Adoni, hurried towards the back of the cottage.

She was barely out of sight when the other man spoke. 'I expect to see Alice come home looking much less peaky.' He swivelled and Adoni was surprised at the force of his piercing gaze. 'You haven't done a good job looking after her so far, for all your money.' His gaze skated over Adoni's tailored clothes with disapproval. 'She's not entirely friendless. If you hurt her—'

Adoni lifted his hand, palm outward. 'I have no intention of hurting her.' He was torn between annoyance at the man's presumption and curiosity that Alice had such a vehement champion. 'If I'd had my way she'd have been on vacation a week ago.'

'Ah,' Jasper said. 'She always could dig her heels in. Just as well, or she'd never have been able to manage this place.'

Adoni frowned. 'Manage *this* place? The estate?'

The old man nodded. 'Ridiculous, isn't it? People thought David mad to hand over the reins to a slip of a girl. But she was a quick learner and she knew the place like the back of her hand. She loves it. Unlike that bumptious nephew of David's. He'd run it into the ground.'

'You're telling me Alice Trehearn managed this whole estate?' It wasn't possible, surely. In addition to the manor house, which was in pristine condition, there were farms and woodlands, this cluster of cottages, all by the look of them in fine order, and—

'She did.' The old man's smile faded. 'Not that I approve of what David did, mind you. Say what you will, it was selfish of him burdening her. But who could blame him?'

Adoni was torn between curiosity and a deep reluctance to hear details of her life with her sugar daddy.

'Here we are.' Alice appeared, brandishing a jar of jam, surveying them speculatively.

Adoni's mind raced. Was she a gold-digger with a talent for good management? Jasper Hyde didn't seem the sort to be seduced by a pretty face yet he was protective of Alice. Clearly too she'd left the estate in good condition, though her own financial circumstances were dismal.

Was her poverty real, or a ploy for sympathy?

Not having answers drove Adoni crazy.

He stirred from his reverie as Alice kissed Jasper on the cheek, promising to send photos of Greece. Jasper growled something about being careful, then Alice and Adoni turned back to the path through the woods.

'What were you and Jasper talking about?' Her voice was high, almost breathless.

'You.' Adoni saw her start.

'What about me?'

He was tempted to string her along, sure he'd discover more about her if she was on edge. But he preferred the truth. 'About you running the estate. Why didn't you mention it?' His investigators had neglected to add that, though they had referred to her having access to Bannister's accounts. Adoni had taken that as proof of her avaricious ways.

'Why should I? It's not relevant.'

Adoni disagreed. Anything about her character was relevant while he tried to determine who the mother of his child was.

Especially when he responded to her more than was desirable. Like now as she marched beside him, her narrow jaw set and a frown knotting her brow. They passed through the perfumed dell and Adoni wanted to pull her close, discover if her hair still smelled of orange blossom and if her skin was as satiny as he recalled. If she'd sigh a welcome as he took her voluptuous mouth. How would she respond if he powered her down into the swathe of bluebells and—?

'You let me think you were just David Bannister's lover.'

Instantly her full lips pinched and her nostrils flared in distaste. 'I did no such thing! *You* came to that conclusion.' She paused, her breathing fast and shallow. 'I don't need to explain my past. Besides, you wouldn't believe the truth if it rose up and bit you.'

Adoni looked into bruised blue eyes and felt his chest constrict. 'You could try me.'

'Could I, indeed? That wasn't what you said in London.' Her hands jammed onto her hips and her chin tilted. 'Besides, you've set yourself up as some sort of judge! It's none of your business.'

She whirled round, her skirt belling around shapely legs, and stalked down the path.

Adoni watched her go, grumpy yet tantalisingly sensual as she strode away. Dappled sunlight picked out the dark auburn in her hair and the natural sway of her hips ignited a pulse of unwilling, inevitable awareness.

She was the mother of his unborn child.

Adoni was stuck with her. He needed to know her, understand her. For his own sake.

Because he wanted her still. Again.

And he intended to have her, on his terms.

But he refused to be duped again.

CHAPTER NINE

'WHAT ARE THOSE THINGS?' Alice peered from the helicopter at the square towers rising from the tiny village below.

She'd got over her initial nerves about flying in the machine soon after they left Athens. Now she was storing impressions of the country she'd only seen on film. She'd expected Greece to be all white beaches and endless blue skies, but there was much more.

Adoni turned, his eyes locking on hers, making her skin tingle. 'Houses.'

'Houses? They don't look like it.' They were like windmills without the sails, or watchtowers.

An expression she couldn't decipher played around his mouth. 'Welcome to the Mani. It's a peninsula at the southern end of mainland Greece. We do things differently here.' The pilot said something in Greek and Adoni laughed.

'Why do they have towers?'

'Because the locals are known for holding grudges. In the old days their feuds sometimes lasted years. They were renowned as proud fighters. Each tower—' he waved a hand '—was once the secure part of the house. The windows are small so defenders could shoot at their neighbours.'

Alice shivered. 'It sounds grim.'

He smiled. 'We don't generally shoot these days.'

'You're from here?' Alice gazed at the barren mountains whose folds plunged into the sea. Some seemed almost bare and others were carved into narrow terraces. It looked wild and windswept yet majestic. Here and there more fertile areas showed green.

They passed another village, a cluster of stone houses and square towers.

'Yes, I'm a Maniot. I was born in Athens but my...father's family is from here.' Alice heard repressed emotion on the word *father* and winced inwardly, remembering what Adoni had said about his parents. He didn't know who his biological father was. 'This is where we came for feast days and holidays. It's where I've built my own retreat.'

As if on cue the helicopter swooped low. Ahead was a cove, its waters aquamarine. A cluster of buildings sheltered at its centre and small boats floated on the crystal sea. On the far side was a headland with a tumble of houses and a now familiar tower.

But it was the building on the nearest headland that caught her breath. Built of local stone, it resembled a traditional tower. But there the resemblance ended. This tower had windows so large she saw right through to the other side. And below it on ground level sprawled a stone and glass building that extended to hang suspended over the steep slope to the sea. The result was unique, daring but elegant, yet part of the landscape.

'That's your house?' Alice turned to Adoni as the chopper came in to land. She hadn't expected this. His grand London hotel and David's estate in Devon that he was negotiating to buy were both traditional.

'It is.' His eyes met hers but she had no idea what was going through his mind.

'It's...amazing. Truly original.'

Those winged eyebrows soared. 'I'm glad you like it. I didn't know you had an interest in architecture.' Was that approval in his expression? Warmth?

Alice's breath thickened, her skin tingling as it too often did around Adoni. Even when she thought she might hate him for his high-handed ways and his determination to think the worst of her, she couldn't quite kick that fillip of excitement when she got close to him. When he looked at her like *that*.

Deliberately Alice turned to watch as the pilot landed on the helipad behind the house.

'There's a lot we don't know about one another.'

Those words proved truer than she'd realised.

First there was the welcoming committee. Not just employees, though there'd been some of those and Alice noted that Adoni treated them like everyone else—with a smile. There were also neighbours who came up from the village to welcome him.

'This is the first time I've visited since the house was finished,' he told her. 'They're curious to see it.'

But it was more than curiosity Alice read in their smiles. It was genuine welcome.

Adoni had urged her to go and rest, saying there was no need for her to stay if she was tired, but she wouldn't have missed the impromptu party for anything.

It wasn't how she'd pictured a billionaire's housewarming.

There was no couture fashion though Adoni, in snugly tailored black trousers and a green shirt that almost matched his eyes, looked like a model for an upmarket magazine.

There were no socialites, but, judging by the callused hands she shook again and again, people who worked hard. There were old folk in dark colours, their faces weathered, and younger ones who were happy to practise English. Children raced across the terrace, laughing, making Alice smile.

She'd been nervous coming here, worrying that she handed Adoni too much power, being in his territory for the discussion about the baby. But as the afternoon drew into evening Alice felt more relaxed than she had in months.

Home cooking scented the air as people arrived with

platters and a spit roast was set up. Instruments appeared and music, unfamiliar yet enticing, began in competition with the babble of people having a good time.

'How are you bearing up?' That dark voice feathered her ear as long fingers gripped her elbow. Instantly her insides did that funny roll and flip as sensation shot from Adoni's touch to the apex of her thighs.

Alice frowned at the fruit juice in her hand. She couldn't even blame alcohol for that response.

Throughout the evening Adoni had kept checking on her. She'd look up to find his eyes on her. Inevitably her thoughts would tangle and she'd lose track of the conversation.

'What's wrong?' Concern tinged his voice. 'Are you feeling ill?'

Alice made herself meet his gaze. There it was again, that whump of sensation when she got too close to Adoni.

It was hard, staring up into that solicitous expression, remembering that he thought her a *femme fatale* who preyed on men.

She swallowed a bubble of laughter. Anything further from the truth she couldn't imagine.

'I can rest later. I'm enjoying myself. Everyone is so friendly.'

He shrugged. 'It's a small community.'

But it wasn't just that. Alice had already heard from several people how Adoni had helped out when a fishing boat had been destroyed in a winter storm. How he'd found work for someone else. How he'd ensured there was a better medical service for the area.

Adoni Petrakis, international tycoon and bane of her life, was respected and liked.

'You're popular,' she murmured and was surprised at how easily she accepted it. Despite the atrocious way he'd behaved when she'd told him about the pregnancy, despite his take-control attitude, Alice grew convinced that Adoni Petrakis was a decent guy, most of the time.

Those wide shoulders lifted. 'They know me. I've been coming here since I was born.'

'The locals back home know Miles Dawlish but they don't welcome him like this.'

As soon as the words slipped out Alice knew she'd said the wrong thing. Adoni's forehead scrunched up in a furrow of displeasure. He dropped her arm as if stung. Alice was sure he'd got the outrageous story about her being David's lover from Miles. The guy was poison and he judged by his own standards. Miles couldn't believe she hadn't been interested in David's money, grabbing what she could for herself. Clearly, he believed any friendship between a man and a woman must be based on sex. He knew nothing of respect, caring or obligation.

The reminder was a sluice of icy water down Alice's back.

'You're wanted.' She nodded to a man approaching from a cleared space on the wide terrace. He said something in Greek, a grin splitting his face. Around them clapping started in time with the music.

Adoni turned, paused briefly, then with a nod left her. He joined the older man at the centre of the terrace. Another joined them, then another.

'You like dancing?' It was a woman she'd spoken with earlier.

'I don't know. I've never really tried.' There hadn't even been a dance at the wedding, since her groomsman partner had been too drunk. Before that she'd been too busy for dances.

'Really? We'll fix that, later. But first watch. You'll enjoy.'

And she did. The music, slow at first, had a rhythm that caught the blood. It was the perfect vehicle for the men to show off. For that was what the dance seemed all about. They formed a line, moving slowly in time with the tune.

At their head the leader, sometimes Adoni, sometimes another, would leap, drop and spin with a measured grace and a rampant athleticism that was all the more impressive for being carefully controlled.

Alice found her gaze following Adoni even when he wasn't in the lead. Watching the rhythmic sway of his body, the proud, upright posture, the deliberate, steady movement of his feet. She recalled his talk of the tough, warlike people who'd carved a life for themselves out of this beautiful, harsh environment.

Swallowing hard, she followed the twist and dip of his broad, straight shoulders, the arrogant angle of his jaw, the strength and potent masculinity in those long legs with their muscled thighs.

As if sensing her regard, Adoni turned, eyes locking with hers.

Something passed between them, as quick and devastating as an earthquake. It rumbled up from the soles of her feet, through her belly where, amazingly, their baby lay cradled, to her chest. It interfered with the beat of her heart, making it quicken and jolt.

Still Adoni held her gaze. From this distance, in the failing light, his eyes looked like dark velvet. Her attention dropped to his mouth and the tremor intensified.

He felt it too. She could tell. It was there in the cut glass angle of his cheekbone where the skin pulled too tight. In the jut of his jaw and the flare of his nostrils.

The heat eddying in Alice's belly flared into a conflagration that roared and swirled, blotting out the music, singeing her nerve endings.

'Excuse me,' she murmured to the woman beside her and swung away.

Adoni farewelled the last of his neighbours. One final pat on the back, a promise to catch up over a game of *tavli* and a glass of ouzo, and he stood in the moonlight, watching the stragglers head down the road.

He was glad of the dim light, for their welcome had moved him. He hadn't lived here for years, though he'd been back often lately, keeping an eye on building progress. Yet the whole community had come out to welcome him.

It was more than he'd got from the people he'd been brought up to think of as family.

He glanced at the large home on the opposite headland. At this late hour there were no lights on. The owner was probably asleep. He hadn't come to the party like everyone else within a thirty-minute radius.

But then Vassili Petrakis hadn't spoken to him since the day he'd kicked Adoni out of his house. The day he'd told him he had no right to the Petrakis name or fortune.

The name Adoni had kept, for he had no other. The lack of fortune had been a blessing in disguise, spurring him to succeed on his own. His only real regret was never seeing the boys he'd grown up thinking of as brothers. They were old enough now to decide if they wanted to see him, but Adoni wouldn't go behind the old man's back to initiate the connection.

Mouth firming, Adoni swung round, surveying his new house. It was innovative, modern, yet with a nod to local traditions.

Vassili probably hated it. Just as he hated Adoni, the living proof his first wife had played him for a fool.

Good. Adoni hoped the old man got gut-ache every time he looked across the bay.

He breathed deep, inhaling the scents of sea salt, wild herbs and something that surely was the very bones of the earth, unique to this place. Instantly he felt calmer. Though he'd lived most of his early years in the city, this stretch of coast was the home of his heart.

What did Alice think of it? She'd seemed fascinated by the scenery and openly admiring of the house.

Adoni's brow scrunched. Did it matter what she thought? She was only here while they sorted out their child's future. And till he was sure she was strong enough to look after herself.

Though now he thought about it, he didn't like the idea of her returning to that cramped bedsit and long hours at the café. Not while she carried his child.

He'd wanted to go after her this evening when she'd left the party. But his housekeeper had reported Alice had decided to turn in.

Their conversation could wait till tomorrow. But something, whether being back in Greece, in the place that felt like home, or bringing Alice into his private space, left him unsettled.

He stalked through to the master suite that had been finished in his absence. Not bothering to turn on the light, he crossed the vast space, passing the comfortable bed, the newly acquired artwork on the opposite wall and the couple of lounge chairs grouped by the window. The enormous glass door slid silently open and he stepped out onto the cantilevered deck suspended above the bluff.

Another deep breath, another draught of clear air that tasted of the earth and the sea. He didn't know why he felt so restless.

A sound made him whirl.

At the far end of the balcony was a pale glimmer. A glimmer that resolved itself into long, slender legs and some short, pale garment as Alice unfolded herself from a chair.

It seemed his housekeeper had put her in the one guest room near his own, assuming Alice was his lover.

It was an understandable assumption. Yet Adoni cursed under his breath as he took in Alice's bare arms and legs, the cloud of dark hair around her shoulders. Her nightdress, held up by narrow ribbon straps, ended high on her thighs.

As if reading his thoughts, she tugged at the hem, curving her shoulders down as if trying to find another few centimetres of cloth to cover her legs.

Her shapely, inviting legs. Silky too—he remembered the feel of them under his palm, their softness as he'd lifted her thighs around his hips as he thrust into her.

Adoni swallowed, surprised how difficult that simple act was. His throat was tight and his tongue thick. In his belly energy whooshed like a match igniting a gas oven. Sure enough, his temperature rocketed as he took in the graceful lines of her limbs and her breasts pushing against her short nightgown.

She crossed her arms as if cold and the movement hoisted the hemline even higher. Did she wear panties or was she naked beneath the flimsy fabric?

His pulse chugged hard around his body, thrumming at his temple as all the urges he'd suppressed around Alice roared back into life. The need to touch, taste, inhale the sweet fragrance of her skin. To test again the lush softness of her feminine core with the hardness rearing even now between his thighs.

Could she see his arousal? Was that why her breasts rose and fell so jerkily?

'What are you doing here?' She sounded out of breath, genuinely surprised. As if she hadn't been waiting for him.

Once again Adoni was torn between believing she was the woman she purported to be and the idea she connived at his undoing, as Dawlish warned. Just as his mother had fooled Vassili Petrakis.

Yet more and more he harboured doubts about that scenario. And there was no doubt Alice carried his child.

The idea, which should direct his mind to legalities, instead fired his rampant libido.

His gaze dropped to the fabric covering her abdomen. There was something primal and sexy about the notion Alice was pregnant with his baby. That her svelte body grew ripe with his seed.

Heat flashed, searing away all thoughts except the need he'd repressed too long. The need to touch her. To relive the bliss he'd found in her body. Memories of that night had haunted him ever since, and not merely because of the pregnancy.

'It's my house, remember?' His voice was tight and low, grinding past cramped vocal cords. 'I came to look at the view.' And hadn't he got an eyeful? He couldn't rip his gaze away. 'I thought you'd be in bed.'

He imagined her sprawled there, beneath him, as responsive and delectable as she'd been in London.

Adoni took a step forward, then another.

Part of his brain screamed that he'd be crazy to get involved with a woman he didn't trust. But he didn't care.

Through all the emotional tangle of discovering he was going to be a father one thing had remained implacably certain—that Alice triggered something more intense, more primitively needy than he'd ever felt. Right now, right here, he gave up fighting it.

'I had trouble sleeping.'

Adoni moved, close enough to see how she swallowed, her face lifting towards his.

'Adoni?' Her voice was sharp but he was damned if he heard fear. It was something else. Something, if he wasn't mistaken, remarkably close to the urgency that swept him.

Alice stepped back, straight into a chair. It scraped across the balcony, loud in the humming silence.

Abruptly she dropped her arms to her sides, flexing her fingers. 'What do you want, Adoni? It's too late to discuss—'

'Who said anything about talking?'

Her breath hissed. 'I don't understand.' Her head jerked higher, the line of her jaw sharp in the moonlight. 'You brought me to Greece to discuss our baby's future. Of course we're going to talk.'

Adoni lifted his hand to stroke the soft wave of dark hair cascading over her shoulder. It felt like rippling satin. Slowly he lifted her hair to his face, bending so he could inhale the evocative scent of orange blossom.

Instantly his body was in lockdown, each muscle and tendon tense with the force required not to haul her up and plunder her mouth—and more.

'We'll talk, tomorrow.' The words grated out. 'But now it's not words I want. It's you. *Se thelo.*'

CHAPTER TEN

ALICE'S BRAIN SHORTED as thousands of volts jolted through her. Her legs trembled when Adoni buried his face in her hair, his big body so close heat radiated out, encompassing her.

She recognised desire from that night in London. It quaked through her. Just like when she'd watched Adoni dance. Others had danced too, arms extended, lunging and leaping, but she'd noticed only him.

He'd done something to her from the start. It was more than attraction, stronger than desire. She had no vocabulary for it except, perhaps, need.

Was it because he'd introduced her to sex so she was conditioned now to respond to him? Except, if it were just sex, why did she want to discover everything about Adoni? Why had she been so eager for information about him from tonight's guests?

Abruptly Adoni lifted his head, his eyes on hers, and the breath escaped her lungs in a rush.

'I want you, Alice.'

It was a statement, bold and direct. Yet surely a question too, for he didn't move a muscle. She felt tension in the air, transfixing her.

Or maybe it was her wayward body refusing to be sensible and retreat. Surely if she moved he'd release her?

Except she didn't want to retreat. She shut her eyes and felt the ripple of excitement spread to her breasts, peaked and full against her nightie, to her womb and the damp place between her legs, right down to her toes and even up to her ears. Her body was one eager erogenous zone, twanging and shivering in anticipation of his touch.

'And you want me.'

Her eyes snapped open. In this light she couldn't make out the colour of his eyes, but there was no mistaking the intensity of that glittering gaze.

Alice couldn't even think of lying. The truth had haunted her since the night they'd met.

'Yes.'

The word came on a huge sigh of relief. Pride and fear had made her try to hide it but it was undeniable.

'Well, then.' Adoni's mouth kicked up in a smile that jolted through her. 'Let's not waste any more time.'

He scooped her up, one arm at her back, the other beneath her bare legs, and strode back the way he'd come. As he stepped into a large shadowy bedroom, Alice wondered if she'd left her common sense behind on the balcony. But she didn't care. She'd never wanted anything so much.

He lowered her to the floor beside the bed. In almost the same movement his hands swept up, collecting her threadbare old nightie and briskly, ruthlessly whipping it up over her head.

Alice's breath snagged in surprise. Automatically she slid one arm across her breasts, the other hand down to the V between her legs.

Adoni's chest rose and fell abruptly, as if he couldn't get his breath. He said something she didn't catch, something in Greek that buzzed along her skin like swarming bees, soft yet dangerous.

It took everything she had to stand, facing that intense stare. But she wanted him, so badly.

'Why hide such a beautiful body?'

She opened her mouth to say she'd never bared herself to any man except him, and then he'd held her, not stood, surveying her. But she bit her tongue. He wouldn't believe that.

How could she want to give herself to a man who distrusted her?

Yet she did. Especially when he gently tugged her arms wide and sighed his pleasure, his eyes devouring her.

Adoni wasn't an ogre. Look at the way he'd cared for her, twice, when faced with her morning sickness.

Now, instead of embarrassment, Alice felt a surge of power and pride, reading his dazzled expression and the faint tremor in those hard hands. His gaze dropped to her stomach and he planted one large palm gently there, where deep inside their baby nestled.

This time the throb of sensation passing through her was pure emotion. A mix of feelings she couldn't untangle, but awe was there at the miracle they'd created, and delight as she read the same in his face.

Warmth spread, a desire to protect and nurture, not just her child but, to her amazement, the man before her. It was akin to the need she'd felt to cuddle him close when he'd spent himself inside her and, for a few precious moments, collapsed in a gasping huddle on top of her.

'You've got too many clothes on,' she murmured.

Adoni blinked, then one corner of his mouth tipped up in a half smile that almost took her out at the knees. His hold on her arms tightened, holding her steady.

'Then you'd better help me.' He drew her right hand to his belt, one wicked eyebrow lifting in challenge. His hands went to his shirt, speedily undoing buttons.

Alice should have felt conspicuous, standing naked with her hand on his belt. But she didn't. She drew the leather through the buckle with a flick, pushed the tongue of the buckle free and dragged the belt undone.

In her peripheral vision she saw the hard, shadowy planes of his chest emerge as his hands raced down the buttons, tugging his shirt free. Alice didn't let herself get distracted. Instead she grabbed his trousers, her knuckles brushing hot flesh that retracted at her touch. A shiver shook Adoni.

Delighted, she wrangled the unfamiliar fastening undone, tugging the zip low, brushing the length of his mighty erection.

Another flinch, this time a shudder, and a hiss of breath from above her.

'*Se hriazome.*'

'I don't understand Greek.' But she understood the message of his aroused body. Alice watched, her insides spiralling into ever tighter coils of want, as he shucked his shoes, thrust down his trousers and boxers, then bent to strip away his socks.

'*Se thelo.* I want you.'

The fire in her veins turned into a roaring inferno as she surveyed him, proud and utterly masculine, strong lines of bone and taut muscle.

'*Se hriazome.* I need you.' His voice burred across her skin, pulling it tight as goose bumps erupted everywhere.

Alice had seen her share of naked males, but they were all on the pages of art books or safely cast in bronze or carved from stone. She'd thought she remembered Adoni's body from that night in London but memory didn't do justice to his magnificence.

She shuffled back, overwhelmed. Surely she shouldn't feel so…overcome?

'Alice?' That deep voice held a new note. 'You're not scared?'

Scared? She was petrified!

She swallowed, her throat constricting. It didn't make sense. He wasn't going to hurt her.

Every part of her clamoured for the pleasure he promised. It wasn't as if they hadn't already done this.

Yet…

His hands curled into fists at his sides and Alice forced

her gaze up to his face, as perfect and imposing as the rest of him. 'You cried that night in London, after we had sex. Did someone hurt you?'

The only man who'd hurt her was Adoni when he'd turned on her. But surprisingly his words settled her.

Sex, that was what this was. What they'd shared in London. Only sex. Nothing to be frightened of.

For a moment there, dumbstruck by the sight of him and the strange feelings making her heart career wildly, she'd feared this might be something else. Something far more dangerous. Her heart still hammered at the idea.

'Alice?' Even in the gloom she made out the tense bulge of muscle and sinew.

'Nothing's wrong. You're just a bit daunting.' Better she share that than the fact that obliterated everything else— that she *felt* more for Adoni than she should.

Yet, instead of smiling or puffing out his chest with male pride, Adoni stood still, watching her.

'You're safe with me, Alice. I swear it.' The words, slow and deliberate, were a pledge.

She quivered and rubbed her hands up her arms, suddenly too aware that she was stark naked.

'If you want to go back to your room I promise not to follow you.'

Alice couldn't help it; her gaze dropped to the impressive rampant erection pointing directly at her belly like some heat-seeking missile locked on its target.

Adoni's rusty chuckle surprised her. 'I don't say it will be easy, but I can do it. If you want.'

The weight of his words filled the silence. She looked up, read the truth in his expression.

'I'll stay.' She had no choice. Her feet were clamped to the floor. Leaving without feeling that beautifully sculpted body against hers would be criminal.

'Good.' He reached out and snagged her hand, pressing his mouth to her palm. His tongue swiped her skin.

Immediately her nipples budded as sparks showered from her hand through her body, coalescing into a searing arc of fire that shot to the aching, empty place between her legs.

Alice shuddered and moved closer, only to halt when Adoni gripped her hips and dropped to the floor before her. Eyes huge, she watched as he bent low, his mouth skimming the skin below her navel.

His hand splayed across her belly. 'I can't describe how it makes me feel, knowing you're cradling our child.'

Another gentle kiss then another, his hands holding her close.

'Try,' she whispered. 'How does it make you feel?' Adoni hadn't spoken about anything but practicalities, about paternity and obligations. What did he *feel* about this child they'd made?

'Humble.' He planted a kiss near her hip. As well as his soft lips, she felt delicious friction where his stubble had begun to grow.

'Excited.' Another kiss, further across her belly. 'Determined.' His lips skimmed wider, trailing heat across her abdomen as if he spun a web of delicate sensation with each caress. 'Nervous.'

Alice looked down at his dark head bowed over her pale skin and her heart went into free fall. There was more honesty between them now, more true feeling than there had ever been.

She threaded her fingers through his crisp hair, intending to turn his head up so she could meet his eyes.

Instead Adoni ducked lower, sitting back on his heels, his gaze fixed on the triangle of darkness at the apex of her thighs.

Alice breathed shakily, vulnerable and needy at the

same time. Then her thoughts frayed as he lifted his hand. His finger traced a line down through dark hair, slipping through her folds. Sparks ignited again and she shuddered. Internal muscles grabbed hard, more than ready for him. Yet Adoni took his time, tracing that sensitive bud then sliding his finger lower, deeper.

Alice gasped, her hips jerking as this time her muscles had something to tighten on.

'Please.' Did she whisper it aloud or was the word in her head?

Adoni didn't look up. He moved closer, grasping her thigh and pushing it wide. Then his mouth was on her, his tongue, and Alice was sure she'd collapse as a fierce tug of erotic pleasure juddered through her.

Surely it was only his hands on her thighs keeping her upright?

'Adoni? I can't...' Her voice was blurred, almost non-existent, like the shimmer of heat over boiling water.

He pulled back and everything inside her gave a throb of loss. Tremors ran through her and her legs shook so hard it was a wonder her teeth didn't chatter. His eyes met hers and something zapped between them. The air felt different—charged, and her nostrils flared at the rich scent she'd only smelled once before—pheromones and sex. Arousal.

Adoni rose on his knees, hands still on her hips, and pushed her back. Unresisting, she went, surprised to find the mattress immediately behind her. She'd forgotten the bed was there.

Alice opened her eyes and her arms at the same time, ready to hold him as he sank down on her. But he held back, kneeling on the floor between her open legs while she was supine on the bed.

'No.' One warm hand skimmed her stomach, making her quiver. 'This time I want to see all of you when you come for me.' The low words in that gravel and velvet voice thrilled her.

Adoni's eyes held hers as he anchored his hands on her hips and slid her closer to the edge of the mattress. Closer to him, for in the same movement she felt him against her, then entering, then gliding hard and high within her.

Alice caught her breath, her teeth biting her bottom lip at the wonder of them together, made all the more intense by Adoni's unwavering stare.

'Does that hurt?' He was withdrawing when she leaned up, reaching for his arm.

'No, don't! It doesn't hurt. It just feels—' He moved within her again, just a smidgeon, and her eyelids fluttered.

'Good?' His mouth stretched into what might have been a smile but looked more like pain.

'Better than good.' Her hand trailed his forearm, rigid muscle and soft hair, as she flopped back on the bed.

He moved again, sure and slow, and Alice thought she'd die of pleasure. Adoni kept one hand planted possessively at her hip but he used his other hand to stroke fingers up her side to her breast, circling the nipple till she gasped and writhed, lodging him more firmly at her core. Then his caress slid low, back to her belly, circling the place where their child rested.

A force swelled within her, hard and compelling as she watched him watching her, felt the oh-so-gentle sweep of his fingertips, a counterpoint to the steady, demanding invasion of his body. Her skin tightened, there was a moment of absolute perfect stillness as his gaze devoured her. Then he muttered something guttural and urgent in Greek, his next thrust hard and true, and her body erupted in bright flames.

Alice was soaring high, jerking and arching in release, when he moved forward, propping himself over her on powerful arms.

He was still too far away. Even as she clamped around him and released with ever-diminishing strength, Alice wanted more. She wanted his chest against hers, his arms around her. His head buried at her neck or his lips on hers. She wanted to wrap her arms around him and not let go.

She wanted them to be *together*.

'Please.' She grabbed his shoulders, curling needy fingers around his smooth, rounded flesh, and tugged.

For a second more he held back, before lying like a living blanket over her—hot, silky flesh with a scattering of crisp chest hair.

Alice took her hands from his shoulders and slid her arms around his ribs, squeezing tight. Then Adoni lowered his lips to her throat, lavishing moist kisses across hypersensitised flesh so she shuddered as the dying embers of pleasure sparked anew.

He shifted between her open thighs, the angle of his penetration changing, stealing her breath all over again.

Was it crazy? This leap of the heart as they melded into one being?

Yes, it was sex, simple physical coupling. But there was more too. Something about being this near to Adoni, his heart thundering against hers, his breath sharp and humid on her skin. One strong arm tucked under her hips to angle her for his pleasure, but the other cordoned her as close as if they were one.

Adoni dipped down to kiss a trail to her breast. Then his mouth settled on her nipple, dragging it hard into his mouth as he withdrew and thrust into her. The harder he sucked, the quicker his tempo, till her blood sprinted in her arteries, her breath ragged as she strived to match his rhythm.

It wasn't enough. She lifted a leg, anchoring around his hip, and was rewarded by a growl of approval that aroused her almost as much as what he was doing to her body. Alice slid her other leg high, jostled against him as she curved her calf over him and locked her ankles.

Adoni lifted his head, his eyes dark as he powered into her, his mouth a flat line of concentration. When he loosened his grip Alice almost protested, except he slid his hand down her belly to the place where they joined and pressed hard on that sensitive nub.

One thrust, their bodies moving as one. Another. And on the third Alice's hands curled in hard, like talons against the slippery satin of his back. She arched her head back and screamed his name, feeling the writhing force swirl and rise and explode so hard she shattered. Ecstasy took her, sharpening every sense. So when he jerked, spine bowing, a stream of words tumbling from his lips as he ejaculated in throbbing waves, Alice felt everything with exquisite clarity.

They clung through the aftershocks, cradling, soothing, as if afraid to pull away.

At least that was how it felt to Alice.

Maybe it was like this every time with Adoni.

She was so wrung out, teetering even now, as if on the brink of a great height, she wondered if it was possible to pass out from pleasure.

'Are you okay?' The words feathered against her neck. She felt the shape of them more than heard them. He cleared his throat. 'Alice?'

'Yes. Fine.' Part of her, the only part with any energy left to expend, silently laughed.

If that's fine, what's good like?

'Too heavy.' His words sounded slurred as his muscles tensed, ready to move.

'No! Stay.' Alice wanted to remain like this as long as she could. She felt joined, not just physically but mentally. She and Adoni together were somehow greater than they were separately.

He gently kissed her chin, half propping himself on one elbow to take some of his weight but not moving away.

Well-being hummed through Alice. Pleasure, contentment. And when he kissed her again, lingering as if addicted to the taste of her, something far more profound consumed her.

She felt as if she belonged.

Pink and apricot streaks of sunlight brightened the dawn sky when Adoni caressed her awake. She'd stretched, slow and cautious, feeling the unfamiliar sensations in her body after last night's lovemaking. But they hadn't stopped her responding enthusiastically.

Now, after a long, satisfying and educational bout of foreplay, Alice gasped as Adoni finally filled her. She arched her back, feeling the depth of his possession in every rioting pleasure point. Hands and knees sinking a little into the mattress, she pushed back just as he moved against her from behind and drew a low groan of pleasure from him.

The sound made her heady with pleasure. *She* made him feel like that. Nor was her satisfaction just from a sense of power. She wanted him to enjoy his own release. She'd had her own climax this morning. It was his turn.

Yet as she slowly found and met his rhythm, felt the needy grasp of his hand at her hip and his other at her breast, excitement zinged through her. She'd always assumed sex in this position would be all about a guy's pleasure, not the woman's. She'd been wrong.

For when Adoni had turned her over onto her stomach and lifted her hips, driving into her with a power that rocked her on her knees, she'd waited to feel used. Instead, with his shaky hands, so at odds with the determined rhythm of his body, he worshipped and caressed. She felt his dominance but at the same time every breath, every shudder proclaimed his need for her.

Everything he did with her in bed made her feel glorious.

Adoni's breath was hot on the back of her neck as his pace picked up, his thighs jolting against her with each quick thrust. Alice lifted one hand from the bed and covered his hand, pressing it harder against her breast. Over the thud of her pulse she heard his breath hiss. That smooth rhythm fractured as he shuddered, and she bit down on a smile.

Then his hand at her hip slid down to her slick centre on his next thrust. She felt teeth graze the place where her neck met her shoulder and abruptly her self-satisfaction disintegrated. Out of nowhere, rapture took her, sucking her under just as it took Adoni. The bright morning light cracked into a thousand shards of brilliance.

Afterwards Alice lay spent. Adoni drew the sheet over her and all but vaulted out of bed. She wondered at his energy as her eyes slid shut. Was it pregnancy that made her so lethargic, or the unaccustomed sex?

She listened to the shower and wished she had the strength to get up and join Adoni. Exhausted as she was, she longed to explore his body again. Who knew what possibilities there'd be as she slicked soap over him?

Not that he'd invited her to join him but—

Why would he? You've already given him what he wants.

Did she really think anything had changed? He didn't believe she'd been a virgin. He believed she'd slept with David for money. He probably thought she'd put out because that was what women did—gave men sex to get what they wanted.

Because, tellingly, despite his sometimes protective attitude, Adoni had never retracted that allegation. It hovered between them, making her feel sullied when she thought of it.

He probably thinks last night was you softening him up for the discussion you're due to have about the baby.

Alice jack-knifed up in the bed and clamped a hand to her mouth, horror filling her. Could that be true? Her gaze fixed on the bathroom door.

After all they'd shared Adoni hadn't kissed her or touched her before getting out of bed. He hadn't uttered a word. Suddenly that seemed important.

For the first time this week nausea churned through her. But it wasn't morning sickness.

Desperately Alice replayed last night's events. Adoni had spoken of wanting her, needing her, that was all. There'd been mutual pleasure, but maybe that was about masculine pride in ensuring his partner was satisfied.

And the pang of delight and emotion that had ploughed through her when he'd spoken of their baby, kissed her belly and made love to her so wondrously?

Alice gnawed her lip.

Her emotions were unbalanced with pregnancy hormones. She'd believed Adoni had begun to feel something for her, mirroring her own growing feelings for him.

Yet there was no evidence of that. He felt strongly about the baby and he'd been kind when she was sick. But he'd brought her across a continent, far from any friends who'd help her stand up to him, when it was time to clinch a deal on their child's future. At the very first opportunity he'd seduced her, taken her into his bed as easily as if it was to be expected, not the momentous turning point it had been for her.

Alice's legs were appallingly wobbly when she planted her feet on the floor and stood.

Behind her water still gushed in the bathroom. Her revelation had taken mere minutes.

Stumbling, swerving to grab her faded old nightdress from the floor, she made her way via the terrace to her room. Now the elation had ebbed she felt stiff and achy, and more miserable than she'd been in weeks.

They'd had sex only because Adoni believed her to be available…easy.

She'd never felt so *used*. So sullied. So stupid.

Carefully she locked the doors to both the balcony and the hall, then crept into the bathroom.

She didn't want to see Adoni for a long, long time.

CHAPTER ELEVEN

ADONI ENDED HIS long-distance phone call and scowled.

Originally he'd planned to spend the morning inspecting the newly completed house instead of dealing with a work crisis.

Some things here still needed finalising. It would have been easier to bring in a top building team, especially given the architect's challenging design. Adoni's choice to use locals, specifically young workers still developing their skills, under strict supervision, had puzzled many.

But Adoni knew what it was like to be young and without resources, fighting for a toehold in a career.

Shoving his chair back from the desk, he prowled to the picture window looking over the sea.

His restlessness wasn't because he'd been side-tracked by work. It was because Alice had derailed him.

Waking beside her this morning, he'd quickly re-evaluated his plans and decided a few more hours in bed would suit him fine. Even thinking about it now tightened his jeans across his crotch. She had that effect on him.

But she'd been exhausted, reminding him of how delicate she'd looked in England, and how recently she'd been ill. He'd torn himself away, deciding a shower would give Alice time to recuperate before they took their pleasure again.

But on his return she'd disappeared. She hadn't even knocked on the door to say she was going, and when he'd gone to her room the door was locked!

Adoni rolled his head to one side, easing stiff neck muscles.

He couldn't figure her out. Alice had been willing. More

than willing. The way she'd come apart at his touch! The way she'd opened herself to him, giving him all he'd demanded and more than he'd expected...

He froze, his mind jammed by the memory of her gasping out her pleasure then wrapping herself around him, hauling him close with arms and legs locked at his hips. She'd held him so tight his control disintegrated. He'd lost track of where he ended and she began.

It had felt profound in a way sex never had.

They had felt different.

Because she was pregnant with his child?

That had to be why.

He glanced at his watch. Almost midday. He'd been caught up in work for hours. It was time he found Alice and talked about the future.

Then he could get to the bottom of why she'd run.

He found her, eventually, by the infinity pool at the end of the cantilevered deck. But she wasn't swimming or sunning herself. She was with one of the young workmen Adoni remembered from a previous site visit. They were huddled, heads together, beyond and below the stone-flagged terrace, where the land dropped away suddenly.

'What are you doing?' Adoni scowled as anger shafted through him. What was the guy doing so close to Alice?

Two heads yanked up as if pulled by strings. The youth looked nervous but Alice just tilted her head in query, eyebrows arched. She wore faded denim shorts that rode high on her slim legs as she crouched, and a sleeveless blue shirt tied at the waist. Sunlight turned her hair from dark to verging on auburn. When she moved russet highlights glinted seductively.

Something inside Adoni rolled over. She looked fresh as dew, except for a hint of tiredness around her eyes and a smudge of dirt on her chin. It was all he could do not to vault off the terrace and gather her up.

Had he ever felt this way about a woman? He tried to remember such a visceral response to Chryssa, his ex-fiancée, and failed. He'd felt desire and pride but his heart hadn't thumped out of control at the sight of her. Nor had he ever seen her dressed so simply. Chryssa had always worn expensive clothes and immaculate make-up. After they made love she'd hurry to the bathroom to primp and tidy her hair. No lying about in an abandoned tangle of bodies like Alice and he had done last night.

'Fixing the pool pump.' Her tone was cool.

'Sorry?' Adoni blinked and tried to focus. The guy with Alice got to his feet, putting a few steps between them, but she remained hunkered where she'd been. She was facing the motor and other workings for the pool, hidden beneath the edge of the flagged terrace where he stood.

'Fixing the pool pump. It wasn't installed properly but it's like the one on the estate in Devon.'

Adoni stared. He'd never pictured Alice doing pool maintenance. Had running the estate in Devon been that hands-on? He knew so little about her.

Alice turned to the youth. 'Here, Costa. Like this.' She beckoned him closer and with one darting look at Adoni the kid approached. She fiddled with something then sat back. 'Try it now.' The boy leaned forward, made an adjustment and the motor hummed into life. The kid beamed at Alice, then seeing Adoni's expression, wiped the smile off his face and quickly moved away.

'Thank you, miss.'

'No problem. I'm glad to help.' She rose and dusted off her hands and knees, watching the youth move away, presumably to report to his supervisor who was overseeing the final jobs on site.

Alice watched him go then turned to Adoni, her expression shuttered. 'What's wrong? You look angry.'

Adoni leaned over and offered his hand. He *was* angry, and it unsettled him.

The hot rush of blood to the head when he'd seen Alice with another man had taken him by surprise. They might not be committed to each other, but she'd been in his bed mere hours ago. That had to explain the raw possessiveness priming his body to high alert. Adrenaline buzzed in his blood as if in preparation to fight a rival.

Finally her smaller hand touched his and he firmed his fingers around it, hauling her up till they stood toe to toe.

'Adoni?' She tilted her head to one side, reading his face, then abruptly she stepped away, ripping her hand free. Her nostrils flared in anger even as something that looked like hurt tightened her face. 'You thought I was coming on to him, didn't you?' Her eyes grew huge in her pale face. 'That's the sort of woman you think I am.'

'No, it wasn't like that.' He hadn't thought she'd instigated anything. He'd wanted to *protect* her. Did she have any idea how alluring she looked with her bare limbs and sweet curves?

'Yeah, right.' She marched over to pick up a book he hadn't noticed beside one of the sun loungers.

Adoni followed, determined to convince her, when a picture on an open page caught his eye. It was a sketchbook and even from a couple of metres the delicate work in it looked exquisite.

'What's that?'

Alice looked down. 'A drawing.'

'*You* did that?' He thought back to her threadbare bedsit with those wonderful botanical studies, so perfect and so out of place in such drab surroundings. Were they Alice's? He'd thought them done by a professional.

'Yes, I did.' She dropped the book onto the lounger and turned, hands on hips. Her breasts rose as she sucked in a deep breath. 'What's wrong? You think *gold-diggers* can't draw?' Fire flashed in her eyes, lightening them from dark slate to something more vibrant. 'You think we're so busy seducing every man we meet we don't have time for—'

'Stop it!' He closed his hands around her upper arms, yanking her against him. How had they got to this when hours ago they'd been locked together in bliss? His gut twisted at her jarring words and the whisper of guilt they evoked. For he had accused her, hadn't he? He couldn't remember if he'd called her a gold-digger but he'd said something similar.

'I won't stop it.' Her chin angled defiantly. 'It's what you're thinking, isn't it?'

'No, it's not.'

He felt a mighty shudder run through her, saw her teeth sink into her bottom lip as if to stop it trembling and watched pain shadow those accusing eyes.

Adoni wanted to slam his mouth down on hers. He wanted to expunge the hurt he saw in her face and rewind the clock to this morning, when they'd been in bed. The day had gone downhill since he'd left her there. He should have stayed. Of course if he had they'd probably still be having sex. They might have stayed there all day. Yet now Alice hissed at him like a wounded animal, her eyes huge and accusing.

He could kiss her into silence, maybe even into his bed. But that would solve nothing.

Except to relieve that burn in his groin.

You want her again, don't you? Even when she's fighting and spitting at you.

'I said, let me go.' She pulled, trying to free her arms. Adoni had to force himself not to tighten his hold. Brute strength wasn't the way.

He let her go, holding his hands up in a placating gesture. 'It's not what you think, Alice.'

'Sure.' He hated the cynicism in her tone almost as much as the pain in her eyes and crumpled mouth.

'We need to talk.'

'About the baby, I know.' She gathered the sketchbook and a leather pouch he assumed held pencils and clutched them to her chest as if for protection.

Guilt was a corkscrew drilling through him. It was true that in the beginning he'd thought the worst, primed by Dawlish's information. But it was a long time since he'd felt that way. He knew Alice better now. She wasn't a cardboard cut-out villainess. He wouldn't have taken her into his bed last night if she were.

But he'd never told her that, had he?

'Not the baby. That can wait.' Her stunned gaze locked on his. He surprised himself too, for he needed to secure his child's future. But this was overdue. 'We need to clear the air first.'

Which was how Alice found herself beside Adoni in the vast lounge room that hung out over the sea. Their chairs, so comfortable it was like being cradled, were drawn up together as if they were friends enjoying the spectacular view together.

But Alice couldn't relax, nor let herself be lulled by the scenery or the quiet luxury. She watched Adoni take a sip of coffee from a tiny cup then place it on a side table. It struck her that he didn't look as sure of himself as usual.

Alice ignored the porcelain teapot beside her and the tantalising aroma of the brew within it. Instead she watched Adoni. The thick glass windows protected from the midday heat but didn't dim the sunlight. Her heart sank as her gaze traced his profile. He was impossibly, arrogantly gorgeous, enough to make her heart trip.

'You're wrong, Alice. I don't think you're a gold-digger.'

'You implied it.' She sat straighter. 'No, you *said* it, even if not in those words.'

'I'd never intentionally take such a woman into my bed. So how do you explain last night?'

His gaze bored into hers and she shrugged, the movement jerky. 'Maybe you weren't thinking with your head.'

That surprised a laugh out of him and, to her horror, the warmth of it coursed through her like hot syrup, making her shift in her seat.

'You could be right.' Suddenly his expression sobered. 'But, for the record, I'd never have slept with you if I thought that. Or brought you into my home.'

Alice stared into those beautiful eyes and wished she could tell if it were true. 'Then why accuse me in the first place? I know you were shocked about the pregnancy, but I was too. That was no excuse. You were so ready to believe the worst gossip about me and David.'

Adoni sat forward. 'You have to expect some response when a guy finds you rifling his wallet.'

Instantly her face flamed. She'd forgotten that. 'How did you know?' She'd left the room before he'd returned from the bathroom.

One black brow rose in a slashing line. 'You didn't put the cards back properly.'

Alice nodded. She'd been in a hurry and when she'd heard him coming she'd dropped the wallet and run for the door.

'If you'd needed money for a taxi—'

'It wasn't that. I just…' She turned and stared at the sea, noticing how the clear shallows gave way to aquamarine then the distinctive green-blue of Adoni's eyes, before deepening to a rich navy.

She turned back, thrusting aside embarrassment. 'I couldn't remember your last name.' The words tumbled out. 'You told me but all I could remember was Adoni. It seemed important that I knew your name because...' She clamped her lips shut rather than say that he'd been her first lover. She'd told him that and he hadn't believed her. 'I didn't like the idea of having sex with someone and not knowing their name.' She stared at him, defying him to laugh.

Adoni's expression was arrested. 'But why leave? Why run?'

Because she'd looked around the stunning, incredibly expensive suite and realised she didn't belong. It was only Adoni's warmth and charm, and the invitation in his eyes, that had made her forget that.

She settled for sharing part of the truth. 'I'd never had a one-night stand and I was out of my depth. I didn't know if I was expected to leave while you were in the bathroom. I didn't know the protocol.' She'd had a horror of outstaying her welcome. She'd already behaved foolishly, even if the sex had been the most wonderful thing she'd ever experienced.

Adoni shook his head. 'I was looking forward to spending the rest of the night with you.'

'Really?' Alice bit her cheek as she heard what sounded like delight in her voice. Was she so easily pleased?

But Adoni didn't seem to notice. He leaned forward, forearms braced on his thighs, hands clasped. 'I must apologise. The day you made the appointment to see me, my temporary PA mentioned you in front of Miles Dawlish.'

Alice's nape prickled. 'Let me guess. He told you about me?'

Slowly Adoni nodded. 'I realise now he had an axe to grind.'

'You can say that again.' Alice hunched her shoulders and rubbed her hands along her arms, remembering years of verbal abuse from the man, every time he'd wanted a loan from David's estate and been turned down.

'Why don't you tell me about it? About *you*. There's nothing to be gained by keeping it to yourself, is there?'

Adoni was right. By letting him believe the worst she'd only made things more difficult. Though had she *let* him? When she'd tried to explain he'd brushed her words aside. Yet once he'd made his opinion clear, her pride had dug in and she'd refused to make the effort.

This man was her baby's father. He'd be in her life from now on. Her belly clenched at the realisation.

'After all, you know about my past. There are only two other people who know the truth about my parents.'

Alice's eyes met his and she felt again that whump of sensation, a deep throb at her core. At the time she'd been moved by his revelation, but too caught up in her own concerns to really consider what it had meant for him to share that secret. It made her past problems fade. At least she'd had people who genuinely loved her.

'Okay.' He was right—it would help if he knew it all. Yet, though her life was an open book, she was reluctant. She tried to live in the present, not dwell on the past.

As she hesitated Adoni leaned forward and poured tea into the delicate porcelain cup on the table beside her, adding milk. At her raised eyebrows he murmured, 'I know how you like it.'

The words took her back to her shabby room in Devon. To Adoni prowling the tiny space like a Greek god come down from Olympus to find himself in a cramped bedsit. He'd been annoying and bossy but...kind.

'Thank you.' She lifted the cup to her lips, inhaled the fragrant steam then sipped. Instantly she felt better. She shuffled back in the chair, letting it embrace her, and turned her head to find Adoni watching her, his lips twitching. 'What?'

'You English are addicted to your tea, aren't you?'

She shrugged, glancing at the tiny cup of intensely dark coffee beside him. 'Like you Greeks and your coffee.'

He lifted his shoulders in a casual shrug that tugged at her feminine centre. It made Alice remember the power in his tall frame, and the way he'd carefully leashed it to ensure her pleasure before his own. Her gaze dipped to her tea as she fought a quiver of excitement.

'I don't have any big secrets and you know most of it.' She paused, annoyance flickering because he'd investigated her. But the investigator obviously didn't know everything. She lifted her eyes to the soothing view of sea and sky that reminded her of her happy childhood.

'I'm an only child and grew up in Cornwall. We were a close family. My mother was a talented portrait artist.'

'That's where you get your artistic talent.'

Alice felt the words sink in. It had been too long since she'd thought of herself as having real talent. She'd longed to attend art school but life and a lack of funds had got in the way. This morning was the first time in ages that she'd picked up a sketchbook.

'From my father too. He was a commercial cartoonist.' Even in his wheelchair, as his body slowly failed him, he'd worked desperately hard, trying to support them. 'His cartoons were so insightful, yet they made you laugh.'

'You're proud of him.'

'Of course.' She met Adoni's probing gaze. 'I'm proud of both of them. Not just because of their talent. They were lovely people.' She still missed them.

Alice took a fortifying sip of tea.

'We were caught in a motorway accident when I was twelve. A lorry skidded on ice and crossed several lanes to slam into us. My mother died instantly but it took ages for them to cut my father out.' Her throat closed and she pretended to take another sip.

'I'm sorry. That must have been…' He paused. 'I can't begin to imagine how hard it was.'

Alice nodded. 'Somehow it seemed worse that I came out of it with only bruising and a cracked wrist. It took a long time before I stopped feeling guilty.' It had almost felt as if it was her fault her mother had died.

She saw Adoni's hand move as if to touch her, then he pulled back. Alice was grateful. Talking about this still choked her up.

'After that we had to give up the house in Cornwall because Dad was in a wheelchair and couldn't cope with the stairs.' And because money had been so tight they couldn't afford the mortgage. 'An old friend of my parents offered us a place in Devon. It was ideal, on one floor and with doorways wide enough for Dad's chair.'

Alice turned to Adoni. 'David Bannister was my god-father. He and his wife saw my mother's work when she was a student and encouraged her. She sold her first painting to them.' She paused, waiting, but Adoni's expression was unreadable.

'David was very good to us. More than a landlord, he was a friend, and we needed all we could get.' Her mother's death had strained relations with their only relatives. Her mother's sister had blamed Alice's father for the accident, despite the evidence. There'd been a rift between the families ever since, till Alice's cousin Emily had invited her to attend the wedding.

'Dad's injuries were complicated. His condition worsened till eventually he couldn't work. Then David waived our rent and there was always a basket of fresh produce from the estate or our neighbours. We lived in the artists' colony you saw.'

'No wonder Jasper is so protective.'

She shrugged. 'Everyone pitched in together.' Alice drew a deep breath. 'Dad fought his health problems but he died when I was seventeen. Soon after, David asked me to come and live at the big house.'

Alice turned narrowed eyes on Adoni, waiting for a re-action, but he merely nodded.

'He was a widower and missed his wife dreadfully. He said he was lonely rattling around by himself. But he did it for me. So *I* wouldn't be alone.' Her lips tightened as she remembered the lies Adoni had believed. Her stom-ach churned in indignation. 'For the record we were never lovers. He didn't seduce me. He was like a grandfather or an uncle.'

'It was good you had someone to care for you when your father died.' There was no doubt in Adoni's deep voice, just statement of fact.

Alice dipped her head in agreement. 'It wasn't supposed to be long-term. I was researching art schools. I wanted to go as soon as I could, after I'd worked to save enough money. David was talking of giving me an interest-free loan. But then he was diagnosed with a degenerative ill-ness.'

She reached for her tea, taking a long drink as she re-membered her devastation. 'He was upbeat, said the treat-ment would help. But it didn't work as well as hoped and he needed assistance sooner than expected.

'In the beginning he urged me to leave, but I refused. I wanted to be there for him, as he'd been for us.' Sometimes she wondered if she'd clung to him so desperately because he was the one person who'd always been there.

'As he grew worse, he relied on me more and more. He didn't advertise his illness, didn't want people feeling sorry for him, so Miles Dawlish never knew till late. Dawlish is David's wife's nephew and, as the estate came from her family and she never had any children, he was the heir. And a bumptious little man too.'

'He is. Thoroughly unlikable.'

Alice swung round to stare. 'But you believed what he said about me.'

Adoni stared straight back. 'I didn't know he was biased. But yes, it wasn't one of my finer moments.' A flicker of a smile appeared at the corners of those mesmerising eyes, arresting Alice. 'I was out of sorts because the fascinating woman I wanted to spend the night making love to had disappeared, presumably to siphon off my credit cards.' He spread his hands. 'I'm sorry.'

She shook her head, her pulse thrumming at the admission he'd wanted to make love to her all night. As if he couldn't get enough of the passion they shared either. 'I suppose it was understandable in the circumstances.'

She took a deep breath and hurried on, eager to get this over. 'The sicker David became the more I helped. At first it was just correspondence and keeping him company but then it was running the estate.'

'Like fixing the pool?' Adoni's half smile did strange things to her insides.

'And more. Organising improvements. Checking on tenants, doing the books. That's where Dawlish and I came into conflict. David couldn't bear the guy and he kept trying to borrow money. After the first few times David refused to see him and I was the messenger.' Alice lifted one shoulder. 'That's when he turned ugly. Accused me of sleeping with David to get money.' She laughed, the sound bitter. 'Actually, most of the money was tied up in the estate, then there were charity commitments like the artists' colony. What was left over went on David's care.'

Poor David—he'd been so determined to keep some of his personal funds aside so Alice could study art. In the end she'd had to lie and pretend it hadn't been spent on palliative care, so as not to distress him.

Silence descended. Not a combative one, but a reflective one. Alice curled back in her chair and finished her tea, feeling strangely lighter.

'Thank you,' Adoni said eventually. 'I appreciate you telling me.'

She turned to find his eyes on her. She couldn't decipher his expression. 'Where does that leave us?'

'Ready to move forward.' It was a statement but she read the question in his eyes, as if he sought her agreement. Slowly she nodded.

'So now you want to talk about the baby.' She straightened her shoulders, trying to dredge up energy though she wilted after the emotions of the last half hour.

'That can wait.'

'Really?' Surely the baby's future was uppermost in his mind? It was the sole reason she was here.

'Really.' His mouth tipped up at one side in a slow smile and reaction jangled through her. He wasn't even touching her and she wanted— 'I find I have to go to Athens for business. I'll be away overnight.'

Alice fought not to show a reaction though her stomach dipped at the news. As if she didn't want him to go.

'Would you like to come? You didn't see anything of the city except the airport.' He paused. 'There's an art exhibition you might be interested in too.'

Instantly Alice nodded, delight filling her. But was it delight at the idea of seeing some of Greece's artistic wonders?

Or relief at delaying their negotiations about the future?

Perhaps it was simply because they'd cleared up the doubts and distrust between them.

Alice had a terrible suspicion her delight was because she'd be with Adoni.

CHAPTER TWELVE

ALICE BRUSHED HER hands down the delicate folds of her dress. The material was finer than anything she'd ever worn, soft as gossamer.

Initially she'd refused Adoni's charity—the gift of a dress and shoes to wear tonight. She hated being beholden. The fact he'd already paid her next month's rent was still a bone of contention. It was fine for him to contribute to their child's upbringing but *she* wasn't after his money.

It was only the realisation her holiday wardrobe contained just shorts, jeans and two well-worn summer dresses that changed her mind. Plus meeting Adoni's chic, exquisitely dressed assistant in Athens. Effie had assured her Adoni was right, that the guests at the exhibition opening tonight would be dressed to the nines.

Reluctantly Alice had been persuaded, accepting Effie's help to negotiate what she suspected were Athens' top boutiques. There were no prices on display and Alice shuddered to think how much her outfit cost. But she *had* enjoyed herself. Despite her glamorous air, Effie was fun, down-to-earth and had an eye for fashion.

Alice had never looked so good.

She twirled before the mirror, the narrow sapphire pleats of the short skirt flaring around her. The glittering fitted bodice and thin shoulder straps sparkled as if crusted with gems rather than sequins and beads. Even her shoes of sapphire silk had tiny beads on the spindly heels that winked and flashed when she moved.

Adoni couldn't ignore her dressed like *this*.

The thought speared through her before she could stop it. Not that he'd ignored her after yesterday's discussion.

He'd been…considerate. So considerate he'd left her straight after dinner, telling her he understood she must be tired, and headed to his office to work.

Alice had lain awake for hours, waiting for him to join her in her vast bed, waiting for him to make love with her again, but he hadn't. She'd woken this morning, late, and just in time for their trip to Athens, feeling out of sorts and needy.

She didn't know what worried her most, her neediness or the possibility he'd decided sex with her wasn't as satisfying as he'd expected. Had he grown tired of her?

Or was it the retelling of her past that made him pull back?

But Alice refused to feel like a victim. She fitted her one piece of good jewellery around her throat and told herself she didn't care about his withdrawal. Much.

Her hand swiped her flat abdomen. She was here to plan her child's future. And to see a little of Greece. Not to pine after Adoni.

This afternoon she'd visited the Parthenon and the Acropolis Museum, marvelling over sculptures she'd seen in books but only dreamed of viewing in person. She'd marvelled at the workmanship, the beautiful images. Yet all the time she'd been thinking of another sculpture, this one warm and supple. A living man whose honed muscles and lean strength made her pulse quicken and her insides melt.

Alice now understood the ancient Greeks' fascination with the nude male form. When that form was like Adoni's—

'Alice?' A knock sounded at her door. 'Are you ready?'

Her eyes widened in the mirror as excitement throbbed through her. Excitement and anticipation.

She'd never been to an exhibition opening. Never been out on the town, unless you counted a meal at the local pub with workmates. But the real reason for her excitement was altogether different.

She wanted Adoni.

It was foolish. They came from different worlds and would separate after they'd agreed on a plan for their baby's future. But meanwhile Alice was determined to grasp what she wanted. She had too much experience of life passing her by.

'Coming!' She spun towards the door. Her skirt flared, caressing her thighs and making her smile.

Oh, yes, she knew what she wanted.

'You look fantastic.'

Original, Petrakis. Can't you do better?

But it was true. Alice looked good enough to eat. His mouth watered at the thought of kissing his way up those bare legs and—

'So do you.' Alice's smile was wide, her eyes sparkling. Adoni hadn't seen her smile like that since the first night in London. It did crazy things to his self-control. A control undermined by the fact she didn't *look* pregnant, or like a woman who needed careful handling.

Last night, with her revelations fresh in his mind and those smudges beneath her eyes, partly because he'd kept her from sleep the night before, Adoni had avoided her bed. Just. It had been touch and go. In the end he'd spent hours testing his new gym, then doing laps in the pool, trying to burn off his hunger for her.

It had hit him anew how wrong he'd been about her. How she'd actually been a virgin when they'd met in London. Adoni remembered that night, the moment of tense stillness and shocking doubt, which he'd dismissed as an impossibility. Now, remembering it, he felt obliged to exert restraint. Alice was pregnant, inexperienced and needed rest.

How was he to keep his hands off her when she looked like this?

'Effie has great taste in clothes.'

Adoni flattened his lips rather than blurt out that it was the woman, not the clothes that dazzled.

Her hand went to her throat in a nervous gesture that belied her confident smile.

'That's a beautiful piece.' He leaned in, pretending to examine the black choker with its fiery opal centre stone. 'Expensive too.' He was speaking at random, hiding the swift inhale that dragged the scent of warm feminine skin and orange blossom deep into his lungs.

'It was an eighteenth birthday gift from Jasper, our old neighbour in Devon.' Her chin notched up in challenge. 'He's a jewellery designer.'

No mistaking her crisp tone. It confused Adoni till he remembered his earlier accusation that she lived off older men. Heat scored his cheeks, guilt biting. He was a proud man, not used to feeling in the wrong.

'He's very talented. The dark blue matches your eyes but the flashes of red and green bring it to life. It suits you—vibrant and with hidden depths.'

'Adoni?' Her head tilted to one side in that endearing way. 'I *think* that's the nicest thing you've ever said to me.'

He took her hand and kissed it, pleased at her shiver and the sudden widening of her eyes. 'The night's still young.'

'This one's intriguing. I love the unusual perspective.' Alice sounded thoughtful but with that hint of excitement he'd sensed all night. Standing beside him, her attention was on a larger-than-life portrait.

The chatter and noise of the exhibition's opening night continued, but in this corner it was muted. Perhaps it seemed so because Adoni's attention was fixed on her.

The artist, who'd followed Alice, spoke enthusiastically

about using light and perspective to reveal character. Instead of listening, Adoni watched Alice.

As if sensing his regard she flashed him a smile, then she took a half-step back, inviting him to join the discussion.

She'd been doing that all evening, favouring him with that wide smile. It dazzled more surely than the exquisite opal at her throat that flashed fire every time she moved.

Did she know how that invitation affected him? That it made him want to plough her back against one of the stark white walls and reacquaint himself with every centimetre of her svelte body?

The dancing light in her eyes suggested she did.

He'd have dragged them out of here and found relief for the hunger riding him hard, but for something else. Alice was having the time of her life.

She was in her element. It shouldn't surprise him, given her family history and her own talent. Yet Adoni was transfixed by the sheer joy she radiated, being here.

She loved the party, mingling with people, striking up conversations. Laughing over the occasional language difficulties and gamely trying out the few Greek words she'd got from who knew where.

It was like discovering a completely different woman.

No. Not that. This was the same woman whose humour and forthright attitude, and sexy body, had seduced him that first night. Who'd intrigued even when he'd railed that fate had tied him to what he'd thought was a conniving gold-digger.

He'd got in the habit of thinking of Alice in simplistic terms. First as a *femme fatale*. Then as someone needing protection. Morning sickness had made her fragile and her living conditions had appalled, making him want to take care of her.

Now he saw depths he hadn't fully appreciated.

'Adoni admired the portrait in the first room,' she told

the artist. Lightly she touched Adoni's hand and lightning shot through him, making his blood fire and his heart drum. 'The one of the old lady.' She turned to him. 'It reminded you of someone, didn't it?'

How had she known? He hadn't said anything. Add perceptive to her list of qualities.

He nodded. 'Our housekeeper when I was a boy. She looked old but when you met her eyes you realised she was young at heart.'

Memory blanketed him. Suddenly he was a scrawny kid again, always in the kitchen because meal times couldn't keep up with his growth spurts. Maria had teased him but she'd shown more warmth and understanding than he'd ever got from his mother.

Alice threaded her fingers through his and squeezed. Her dark gaze was soft with understanding.

How did she *do* that?

He didn't need understanding. His life was exactly as he wanted it.

'I think—' Alice turned to the artist '—you'd better mingle with your guests. We don't want to monopolise you.'

The guy shrugged, obviously happy basking in Alice's enthusiasm. And enjoying the delectable picture she made in that short dress.

Adoni leaned closer. 'Yes, it's important you circulate. It will help sales.'

The guy took one look at Adoni's face and agreed.

'You've got an admirer. He looked smitten.' Adoni smiled when Alice's gaze instantly left the artist and turned to *him*. Their eyes met and he felt that familiar buzz. Anticipation. Possessiveness.

It should bother him. It had been years since he'd felt proprietorial about a woman. Yet somehow—

'He was hoping for a sale, that's all.' She gave a self-deprecating smile. 'He probably thought I had the money to buy one of his works.'

Did she really not understand how attractive she was, with her elegance and vivacity?

All night she'd been a flame drawing moths as other guests responded to her. She was bright, fun and truly interested in them.

'Adoni!' A blonde socialite air-kissed him with enthusiasm then turned to Alice. 'Here he is, Alice.' She introduced a young man as an aspiring jewellery maker. 'He's interested in the artists' colony you mentioned, *and* seeing that stunning choker up close.'

Adoni watched, annoyed, as the guy moved in for a close-up view that included the top of Alice's breasts above her low-cut gown. Had her breasts always been that full or had they changed with pregnancy? Two nights ago they'd filled Adoni's hands to perfection.

He reached out to yank the guy back by the scruff of his neck when Alice's fingers caught his. Her intimate smile momentarily derailed his thoughts.

Then she freed her hand and unclipped the necklace. Handing it to the jeweller, she leaned into Adoni. 'It's the necklace he's interested in.'

Adoni merely raised one eyebrow and hauled her hard against his side, staking his claim.

For a second Alice looked surprised, then she smiled a cat-that-got-the-cream smile that made Adoni's temperature spike. If she kept looking at him like that...

Yet Adoni forced himself to be patient, not cut her evening short. There was a different sort of pleasure in being with her here.

When he'd taken Chryssa out, she hadn't engaged with others so much as thrived on their adulation as she paraded her latest expensive outfit. He'd realised too late he was a trophy to show off, a means to climb the social ladder and fund her lifestyle.

Alice, by contrast, was interested in people, vibrant and amusing as she chatted, not about herself but about them and art and a hundred other things.

Plus she responded to him as a man, a companion, not a shortcut to the good life, turning to him again and again, drawing him into the conversation.

She was as genuine as he'd first thought her. After a lifetime dealing with people whose professed love masked pride and selfishness, he appreciated how special that was.

But below that, humming through each pulse of his blood, was a demand he could no longer ignore.

Finally, after another half-hour, Adoni murmured in her ear, 'We need to leave.'

Questioning eyes met his. What she read in his face he didn't know but she blushed and her pupils dilated. He felt her shudder and her back arched to his touch as if inviting a caress.

'Now!' His voice cracked on the word. He'd stayed for her sake but if he didn't have her soon he'd combust.

'Yes.' Her whisper feathered his chin, evoking a surge of pure triumph.

Their goodbyes were rushed. No doubt everyone guessed the reason for their sudden urgency but Adoni didn't give a damn. All he cared about was Alice, wrapping his arms around her, sinking into her slick, tight body and losing his mind.

'Adoni!' Her breathy voice almost undid him as he strode out onto the pavement. 'Wait. I can't go this fast in heels.'

For answer he simply swept her up into his arms, carrying her to his sports car, just down the street. He couldn't wait for the valet to drive it up.

Her gurgling laugh caressed like warm satin, drawing nerves to the verge of breaking point. Adoni ignored the sea of faces turned towards them and within seconds they were in the car, peeling away into the traffic.

Neither said a word as he drove. Adoni was hyper-aware of Alice's every movement. Of her quickened breathing and the slide of her dress as she crossed her legs, then uncrossed them. Either she was as turned-on as he was or she was intent on driving him crazy. With every restless movement he imagined her bare leg sliding against him, up over his hip and—

'We're here.' He swung through the electric gates and up, past cypresses and colourful oleanders lining the driveway, into the garage beneath his high-set home.

Adoni switched the engine off, the only sound the tick-tick of the motor and the thud of his pulse. He drew a deep breath, willing his body to relax, but it was impossible. He was too wound-up. Clicking the remote control to shut the garage door behind them, he got out and went round to the passenger side, helping her out.

'Thank you, Adoni. I had a lovely evening.'

Her hand was small in his, her eyes bright with sapphire depths. She stood so close her breasts teased his torso. The light imprint of her body fuelled the fire burning within.

'It's not over yet.' He pulled her wrists up and over his shoulders, gripping her waist, marvelling at how perfectly its seductive curve fitted his palms. Adoni tugged and she came willingly, leaning up on her toes and planting those lush lips against his mouth.

Adoni groaned and lashed his arms round her, accepting her invitation and driving down with his tongue, plundering the velvety heat of her mouth. She tasted so impossibly good. Alice arched, supple yet taut, and a rolling wave of lust engulfed him. At this rate it would be a miracle if they made it upstairs to a bedroom.

Her fingers channelled through the hair at the back of

his scalp, sending trails of flame racing down his spine then circling round to his groin.

'Alice.' He groaned it against her mouth, desperation rising. He closed his eyes, inhaling orange blossom, motor oil and musky pheromones.

He shuddered and dragged his mouth from hers. 'We need a bed.'

Air filled his starved lungs as he snapped his eyes open and made himself step back. But he kept her prisoner with his hands. It would take a moment before he found the strength to let her go.

Heavy-lidded eyes met his. Her mouth, always outrageously seductive, was a reddened pout, ripe from his kisses. His fingers tightened.

'I can't wait that long.'

Adoni's clothes felt far too tight, restricting. It took everything he had not to move. He shook his head, the movement straining already taut muscles. 'Don't say that or I'll forget about behaving like a civilised man and take you here, in the garage.'

She blinked, her pupils dilating, drawing his fascinated gaze. 'I don't feel very civilised, Adoni.' Her voice grew husky on his name, turning it into a caress. 'I've wanted you all night and...'

He lifted her off the floor and up against his hardness, his gaze sweeping the long garage. *There.* Just metres away—a work bench against the wall.

Adoni had just enough control to check the surface—like everything else in the property it was pristine—before he lowered her onto it. Instantly, gratifyingly, she opened her knees and he stepped in, tucked hard between her splayed thighs.

'Yes!' Her head fell back against the wall as he ground himself against her.

Adoni lifted his hand to stroke the perfect pale arch of

her throat, stunned at how erotic it was and how his hand shook. What was it about Alice that turned him on so hard and fast? The fact he'd planted his baby inside her? Yes. No. It was more than that.

There was no time to solve that riddle now. Her hands were on his belt as he shoved her floaty skirt up her bare legs. He tugged her hard against him.

She moaned and he bent, nipping at that sensitive spot where her neck curved down to her shoulder. She moaned again, ripping his trousers undone while he slipped his hand between her legs. She shuddered as he tore her panties aside and stroked her.

'No!' Her hand clamped his wrist. 'I want *you*,' she said. 'Just you.'

Adoni worked on autopilot. He wasn't conscious of anything but the expression on her face and his desperation to give her—give them both—what they needed.

He'd never been so aroused. So when he thrust, slow and sure, right to the core of her, it was no surprise when that glorious slide ended in ripples of pleasure. They grew into shudders of ecstasy, engulfing them and sending them spinning towards the stars.

Later–much later—they made it to his bedroom. Again they came together in a glorious conflagration that wrung them out and made a mockery of Adoni's belief that he knew the full measure of physical ecstasy.

Now he lay in bed with Alice curled up against him, her leg across his hips, her soft little belly, where their baby rested, pressed into his side.

Adoni just had the strength to stroke the dark tresses spilling over her shoulders.

In the distance Athens hummed, the cityscape visible through the wide windows. But his mind wasn't on the floodlit Acropolis or the network of streets. It was on the woman in his arms. And the future.

In the beginning he'd wanted only his child. To love it and give it the life it deserved.

Now Adoni wanted more.

He wanted Alice.

He breathed slowly, testing the idea.

It was crazy to want any woman long-term, given his history. Crazy after knowing her such a brief time. Yet he did, and Adoni trusted his instinct. Instinct had got him the most important breaks in his career. Instinct came through when carefully laid plans failed.

Instinct told him he wanted Alice. That he'd *keep* wanting her. This wasn't a passing attraction.

She'd make a good mother, unselfish and caring. She'd do her best for their son. For some reason Adoni was convinced it was a boy.

The more Adoni knew about Alice's story, the more he realised she took family, caring and duty seriously. She had her dream of art school but had deferred it to look after the man who'd supported her family. She paid her debts. She was honourable.

Honourable. Caring. Sexy. Even her obstinacy, her feistiness were assets, or would be when directed towards nurturing their son. And weren't two loving parents better for a child than two parents living apart, turning their child's life into a schedule of travel and disrupted routines?

More than that, there was something vital, adorable, unfettered about Alice. She was a breath of fresh air—so different from him and yet, he was discovering, so similar in the ways that mattered.

She shifted, her breath stroking his skin. His nipple tightened at that phantom caress and his loins stirred.

It was tempting to wake her again. He was insatiable. He'd told himself it was due to the child she carried. Or because she really had been a virgin when she came to him. However politically incorrect, there was something viscerally exciting about knowing he was her first lover. He could, if he wanted, be the only lover she ever had.

The idea solidified his determination. He just had to figure out how to get everything he wanted.

CHAPTER THIRTEEN

THEIR OVERNIGHT STAY in Athens became a week as Adoni worked and Alice explored, discovering and delighting in what the city had to offer. Evenings were spent dining out, enjoying the nightlife, then hurrying back to his sleek white mansion and making love into the wee hours.

Neither mentioned the future, or her leaving. It was as if they both realised this bubble of mutual delight was fragile. They didn't want to spoil it with the nitty-gritty negotiations that must eventually come.

Alice knew she should think of leaving but couldn't summon the energy. England with its dismal spring weather and her tiny, cold room seemed a million miles away.

Was it so wrong to accept Adoni's hospitality and not worry about her rent for just a little longer? As he'd said, she really was feeling better for the rest and surely a healthy mother was better for the baby?

Or maybe you're looking for excuses to stay because you can't imagine leaving him.

It was true. She didn't *want* to go.

So when Adoni presented his plan a few days after they returned to his villa in the Mani, Alice stifled her amazement and actually considered his proposition.

'We both want what's best for our baby.'

Alice nodded. 'Of course.'

Adoni smiled, distracting her as he stroked a finger down her bare arm.

They sat on the balcony outside the master bedroom, enjoying the early evening air, scented by the wildflowers that bloomed so prolifically around the house. The rhythm of waves soothed when her pulse beat hard at Adoni's touch.

One touch was all it ever took, sometimes just a look, for her to melt. Alice shivered and tried to concentrate.

'We both need to build a relationship with him.'

'Him?' Alice raised her brows but Adoni merely smiled. That wry tilt of his lips was so ridiculously attractive it stole her breath.

'What can I say? I believe our child is a boy.'

Alice said nothing. Not because of Adoni's bizarre claim, but because when he said *our child* it did strange things to her insides. As if they were a couple, a family.

The notion, like an elusive wisp of aromatic smoke, tantalised before fading into nothing. They weren't a couple; they were sharing pleasure for a short time, no strings attached.

Alice shifted in her chair, refusing to acknowledge the swift plunge of her belly that felt like disappointment.

'It will be better if he has both of us in his life, *ne*?'

'Yes.' Alice tilted her head, searching Adoni's face. His use of the Greek word *ne* for yes caught her attention. He rarely used Greek with her, except when they were naked. He reverted to his native language in the throes of passion and Alice adored it—he sounded so desperate, so out of control then. Was Adoni *nervous*?

'And we agree security is vital to a child.'

Again Alice nodded. 'Where are you going with this, Adoni?' While they hadn't formally discussed future arrangements, occasionally one or the other would remark on some aspect they believed important. It had been a relief to discover their views coincided—a good relationship with both parents. Time in both Greece and England, and raising their child as bilingual, enriched by the cultures of both parents. 'You're going over what we've already discussed.'

'Patience, *glyká mou*. This is important.' He threaded his fingers through hers, engulfing her hand. Alice wished she didn't enjoy that easy touch so much.

She'd miss it when she went back to England.

'Go on then.'

Deliberately she turned away from his proud, handsome profile, staring over the rough ground where she'd sketched this afternoon. There'd been bright red peacock anemones and carpets of white daisies, delicate pink orchids and so many other flowers she didn't have names for. She could spend days, weeks, years here, painting.

It was paradise.

And not just because of the plants. Or the sunlight or the friendly locals.

Paradise because you've never been happier than here, with Adoni.

She stilled, arrested by what that told her.

'I've thought about how we can achieve that and ensure our son isn't continually in transit between us, especially when he begins school. Continuity will be important.'

Alice sat straighter. What was he leading up to? Continuity? Did that mean their child living with Adoni since he could provide everything money could buy? Alice's tension notched up. Would she have to fight for her rights?

His expression was intent, still as a predator about to strike, or a tycoon about to deliver a *coup de grâce* to some underperforming executive.

Had she misjudged him? Was he going to fight for sole custody? Surely not! That didn't fit with the man she'd come to know and—

'I believe we should raise him together.'

'Sorry, I thought you said—'

'I did. I believe the pair of us should raise him.'

She angled her head as if that might help her read his thoughts but he looked more guarded than ever.

'Define *together*.'

'As a couple. As a mother and father, raising their child in the usual way.'

Alice blinked but Adoni looked just the same. 'You mean *living together*?' Her voice betrayed her, growing hoarse.

'*Ne.* Yes.' He caressed the pad at the base of her thumb. Was it an unconscious gesture or was he trying to soothe her, knowing he'd dropped a bombshell?

'Adoni.' She sat forward, her gaze locked on his. 'You need to spell this out. It sounds like you're talking about us living as…as…'

'Partners. Parents. Lovers.' Each word, in that deep voice, was like a mighty stone dropping into a still pool. Alice felt the ripples grow and crest in waves of emotion.

'You want us to *marry*?' Her voice cracked. Adoni hadn't struck her as conservative but he was Greek and she guessed traditions like marriage and legitimacy might be more important to him than to many.

She had her answer in his instantaneous withdrawal and the blaze of horror in his widening eyes. He slammed against the back of his chair and his hand dropped hers as if he'd discovered it was a live bomb.

'Not that!' He shook his head for good measure. Then, as if reading something in her gaping expression, he continued. 'I don't intend to marry, ever. I'm sure you understand, given my history.'

Alice inclined her head. He meant his mother, who'd married only for money and security. The woman who'd lied and connived and never divulged the identity of Adoni's real father.

Adoni's distaste for marriage was understandable. Yet that didn't diminish her hurt at his horror. Or her poignant sense of loss that it could never be an option.

What was she thinking?

Her nape prickled as she identified the direction of her thoughts.

Was she really pining because Adoni would never offer to marry her? It wasn't as if they loved each other. Marriage would be a farce, a sop to convention because of the child they shared.

Alice clasped her hands tight in her lap, as if by reining in her physical response she might control her wayward thoughts.

'So,' she said slowly. 'You want us to live as a couple.' She paused, watching him nod. 'To be lovers and parents together.'

'A family. Yes.' He leaned towards her then, his mouth curving invitingly.

It's safe for him to get close now he's made it clear you can never be his wife.

Alice cursed the cynical voice in her head and tried to focus. Just because *she* believed in love and marriage didn't mean everyone did.

'But we don't…' She hesitated to use the word *love*. 'You're talking about a permanent commitment?'

His eyebrows lifted as if in surprise. 'Won't raising our son be a permanent commitment?'

'Of course. But that's different.'

'Why? We agreed stability and strong, loving relationships will be best for our child.'

There it was again. That zap of sensation on the words *our child*.

'That doesn't mean we have to *be* together.' Even if her insides were doing cartwheels at the prospect of being Adoni's long-term lover. Of sharing her days and nights with him while they brought up their son together.

Listen to her. Now she was buying into his crazy idea, even down to the sex of their child!

Adoni's gaze dropped to her mouth, then her breasts, completing a leisurely survey then lifting to her eyes. By that time Alice's breathing was short and sharp and hot needles prickled her flesh. She wanted to be outraged but instead identified her reaction as excitement.

She had it bad, this attraction for Adoni.

'We don't have to be together but I *want* to, Alice.' His voice hit that low, resonant note that did disastrous things to her determination to resist. 'You'll be a wonderful mother. You're warm, generous and attractive. I like your down-to-earth attitude and your honesty.'

Honesty? He'd come so far from the man who'd accused her of sleeping with him for gain.

'Thank you, but—'

'Plus, I want you as I've never wanted any other woman.' The words left her speechless, mutely blinking up at him. 'I think we could make each other very happy, Alice.' He reached for her hand again, raising it to his lips and pressing a kiss there that sent hope, desire and all sorts of impossible emotions shivering through her.

'This is very…unexpected.' Alice couldn't think what to say. Her one conviction was that she mustn't—absolutely must *not*—throw herself at him and say yes. Though the temptation was strong. She needed time to consider.

He might have read her mind. 'You need to think about it.' His sober tone conflicted with his heated, hungry eyes. Those spoke a different language, not of caution and negotiation but of rampant ownership. The fire in his eyes made her whole body tingle.

Alice frowned. Adoni, *possessive*?

'You needn't worry that you'll be disadvantaged in any way,' he said quickly, making her wonder how he'd interpreted her frown. 'My legal team has drawn up an agreement so you'll be looked after.'

'Looked after?' She sounded like a parrot but she had trouble following his logic. She'd thought Adoni would look after her, and vice versa. Surely, if they were partners—

'While I'm alive and even if anything should happen to me, you'll be taken care of.'

'I think you need to explain.'

Adoni nodded. When he spoke his tone was brisk. Yet still she saw a glaze of heat in his scrutiny. 'We sign a contract. I will support you with a generous allowance.' He named a sum so large it made her head spin. 'That will continue even if I predecease you, so long as you are supporting our child and he's thriving under your care. But you'll have no other claim on my estate—it will all go to the boy.'

Alice felt her eyes round. Anger spiked that there was any doubt their child would thrive under her care! Was Adoni going to appoint observers to check that?

Then she recalled how his parents had treated him and, though still angry, managed to swallow her pride. He was trying to ensure their baby was well cared for. She couldn't fault Adoni for that.

'And what would I be agreeing to?' Her voice didn't sound like her own.

Adoni shrugged. 'To live as my partner, help bring up our son. Not take any other lovers.'

Did his gaze sharpen on the words?

'And would you make a similar commitment?' Her chin hiked up.

'*Yes*. I have no intention of undermining the family I want to build for our child.'

Our child. There they were again, those magic words. Only this time, instead of making Alice feel warm and fuzzy, they made a warning bell clang discordantly. No matter how tempting it was to think of being Adoni's lover, his partner, this was about the baby. Not them.

Alice shook her head. 'I don't know. It's too…'

'Too what?' Adoni leaned in, his wide shoulders and intent expression crowding her back in the seat.

Too bizarre! A binding contract to ensure she cared for her child and didn't cheat on her lover!

Whoever heard of such a thing?

Adoni, obviously. It was a reminder that, however relaxed she felt with him, they were from different worlds.

'Unexpected,' she said flatly. A weight pushed down on her, crushing her earlier pleasure at being with him.

Clearly that wasn't enough for Adoni. His mouth thinned. She could almost hear his mind working.

'It's more than fair, Alice.' His eyes flashed and his jaw angled up in that unconsciously arrogant expression that both thrilled and annoyed her. 'I've even stipulated that all decisions about the child's future will be mutually agreed between us. I'm trying to make things easier.'

Part of her recognised he was right. In his own outlandish way, he was ensuring their child had a family who loved and cared for it.

'What if I want to do something in addition to being a mother? Like go to art school and work as an artist?' She'd already buried that idea, at least for the foreseeable future, because it would take all her time and resources to care for her baby. But she wanted, one day, to pursue the dream she'd deferred so long.

'Alice.' Adoni took her hand in both of his, his clasp ridiculously reassuring. 'I'm not a bully. Of course you need your art. You're talented and it's a tragedy you haven't had a chance to pursue that properly.' His words buried themselves deep within her. Pleasure glowed at his belief in her.

'I don't intend to give up my business but I'm sure I can delegate more so I spend time with you and our boy. If you want to work too, you should. So long as there's a balance between career and home.'

Alice shook her head, striving to take it all in.

'What?' Adoni's hold tightened. 'What have I said that you don't like?'

She smiled ruefully. 'Nothing. You're being so…reasonable, it's a shock. I thought you might demand I devote myself solely to hearth and home.'

His lips quirked up. 'It's true we Greeks can be traditional about that.' His thumb rubbed the underside of her wrist and her pulse fluttered. 'But I want what's best for our child. I believe that means mutual respect and parents who are happy and fulfilled, not sniping over petty grievances.'

'You don't envisage disagreements?'

'I'm counting on them.' He leaned so close his breath tickled her face and Alice felt heat sear her throat and cheeks. 'I love your spirit. The way you stand up for yourself. I anticipate our love life will be fiery and incredibly satisfying.'

The bloom of damp heat in the space between her legs told Alice she'd enjoy it too.

But beneath it all, like a sour note she couldn't eradicate, was regret. More than regret. Disappointment.

That Adoni would love their baby but never her. He'd excised the very notion and, no matter how tempting it was to believe she could change him with time, she had to face facts. Adoni didn't believe in romantic love. It wasn't even on his radar.

They could have a mutually enjoyable, respectful relationship, dedicated to the well-being of their child.

But there would be no love.

Could she live with that? Give up what, she realised now, she'd hoped to find one day. Could she accept something that was its mere shadow?

She swallowed, tasting that sourness on her tongue.

'You'll have to give me time to think.'

Adoni ended the conference call and shoved his chair from his desk. Here in the tower above the house, he had spectacular three-hundred-and-sixty-degree views. Usually the panorama of sea and land was soothing.

Not today. Not even his company's impending software

release, which promised to be its most successful yet, made him smile.

He stalked to the window facing the coast.

His software enterprise was steadily increasing market share. His plan to widen his investment base with a portfolio of luxury boutique hotels was proving profitable, despite economic uncertainties. Even the Devon property was available for purchase at the price he wanted.

Yet he felt no buzz of satisfaction.

Shoving his hands in his pockets, he surveyed the slope to the beach. Alice had taken that route. She'd talked of capturing some shots of wildflowers for the portfolio she was preparing. No doubt she was immersed in her art.

Her talent made his own capacity with numbers and technology seem a paltry thing, mere money-making.

Because somewhere along the line his passion had become business?

No, he wasn't such a naïve purist. He revelled in his work, got satisfaction out of developing better and more user-friendly software. It had taken talent as well as incredible hard work to achieve what he had.

Yet still he felt that niggle of dissatisfaction.

Adoni peered at the coastal track. Was she coming back yet?

It had been weeks since he'd suggested they live together permanently, yet Alice still hadn't agreed. He'd pulled back, giving her time to consider. Lately, when he'd raised the subject, she'd looked so troubled he hadn't persisted, telling himself to be patient. He'd bided his time. Surely these halcyon days were a precursor to the future he envisaged.

Alice was as responsive as ever. His sex life had never been so good. And living with her had convinced him a long-term arrangement made eminent sense. He felt energised by her presence. Even chatting over dinner was a delight rather than the chore it had sometimes been on dates.

It was only a matter of time before she said yes and signed the agreement that would bind them into a family.

He frowned, his mind snagging on her expression as he'd shown her the contract. Was it the penalty clause for disloyalty that made her hesitate? If she slept with someone else she'd lose all financial support.

But that was non-negotiable. Adoni couldn't countenance the thought of Alice having sex with someone else. His fingers bit into the windowsill.

She was *his*. They'd be a family. He wasn't sharing her with anyone but their child.

As ever, thought of that fragile new life sent a shaft of pleasure/pain through his chest. Pride and excitement vied with fear of what could happen if Adoni didn't take every precaution to protect his son.

He looked at the westering sun, turning the navy blue sea to shades of apricot and neon pink.

It was late, in more ways than one.

He'd been patient long enough.

CHAPTER FOURTEEN

ADONI WAS WAITING for her when Alice entered the master suite, sketchbook in hand. Her skin was flushed despite the broad-brimmed hat that protected her from the sun.

'We need to talk.' He hadn't meant to blurt it out but his phenomenal patience had frayed.

He needed to close this deal. Now.

Besides, when she swept the hat away, releasing a tumble of auburn-tinted hair that caught the dying light like rubies, when her pert breasts pushed with every quick breath against her shirt, it was talk or take her to bed.

For weeks Adoni had revelled in the sex. It was time he developed control.

'Sure.' She surveyed him with her deep slate-blue gaze then turned to put away her art equipment. 'Is there time for a shower first?'

'No.' If she showered he'd join her. There'd be no talking—no *sensible* talking—for hours. 'It's time to sort this.'

She didn't ask what *this* was. She must have been expecting this discussion.

'Okay. But let's go to the pool. I can soak my feet while we chat.'

Adoni nodded and motioned for her to lead the way. His eyes traced the curves of her hips beneath denim shorts and the way her pale T-shirt clung. Was that a slight thickening of her slim waist? He loved her body just as it was, but he eagerly awaited visible signs of pregnancy. The thought of her cradling his child in her body was still one of the most powerfully erotic things he'd ever known.

'You want to talk about the contract?' she said when they

were settled, he in a lounge chair and she on the flagstones, her bare feet in the pool as she leaned back on her hands.

It struck Adoni that this way he saw her only in profile, not face-on.

'We need to prepare for our child's arrival.' Better to mention that than the fact he, Adoni, was unsettled that they hadn't arrived at an agreement. His nights had been spiked lately by dreams where Alice shoved the contract at him then strode off, carrying their infant son whose outstretched arms and cries tore Adoni from sleep.

He set his jaw. That *wasn't* going to happen.

'You're right.' She paused and her forehead wrinkled as she stared across the pool. 'But you're asking a lot, Adoni.'

He locked his jaw. He'd *been* patient. This was the best way to proceed. They'd all win.

'What will it take to convince you?'

Slowly Alice turned. Her expression was more sombre than he'd seen in weeks. Adoni's belly tightened as premonition drilled through him. Had something happened on her outing? She'd been all smiles when she left.

'Tell me about Vassili Petrakis.'

Adoni reared back, shock smacking him.

'What's he got to do with us?'

Alice shrugged. 'I need to understand you before I commit to living with you.'

Adoni strove for control. If hearing this again helped persuade her, what did it matter?

'We thought he was my father. Then we discovered he wasn't.' Adoni kept the words brief. 'He was furious that my mother had deceived him and he'd raised a cuckoo in the nest.' Adoni's skin crawled. He could still hear the bass rumble of disgust in the old man's voice. 'He kicked me out and I've never seen him since.'

Adoni rubbed his collarbone as if there was a phantom ache from the old fracture. Vassili had been so furious that day. When Adoni hadn't instantly obeyed and left the house, Vassili had tried to shove him out of the door. Adoni, angry and heartsore, but above all stunned at the rejection, had lost his footing and crashed onto the stone doorstep. The old man had shut the door so fast he probably didn't even realise Adoni had been injured.

Slim fingers gripped Adoni's other hand. He turned to find Alice leaning close, sympathy in her eyes.

'It must have been dreadful.' Her brow knotted. 'But don't you want to see him again? He raised you after all. He must have felt so betrayed. Maybe he regrets how he behaved.'

Adoni turned his hand, capturing her delicate wrist, feeling the strong pulse hammer there. Alice was nervous. Why?

'I have no interest in seeing him. He disowned me. Barred me from seeing my brothers.' Though of course they were brothers in name only. 'Because of him I was homeless, penniless and I lost my fiancée too.' Which had been a blessing in disguise, but that didn't pardon Vassili's rejection.

Alice blinked, suddenly breathless. Adoni's words stripped the air from her lungs. He'd been *engaged*?

Finally she found her voice. 'Weren't you young to be engaged?'

'Nineteen.' His voice was grim. 'I thought I knew it all. Just as I thought Vassili couldn't be serious about disowning me.'

'What happened? To your fiancée?'

'Nothing.' Adoni's mouth curved up in a smile that made Alice shiver. It looked *feral*. 'When she realised I had no money or prospects she ditched me.'

Alice watched Adoni's face stiffen into an implacable mask. Clearly he'd never forgiven the woman.

Then it hit her—first his mother, then his fiancée, both teaching him women weren't to be trusted. One such betrayal would warp any man's opinion. But two?

No wonder he demanded she sign a contract. Everything had to be checked and double-checked by lawyers, because simple trust was impossible.

Alice sucked in a frantic breath as her stomach hollowed. It felt as if her insides were collapsing. Or maybe that was her stupid daydreams.

Fervently she wished she could turn back the clock to this morning, when they'd laughed together in Adoni's vast bed. He'd teased her, kissing the couple of freckles on her nose, then proceeded to examine her all over, pretending to find and kiss more freckles in the most unlikely places. They'd been so *happy*, so in tune.

She remembered the heavily lined face of the man she'd met this afternoon. The pain in his eyes that she suspected had nothing to do with his physical problems.

'I saw him today.' Just in time she stopped herself from saying *your father*. 'Vassili.'

'You *what*?' Adoni's grip tightened, making her wince. Instantly he released her. 'Where was this?' He drew himself up, his expression ominous. He looked like a warrior preparing for battle.

'Down near the shore. He saw me drawing.'

Adoni breathed deep. On the exhale he whispered a string of soft, savage words in Greek. 'He knew who you were?'

Of course he did. It was a small community and she'd just learned his house sat on the next headland. She could see it now. Adoni must have built here to thumb his nose at the man who'd raised then rejected him. Alice shivered, recalling what Adoni had said about long-held grudges in this part of the world.

Was that the sort of world she wanted her child to grow up in?

'He knew where I was staying. He asked how you were.' Alice had read the effort it took for the older man to ask. With his chunky stature and square face he looked nothing like Adoni but in one thing they were the same—that look of austere pride. Adoni wore it now like a warning sign.

'You didn't answer him?'

Alice rubbed her hands up her suddenly chilled arms. 'I told him you were well. I told him your business is thriving and...'

'He has no right to hear any of that.' Adoni's voice was harsh, like forged metal.

'I felt sorry for him. He's had a stroke, I think. His face was lopsided and he walked with a stick.' It was obvious he'd made a monumental effort to reach her. A man with his physical limitations didn't just happen along the track where she painted. She'd ended up walking him back to the village, concerned despite his protestations.

Adoni said nothing. Nor did his expression soften.

'I think...' She hesitated. 'I'm sure he'd like to see you, maybe make amends.' The old man's sorrow touched her. 'If he contacted you would you...?'

Alice stopped as Adoni's expression flickered.

'He *has* contacted you, hasn't he?'

Adoni shrugged. 'We have nothing to discuss.'

Alice stared. 'I know he did wrong, Adoni. But he was your father. Don't you want to see him? See your brothers?'

The flicker became a scowl. 'He made it clear they're not my brothers.'

'Adoni!' Alice swung her legs out of the pool and knelt before him, putting her arms around him and squeezing tight. But he held himself rigid. There was no softening. No acceptance of the comfort she offered.

'Isn't it worth *trying*?'

Adoni captured her wrists and unwound her arms, distancing her as he held her hands before him. His eyes were hard as diamonds. 'The past is over. What's important is our child. Our life together. When you sign the contract—'

'I'm not saying you can change the past. Just that it's better not to hold hate in your heart.' And distrust. She wanted to tell Adoni she was fighting for *him*—for them, and their child. For she wasn't sure she could commit to a family where her partner was better at grudges and distrust than loving.

Especially now she knew it was love she wanted from this man. She'd finally worked out what all her feelings for him meant. Trust, desire, frustration, pride, tenderness and hope—so much hope.

Together they added up to love.

She'd been falling in love with Adoni from the night she'd barged into him and looked up into those amazing blue-green eyes that shimmered with amusement and tenderness. She'd fallen further the more she knew him. These last weeks, living and laughing with him, had simply set the seal on her emotions.

She was in love with Adoni Petrakis.

She wanted him with all her heart and soul.

But she wasn't prepared to settle for less than love. She needed more.

Even the *hope* of love in the future would do to begin with.

But was he capable of that? Could he weather the inevitable ups and downs of a close personal relationship with positivity and a willingness to meet her halfway?

'You ask too much.'

Maybe she did. Maybe this was crazy, none of her business. But it felt vital she try.

'I know I'm asking a lot.' Alice pressed close, willing him to understand. 'I don't ask you to forgive and forget.

But just listen, that's all. He said his sons—' just in time she stopped herself from saying *your brothers* '—miss you. They want to contact you but feel it would be disloyal while there's a breach between you and Vassili.'

Surely Adoni would relent if it meant reuniting with the young men with whom he'd shared his youth?

'You're not listening, Alice. The past is the past. I want to move on.'

Alice sat back on her heels, drawing her hands from his. Despite the warm air and the heat of the flagstones, a chill enveloped her.

It was tempting to say nothing, to sign his precious contract and hope for the best. But everything inside her screamed that was wrong. It wasn't the way things were supposed to be between two people who truly cared—

'Alice? This has nothing to do with *us*.'

'How can you say that? The past isn't over for you, Adoni. It's driving the present and it's shadowing your future, *my* future. Our *child's* future.'

She hefted a sustaining breath. 'It's not just about you and Vassili. It's deeper than that. You're asking me to sign my life away in a legal contract.' Before he could speak she raised her palm. 'I understand you're wealthy and need to protect that wealth. But—' Alice shook her head '—I want us to be about more than that.'

'What are you saying? That you'll agree to my plan only if I talk to that man?' Adoni looked strained, the flesh tight across the strong bones of his face. 'Or that you're offended by me wanting to protect us all with a written contract? You want to live with me but not accept my terms?'

Alice tried to read his expression. Was that anger there? Scorn? She couldn't tell. Something about the hollow timbre of his voice spoke of disappointment, but maybe she projected her own feelings.

She shook her head. 'I don't know. I'm sorry, I honestly don't know.'

She lifted her knees and wrapped her arms tight round her legs, trying to protect herself from the onslaught of fierce emotions that charged the atmosphere. Her nape prickled as if from static electricity and she wouldn't have been surprised to hear the hiss and crackle of something combusting.

'I *care* for you, Adoni.' She wasn't brave enough to tell him the truth, that she loved him.

'But…?' One of those sleek winged eyebrows that she found so appealing flicked high, making his expression simultaneously superior and disappointed.

'I've been thinking about your contract. I was going to tell you I'm ready to sign—'

Instantly his demeanour changed. Adoni leaned forward, his knuckles gently brushing her cheek. His smile made him a different man. The man she loved. 'That's wonderful!'

Alice pulled back, torn between loss and relief when his hand dropped away.

'But then I thought about what would happen if I got pregnant a second time.' His smile was back, that familiar, slow, delicious one she saw most often in bed. 'It's quite likely, you know. We used a condom last time but I still fell pregnant and you're so—'

'Virile? Insatiable?' He shrugged. 'It's not just me, *glyká mou*. You're as highly sexed as I am.'

Alice flattened her mouth, biting back a retort that it wasn't about being highly sexed. It was about being with the person you *loved*.

'If we are blessed with a second child, or a third, I won't complain.'

She believed him. In fact, Adoni positively beamed. But he hadn't thought this through as she had.

'But what will be your *first* response? You want me to agree in front of lawyers, to lose financial support from you and actually pay a fine if ever I'm caught having an affair. You've arranged it so that if you die and I'm left raising our son…' She blinked, her eyes prickling. Damn it, again she was buying into his belief it was a boy. 'Raising our *child*, someone will check I'm doing a good job before letting me have that allowance.'

'You—'

'Let me finish, Adoni. Please.'

Eyes narrowed, he nodded.

'What that tells me is that you don't trust me. Even now you know me better, you don't *trust* me. You reserve the right to believe I might live down to your worst expectations.'

Alice snatched another shallow breath, her lungs too tight to allow anything more substantial. 'So if I come to you and tell you I'm expecting another baby, will you arrange another paternity test, just to be sure? Will you calculate your travel over the previous months and check where I'd been without you? Perhaps get investigators to see if I've had any male visitors? When will we celebrate—when I break the news or when we get the results back from the lab?'

Adoni's face was stony, the frantic pulse at his jaw the only sign of life.

'And if there's a third pregnancy, do we do it all over again because though you might *want* to trust me, you can't quite manage it? Just as you find it hard to forgive?'

Alice blinked, swallowing tears that threatened, for she knew, she could see in his eyes, that he *wanted* to trust her.

'I know your mother and father hurt you. I know your fiancée let you down. If I could get my hands on that woman I'd make her sorry for how she damaged you. I'm so jealous of her. Because you *loved* her.' Alice gulped, knowing she'd revealed too much. 'I'm sure you didn't make *her* sign on the dotted line and—'

'Which is exactly why a contract is necessary. I've learned my lesson.'

'Not everyone is out to betray you, Adoni. *I'm* not.'

'Yet you find it impossible to prove that by simply signing your name.'

Alice's shoulders slumped. She couldn't get through to him, didn't have the words to make him understand how she felt. She couldn't bear this any more. It felt as if her heart cracked from top to bottom.

'You don't know how much I want to sign,' she whispered. 'If I did I'd have it all, wouldn't I? You and our baby and our life together.'

It was a struggle to swallow over the lump in her throat.

'But every time I've tried I just can't. It doesn't feel *right*, selling myself like a commodity in a deal picked over by lawyers. I don't expect you to love me—I know you don't. But I need *something*. A sign that maybe, one day, you'll smash through that shell you've built around your heart and really care.' She turned and looked away, her gaze turning to the mansion on the next headland.

'I thought if you agreed to listen to Vassili, or meet your brothers, it would be proof your heart hadn't completely hardened—'

'Alice. Don't.' A large hand brushed her cheek, smearing the trickle of moisture she hadn't even noticed. 'Don't cry.' His voice was rough.

Savagely she rubbed her face, banishing the tears, though they tasted bitter at the back of her throat. She got to her feet, her knees as creaky as those of a woman four times her age.

'I'm sorry, Adoni.' She met his eyes, saw a bleakness there that matched what she felt. 'It's totally unreasonable to expect you *not* to insist on a contract. I don't know exactly *what* I want.'

Liar—you want him to love you!

'I just know it's not this.'

Alice drew a shaky breath, waiting for him to argue, to insist. But he said nothing. He looked as shell-shocked as she felt.

Gathering up her strength, she said what she should have weeks ago. 'Thank you for the generous...proposition. It's very tempting but it won't work. When I commit to a man for life I want it to be for love, not convenience.' She swung away, her vision blurring.

'I'd appreciate it if you could arrange my flight back to England. Have your lawyers draw up papers for shared custody, time with you and time with me. I won't fight you on that.'

She swallowed, her face crumpling like her heart as she walked away. 'Goodbye, Adoni.'

CHAPTER FIFTEEN

ADONI SHRUGGED AND straightened his jacket. Tailor-made, it fitted perfectly, but this evening it didn't seem to.

He hooked a finger into his collar, trying to ease the constriction there, though he knew it was just nerves. Even the phantom pain in his collarbone was back.

Too much rode on tonight's outcome.

Everything rode on it.

He'd realised the moment Alice had left him in Greece, even *before* she'd left, that the arrangement she suggested was untenable. He had no intention of sharing their child, like a boomerang flying backwards and forwards between them. Of not seeing Alice except at each handover.

He rubbed the heel of his hand over his clavicle. He knew what he wanted. And he was a man who got what he wanted. Yet that knowledge inspired none of his usual confidence.

For the first time in years Adoni felt nervous. Scared his plan might not work.

Catching the direction of his thoughts, he stiffened his spine and strode to the door of the plush London gallery. He'd never been a coward. He couldn't afford to start now.

The first room was empty. The exhibition wouldn't open for another hour and the gallery was technically closed. In the distance he heard the clatter of plates from a back room—caterers preparing for tonight's party.

Adoni strode deeper, barely glancing at the portraits on the white walls. When he'd come here to see Felix Christow earlier, these works by Alice's mother had moved him immeasurably. They conveyed such depth of emotion, such understanding, it was impossible not to be entranced. Especially when the subject was someone she loved. The portrait of her husband, captured at his drawing board, with his sleeves rolled up and his hair unkempt, conveyed such warmth and affection Adoni felt as if he'd intruded into an intensely private world.

That was the world Alice had inhabited as a child. A world of love and intimacy, of happiness and trust such as Adoni had never known. No wonder she hadn't been ready to accept his bloodless contract!

Murmuring voices drew him into a vaulted space, the second last room in the exhibition.

There she was.

Adoni's heart slammed his ribs so hard it felt as if it had yanked free. That it might at any moment tumble right out of his body.

It had been just a week since he'd seen her but it seemed a century.

His pulse skipped as he realised she wore the dress he'd given her. She'd left it in his home. The sight of it, alone in the empty wardrobe, had reinforced his isolation, his loneliness, after she'd gone.

He'd wrenched it out but, instead of tossing it away, his hands had gentled on the soft fabric she'd worn against her flesh. The next day he'd had it hand-delivered, with a note asking that she keep the gift as proof of goodwill between them.

His relief when she'd accepted had been matched only by his determination to make Alice accept more than a mere dress.

Now the dark blue gown graced her slim form. The beaded bodice scintillated as she moved and the short skirt flirted around her pale legs. Her dark hair, with its rich hint of auburn, was simply styled up, leaving her creamy neck bare except for that glowing opal necklace.

And Adoni wanted her as he'd never wanted any woman in his life.

That was what drove him across the room, heedless of the fear jamming his throat.

'Ah, Mr Petrakis. How good to see you.' Christow, the gallery owner, was calm and urbane, everything Adoni wasn't at the moment. Adoni stared down into Alice's stunned face, feeling the charge of adrenaline rush his body.

He must have responded to Christow's welcome, even answered, but he had no recollection of it. He was so engulfed by emotion as he drank her in he barely noticed the other man leave.

'He was expecting you.' Alice's voice was uneven. The beads over her breasts trembled and shimmered as she drew an unsteady breath.

'Sorry?' Adoni forced himself to focus on Alice's words.

'Felix expected you.' It was a challenge. Or perhaps an accusation.

Adoni shrugged. He wasn't going to apologise for persuading the gallery owner to arrange this time with her. Christow had been only too eager to assist a collector of Adoni's stature.

'I mentioned I'd like an early viewing.'

Who are you kidding, Petrakis? Pride has no place here. It's already done more harm than good.

'I needed to see you.'

Alice lifted her hand to her opal choker, fingers closing around it like a talisman.

'We've said everything, Adoni. Let's leave it to the lawyers.' Her eyes shimmered, over-bright, and he wanted to reach out and pull her close, assure her everything would be okay. Except the curl of raw terror in his gut was proof everything was far from okay.

'No lawyers.'

'Sorry?' Her grasp on the necklace tightened.

'What's between us…' For the life of him Adoni couldn't prevent his gaze dropping to her flat stomach. 'It's not a matter for lawyers.'

If he'd thought that might convince her to listen, he was doomed to disappointment. Her pale face froze and her beautiful mouth tightened.

'I'm sorry, Adoni.' Her voice sounded stretched tight. 'I can't do this. Not here, not now.' A jerky movement indicated her mother's art on the walls. 'This is already… difficult.'

He stepped closer. 'I can imagine it is. But wonderful too. To see so much of your mother's work in one place must be gratifying.'

Slate-blue eyes caught his, widening as if she were surprised at his understanding.

'Your mother was very talented. Like you.'

Instantly Alice shook her head. 'There's no comparison. I'm just—'

'An incredibly gifted artist.' He could resist no longer. Adoni reached out and touched her bare arm, his fingertips tingling at the contact. She stilled, her breath locking in her lungs just like his. The touch became a caress, light as a windblown leaf, and he felt her shiver.

But she didn't pull away.

His fingers encircled her arm, gently capturing her.

'You're right,' he murmured, inhaling the aroma of sweet blossom and femininity that was Alice's signature scent. 'This isn't the place.'

He pulled gently, inviting her into the exhibition's final room. 'There's something I want you to see. *Please*.'

Adoni's tension eased, just a little, when she moved with him. They turned a corner, into a dimly lit space where lights illuminated the sole painting in the room. An exquisite portrait in oils of a mother and child.

Alice froze. He heard the hiss of her breath.

'How?' She swallowed hard. 'Felix didn't mention this!' She took a step closer, eyes on the painting, and Adoni released his hold.

'It was a late inclusion.' Adoni didn't spare the painting a glance. All his attention was on Alice and the stark emotion in her taut frame. Had he done the right thing? 'I hoped you'd like seeing it again—'

'*You* arranged this?' She swung round and met his stare, her eyes shocked.

Hell! It was meant to be a pleasant surprise.

'I've been negotiating for weeks to buy it. I was going to give it to you—' he paused, not wanting to say the words, but knowing he must '—when you agreed to stay with me.'

Alice blinked and, to his horror, tears glistened in her eyes. Furiously she blinked them back. 'That was a very kind gesture.'

Kind? He wasn't kind. He'd wanted to make her as happy as he'd known he'd be when she agreed to be his.

Except it hadn't worked out that way, had it?

'I'm sorry. I didn't mean to upset you.'

Alice stared up into Adoni's strong face, noting the meticulously shaved jaw, the tautness in those proud features and the flicker of unease in his eyes. She'd never sensed such vulnerability in him. She didn't know what to make of it.

'You didn't upset me. You…surprised me.' She turned to the portrait, her pulse thumping madly. It showed a young woman with auburn hair and laughing blue eyes. On her lap sat a little girl of three, clasping a ragged old teddy. Alice knew she was three because her parents had told the story often, of how they'd had to cajole her to sit still long enough for her mother to complete the self-portrait. Of how Alice had squirmed and shifted until her father handed her Old Ted.

'It was the last painting of hers that my father sold. He

didn't want to part with it.' Her throat closed on the words. Money had been so tight when David offered them somewhere to live.

'It's yours.' Adoni's voice was gravel.

'But I can't.' She swung to face him. 'I didn't accept your—'

'This is a gift. No strings attached. It should never have left your family.' His voice softened. 'It belongs with you, Alice. I know how important family is to you. You need to have this.'

'But…' His expression stopped her protests. She couldn't define what she saw there, except that it was unfamiliar and compelling. Emotion rippled through her, right to that place inside that had felt hollow since the day she'd left Greece, left Adoni.

Abruptly, to her horror, tears filled her eyes again.

'Don't, *karthia mou*.' His warm hand cupped her cheek, his thumb stroking the moisture away, making her shudder with the effort of restraint. She wanted to bury her head against him, wrap him close and not let him go. She'd been so *lonely* without him. As if she'd left part of herself behind in Greece.

'It's too much.' She blinked and lifted her chin.

His eyes captured hers. 'It's yours, Alice, as it should always have been. It's a work of great beauty and passion and I want you and our child to have it.'

Alice's mouth crumpled. It would be so much easier if she could dislike Adoni, but that was impossible. With every word he made her decision harder to bear.

'If it makes you feel better about accepting, perhaps you'd consider doing me a favour in return?'

'What's that?' Alice gave up trying to pretend she wasn't crying. She sniffed, wiping her eyes.

'Be with me when I meet Vassili and his sons.'

Alice's mouth dropped open. 'You're meeting them?'

The grim lines around Adoni's mouth and the tension in his tall frame gave his answer. 'Yes.' He lifted a hand to his collarbone then dropped it. 'I've been thinking about what you said.' He shook his head. 'I've thought of nothing else. And I decided you were right. I've been a coward.'

'Adoni!' She reached out to touch him, then curbed the gesture, withdrawing her hand. 'You're not—'

'I am.' He straightened to his full, impressive height. 'I pretended family didn't matter. That the past didn't matter, but I was living a lie.' His voice softened. 'So I rang him.'

'You did?' Alice didn't hesitate this time. She grasped his hand, feeling the tremor that ran through him. Worry stabbed her. She'd been so ready to give advice, to tell him what was wrong with his life. But who was she to judge? 'Was it...?'

'It was difficult. Stilted.' Adoni's mouth rucked up at one side. It wasn't a smile yet Alice's heart flipped over. 'I'm not sure about forgiving him, but I'm willing to see. And I want to see the boys. I've missed them.' He covered her hand with his. 'Thank you, Alice. Without you giving me a kick I'd never have made the first move.'

'I didn't do anything. I—'

'You did, *karthia mou.*'

The expression in his eyes, that caressing tone of voice did terrible things to her willpower.

'I wish you wouldn't say things I don't understand. You know I—'

'*Karthia mou* means *my heart.*'

Alice's own heart gave a mighty leap at his words.

'*S'agapó*, Alice. I love you.' He lifted her shaking hand to his mouth and kissed it, slow and gentle, and suddenly her knees were so wobbly she thought she'd collapse. Except he lashed his other arm around her, enfolding her in protective heat.

'Adoni? I don't understand. You don't do love. You don't trust or—'

'*Didn't.* Past tense.' He smiled and it was like sunshine after a month of grey skies, warming her to the core. Yet his eyes didn't smile. His eyes were sombre. 'I thought I loved Chryssa but I was too young to realise it was infatuation. What I feel for you is far beyond that. And, before you ask, it's not just because of the baby. It's *you*, the woman you are, the way you make me feel.'

He pressed another kiss to her hand, her palm this time, and desire shot through her like flaming ribbons. Desire, hope and disbelief. This couldn't be happening.

'*Tha doso ta panta gia na ime mazí sou.*'

Before she could ask he translated.

'I will give anything to be with you. Anything.'

'Adoni?' Her voice cracked. It was too much—far too much—after a week nursing a shattered heart. 'What do you want from me?'

'*You.* I want you, Alice. On any terms you like. Come and live with me, or I'll live with you in Devon. Or marry me.' He paused, his features grave. 'Above everything I want to marry you, but I understand that might be asking too much just yet.'

Alice wished she were strong enough not to reveal how his words affected her, but she wasn't. This week had sapped her strength. Walking away from the man you loved did that.

She clung to him, fingers curling around his. 'Don't talk like that! I know you don't want to marry.' It hurt that he'd say it, when she knew it wasn't possible.

For answer he scooped her up in his arms and strode to the padded bench seat in front of the portrait. He sat and settled her on his lap. Alice felt the hammer of his heart against her and his rough breathing teased her hair.

'I want marriage, Alice, because I want you, for ever.

No contracts, no lawyers, just two people pledging themselves. I *trust* you, Alice. I believe in you.'

She stared up into those stunning eyes and realised he spoke the truth.

Something caught at her chest. Hope?

'When you left I knew I'd been wrong, clutching the past. I knew I wanted you, no matter what. I love you and I want us to be together, simply because we love each other.' His voice dropped to a low note that tugged at her very core. 'I want a chance to prove myself and win your love, Alice. However long it takes.'

It was too much to take in. Too much like the daydreams she'd harboured though she'd tried to be sensible. She shook her head. Instantly he stiffened.

'Please, Alice. I need you. Give me a chance.'

'I'm trying to understand.'

'Maybe you'll understand this.' He tilted her chin and placed his mouth on hers. It was a gentle kiss, so tender, so tentative. A mere brush of soft lips, the silken slide of his tongue, the shuddering breath of a man on the edge.

Suddenly it was too much, and not enough. Her caution disintegrated and desperate yearning took over. Alice speared her hands through his thick hair. She opened her mouth, sucking his tongue inside. Adoni met her caress for caress, till she saw stars and her whole body was afire.

When he pulled back enough to meet her eyes, he looked both triumphant and desperate.

'Tell me you'll give me a chance. I need—'

'You don't need a chance, Adoni.' Alice kissed the corner of his mouth, stunned and grateful that she had the right to. 'I fell in love with you in Greece. I think I even began falling for you that first night.'

There was awe in those eyes that ate her up. And pride and possessiveness and love. Alice guessed they mirrored what was in hers.

Happiness welled, a surge of glorious feeling such as she'd never known. Here, on Adoni's lap, surrounded by those strong arms, caught in his hard embrace, Alice felt she'd finally come home.

'You're willing to take a chance on me, Alice?'

'I am, Adoni. If you are.'

'Always, *karthia mou*. For ever.'

EPILOGUE

'READY, *KARTHIA MOU*?'

Alice looked up into dancing eyes. Eyes as bright as the sea, as bright as the joy she'd found with this man. A little shimmy of excitement wriggled through her. Every day with Adoni was an adventure in love.

'Of course. So long as you promise not to drop me.'

Those wicked eyebrows rose, giving her darling husband a devilish look that always made her pulse race. 'It would take more than a couple of steps to make me let you go, Alice.'

He drew her close to his hard chest, reminding her how very strong he was, and how easily he'd scooped her off her feet. Her thrumming pulse quickened. She loved his strength and protectiveness even if occasionally she had to battle his desire to wrap her and Sophia in cotton wool.

Alice glanced down at the pram parked just inside the open door to the home Adoni had built for them. Sophia Rose Petrakis was fast asleep. With her rosebud mouth and eyes the colour of the sea, she was more beautiful than Alice could have imagined. And she was the light of their lives. Adoni had fallen for their daughter in an instant, despite his earlier conviction they were having a boy. Seeing her husband and daughter together was one of life's most precious gifts.

'She'll be fine for a few moments.' Adoni's deep voice soothed. 'Long enough for me to carry my bride over the threshold.'

'Bride? We've been married a year!' But Alice laughed as he strode into the vestibule and slowly lowered her to the floor.

'But this is the first home we've made together. We needed to mark the occasion.' His meaning was clear.

'You have sex on the brain, Mr Petrakis.'

A slow tilt of his mouth and Alice was swaying against him, wrapping her arms around him.

'And that's bad?' he purred, cupping her face, his hands gently caressing her cheeks.

Emotion welled. She was so very lucky. Who'd have thought life would be so good?

'Alice? Is something wrong?'

Instantly she shook her head then pressed her mouth to his. His kiss reminded her of everything that was right in their lives. Love and trust and a determination to work at a relationship that would last a lifetime.

They spent their time between London and Greece. Adoni had even offered to make a home on the estate where she'd once lived. But the beautiful period property had been David's home, his dream, not hers. So Adoni had found this site looking over the coast nearby, and built a home for them here. A home that would echo with children's laughter and give space for her painting and allow Adoni to work whenever they decided to live in England.

'No, *agape mou.*' The Greek words came easily to her now. 'There's nothing at all wrong. You make me so happy I sometimes can't quite believe how lucky I am.'

'Not lucky, Alice. Loved.' He dipped his head to hers and kissed her with such joy and tenderness that her heart sang.

* * * * *

MILLS & BOON

Coming next month

IMPRISONED BY THE
GREEK'S RING
Caitlin Crews

Atlas was a primitive man, when all was said and done. And whatever else happened in this dirty game, Lexi was his.

Entirely his, to do with as he wished.

He kissed her and he kissed her. He indulged himself. He toyed with her. He tasted her. He was unapologetic and thorough at once.

And with every taste, every indulgence, Atlas felt.

He felt.

He, who hadn't felt a damned thing in years. He, who had walled himself off to survive. He had become stone. Fury in human form.

But Lexi tasted like hope.

"This doesn't feel like revenge," she whispered in his ear, and she sounded drugged.

"I'm delighted you think so," he replied.

And then he set his mouth to hers again, because it was easier. Or better. Or simply because he had to, or die wanting her.

Lexi thrashed beneath him, and he wasn't sure why until he tilted back his head to get a better look at her face. And the answer slammed through him like some kind of cannon-ball, shot straight into him.

Need. She was wild with need.

And he couldn't seem to get enough of it. Of her.

The part of him that trusted no one, and her least of all, didn't trust this reaction either.

But the rest of him—especially the hardest part of him—didn't care.

Because she tasted like magic and he had given up on magic long, long time ago.

Because her hands tangled in his hair and tugged his face to hers, and he didn't have it in him to question that.

All Atlas knew was that he wanted more. Needed more.

As if, after surviving things that no man should be forced to bear, it would be little Lexi Haring who took him out. It would be this one shockingly pretty woman who would be the end of him. And not because she'd plotted against him, as he believed some if not all of her family had done, but because of this. Her surrender.

The endless, wondrous glory of her surrender.

**Continue reading
IMPRISONED BY THE
GREEK'S RING
Caitlin Crews**

Available next month
www.millsandboon.co.uk

LET'S TALK

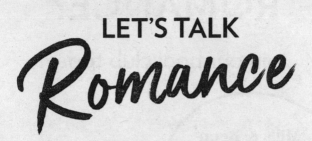

For exclusive extracts, competitions
and special offers, find us online:

f facebook.com/millsandboon

○ @millsandboonuk

𝕎 @millsandboon

Or get in touch on 0844 844 1351*

For all the latest titles coming soon, visit
millsandboon.co.uk/nextmonth

*Calls cost 7p per minute plus your phone company's price per minute access charge

Want even more
ROMANCE?

Join our bookclub today!

'Mills & Boon books, the perfect way to escape for an hour or so.'

Miss W. Dyer

'Excellent service, promptly delivered and very good subscription choices.'

Miss A. Pearson

'You get fantastic special offers and the chance to get books before they hit the shops'

Mrs V. Hall

**Visit millsandbook.co.uk/Bookclub
and save on brand new books.**

MILLS & BOON